STORIES FROM
THE BLUE MOON CAFÉ II

Edited by Sonny Brewer

MacAdam/Cage
155 Sansome Street, Suite 550
San Francisco, CA 94104
www.macadamcage.com
Copyright © 2003
ALL RIGHTS RESERVED.

Library of Congress Cataloging-in-Publication Data

Stories from the Blue Moon Café II / edited by Sonny Brewer.
    p.cm.
  ISBN 1-931561-43-5 (alk. paper)
1. Southern States—Social life and customs—Fiction. 2. Short stories,
American—Southern States. I. Brewer, Sonny.
PS551.S743 2003
813'.0108975—dc21

2003013976

Several of these stories have appeared elsewhere, in some cases in a different
form: "A Roadside Resurrection" by Larry Brown in *The Paris Review* and *The
Christ-Haunted Landscape: Faith and Doubt in Southern Fiction*, University Press
of Mississippi; "My Heroes Have Always Been Grill Cooks" by John T. Edge in
Oxford American magazine; "The Saint of Broken Objects" by Tom Franklin
and Beth Ann Fennelly in *The Southern Review*; "Dialogue of Men and Boys"
by David Wright in *64 Magazine*; "A Fairhope Alien" by Gregory Benford in
The Magazine of Fantasy and Science Fiction; "Last Days of the Dog-Men" by
Brad Watson in *Last Days of the Dog-Men*, W.W. Norton & Co.; "Speckled
Trout" by Ron Rash in *The Kenyon Review*; "Veneer" by Steve Yarbrough in
Oxford American magazine and *Veneer: Stories*, University of Missouri Press;
"Jubilee" in the anthology *Literary Mobile*.

Manufactured in the United States of America.
10 9 8 7 6 5 4 3 2 1

Book and jacket design by Dorothy Carico Smith.

STORIES FROM
THE BLUE MⵘN CAFÉ II

Edited by Sonny Brewer

MacAdam/Cage

TABLE OF CONTENTS

This book is dedicated to you.

Acknowledgments

Thanks are always in order when a task is completed, when an idea is rendered, when a gift is given. The authors and poets in this book are first on my list, sharing their eccentric passion for words, side by side with Diana and my kids, my family, *Mamanem*—Kendra, Carolyn, and Joe, and the rest of the in-laws and outlaws—for giving me their support and cutting me the slack to get the work done. Martin Lanaux for being the bookseller and more at Over the Transom Bookstore while I'm blinded by blue moons. Jim Gilbert for mastering the web we weave in cyberspace, and killing the snakes in the barn. Suzanne Barnhill for her eagle-eye copyediting. Frank Turner Hollon, Tom Franklin, and William Gay, the original Three Musketeers of Southern Writers Reading. Every bookseller everywhere, and especially my pal John Evans with his crew at Lemuria, Jamie and Lyn and the Square Books gang, and Alabama Booksmith's Jake Reiss and his staff. And every reader everywhere. Librarians, too—Charlotte and her ilk. From MacAdam/Cage: in the front office, David Poindexter, Pat Walsh, Scott Allen, Anika Streitfeld, Avril O'Reilly; the Denver marketing gurus, Melanie Mitchell, Tasha Reynolds, Amy Long; and Dorothy Carico Smith (cover art Goddess and graphics Genius). Then there's Rick Bragg who had nothing to do with this book, but who's buying me a barbecue sammich now that it's put to bed.

Sonny Brewer

The waitress swiveled her hips to negotiate the space between two chairs pushed back from their tables, making her way toward me, dutifully keeping tabs on the level of coffee in my cup.

"Writin' a novel, sweetie?" she asked. Her black-and-gold name tag said "Becky."

Fair enough question, there in Fort Lauderdale's Marina Marriott, the site of the 2002 Southeastern Booksellers Association trade show. Outside the La Marina café, a conference gathering of authors and booksellers swirled and hummed. But her query was a little facetious. It was a cocktail napkin my pen was scratching upon.

"Yeah." And so is my dentist writing a novel, and his car mechanic, and the bellhop at the front door of this hotel. Everybody who got past the seventh grade and who has a computer or a pencil and paper is writing a novel. "But this ain't it," I said.

"Your Christmas gift list?" Becky persisted. "Is my name on there?" She had pulled in close enough to see that it was a list of names coming together there on the folded rectangle of soft white paper.

"Well, not yet. Warm up my coffee, and I'll put your name right to the top."

"Who's on the list with me? You on the list?" she said to William Gay, seated next to me, sipping his beer. She looked back at me before he had a chance to answer.

"This is a list of the writers I've asked to be in this anthology I'm working on. I've asked three or four people here at the conference, and it occurred to me a few minutes ago I'd better get down who promised me a story."

"You a writer then?"

"Not really. I'm the editor."

"What's it called?"

"*Stories from the Blue Moon Café.*"

"Oh, I've been there." And before I could tell her that the café in this title did not actually exist—that it is an archetype for all good cafés where a writer might want to park in a back booth and pencil some good lines into a worn notebook—she said, "The Blue Moon Café in Savannah. That's such a neat place. And it's haunted. You probably know that."

No, I did not know, had no idea, that there was a haunted Blue Moon Café in Savannah. But that's where I'm sitting now. Laptop on the table, typing this introduction to the second volume of *Stories from the Blue Moon Café*. The windows are open, and there's a damp breeze moving the curtains. The waitress is at the cash register, taking a customer's money.

Hold on! I'm not sitting in a café in Savannah. See, I had *planned* to go there, to find the joint Becky told me about, take a seat, order a coffee, and do just what I said in the preceding paragraph: beg the ghosts' pardon, pull up a chair, open my laptop, and finish this introduction. I wrote the first of it a while back, stored it to my hard drive, and figured to finish it off inspired by the company of *les hantons* in an actual Blue Moon Café. But when I called my friend in Savannah, a publisher, Deric Beil, who knows all there is to know about the city, he said, "Sorry, Sonny. We've got lots of haunted places in town, but no Blue Moon Café."

"You sure about that? I mean Becky said she sat in a booth there not three months ago."

"I'm sure. Who's Becky?"

"Never mind."

"You know, you might call one of those 'See Historic Savannah'-type tour groups. Maybe one of the cafés was once called that, or is nicknamed Blue Moon. Might be worth a try."

I could see my Savannah road trip going melting like an ice cube in a hot cup of coffee. I got on the Internet and found a number for the Chamber of Commerce, and another for a horse and carriage outfit. I got on the phone. Twenty minutes later, and I'm certain: No Blue Moon Café in Savannah. No question.

Okay. I called down to the Fort Lauderdale Marriott, got the La Marina café, asked for a waitress named Becky, and got her on the phone, reminded her of our conversation months earlier. "Are you sure it was the Blue Moon Café?"

"Yes."

"Are you sure you were in Savannah?"

"I'm sure, sweetie. Hey, you know I was telling my girlfriend just today about that guy with you from Tennessee—this is so weird, you calling me today when I was just today talking about you writers, and it's been, what, six months since you were here? That William Gay guy. He was so nice to talk to me. I asked him how he got to be a writer, and I was telling my friend, he said 'I just started writing.' He was serious, too."

Yeah. He was serious. I thanked Becky, told her to pick up William's new book of stories, and I'd see her later. So there went my haunted Blue Moon café.

Now, kicked back in my study at home, hands behind my head and staring out the window, it occurs to me that, like the glasses you cannot find parked on the end of your nose, I'm square in the middle of the haunting. Here it is—it's this book in your hand. The ghosts rising and flowing, descending and retreating, beckoned by the words marked down by these writers, spells cast by their stories. Strangely connected events, absent the bond of planning and proximity, proving that faith in the unseen is not necessary. Experience stands, hands on hips, squarely in its place. A phone call on the right day. Weird.

So this is the Blue Moon Café, where everyone has been and whose address somewhere south of the Mason-Dixon line no one knows, whose stories pulse and echo in the rooms and hollows of your heart like the blood of unknown ancestors. The voices we hear, the voice we raise down here.

A ROADSIDE RESURRECTION

Larry Brown

Story opens, Mr. Redding is coughing in a café by the Yocona River, really whamming it out between his knees. He's got on penny loafers with pennies in them, yellow socks, madras shorts, a reversible hat and a shirt that's faded from being washed too many times. His wife, Flenco, or Flenc, as he calls her, is slapping him on the back and alternately sucking her chocolate milkshake through a straw and looking around to see who's watching. She's got a big fat face, rollers in her hair, and she's wearing what may well be her nightgown and robe. Fingernails: bright red.

"Damn!" Mr. Redding coughs. "Godamighty...damn!"

Flenco hits him on the back and winces at his language, sucking hard on her straw and glancing around. Mr. Redding goes into a bad fit of coughing, kneels down on the floor heaving, tongue out and curled, veins distended on his skinny forearms, hacking, strangling, and the children of the diners are starting to look around in disgust.

"Oh," he coughs. "Oh shit. Oh damn."

Mr. Redding crawls back up in the booth and reaches into his shirt pocket for a Pall Mall 100, lights it, takes one suck, then repeats the entire scenario above. This goes on three times in thirty minutes.

Customers go in and out and people order beers and drink them at the counter on stools, but Mr. Redding lies back in the booth while his wife mops his feverish forehead with wetted paper towels brought by a waitress from the kitchen, along with another milkshake just like the last one. The hair on Mr. Redding's forearms is dark and scattered like hair on a mangy dog just recovering, and his sideburns sticking out from under the reversible cap are gray. Twenty years ago he could do a pretty good imitation of Elvis. Now he's washed up.

"Oh crap," he says. "Oh shit. Oh hell."

Flenco mops him and sops up his sweat and sucks her big round mouth around the straw and looks at people and pats him on the back.

Truckers come in with their names on their belts and eat eggs and ham and wash down pills with coffee and put their cigarettes out in their plates, stagger back outside and climb up into their sleepers. Flenco looks down the road and wonders what road she'll be on before long.

"Oh shit," Mr. Redding wheezes.

Miles away down the road a legendary young healer is ready to go raise the roof on a tent gathering. Sawdust is on the floor and the lights are bright and a crippled boy in a wheelchair has been brought forward to feel his healing hands. The boy lies in his chair drooling up at the lights, hands trembling, the crowd watching on all sides, spectators all piled up along the back and sides and others peeking in the opened opening, some lying on the ground with their heads stuck up between the tent pegs. The crippled child waits, the mother trembling also, nearby, hands clasped breastwise to the Holy Father Sweet Mary Mother of Saints heal my child who was wrong from the womb Amen. The lights flicker. The healer is imbued with the Spirit of God which has come down at the edge of this cotton field and put into his fingers the strength of His love and healing fire. Outside bright blades of lightning arch and thunderclouds rumble in the turbulent sky as the healer goes into his trance. His fine dark hair is sleek on the sides of his head and he cries out: "Heeeeeeal! Heal this boy, Lord! Heal him! Dear sweet merciful God if You ever felt it in your heart to heal somebody heal this boy! This boy! This one right here, Lord! I know there's a bunch of 'em over there in darkest Africa need healing too Lord but they ain't down on their knees to You right now like we are!"

The healer sinks to his knees with these words, hands locked and upflung before him. Ushers are moving slowly through the crowd with their plates out, but nobody's putting much into the plates yet because they haven't seen the boy get up and walk.

"Lord what about Gethsemane? Lord what about Calvary's cross? Lord what about Your merciful love that we're here to lay on this child? There's his mama, Lord. I guess his daddy's in here, too. Maybe all his brothers and sisters."

"He's a only child," the mama whispers, but nobody seems to notice. The rain has started and everybody's trying to crowd inside.

"Neighbors? I don't believe there's much faith in this house tonight. I believe we've done run into a bunch of doubting Thomases, folks who want to play before they pay. Maybe they think this ain't nothing but a sideshow. Maybe they think this boy works for me. Because I don't believe they're putting in any money to further our work."

The ushers make another pass into the crowd and collect six dollars and fifty-two cents. The boy lies in the wheelchair, legs dangling. This child has never walked before. The mother has told the healer his history. He was born with spinal meningitis, his heart outside his body, and she said God only gave him one kidney. She said on the day she goes to her grave she will still owe hospital bills on him. The healer can see that the congregation thinks nothing is going to happen. He can almost read their faces, can almost read in their countenances the unsaid accusations: *Ha! Unclean! Impostor prove your worth! Make him walk!*

The healer comes down from the podium. The fire of God is still in him. The wheels of the wheelchair are mired in the sawdust. The mother has already begun to feel what has come inside the tent. She faints, falls over, shrieks gently. An uncle stands up. The healer lays his hands on.

"Now I said *heal!* I don't give a damn! About what's happening over there in Saudi Arabia! I don't care what else You got on Your mind! You got to heal this boy! Either heal him or take him right now! Heal him! Or take him! We don't care! He's with You either way!"

The child wobbles in the wheelchair. The healer digs his fingers down deep into the flesh. More people stand up to see. The mother wakes up, moans and faints again. The lightning cracks overhead and the lights go out and then come back on dim. The ushers are moving more quickly through the crowd. An aura of Presence moves inside the tent to where everybody feels it. The child grips the armrests of his chair. His feet dig for purchase in the sawdust. He cries out with eyes closed in a racked and silent scream.

"Yeah!" the healer shouts. "Didn't believe! Look at him! Watch him walk!"

The boy struggles up out of the chair. People have come to his mother's side with wet handkerchiefs and they revive her in time to witness him make his stand. He rises up on his wasted legs, the healer's hands octopussed on his head.

"Heal! Heal! Heal! Heal! Heal! Heal! Heal!"

The boy shoves the hands away. The mother looks up at her son from the dirt. He takes a step. His spine is straight. He takes another step. People are falling to their knees in the sawdust. They are reaching for their purses and wallets.

Mr. Redding has to be taken outside because he is bothering the other customers. Flenco lets him lie on the seat of the truck for a while and fans him with a Merle Haggard album.

"Oh shit," Mr. Redding says. "Oh arrrrgh."

"It's gonna be all right, baby," Flenco says.

Mr. Redding is almost beyond talking, but he gasps out: "What do…you mean…it's…gonna…be…all right?"

"Oh, Flem, I heard he'd be through here by nine o'clock. And they say he can really heal."

"I don't…believe…none of that *bull*shit!"

Mr. Redding says that, and goes into great whoops of coughing.

A lot of money in the plates tonight. The mission can go on. But some helpers have wives back home, trailer payments have to be met, others want satellite dishes. The healer requires nothing but a meal that will last him until the next meal. He gives them all the money except the price of steak and eggs at a Waffle House and heads for the car. The road is mud. The tent is being taken down in the storm. The memory of the woman is on him and he doesn't feel very close to God.

"Oh shit," Mr. Redding says. "Oh damn oh hell oh shit."

"Baby?" Flenco says. "Don't you think you ought not to be cussing so bad when you're like this?"

"Li…iii…iiike what?" Mr. Redding spews out.

"When you're coughing so bad and all. I bet if you'd quit smoking them cigarettes you wouldn't cough so bad."

She pats him on the back like she saw the respiratory therapist do and feels she knows a little about medicine.

"Oh crap," Mr. Redding says. "Oh *shit!*"

Flenco mops his sweaty head and fans hot air with her hand. She has heard that the healer drives a long black Caddy. They say he refuses to appear on network television and will not endorse any products. They say he comes speeding out of the dusty fields in his dusty black car and they say the wind his machine brings whips the trousers of the state troopers before they can get into their cruisers and take pursuit. They say he lives only to heal and that he stops on the roadsides where crippled children have been set up and where their mothers stand behind them holding up cardboard placards painstakingly printed HEALER HEAL MY CHILD. They say that if the state troopers catch up with him while he is performing some miracle of mercy on one of God's bent lambs, the people pull their cars out into the road and block the highway, taking the keys out of the ignitions, locking the doors. It's said that in Georgia last year a blockade of the faithful ran interference for him through a web of parked police cars outside Waycross and allowed him to pass unmolested, such is the strength of his fame. Flenco hasn't a placard. She has rented a billboard beside the café, letters six feet tall proclaiming HEALER HEAL MY HUSBAND. Telephone reports from her sister-in-law in Bruce confirm the rumor that he has left Water Valley and is heading their way. Flenco imagines him coming down out of the hilly country, barreling down the secondary roads and blasting toward the very spot where she sits fanning Mr. Redding's feverish frame.

"Oh shit," Mr. Redding says. "Oh God...dang!"

"Just rest easy now, honey," Flenco says. "You want me to go get you some Co-Coler?"

"Hell naw I don't want no goddamn Co-Coler," Mr. Redding says. "I want some...want some goddamn...I want some...shit! Just carry me...back home and...goddamn...let me die. I'm...goddamn...burning up out here."

Flenco hugs his skinny body tight and feels of his emaciated wrists.

Hands that used to hold a silver microphone hang limply from his cadaverous arms, all speckled with liver spots. She wants him to hold on a little longer because she doesn't know if the healer has worked his way up to raising the dead yet. She knows a little of his scanty history. Born to Christian Seminoles and submerged for thirty-seven minutes in the frigid waters of Lake Huron at the age of fourteen, he was found by divers and revived with little hope of ultimate survival by firefighters on a snow-covered bank. He allegedly lay at death's door in a coma for nine weeks, then suddenly got out of his bed, ripping the IV tubes out, muttering without cursing, and walked down the hall to the Intensive Care Unit where a family of four held a death vigil over their ninety-year-old grandmother, fatally afflicted with a ruptured duodenum, and laid his hands on her. The legend goes that within two minutes the old lady was sitting up in bed demanding Fudge Ripple on a sugar cone and a pack of Lucky Strikes. Fame soon followed and the boy's yard became littered with the sick and the crippled, and the knees of his jeans became permanent grass-stained from kneeling. The walking canes piled up in a corner of the yard as a testament to his powers. A man brought a truck once a week to collect the empty wheelchairs. He made the blind see, the mute speak. A worldwide team of doctors watching him cure a case of wet leprosy. The President had him summoned to the White House, but he could not go; the street in front of his house was blocked solid with the bodies of the needing-to-be-healed. People clamored after him, and women for his seed. The supermarket tabloids proclaim that he will not break the vow he gave to God in the last few frantic moments before sinking below the waters of Lake Huron: if God would bring him back from a watery death he would remain pure and virginal in order to do His work. And now he has come South like a hunted animal to seek out the legions of believers with their sad and twisted limbs.

"Flenc," Mr. Redding coughs out, "how many goddamn times I told you...oh shit...not to...aw hell, ahhhhh."

The tent is down, the rain has ceased. The footsteps of many are printed in the mud. He's had to sign autographs this time, and fighting the women off is never easy. They are convinced the child they'd bear would be an Albert Einstein, an Arnold Schwarzenegger, a Tom Selleck with the brain of Renoir. Some tell him they only want him for a few moments to look at something in the back seat of their car, but he knows they are offering their legs and their breasts and their mouths. He can't resist them any more. He's thinking about getting out of the business. The promise has already been broken anyway, and the first time was the hardest.

His bodyguards and henchmen push with arms spread against the surging crowd and his feet suck in the mud as he picks his way to his Caddy. All around sit cars and pickup trucks parked or stuck spinning in the mud as the weak sun tries to smile down between the parting clouds.

He gets into the car and inserts the ignition key and the engine barks instantly into life with the merest flick of the key. The engine is as finely tuned as a Swiss watchmaker's watch and it hums with a low and throaty purring that emanates from glasspack mufflers topped off with six feet of chrome. He tromps on the gas pedal and the motor rumbles, cammed up so high it will barely take off.

He hits the gas harder and the Caddy squats in the mud, fishtailing like an injured snake through the quagmire of goop. The crowd rushes the bodyguards, pushing their burly bodies back and down and trampling them underfoot, stepping on their fingers, surging forward to lay their once-withered hands on the dusty flanks of the healer's automobile. Faces gather around the windows outside and the healer steers his machine through the swampy mess of the pasture and over to a faint trail of gravel that leads to the highway. Many hands push and he guns the car and mudballs thwack hollowly and flatten on the pants and shirts of the faithful left gawking after him in his wake. They wave, beat their chests to see him go. Liberated children turn handsprings in the mud and per-form impromptu fencing matches with their useless crutches and these images recede quickly through the back window as the car lurches toward the road.

The healer looks both ways before pulling out on the highway. Cars are lined on both sides all the way to the curves that lie in the distance.

Horns blare behind him and he turns the car north and smashes the gas pedal flat against the floorboard. The big vehicle takes the road under its wheels and rockets past the lines of automobiles. Small hands wave from the back seats as he accelerates rapidly past them.

The needle on the speedometer rises quickly. He eyes the gas gauge's red wedge of metal edged toward FULL. He finds k. d. lang on the radio and fishes beneath the seat for a flask of vodka his bodyguards have secreted there. The prearranged destination is Marion, Arkansas, where droves of the helpless are rumored to be gathered in a field outside the town.

He takes one hit, two hits, three hits of vodka and pops the top on a hot Coke while reaching for his smokes. His shoes are slathered with mud and his shirt is dirty, but fresh clothes await him somewhere up ahead. Everything is provided. Every bathroom in the South is open to him. The Fuzzbuster on the dash ticks and he hits the brakes just in time to cruise by a cruiser hidden in a nest of honeysuckle. At 57 mph.

He feels weak and ashamed for breaking his vow, but the women won't let him alone. They seem to know the weakness of his flesh. A new issue of *Penthouse* is under the seat. He reaches over and takes his eyes off the road for a moment, pulls the magazine out. He flips it open and the pictures are there, with nothing left to the imagination, the long legs, the tawny hair, the full and pouting lips. With a sharp stab of guilt he closes it up and shoves it back under the seat. He can't go on like this. A decision has to be made. There are too many who believe in him and he is the vessel of their faith. He knows he's unworthy of that trust now. It's going to be embarrassing if God decides to let him down one night in front of a hundred and fifty people. The crowd might even turn ugly and lynch him if he's suddenly unable to heal. They've come to expect it. They have every right to expect it. But they don't know about his needs. They don't know what it's like to be denied the one thing that everybody else can have: the intimate touch of another.

Mr. Redding lies near comatose under the shade tree Flenco has dragged him to, and people coming out of the café now are giving him queasy looks. Flenco knows that some good citizen might have an ambulance called.

"Just hold on now, baby," Flenco says. "I feel it in my heart he's coming any minute now."

"I don't give a...give a good...a good...a good goddamn...I don't give a shit who's coming," Mr. Redding hacks out. His lips are slimy with a splotching of pink foam and his breath rattles in his chest like dry peas in a pod. He quivers and shakes and licks his lips and groans. Flenco cradles his graying head in her ample lap and rubs the top of his hat with her tremendous sagging breasts. Her rose-tipped nipples miss the passion that used to be in Mr. Redding's tongue. Flenco deeply feels this loss of sexual desire and sighs in her sleep at night on the couch while Mr. Redding hacks and coughs and curses in the bedroom and gets up to read detective magazines or rolls all over the bed. She's ashamed of her blatant overtures and attempts at enticement, the parted robe, the naked toweling off beside the open bathroom door, the changing of her underwear in the middle of the day. Mr. Redding appears not to notice, only lights one Pall Mall after another and swears.

She has sent a little wide-eyed boy inside for another chocolate milkshake and he brings it out to her under the tree where she holds the gasping wheezebag who used to belt out one Elvis song after another in his white jumpsuit with the silver zippers. He'd been nabbed for bad checks in Texas, was on the run from a Mann Act in Alabama, but Flenco fell in love with his roguey smile and twinkling eyes the first time she saw him do "You Ain't Nothin' But a Hound Dog" at the Junior/Senior Prom. His battered travel trailer had a cubbyhole with a stained mattress that held the scented remnants of other nights of lust. But Flenco, pressed hard against the striped ticking with her head in a corner, found in his wild and enthusiastic gymnastics a kind of secret delight. Shunned by her schoolmates, sent to the office for passing explicit notes to boys, downtrodden by the depression caused by her steady eating, Flenco was hopelessly smitten in the first few minutes with his hunk of "Burning Love."

Now her lover lies wasted in her lap, his true age finally showing, his wrinkled neck corded with skin like an old lizard's as he sags against her and drools. She's not asking for immortality; she's not asking for the Fountain of Youth; she's only asking for a little more time. The hope that burns like a bright flame in her heart is a candle lit to the memory of physical love. She wipes his hot face tenderly with a wadded napkin soaked in the cold sweat from the milkshake cup. Mr. Redding turns and digs his head deeper into her belly. People at the tables in the café are staring openly through the windows now and Flenco knows it's only a matter of time before somebody calls the lawdogs.

"Can I do anything for you, baby?" she says.

Mr. Redding turns his eyes up to her and the pain buried in them is like a dying fire.

"Hell yeah you can...do...something...goddamn...do something... oh shit...for me. You can?...goddamn... oh shit...you can...just...hell... by God...shoot me."

"Oh baby, don't talk like that," Flenco says. Her eyes mist up and she covers his face with her breasts until he reaches up with both hands and tries to push the weighty mass of her mammary monsters up out of the way.

"Goddamn, what you...what are you trying to...trying to...I didn't say...smother me," Mr. Redding says.

Flenco doesn't answer. She closes her eyes and feels the former flicks of his tongue across her breastworks in a memory as real as their truck.

The road is straight, the cotton young and strong, and the Caddy is a speeding bullet across the flat highway. The needle is buried to the hilt at 120 and the car is floating at the very limit of adhesion, weightless, almost, drifting slightly side to side like a ship lightly tacking on the ocean in the stiff edges of a breeze. The blue pulses of light winking far behind him in the sun are like annoying toys, no more. The healer dips handful after handful of roofing tacks out of the sack beside him and flings them out the open window, scattering them like bad seeds. The blue lights fade, are gone, left far behind. Others of like bent are waiting probably somewhere ahead but he'll deal with them when the time comes.

Fruit and vegetable stands flash by the open windows of the car, junk peddlers, mobile homes, stacked firewood corded up on the side of the road for sale, waving people, fans. It is these people he heals, these people crushed and maimed by the falling trees, by the falling house trailers, by the falling cars and junk. These innocents carving a life out of the wilderness with their hands, these with so much faith that he is merely an instrument, a transmitter to funnel the energy required to make them stand up and throw away their braces. He thinks of the promise he made going down reaching for the surface of Lake Huron. He gets another drink of the vodka and lights another cigarette and shakes his head as the hubcaps glitter in the sun.

"Lord God I wouldn't have touched her if I was the Pope!" he suddenly screams out into the car, beating his fist on the seat. He turns his head and shouts out the open window. "Why didn't you let me die and then bring me back as the Pope? Huh? You want to answer that one, Lord?"

He takes another quick suck of the hot vodka. His shoulders shiver, and he caps it.

"I cain't cure everbody in the whole world!"

He slows down and rolls to about 15 mph and shouts to a God maybe lurking behind a dilapidated cotton pen and guarded by a pink Edsel with the hood on the roof.

"You ought not made it so tough on me! I ain't like Jesus, I'm human! I can't do it no more, they's too many of 'em! They's too many women! I take back my promise, I quit!"

The long low surprised face of a farmer in a 1953 Chevrolet pickup with a goat in the back passes by him in slow motion, his head hanging out the window, a woman looking over his shoulder, seeing, figuring the black car and the haranguing finger poking out at a telephone pole, gathering her wits, her thoughts, her breath, to point back, inhale, scream: "It's HIM! PRAISE WONDERFUL GOD IT'S HIIIIIIIM!"

The healer looks. He sees the old black pickup grind to a halt, the one brake light coming on, the woman hopping out the door, arms waving, the farmer leaning out the window waving. For the first time ever the healer is tempted to burn rubber and leave them smelling his getaway fumes, leave behind him unheard the story of their huge drooling son, prisoner of the basement, chained in the garage at the family reunions. But the faces of these two parents are lit like rays of sunshine with the knowledge that a modern messiah has chosen the road that borders their alfalfa patch to receive his Divine instructions.

The woman runs up to the side of the car and lays her hands on the fender as if she'd hold it to keep the car from leaving. Her beady eyes and panting breath and hopeless eternal hope-filled face tell the healer this woman has a task of such insurmountable proportions she's scarce shared the secret of her problem with minister or preacher or parson, that this one's so bad he can't quit now. Holy cow. What pining cripple on his bed of moldy quilts with his palsied arms shaking lies waiting nearly forever for his release? What afflicted lamb has lain behind a curtain to be hidden from company all these years? Here, he sees, are the mother and the father, the suffering parents, here with their pain and their hope and their alfalfa patch and cows and fishponds, their world struck askew by the birth or the affliction or the accident that befell their fallen one, with neither hope of redemption or cure available for what might be eating mothballs or masturbating in dirty underwear or hiding it under his mother's mattress to be discovered when the springs need turning, might be roaming the pastures by night creeping stealthily upon the female livestock.

"Healer," the woman asks, "will you heal my child?"

He's not coming, Flenco suddenly decides. In a burst of thought process too deep for her to understand, a mere scab on the broad scar of telepathy which man's mind forgot to remember eons ago, she knows somehow that another emergency has detained him. She knows, too, that they must therefore go find him. She gets up and catches Mr. Redding under the armpits and drags him through the dust toward the truck, where now in large numbers on the other side of the café windows people stand gathered to track the proceedings and place wagers on the estimated time of arrival of Mr. Redding's demise.

"Oh hope, there's hope," she chants and pants. His heels make two trails of dust through the parking lot but his loafers stay on like a miracle or a magic trick. Flenco gets him next to the running board and stoops to release the precious burden of him, opens the door, gives a hefty grunt and hauls him up into the seat. Mr. Reddings falls over against the horn of the truck and it begins to blow as Flenco shuts the door and runs around to the other side. She yanks open the door and pushes him erect in the seat and reaches across him and locks the door so he won't fall out and hurt himself any worse. Those cigarettes have a hold on him that keeps him from eating, from gaining weight, from not wheezing in the early morning hours when she awakens beside him and lies in the dark staring at his face and twirling the tufts of gray hair on his chest around her fingers. But maybe the healer can even cure him of his addiction, drive the blackness from his lungs, the platelets from his aorta, flush the tiny capillaries in their encrusted fingers of flesh. She seat-belts him.

Mr. Redding sits in a perfect and abject state of apathy, his head keened back on his neck and his closed eyes seeing nothing. Not even coughing.

"Hold on, baby," Flenco says, and cranks the truck. Truckers and patrons stand gawking at the roostertail of dust and gravel kicked up by the spinning wheel of the truck, then it slews badly, hits the road sliding and is gone in a final suck of sound.

With stabbing motions of her arm and hand, index finger extended, the mother directs the healer into the yard. A white picket fence with blooming daffodils belies the nature of the thing inside.

"Please, he's a baby, harmless really, come, in here, behind, I just know you, please, my mother she, my brother too they," she gasps.

The healer turns in and sees the black pickup coming behind him, the goat peeking around the cab as if directing its movement, this Nubian. Before he can fully stop the car, the woman is tugging on his arm, saying, "In here, you, oh, my husband, like a child, really."

He opens the door and starts out as the truck slides to a stop beside him, dust rising to drift over them. The healer waves his hand and coughs and the woman pulls on his arm. The farmer jogs around the hood on his gimpy leg and they each take an arm and lead him up the steps, across the porch, both of them talking in either ear a mix of latent complaints and untold griefs and shared blames for the years this child born wrong and then injured in the brain has visited on this house. The healer is dragged into a living room with white doilies under lamps and a flowerful rug spread over polished wood and a potbellied stove in one corner where a dead squirrel sits eating a varnished walnut.

"Back here, in here, he," the woman rants.

"You know, he, by golly, our field," the farmer raves.

The healer is afraid they're going to smell his breath and he turns his face from side to side as he's dragged with feet sliding to the back room, inside the closet, down hidden stairs revealed by a trapdoor. The farmer unlocks a door in the dark, hits a switch. A light comes on. Gray walls of drabness lie sweating faintly deep in the earth's damp and they're hung with old mattresses brown with spots. The furniture in the room is soft with rot, green with mold. A large, naked, drooling hairy man sits playing with a ball of his own shit in the center of the room, his splayed feet and fuzzy toes black with dirt and his sloped forehead furrowed in concentration. He says, "Huuuuuuuurrrrrnnn......"

The healer recoils. The hairy man sits happily in the center of the floor among plates of old food and the little pies he has made, but looks up and eyes his parents and the paling youth between them and instantly his piglike eyes darken with total ignorance or like the darkest of animals an unveiled hostile threat.

"Hurrrrr," he says, and swivels on his buttocks to face them.

"Sweet Lord Jesus Christ," the healer whispers. "Get me out of here."

"Not so fast, young fella," the farmer says, and unlimbers from a back pocket a hogleg of Dirty Harry proportions, backs to the door behind him, locks it, pockets the key deep in his overalls.

It doesn't smell nice at all in this dungeon and the thing before him begins to try to get up on its knees and make sounds of wet rumbling wanting deep in its throat. The eyebrows knit up and down and together and apart and the healer draws back with his hands up because the man is sniffing now, trying like a blind calf to scent his mother, maybe remembering milk.

Mr. Redding lies back in the seat not even harumphing but merely juxtaposed into the position his wife has seated him in like a form set in concrete while the truck roars down the road. Flenco slurps the sediment of her shake through the straw and flings the used container out the window into a passing mass of sunflowers' bright yellow faces. Her right hand is clenched upon the wheel and her foot is pressed hard on the gas.

"Hold on, baby," she says. "I don't know where he's at but we're going to find him." Her mouth is grim.

Mr. Redding doesn't answer. He sits mute and unmoving with his head canted back and lolling limply on his neck, the squashed knot of his reversible fishing hat pulled down over his ears. He seems uninterested in the green countryside flashing by, the happy farms of cows grazing contentedly on the lush pasture grass, the wooded creeks and planted fields within the industry of American agriculture thriving peacefully beside the road.

Flenco reaches over and gets one of his cigarettes from his pocket and grabs a box of matches off the dash. She doesn't usually smoke but the situation is making her nervous. Afraid that his rancid lips might never again maul her fallow flesh, she scratches the match on the box and touches the whipping flame to the tip of the Pall Mall 100. Deluged with the desperation of despair, she draws the smoke deep and then worries her forehead with the cigarette held between her fingers. Her eyes scan the fertile fields and unpainted barns for a gathering of cripples miraculously assembled somewhere to seek out the ultimate truth. Somewhere between the borders of three counties a black Caddy runs speeding to another destination and she must intercept it or find its location. The rotting fruit of her romance lies hanging in the balance. The sad wreck of her lover must be rejuvenated. All is lost if not.

Flenco remembers the early years with Mr. Redding. Through him the ghost of Elvis not only lived but sang and whirled his pumping hips to dirges engraved on the brains of fans like grooves in records. He could get down on one knee and bring five or six of them screaming to their feet and rushing to the edge of the stage, the nostalgic, the overweight, the faded dyed ever-faithful. Now this sad wasted figure lays his head back on the seat with his lips slightly parted, his tongue drying.

Flenco smokes the cigarette furiously, stabs the scenery with her eyes, roars down the left fork of a road where a sign says HILLTOP 10 MILES. Dust hurtles up behind the pickup as it barrels down the hill. Flenco has the blind faith of love but she panics when she thinks that she might not find the healer, that he might be out of reach already, that he might have taken an alternate road and be somewhere else in the county, doing his work, healing the minions who seek him out, laying his hands on others less fortunate whose despair has eclipsed hers. But as long as there is gas in the truck, as long as Mr. Redding draws breath, she will drive until the wheels fall off the truck, until the cows come home, until they piss on the fire and call the dogs. Until hope, however much is left, is smashed, kicked around, stomped on or gone. Until Mr. Redding is dead.

Flenco eyes him and feels uneasy over his stillness. She's never known him to be this quiet before. She mashes harder on the gas and her beloved sways in the curves.

"Hold on, baby," she whispers.

The healer stands unmoving with the hard round mouth of the pistol in his back. The man on the floor is growling low and grinding his tartared teeth. His hairy arms are encrusted with a nameless nasty crap.

"Aaaarrrrr," he says.

"Yes, darling," the mother coos. "The nice man has come to help us. You like the nice man, don't you, dear?"

"He likes to play," the farmer says. "He plays down here all the time, don't you, son?" the farmer says. "We just keep him down here so he won't scare people," he explains.

The parents see no need to recite the list of stray dogs and hapless cats caught and torn limb from limb, dripping joints of furred meat thrust mouthward without mayonnaise. The six-year-old girl still missing from last year is best not spoken of. The farmer now makes use of a pneumatic tranquilizer gun before laying on the chains and padlocks at night. Delivered at home beside his stillborn twin like Elvis, the hairy one has a headstone over his undug grave.

The warped and wavy line of his dented skull is thick with a rancid growth where small insect life traverses the stalks of his matted hair. He sways and utters his guttural verbs and fixes the healer's face with his bated malevolence and grunts his soft equations into the dusty air.

"He wants to play," the mother says. "Ain't that cute."

"Cute as a bug," the farmer says, without loosening his grip on the pistol.

"I can't heal him," the healer says.

"What did you say?" the farmer says.

"Did he say what I think he said?" the mother says.

"I think you better say that again," the farmer says.

"I can't heal him. I can't heal anything like this."

"What are you saying?" the mother says.

"You heard what he said," the farmer says. "Says he can't heal him."

"Can't?" the mother says.

"I can't," the healer says, as the man on the floor drools a rope of drool and moans a secret rhyme and moves his shoulders to and fro and never takes his eyes off the healer's face.

"I bet you'd like to know what happened to him," the mother says.

"Horse kicked him," the farmer says.

"Right in the head," the mother says.

"Turned him ass over teakettle," the farmer says. "Kicked him clean over a fence."

"Like to kicked half his head off," the mother says. "But you've cured worse than this. That little girl over in Alabama last year with that arm growed out of her stomach and that old man in the Delta who had two and a half eyes. You can heal him. Now heal him."

"We done read all about you," the farmer says. "We been trying to find you for months."

"And then he just come driving right by the place," the mother says. "Will wonders never cease."

The man on the floor is trying to form the rude impulses necessary to gather his legs beneath himself and put his feet flat on the floor. He wants to stand and will stand in a moment and the farmer reaches quickly behind him for the coiled whip on a nail.

"Easy now, son," he says.

A low uneasy moaning begins at sight of the bullwhip and the bared teeth alternate with that in a singsong incantation as he totters up onto his knees and rests his folded knuckles flat on the floor. The hair is long on his back and arms and legs. His face is transfixed with an ignorance as old as time, yet a small light burns in his eyes, and he has a little tail six inches in length extending from the coccyx bone with a tufted tip of bristles. He slides forward a few inches closer to the healer. Old bones lie piled in corners for safekeeping with their scraps of blackened flesh.

"You might as well go on and heal him," the farmer says. "We ain't letting you out of here till you do."

"He's been like this a long time," the mother says.

"You don't understand," the healer says. "I've never dealt with anything like this."

"You cured cancer," the farmer says.

"Raised the dead, I've heard," the mother says.

"No ma'am. Ain't nobody ever raised the dead but Jesus Himself," the healer says, as the thing begins to look as if it would like to grab his leg. He tries to retreat, but the gun is in his back like a hard finger.

"What you think, mama?" the farmer says.

"I think he's trying to pull our leg," she says.

"You think he's a false prophet?"

"Might be. Or maybe he's used up all his power."

"What about it, young feller? You used up all your power?"

"I known it was him when I seen that black car," she says.

"Lots of people have black cars," the healer says dully, unable to take his own eyes off those dully glinting ones before him. What lies inside there will not do to look at, it won't be altered by human hands, probably should have been drowned when it was little. "Don't let him hurt me," he says.

"Hurt you? Why he ain't going to hurt you," the mother says. "He just wants to play with you a little bit. We come down here and play with him all the time, don't we, daddy?"

"That's right," the farmer says. "Hopfrog and leapscotch and like that. Go on and lay your hands on him. He won't bite or nothing. I promise."

"He's real good most of the time," she says. "We just keep him penned up so he won't hurt hisself."

"I can't...I can't...," the healer begins.

"Can't what?" the farmer says.

"Can't what?" the mother says.

"*Touch* him," the healer breathes.

"Uh oh," says the farmer. "I's afraid of that, mama."

"You people have got to let me out of here," the healer says. "I'm on my way to Arkansas."

"Wrong answer, mister," the farmer says.

"Definitely the wrong answer," the mother says.

Their boy moves closer and his snarling mouth seems to smile.

Flenco stands in her nightgown and robe and curlers, pumping gas into the neck of the fuel tank located in the left rear quarter panel of the truck. Years ago Mr. Redding took a hammer and screwdriver to it so that it would readily accept a leaded gasoline nozzle. Flenco pumps five dollars' worth into it and hands the money to the attendant who wiped no windshield and checked no oil but stood gawking at the rigorously mortised figure of Mr. Redding displayed in the seat like a large sack of potatoes. The attendant takes the five and looks thoughtfully at Flenco, then opens his mouth to ask:

"Lady, is this guy all right?"

Flenco starts to go around and get behind the wheel and then when she sees the beer signs hung in the windows of the gas station thinks of the twenty-dollar bill wadded in the pocket of her robe like used facial tissue.

"Well he's been sick," she says, hurrying toward the door of the building.

"I don't believe he's feeling real good right now," he says to her disappearing back. When she goes inside, he watches her heading for the beer coolers at the back of the store and steps closer to the open window of the truck. He studies Mr. Redding from a vantage point of ten inches and notices that his lips are blue and his face is devoid of any color, sort of like, a *lot* like, an uncle of his who was laid out in a coffin in the comfort of his own home some two weeks before. ·

"Mister," he says. "Hey, mister!"

Mr. Redding has nothing to say. Flenco comes rushing back out the door with three quart bottles of cold Busch in a big grocery sack and a small package of cups for whenever Mr. Redding feels like waking up and partaking of a cool refreshing drink. She eyes the attendant suspiciously and gets in the truck and sets the beer on the seat between them, pausing first to open one bottle and set it between her massive thighs. She leans up and cranks the truck and looks at the attendant who steps back and holds up one hand and says, "Don't mind me, lady, it's a free country." Then she pulls it down into D and roars out onto the road.

Flenco gooses it up to about sixty and reaches over briefly to touch Mr. Redding's hand. The hand is cool and limp and she's glad the fever has passed. He'll feel better now that he's had a nap, maybe, not be so irritable. Maybe she can talk to him reasonably. His temper's never been good even when he was sober which hasn't been much these last twenty years. Flenco wonders where all those years went to and then realizes that one day just built onto another one like a mason stacking bricks. All those nights in all those beer joints with all that singing and stomping and screaming and women shouting out declarations of desire for the frenzied figure that was him just past his prime blend together in her mind and spin like carousel horses in a funhouse ride. They billed him as Uncle Elvis, and he's told Flenco a little about his one trip up the river and how they'd hit you in the head with something if you didn't act right, but those days are long gone and what does it matter how since the cars he stole were transient things and even now probably lie stripped and rusted out in some junkyard bog, a hulking garden of flowers adorning their machinegunned sides?

Flenco feels guilty for feeling her faith sag a little when she thinks of all the miles of roads the healer could be on and how easy it will be to miss him. She wonders if it was smart to abandon her big billboard sign by the side of the road and take off like this, but she was feeling the grip of a helpless sudden hopeless inertia and there was nothing to do but put some road under her wheels.

Flenco glances at Mr. Redding who is still oblivious to everything with the wind sailing up his nostrils. She takes a hefty slug of the beer between her legs. She nudges him.

"You want some of this beer, baby? You still asleep? Well you just go on and take you a nap, get rested. Maybe you'll feel better when you wake up."

Flenco hopes that's so. She hopes for a clue, a sign somehow, maybe that gathering of the crippled in a field like she's heard happens sometimes. If she can find him, she'll deliver Mr. Redding into the healer's healing hands herself. But if she can't, she doesn't know what she's going to do. She feels like the eleventh hour is fast approaching, and her beloved sits on the seat beside her in stony silence, his mouth open, his head canted back, the wind gently riffling his thin gray hair now that his reversible cap has blown off.

"I think maybe they need a little time to get to know one another, mama, what do you think?" the farmer says.

"That might be a good idear," the mother says. "Leave 'em alone together a while and maybe they can play."

The healer looks for a place to run but there are no windows in the airless chamber of what his good work has brought him to and no door but the one the farmer guards with the point of a gun.

"You can't leave me down here with him," the healer says, and he searches for some shred of sanity in the seamed faces of the farmer and his wife. His playmate edges closer.

"You could even eat supper with us if you wanted to after you heal him," the mother says. "Be right nice if we could all set down at the table together."

"He makes too big a mess for him to eat with us very much," the farmer says, a little apologetically, gesturing with his gun. "Throws his food everwhere and whatnot."

The farmer turns with the key in his pocket and fumbles down deep in there for it. He takes the key out and has to almost turn his back on the healer to get it in the lock, but he says, "I wouldn't try nothing funny if I was you."

"If you're scared of him biting you we'll hold him and not let him bite you," the mother says.

The key clicks in the lock and the farmer says, "I just don't believe he's much of a mind to heal him, mama. We can go up here and take us a nap and when we come back down they liable to be discussing philosophy or something, you cain't never tell."

"You people don't understand," the healer says. "He's beyond help. There's nothing I can do for him. I don't deal with the mind. I deal with the body."

"Ain't nothing wrong with his body," the mother says. "We just had to slow him down a little."

"His body's in good shape," the farmer says. "He's strong as a ox. Why I've seen him pull cows out of mud holes before. I don't believe he knows how strong he is."

"We'll be back after a while," the mother says, and out the door she goes. "Come on, daddy," she says back. The farmer backs out the door holding the gun on the healer and then the door closes. There are sounds of the other lock being affixed on the other side. The healer backs hard into the corner and eyes the mumbling being in front of him.

"Jesus would heal him if He was here!" the farmer hollers through the thick door. "I done read all about what He done in the Bible! They've done, They've done laid this burden on us to test our faith! Ain't that right, mama!"

"That's right, daddy!" the mother shouts through the door.

"We been tested!" the farmer screams. "We been tested hard and we ain't been found wanting! Have we, mama!"

"You got that right, daddy! Lots of folks couldn't put up with what we've put up with!"

"Just don't make him mad!" the farmer shrieks. "Don't try to take nothing away from him if he's playing with it! He don't like that! He's a little spoiled!"

"He likes to rassle but don't get in a rasslin' match with him cause he gets mad sometimes! Don't get him mad! We'll be back in about an hour! Talk to him! He likes that!"

A rapid clump of footsteps climbing up the stairs fades away to a slammed door above. The healer flattens himself in the corner with his arms bracing up the walls.

"Don't touch me, please," he says, then adds: "I'm not going to hurt you."

The prisoner has made himself a bed of soiled quilts and assorted bedding and he pillows his head with a discarded tire. His nest is knotted with hairs and his lair is littered with lice. The farmer has snipped his hamstrings and Achilles tendon on alternate legs and cauterized the severed sinews while the mother kept the head restrained and the howling muffled with towels rolled and stuffed over his mouth one midnight scene years ago when they became unable to control him. He moves toward the healer, slowly, hard. The healer watches the painful stance, the shifting feet, the arms outspread for balance, and he walks like a man on a tightrope as he makes his way across. Perhaps to kiss? His dangling thangling is large and hairy, swaying there like a big brown anesthetized mole.

The healer watches him come. On the edges of the wasted fields of the South and stuck back in the roadless reaches of timber where people have trails like animals, the unseen faceless sum of mankind's lesser genes quietly disassemble cars and squat underneath trees talking and back of them lie small dwellings of rotted wood and sagging floors where strange children sit wrapped for hours on end slavering mutely and utter no words from their stunned mouths. Pictures of porches full of them all shy and embarrassed or smiling in delight turn up now and again here and there, but no visitor but the documenter of the far less fortunate comes to visit again. It is not that they are not God's children, but that mankind shuns them, bad reminders of rotted teeth and mismatched eyes, uncon-trollable sexual desire turned loose in the woods to procreate a new race of the drooling mindless eating where they shit. He is like them, but even they would not accept him. An old midwife who knew anything would not allow the question. In the first few desperate moments the hand would smother the mouth, pinch the nostrils, still the heaving chest trying to draw in the first tiny breath. The brother and sister above know this. They have known it for years.

The thing comes closer and the healer looks into its depthless eyes, eyes like a fish that lives so deep in the dark black of the ocean and has no need to see. He thinks of the woman's legs in the backseat of the car parked behind a Walgreen's in Sumter and the strength of the promise of God. He thinks not of retribution or outrage, and not even fear any more. He thinks of mercy, and lambs, and he brings his hands out from his sides to suffer to him this outcast. His fingers reach and they touch and he clamps them down hard over the ears. Dust motes turn in the air. They stand in stillness, hardly breathing, locked by the touch of another hand. Their eyes close. The healer fills his chest with air. He prepares to command him to heal.

Flenco sits sobbing beside the road in a grove of trees with a cool breeze wafting through, gently moving the hair on Mr. Redding's head. It's a nice afternoon for a nap, but Flenco has no thoughts of sleep. The search is over and he is cold like a slice of baloney, an egg from the refrigerator. The state troopers cluster behind her and slap their ticket books along their legs, heads shaking in utter solemnity or undisguised amazement. The ambulance crew waits, their equipment useless, still scattered their ambu bags and cardiopulmonary cases over the gravelly grass. The sun is going down and the legendary speeder has not appeared, and the road-block will soon be broken up, the blue-and-white cruisers sent out to other destinations like prowling animals to simply prowl the roads.

But an interesting phenomenon has briefly materialized to break the boredom of an otherwise routine afternoon, a fat woman drunk and hauling the dead corpse of her husband down the road at ninety, sobbing and screaming and yelling out loud to God, and they wait now only for the coroner to place his seal of approval so that the body can be moved. One trooper leans against a tree chewing a stem of grass and remarks to nobody in particular: "I been to three county fairs, two goatropins and one horsefuckin', and I ain't never seen nothing like that."

Some chuckle, others shake their heads, as if to allow that the world is a strange place and in it lie things of another nature, a bent order, and beyond a certain point there are no rules to make man mind. A wrecker is moving slowly with its red lights down the road. Doves cry in the trees. And down the road in a field where someone has stood them stand three giant wooden crosses, their colors rising in the falling sunlight, yellow, and blue, and tan.

Choose Your Travel Partner Wisely

Michelle Richmond

We first spotted them at Gate B27 in Dallas International Airport. Both were tall, blond, and neatly dressed. I got the feeling their physical similarities brought them together, two people looking for near copies of themselves, albeit in the opposite sex. She smiled at me while he was engrossed by his book, a paperback with embossed gold lettering on the cover. The title of the book was *All of Us*.

The woman stared a second too long. I hid behind *The Dallas Morning News*. "Is she still looking?"

"Yes," Jim said.

"What does she want?"

"Maybe she knows you."

"I've never seen her before in my life."

On the plane, the blond couple sat right behind us, so close I could smell the light flowery scent of her perfume. Every now and then I'd peek through the crack between our seats and they'd be whispering to each other. When they caught me spying they'd stop talking.

Finally we descended toward the runway in San Jose Cabo. To the left I could see the desert mountains, sanded a dull brown, and to the right the lush sea, blue and roiling. It was early evening, and a yellow light shimmered over the mountains, the sea, the tip of the airplane's wing. We stepped off the plane into a dry pleasant stillness. After passing through customs, where a crumpled man gave our passports a cursory glance, Jim and I followed a driver named Lupe to an old blue van and climbed in. Minutes later the couple boarded the van and sat behind us.

"Surprise," I whispered. We looked straight ahead, but the man leaned forward and said in an unnaturally loud voice, "Hello. We are the Thompsons. How often do you do this?"

I turned around and got my first good look at him. His face was pleasant and eager, his hair wavy; he looked like one of those guys you see modeling off-brand slacks in the Mervyn's catalog. His wife was a couple of years his senior and was holding a big orange beach bag on her lap. On top of the bag was a brochure for their hotel: *Westin Regina. No Barriers.* The front of the brochure had pictures of surgically proportioned women in small bikinis frolicking in the surf.

"It's our first time to Mexico," I said, vaguely sensing that I wasn't answering the appropriate question, that by *this* he meant something other than vacations to Mexico, although I wasn't sure. "What about you?"

"This is our second year," she said. "Our first to Mexico, but our second time to do this. Last time it was Puerto Rico."

"We live in Chicago," the man said. "I have psoriasis, and the salt air and heat is good for my condition." He held up his arm and showed us a large brown patch stretching from elbow to wrist.

The woman shifted in her seat and looked down at the floor, and he glanced over at her, apologetic-like, and reached for her hand but she wouldn't take it. I got the feeling he was always making inappropriate comments that turned people off to them as a couple, always confessing things best saved for later. I got the feeling maybe she couldn't forgive him for doing this, but it was a habit he couldn't break, born of desperation and a naive kind of honesty.

"Oh," I said. "My dad had that." It wasn't true, but I wanted Mr. Thompson to know I didn't hold the psoriasis against him. I wanted to show empathy, something my husband had been teaching me to do over the years, although I never quite caught on.

"Really?" Mr. Thompson said.

And then I realized "had" was probably the wrong word choice, as it implied that my dad might have died from psoriasis, so I added, "He died of liver cancer." Also untrue. I added a few small details to make the lie more credible: "Last month. He was 73. The funeral was in New Orleans."

There was another awkward pause. Mrs. Thompson said, "I'm sorry to hear that," and Jim said, "It's okay. They weren't close." I marveled at his ability to take a white lie to its logical end, to twist the lie in such a way as to make everyone feel as comfortable as possible.

I looked out the window. Small motels rose up between stretches of unoccupied beach and desert brush. Skinny cacti lined the median. The roadside was crowded with dilapidated billboards advertising perfume and cigarettes, health clubs and tequila. Finally a grand resort came into view, all red and blue stucco lit up against the cool brown evening. Lupe pulled into the long driveway winding down toward the beach. Attractive Mexican youth in hotel uniforms were standing around in the open lobby. The lobby was just a pale elegant slab of marble nestled under some rustling palm trees, no walls or windows. No barriers, as Mrs. Thompson's brochure promised.

The couple got out of the van. "Have fun," I said.

Mr. Thompson looked confused. "Oh, you're not staying here?"

"We're at Solmar."

"We'll be here for a week," Mrs. Thompson said. "Call us. We'll get dinner, drinks, see how it goes."

"Okay, we'll do that," I said, knowing that we wouldn't. They seemed too desperate somehow, too needy. I could imagine them hanging onto us through the whole vacation, sapping our attention, grinding on our nerves. I thought about a girl I knew in grammar school named Doris, who wore fuzzy yarn ribbons in her hair and followed me earnestly from first to fifth grade, each year inviting me to a birthday party at which I was the only guest.

In our room that night, with the sea breeze coming in from the balcony and the sound of fireworks thundering in the distance, we leafed through the complimentary Cabo magazine. On page 57 there was an ad for the Westin Regina. "They have passion," the ad said. "They have fun. They have...*no barriers.*" At the bottom of the page, in big yellow letters: "Westin Regina. Where The Lifestyle meets the sun. Choose your travel partner wisely."

"Why do you think they capitalized The Lifestyle?" I said. "Is that code for something?"

"Swinging," Jim said. "Wife-swapping. You take mine, I'll take yours." He was concentrating on the add, reading the fine print.

I thought of Mrs. Thompson's parting words—*we'll see how it goes.*

"Oh my God. Do you think the Thompsons—"

"Yep."

"Do you think they think we do too?"

"Looks that way."

Jim was in the best mood he'd been in since we left home. I imagined breasts, hands, hairy chests, a spidery tangle of arms and legs. Suddenly I felt nervous, like what if Jim had delved into this before we met, and what if he wanted to do it again? I yanked the magazine out of his hands. "So how did you know what The Lifestyle means, anyway?"

"I had this second cousin from Wisconsin. He was involved with that stuff."

"How come you never mentioned it before?"

"I hardly know the guy. He told me about it several years ago at a family reunion. He was drinking bourbon and Coke and he was depressed and all, and it just slipped. What happened was, I said to Walt, 'Sorry to hear about the divorce,' and he said 'I can't blame Darlene. I have to blame The Lifestyle.' Then he tells me how they used to go down to Boca Raton three times a year to partake. He said it was like some kind of smorgasbord. One minute you have a slab of Wisconsin Cheddar in front of you, and the next minute, you're in The Lifestyle, and whoa, there's this platter with the Wisconsin Cheddar, plus the double crème Brie, the Havarti, the Camembert, the smoked Gouda, the works. And suddenly the double crème Brie looks better than the Wisconsin Cheddar. Walt, see, he's this pale, overweight guy, and he was the Cheddar."

"That's how he put it?"

"Maybe he was the Velveeta. That's not the point. Point is Darlene suddenly saw what life was like with the full cheese board."

I was thinking about Jim's pale fat second cousin, Walt, taking his skinny little wife to Boca Raton, and how there'd be all those tan men down there in their khaki shorts, their muscled legs, their deck shoes, and how Walt must have regretted ever getting Darlene involved in all that.

"Poor Walt didn't stand a chance," I said, putting my arms around Jim's neck. The talk of broken marriages had made me feel affectionate.

"Do you want to make love?"

"Not yet."

"Does that mean maybe later?"

"Of course."

In the old days, if I wanted sex all I had to do was unsnap my bra or pat Jim in a certain way in the small of the back or give him this "Hey, I'm your wife" look from across the room, but lately there always had to be conversation, negotiation, deliberation. I couldn't figure out when or why sex had lost its spontaneity, becoming some official act demanding diplomacy.

"Okay," I said. "What should we do, then?"

"Let's check out the beach."

A light breeze was blowing, and the white hotel rising against the bleached rock in the moonlight reminded me of some place I'd been as a child. The beach was deserted except for an elderly woman in a red swimsuit doing leg lifts on her towel. We asked her to take our picture, which she did, but then she insisted on taking the same picture several times. "Your eyes were closed," she said the first time, then, "I cut your heads off," then, to me, "Hon, suck your stomach in."

After returning to our room and showering we lay naked in bed watching a sexy show. The show was in Spanish and I couldn't understand the words, but I could tell that the characters on the show lived lives of wild abandon, of great passion and sexual urgency. I started rubbing Jim's back. "Seriously," I said. "Would you ever?"

"Ever what?"

"You know. Like the Thompsons."

"It would have to be the right couple," he said.

I traced the spatter of light brown moles on his back, which were sort of in the shape of the Big Dipper. "How would you know when you found the right couple?"

"They'd be about our age," he said, "and good-looking, of course." He rolled over and looked at me. "Like the Thompsons. Maybe we should call them."

"You're kidding, right?"

"Maybe."

That night I dreamt of a famous young Hollywood couple. In the dream, they were sitting in our suite, wearing terrycloth robes. The man, dark-haired and tan, started kissing me. The woman, red-headed and softly lit, offered my husband a drink. She had very pale and lovely feet. She slid her foot up my husband's leg, and then I woke. I couldn't go back to sleep after that. I felt sad and vaguely frightened.

The next few days we lounged on the beach, went snorkeling at the Santa Maria coral reef, and watched whales breaching as they journeyed, slow and slick-backed, from the Sea of Cortez into the wide cold Pacific. We drank a great deal of Tecate and margaritas, ate fried eggs with tomatoes and peppers, lobster tail and shrimp with molé sauce, thick tortilla chips dipped in guacamole. By the time we got back to our room each night we were too tired and hot and full for sex.

On our final evening, nursing sunburns and a vague sense of malaise, we walked into town for dinner. We chose a little restaurant a few blocks from the beach, a thatch-roofed hut run by a man from Croatia. The restaurant was crowded with locals and tourists. A mariachi band was playing by the bar. We took the only available table, which was on the outdoor patio and close enough to the road that we could smell exhaust from passing cars. We had just ordered our drinks when my husband spotted the Thompsons several yards down the sidewalk, walking in our direction. The sidewalk was busy, and they passed without looking into the restaurant.

"Should we invite them to dinner?" Jim asked.

We'd been in Cabo for five days, with only each other for company. By then we'd grown slightly argumentative and bored. "If you really want to," I said.

Jim got up and disappeared into the sidewalk crowd. In a couple of minutes he was back, the Thompsons by his side. Their faces were slightly burnt. She was wearing a strapless top, and bathing suit lines cut across her shoulders. Jim glanced at her breasts. Following his eyes there,

I noticed how good they looked, pressing against the white cotton of her top.

"Hello," they said in unison.

"Hi. I never got your first names."

"Steve," he said. "This is Rebecca."

I told them ours. "Please, have a seat."

The waiter appeared with two more menus, and we ordered a pitcher of margaritas and the seafood sample appetizer. We talked about snorkeling and deep sea fishing, about movies and antique gramophones, the latter of which the Thompsons collected, about UPS versus FedEx. We were having ourselves a regular conversation until, three pitchers into the evening, Jim looked up from his chile relleno and said to Steve, "So tell us about the wife-swapping."

Rebecca looked at him as if he'd just spat in the communion cup. "It's no longer called wife-swapping," she said. "That ended long ago. Now it's called The Lifestyle." She was sitting next to me, and over the course of the evening her chair had mysteriously migrated a few inches in my direction. Every time she reached for her drink, her hand brushed my forearm.

"It's not just the name that's changed," Steve said, scratching his bicep. "The whole system is different now. The nuances are different. For example, a couple may get together and the man go with the man, the woman with the woman." He put a hand on Jim's shoulder when he said this.

I was waiting for Jim to start laughing the way he does when he's nervous, but he didn't. He patted Steve on the back like they were the best of friends, like it didn't bother him one bit where Steve was going with this.

"Or one spouse may choose to sit out and watch the other three together," Steve said. "Everything is a mutual agreement between two spouses, who choose their partners wisely, it is assumed, and together."

"Interesting," Jim said. The waiter came at just that moment, and I ordered another round of margaritas. The question that was on my mind, the question I didn't dare ask, was why they approached us on that first night, why they thought we'd be interested. Did we give off some subtle, deceptive signal that erroneously marked us as swingers?

One hour and two pitchers later, Steve took my husband's elbow in his hand and said, "Would you like to join us for a drink at our hotel?"

I was trying to figure out how to politely refuse when Jim blurted, "We'd love to."

Rebecca and Steve went out to hail a cab, leaving us alone for a moment. "What the hell are you doing?" I said.

"Lighten up," Jim said, kissing me on the cheek. "It's just a drink."

In the taxi, I took the front seat and stared ahead at the black road melting into the darkness, while the others carried on a lively conversation in the back. In the rearview mirror I could see Jim sitting between the Thompsons. Steve's hand rested dangerously high on Jim's thigh, and Jim wasn't doing anything about it. Once, before we were married, Jim had said, "In the sex department, there's nothing I wouldn't try once," but I never believed him. Back then, I thought he was just trying to impress me.

Soon we were at the Westin Regina in a room clearly designed for romance. Suite 127 had a high white ceiling and tile floors, a king-sized bed with red sateen sheets, a heart-shaped hot tub in the corner. We were all standing around trying to act casual, and Steve was looking grateful, and my husband was looking inquisitive, and Rebecca was looking at me, and, feeling that I had to defend myself, that I had to set things straight, I said, "The last time I kissed a girl was in the fifth grade. We were playing spin-the-bottle at Marnie Topeka's house." I remembered Doris with her closed eyes, her puckered lips, the look of sheer excitement on her face as she kissed me. The kiss lasted only a second, but after that I felt I'd done my duty, and I never answered her phone calls again, never went to another one of her lonely birthday parties.

Rebecca stood by the door, her hand draped over the knob like a woman in a champagne ad. The moment we walked into the room, she had transformed into the poster girl for Miss Elegance Perfume. Now, she walked over to me and put a hand on my shoulder. "Mary," she said. "May I call you Mary?"

"Okay."

My name isn't Mary. I don't know how she came up with it. I have to admit it made me feel a little more relaxed, though, being a Mary, as though I wouldn't have to live with the consequences of whatever happened here. Whatever happened here would be Mary's problem.

"Good." She had slipped her hand under my blouse and was tracing my spine with one finger. My skin felt very hot. "You should know, Mary, that we're not going to ask you to do anything you don't want to do. Okay? This is all about what *you* want."

Steve moved toward my husband, and I was wondering if psoriasis was contagious, and I was half hoping they'd pull out an Amway brochure or a Church of Latter-Day Saints pamphlet, and then we could all have a good laugh because this had been a big misunderstanding, and the Thompsons would confess, a bit awkwardly, that all they ever wanted to do was sell us shampoo or eternal life. But then I saw that Steve was actually unbuttoning his shirt, and then Rebecca started taking off her top, and I realized that nothing we were going to do here would get us anywhere close to heaven. I heard the sound of a zipper across the room. I reached over and turned off the light, because there are some things you don't want to see.

It felt like college all over again, that moment in the bunk bed in your dorm room with the guy from Psychology 101 when you think, "I've done it now," because by this point you've let him get so far—due to ill planning, indifference, embarrassment, whatever—that you've reached what is commonly referred to as the point of no return, and you realize there is no graceful way to derail the train, and that doing so would be too much trouble, and besides, being on the train is really no worse than being off the train, and you're just concentrating on getting back to the station, where you can say goodbye and wave politely from the platform. And then Rebecca was talking to me real quiet, and I was too dizzy from drink to understand what she was saying, and I was smiling at her, trying hard not to be prudish, and I could see my husband in the far corner of the room peeling off his socks, and I heard Steve say, "Is that all right?"

I kept trying to catch Jim's eye, waiting for him to indicate we weren't really going through with this, but he wouldn't look at me. I remembered my grandmother's meat Jell-O, no lie, this Jell-O actually had ground beef in it, mixed with cream cheese and raspberries, and it was lime Jell-O, and we had to eat it every Fourth of July, when every other family was eating fried chicken and frosted cupcakes, and in the car on the way to my grandmother's house my dad would say, "She's worked hard to make it a special day and if you don't eat the meat Jell-O there'll be another thing coming." I was remembering how I'd always been so polite when my grandmother passed the meat Jell-O, how I'd never once hurt her feelings, and how my husband was over there not hurting Steve's feelings, and I was not hurting Rebecca's feelings, and how we'd be back at the station any day now.

Then something happened: Jim let out this little moan. It was a sound I'd always thought he shared with me alone, a sound he made when he was really enjoying things. It occurred to me that he was not just being polite; he was getting into this.

I look back now and think I could have done it. I could have, probably would have, if Rebecca's fingers hadn't been so cold, if when she touched my breast I hadn't felt a chill go straight through her fingertip to the center of me, a chill that knocked me back to reality, to the prim and proper constraints of my limited world view. It also occurred to me, as her cold fingers were circling my nipple, that she looked a lot like Ralph Fiennes—something in the eyes, or maybe the jaw. It was too much. "Wait!" I said, gathering my blouse around my shoulders. Rebecca pulled her hand away. Steve looked up.

"What?" Jim said.

Steve ran his hands through his hair slowly, a slick Bee Gees sort of move that made the whole scene even more unsettling. "Is everything okay?"

"Mary, honey," Rebecca said.

They were all staring at me, waiting. I felt like the kid who refuses to smoke pot behind the bleachers, the kid who ruins all the fun. "I'm sorry," I said. "We have to go now."

"Let's just take it slow," Jim said.

"I can't do this." I turned to Rebecca and said, "My name's not Mary."

"Why don't you take a taxi?" Jim said. "I'll meet you back at our place."

"Please," I said. I knew if we did this, things would be different between us. I wasn't sure how, exactly, but it was clear to me that once we took this step, there'd be no getting back to where we were before. For several seconds Jim just stood there, looking from me to Steve, then Rebecca. I could tell he was deciding between us—between this couple we'd just met and me, his wife of seven years.

"Let's talk this out," Steve said. Was it just my perspective, or did Steve have a smug look on his face, like he knew he had this thing in the bag? I imagined a line of uncertain couples stretching out the door, each succumbing, one by one, to Steve and Rebecca's persuasion.

Finally, Jim buttoned his shirt, pulled on his shoes and socks, and patted Steve on the shoulder. "Listen," he said to Steve, "I'm really sorry."

"It's normal to be nervous," Rebecca said as I turned the doorknob; perhaps she still thought she might be able to win me over. Steve sat on the edge of the bed. "It could've been fun," he said. "It could've been really terrific."

Rebecca smiled at me in a way that reminded me of Doris that night at Marnie Topeka's house, the night she spun the bottle and the nozzle pointed at me; after the kiss, during which I kept my eyes open and my lips closed, Doris's big face loomed over me, smiling in a forgiving and disappointed way. "Call us if you change your mind," Rebecca said.

In the hallway, Jim didn't look at me. He didn't say one word on the ride back to the hotel. In our room, he stood staring out the window for some time. Finally, he said, "What happened? You used to be game for anything. You used to be so much fun."

Our evening with the Thompsons remained a closed subject for months. Neither of us brought it up. But I could sense in Jim some lingering disappointment, some silent acknowledgment that I was, in the end, a lesser woman than he'd hoped I could be. I think, after that night, he became resigned to something he'd been suspecting for a long time: I wasn't designed for wild adventures and unconditional generosity. We made love less often, laughed less frequently. Sometimes I would find him gazing at me from across the room, a confused look on his face, as if, for the life of him, he couldn't remember why he'd married me.

Then, one afternoon in April when I was cleaning out the hall closet, I came upon a video. The video was called "The Lifestyle." It was a documentary which, according to the jacket copy, followed ten couples around while they went to various parties meeting other couples who went to the same sort of parties. A reviewer for *The Village Voice* promised "a rollicking good time."

The edges of the box were torn, and the label on the video was faded. I imagined all the places the tape had been. I went into the living room, where Jim sat reading Trotsky's *My Life*, and said, "What were you thinking, bringing this home?"

Jim closed his book. "I was just curious," he said. He looked so embarrassed I almost felt sorry for him.

I popped the tape in the VCR. He pretended to keep reading. In the documentary, staid interviews were interspersed with scenes from parties. At the parties, naked men and women talked about sports and home repair, solar paneling and lawn fertilizer. In the background, other couples were cavorting and moaning. The overall impression was one of mundanity and poor health, rolls of fat jiggling and big breasts swaying, men with triangular torsos saying dirty things while they watched someone else have sex with their wives. The houses in the video all had black Formica furniture and walls covered with bright prints in plastic frames. I couldn't imagine the Thompsons in such a scene. They were too attractive, too healthy, too well-dressed. I almost felt a stab of pity for them. I imagined them stepping into one of these parties, instant prey, the most desirable couple by far in every situation. Their dance cards would be full all night, and they'd go home feeling queasy and slightly used.

In one scene, there were all these naked people sitting around by a pool, and this one guy was working the gas grill, wearing a baseball cap that said Green Bay Packers. He was flipping burgers and talking to another man, also naked, who was holding a stack of Chinette plates. They were discussing the advantages of propane heat.

The video cut from the swimming pool scene to a room inside the house. There was brown paneling on the walls and several mattresses on the floor. One couple was having sex, while across the room a muscular brunette woman played Battleship with a man in red underwear. "You sunk my battleship," the brunette said, just as the other woman reached orgasm in the corner.

"Good timing," Jim said. He was trying to make light of the situation, but I wasn't laughing.

A few seconds later the man on the mattress looked directly into the camera and grunted unpleasantly. "B6," said the man in red underwear. The woman sat up and straightened her skirt. She looked nothing like a person who had just engaged in a pleasurable act. She was straight-faced and serious, emotionless, like someone about to be interviewed for a job in retail. There was something disturbingly clinical about the whole scene.

Jim got up, grabbed the remote from me, and hit the stop button. "It wouldn't have to be like that," he said.

"Why did you want to?" I said. "What did you expect to get out of it?"

"I just thought we could do something different for a change."

He dropped the remote on the coffee table and went into the bedroom, shutting the door behind him. I wished I could go back to that night and do it all again, just close my eyes and let it happen and prove myself to Jim. I didn't know what I'd prove exactly—that I still possessed an adventurous streak? That after seven years of marriage, I could still surprise?

After that, we didn't make love for a long time, almost two months. When we finally did, one night when we were both drunk, pictures from the documentary came to me, big naked men with strange patterns of hair on their bodies, scantily clad women making ugly faces, blobs of potato salad on shaky Chinette plates. I thought of meat Jell-O, Fourth of July, homemade fireworks sputtering over a dirty little pond. Jim came with his eyes closed; he used to always keep them open.

That night, after Jim fell asleep, I tried to think of clever schemes to save our marriage. I began to imagine scenarios in which we encountered the Thompsons again; I almost wished for it to happen. At odd moments when Jim and I were set adrift in some foreign place, I would think of the Thompsons, and would convince myself that we might run into them at any moment. I envisioned this chance reunion, how I would go forward to meet them. There would be no need for conversation, only the quick nod, the slight smile, the touch on the elbow, and they would know from this subtle signal that I meant for them to follow us. In some dark hotel room I would undress without shame, offering myself to Rebecca in a way that I could not do before. Often, in waking dreams, I witness with great clarity the details of this encounter. In the street below, a vendor is selling apples. A group of schoolchildren pass beneath our window. I move one hand slowly over the pale curve of Rebecca's hip. With the other I touch her neck, her collarbone, then, with one quick motion, unhook her bra. Rebecca sighs and pulls me closer, and I look up to see my husband standing in the corner, silently undressing. "It's all right," I say to him, "anything goes."

ROME, ITALY

Fannie Flagg

Mrs. Lenore Simmons Krackenberry, a large, imposing woman with a scarf flowing behind her, was escorted into a private room at the Vatican and apologetically informed that her audience with the pope would be limited to five minutes. She smiled good-naturedly at the young man and in a deep Southern drawl so thick you could cut it with a knife said, "Honey, five minutes is all I need. He's busy. I'm busy. So that's just fine."

She sat with a lace handkerchief on her head bearing the initials LSK and admired the tapestries hanging on the walls while she waited. She had decided to spend her "Soak Up Culture Month" in Italy this year, so she could kill two birds with one stone, and this was one of those birds.

In a few minutes she was ushered into a room where the pope was sitting with his interpreter standing by his side. She walked up and said, "Well, how do you do, I'm Lenore Simmons Krackenberry all the way from Selma, Alabama. And I know one of your darling archbishops from Mobile, Archbishop Oscar Lipscomb. We are both on the board of the International Coalition of Christians and Jews, and while I was in town I wanted to drop by and chat with you about this birth control thing."

The small, thin, nervous man by his side turned to the pope and said in Italian, "Your Holiness, I am afraid I cannot understand what she has said; her English is very poor."

The pope smiled and nodded at Lenore. She smiled back and continued, "Now look, I know you all are against it, but really, you need to change those little rules. I think you really need to get behind this thing and tell all your people to stop breeding so much. Too many people are going hungry.

"Not to mention the overpopulation problem. Why just look at Bangladesh, those poor people are starving to death...I'm head of the Selma chapter of Planned Parenthood and we think it's just cruel to bring children into the world just to have them starve to death. If you can't feed them you shouldn't have them...don't you agree?"

The interpreter said, "I believe the lady is speaking of a drum that is free...or something of this nature."

The pope nodded and smiled. Lenore Simmons Krackenberry smiled back, and asked the interpreter, "What did he say?"

"His Holiness appreciates your interest in this matter."

"Oh? Well good. Tell him I love his outfit, and tell him he should come to Mobile sometime for Mardi Gras. We have all kinds of lovely clothes he would like. Brocades, silks...the King and Queen of Mardi Gras outfits alone cost over one hundred thousand dollars. And we would love to have him. Tell him he could have his own float if he wanted."

The interpreter pulled a long white handkerchief out of the pocket of his cassock and wiped his brow and said, "Your Holiness, I am sorry. But I am sure she will not be much longer."

Lenore looked at the pope. "Your palace is just lovely. I'm a Presbyterian myself but I can certainly appreciate all the time and effort you go to to keep it looking so nice."

The interpreter said, "She says something about..." He faltered, "I cannot be sure..."

The pope smiled pleasantly and nodded at her. Lenore glanced at her watch.

"Well, I'm going to run now...but I did want to put that bug in your ear while I was here..."

The interpreter smiled, "I think she is finished." The pope smiled again and said something pleasant in Italian.

"What did he say?" asked Mrs. Krackenberry, smiling and nodding back.

"His Holiness would like to thank you for your visit. He is always most happy to receive Americans and would like to give you his blessing."

"Oh...well, how sweet."

The pope made the sign of the cross and gave her a long blessing in

Latin. When he finished she did a small Magnolia Trail Maiden curtsy and said, "I loved meeting you. And do come to Selma sometimes, we would just love to have you. Now, if you come, you be sure to call me, I'm in the book…and I'll tell Archbishop Lipscomb you said hello…Arrivederci!"

Lenore walked out and met her friend, Mrs. Pearl Jeff, who had come to Rome with her and who was waiting outside.

Mrs. Jeff said, "Well, did you meet him?"

"I sure did, and honey, he is just precious, the cutest jolliest thing. He couldn't have been nicer."

"What happened? Tell me everything."

"Well we chatted for a few minutes, of course, to be polite. And then I told him what I thought and he seemed to agree."

"Oh, what did he say?"

"Well he didn't say much. He just more or less listened. You know, he doesn't speak a word of English. I had to be interpreted. But at the end he said a little something in Italian. Now you mark my words, I bet we see a big change in that birth control policy in the very near future."

"Really?" said Mrs. Jeff in awe.

Lenore waved away a pigeon that was flying over her head. "Oh, yes, and I invited him to come to Selma. I told him we would love to have him."

"Ohhh, do you think he might come?"

Lenore looked at Pearl. "Well I don't know why in the world he shouldn't. He loves America."

A WALTZ IN THE SNOW

Eric Kingrea

The train rumbled east, toward the frontlines and away from the setting sun, so that Holden had to peer behind him from his window seat to see the light die. He took a closing glance at the light, before the heights of the surrounding mountains consumed it, with only the artist colors painting the sky to mark its fall from view. He shifted, situating himself for the hundredth time on this rough ride.

Holden was a storyteller, a fine one. Told stories to the other soldiers about hunting twelve-point bucks for days on end in his Carolina woods and about all-night moonshine binges busted by revenuers. The men in his company always took his stories with a grain of salt, or maybe a shaker full. Nobody cared if his stories were the truth. Holden's tales kept them warm, made them laugh, calmed their fears. Holden didn't mind when many simply fell asleep in the middle of a story, his voice soothing them like their mother's had when they were children, plump-faced and dirty-nosed, clean and happy, a hundred years ago and a million miles away.

The journey was well into its second hour, and those soldiers who could not sleep were drawn like flies to sugar, one by one, toward the big man, careful not to step on any of their sleeping companions scattered about the floor, gathering around Holden for a tale.

He grinned at the hopeful faces surrounding him. He removed his tobacco pouch, packed it, and put a wad in his cheek. He used a spare canteen of German make for the chew, and spat into it at regular intervals. Sitting there a spell, enjoying the burley, he let the suspense rise, glancing for split seconds at each soldier, then off into the night.

Holden slapped his thigh, spat again into the canteen, and said, "Well, then." And he took another look around at his audience. "Y'all want to hear a story?" A mumble of assent rolled through the men. So he began.

"I'm going to tell you the gospel truth, every word of it. It was a beautiful thing to see. Most times I don't believe it actually happened myself, and I end up thinking that's the thing with remembering—if something happens too fast or too hard, you're stuck with the feeling that maybe it never happened at all. Then I remember something little. Change in the wind, maybe, or some curse I made at the snow. Those little things are what keep this story real to me."

Holden stopped to spit. "Wasn't too long ago this happened. We were surrounded by the Krauts in Bastogne. 'Bout the time when it was coldest, if y'all can remember, and you'd have to be dead in a grave if you don't. Snow was packed tight and the ground froze over faster than you could dig it out for a hole. It was insane, that snow, unnatural and clinging hard to the trees. White for as far as you could see, nothing but white. The trees were white too. I remember how those needles and the snow would shower down whenever artillery hit them. Snow and trees, that was about it. Yeah, and the Germans were peppered about the forest right along with us. Sometimes a man just wandered around—lost—not sure where the hell he was, and just dumb to get lost with all them Krauts around.

"So I was an idiot and got myself lost: me and a couple of the guys—Bishop and Hollinger. Y'all remember Bishop, huh? Scrawny kid, small? Little moustache? And Hollinger, Alabama boy, hard one to forget…"

Someone interrupted.

"Yeah, a hunter, that's right. That boy would parade the fact wouldn't he? Saying how he'd done it all, stalked his deer, him and his dog, with a bow and arrow no less. Smeared himself with its blood and drank it, adding in some whiskey for kick. He kept on saying he wanted to go hunting. Well, that's what we did, we went hunting. We were in a forest. That's where deer live. So, we went looking for deer. We started talking about a big buck that we could roast up. Bishop even had a piece of tent we could use to hide the fire from the Krauts. Hell, we could smell the fat and backstaps on our pans already. Hunger, boys, the hunger did it to us, made us take those risks we knew we shouldn't be taking. That gnawing hunger that every man here has felt. Can't concentrate for the rumbling in your belly, can't think, can't fight.

"We left our holes when night came. There was a full moon, clear sky, we could see fine. It was pretty out there, I'll give it that much, the moon made the white silvery, made it seem like we were sloshing through riches, pure wealth, the silver in the snow and the diamonds in the sky. It was pretty. We drifted through the forests like ghosts—silent as smoke. It was mad, as y'all might be thinking, no sane man would be caught in the dead of that night, wandering around, chasing after some meat hidden in the trees. Red faces, red eyes, we had them, like wolves driven on instinct and hunger, always the hunger.

"Half into the night, I coulda swore on a stack of Bibles that I heard harsh German mumblings coming up from the ground, as if our Mother Earth herself had betrayed us. Those are the tricks your mind can play on you. I tell you, that brain of yours has got a darker sense of humor than the night that's caking us as I speak. We'd stopped for a rest—for Bishop to get feeling back into his feet—when one of those white pines exploded not sixty yards from our position. In the background there was a high screeching, like a train turning ass-over-end off of its rails. Pine needles rained down, sharp and light on the air. I did what I was taught. I found cover, and I laid there, flat as a board, teeth clenched, eyes open and watching. I don't know why I kept my eyes open, but what I saw was pretty too, in its way. I watched the mile-high dirt jumps, the moon shaking from the awesome power being leveled on the earth, exploding trees and pine needles falling like broken snowflakes, all of it in slow motion.

"And Hollinger. I saw he hadn't moved, hadn't made for cover, just kneeled down and put his head into the snow. That's when I saw it. I can't rightly say what kind of thing it was I thought I was seeing, but it was the stuff of children's nightmares. It was such an odd thing, how that German tank had taken on the likeness of some beast, coming on like something gone mad up out of the pits of hell, the Devil himself riding it hard and screaming, driving it with hate and death. There lay Hollinger, in the path of that tank, Satan's creature. He was on his knees, weak. About to be crushed—almost dead then—until Bishop, an angel, little Bishop with his scraggly little moustache, ran out from wherever he'd been, grabbed Hollinger, and dragged him into a ditch. Saved his life, he did, and deserves a medal for it, and I'll be saying that to my grave. Then the tank rattled off to the right, went out of sight over a little hill, and the night got real quiet again, but for the ringing in our ears.

"I walked out, thankful to be alive, and checked on the other guys. Hollinger sat on the ground, his back against a tree, his eyes open wide. Not like in fear open wide, just a stunned wide, wide like they were gonna cover the world. Bishop was with him, talking to him. Then as I walked up he snapped out of it. He blinked his eyes, stuttered through his first couple of words, then promised us that he was all right. Bishop asked him if he was sure, if maybe we should get back to our positions. And Hollinger got a look, his eyes went narrow, said, 'You're still hungry, ain't you?' He grabbed his rifle, that same weapon, boys, he'd dropped in fear, and shuffled off into the snow and the night.

"We followed him. He was different. This man was not Hollinger who'd knelt down afraid out there. Here he goes crashing his way through the snow, with the ugly look of a dog hungry for something to bite. We followed him best we could, but he was always a good ten yards in front, blasting across the frozen ground. He scrambled up a little hill, slipped a time or two, and stopped cold at the height of it, dropped flat. When we caught up, he motioned us to hush. Hollinger pointed to a clump of pines. I looked, and I spotted it. Like it appeared out of the haze. I thought that my scattered mind had conjured up a ghost. We sat there, still as statues, staring at it.

"Not forty paces away was the biggest, most beautiful buck I had ever seen. Had to be my size at least, and muscle, every inch on its body was corded muscle, strong. White as death and the snow we were frozen to. It was a wonder how we ever saw the thing before it saw us. I kept blinking, every time it moved, like it was going to disappear. And fade out like it faded in. Lord, if it had disappeared I'd probably still be bab-bling. But there it was, and there it stayed, pacing. Made not a sound, though. Not a sound.

"Beautiful, that's all I can say about it. The whole world disappeared except for that white stag. Its antlers hung on its head like a live oak's branches, at least fourteen-point, and whenever it got near a tree, its antlers seemed to join with the tree, like they changed into branches. Everything in those woods was focused on that animal, I tell you, on its eyes, on its skin, and the white of that lonesome night was born from that deer, boys, and spread out in every direction from it. The wind stopped hurting, and the only way you knew it was blowing was how it shook the shaggy white coat on that deer's chest, like a wind across a snowdrift."

Someone laughed.

"You call me a liar and you'll eat your shoe. I saw it, and I was there. That's what I saw. The moon was only there to give us enough light to see. I will tell you boys true that our very souls were struck by that ghostly vision. We might've cried just looking at it. But, boys, our stomachs still screamed. Hollinger was the first to unglue his eyes—got those dog eyes again. He mumbled it first to himself and then repeated it to the two of us. 'A clean shot,' he said. 'A simple kill. Y'all hungry, ain't ya?'

"Now, as I look back on it, Hollinger stepping out into the open, it was a fucking mistake. We should have stopped him. But the hunger, the fatigue, the cold, it all took its toll. We weren't thinking right, the world wasn't right in our heads. That's my only excuse for it, and it's a sorry one for such a steep price. Regardless, me and Bishop stayed low and flat."

Holden spit again and looked up, staring at something beyond himself, beyond his memory. He looked sleepy, tired. In the stillness, he breathed, a breath long and slow that sounded in the train car like a muted sob. Then he spoke:

"Hollinger…he went asking that snow stag to a dance. That's all the scene was, really, a little dance with death. I can see it almost, like in some icy ballroom. Hollinger standing there, tall and as proud as a monument, his gun extended like an arm of invitation to dance. The two of them making their small steps. And that buck moving almost without appearing to, looking perfect and beautiful and holy, but at the same time like it had been forgotten, left behind out there in those woods. And us, watching, breathing into the quiet of that night, watching that waltz in the snow."

Holden had never told a story using words like these, spoken with such distant reverence before. Men shifted uncomfortably. It was a strange silence that the big man broke, coming back to his old voice, a little loud.

"Looking back, it's a wonder why Hollinger hadn't already shot the damn thing. Anyway, we never heard what the deer heard, at least until it was too late. It didn't know we were there, didn't know about the plans we had for it, but it tensed suddenly, in the split-second jerk of its kind. Locked and rigid for only a second or two, we knew the thing was poised to haul ass. I looked around. What could've alerted the deer? Thinking, 'Shoot Hollinger! Man, fire on the target!'

"So when a crack rang out across the night, and the buck fell to the ground, shot in the hind quarter, I switched my gaze from the deer to Hollinger, then back to the deer. It got back up and tried to run off, then back to Hollinger...when I realized he had not fired his weapon. He stood there, in the open, his rifle still cold in his hands."

Holden paused, squeezing his spit canteen. His gaze rose quickly to the ceiling and back to meet the eyes of a man sitting cross-legged near his right boot.

"Another crack, and Hollinger's head exploded in a red mist and he dropped. 'Sonofabitch' was what Bishop said, and from the cover that the small rise gave us, Bishop screamed and stood up. The sniper shot him in the shoulder, and he said, 'Sonofabitch' again, and slumped down so I grabbed him and hauled him away from there. Didn't know where in the hell I was going. Back across the forest and through the snow with some notion of getting out of the sniper's line of fire. We staggered and tripped through the forest, scared as rabbits. Then, by God, boys, it's the truth, there was that deer. *It* ran beside us, at least for a time. I remember seeing it, as beautiful as it had ever been, the blood from its wound just a red patch on its back leg. Didn't slow it down a bit. Not dying. Just running along in the snow, regular as can be, not even noticing pain or blood. Back and forth, right to left, making its way across the forest floor, like nothing was wrong. Teasing us like a high-born lady would a low-born man at some fucking debutante ball. Hell, teasing Death herself. Graceful and perfect. I hated the sonofabitch, and I tell you boys, I would have done anything to switch places with it.

"It left us eventually. Disappeared into those endless woods. Somehow, in some way, we made it back, me and Bishop. He pulled through. He was shipped out, back home, to live with a nastier wound, the crazy loss of a friend in pine woods a million miles from home. Hollinger? He stayed where we left him." Holden looked down at his boots. "I have no excuse for that."

Then Holden was silent, and as the silence stretched, men rose and coughed and shuffled off here and there to find free space on the floor to sleep. Holden sat and watched for a time the night passing beyond his window until he felt sleep coming on. He rested his head against the glass, and closed his eyes to protect himself from the sweet and terrible darkness.

Vials of Life

Lee Gay Warren

COME EXPERIENCE THE ONE TRUE HOLY GHOST, the sign by the old Pentecostal church said. Asa slowed to read it, then pulled off onto the gravel parking lot. It was dark and he saw no one about, so he dragged his ladder out of the jumble of tools and junk in the back of his truck and set to work. When he was done moving the letters about on it the sign said MEET THE EXPERT ON CREOLE HONEY HOGS. "Much better," Asa said aloud. He loaded the ladder back up and drove on. The next church on his stop was Shallow Creek Baptist, and today their sign read GET RIGHT WITH GOD BEFORE ITS TOO LATE. There was no apostrophe; there seldom was. Asa often thought that the people who hung the letters on these signs should know how to spell and punctuate. He stood beside his truck, its door still open, and studied the letters, changed them to read TIGGER ATE HOT DOGS WITH LEO BRETT. There were a couple more churches with signs in the next five or so miles, but he was tired, so he headed towards home.

He saw Tina waiting for him on the porch of their little brick house and for a moment was tempted to turn and leave, and if she'd been looking the other way he might have, but it was too late. "You have to go bail Davy out," she said when he stepped onto the porch.

He went around her through the door, into the dim cluttered living room. He sat down on the sagging couch and leant his head against the back of it, closed his eyes. Tina followed him. "Did you not hear me?" she said. "Or what?"

"I heard you," he said. He opened his eyes. She looked a little frantic. The drugs were starting to show. Her hands shook and she had lines at the corners of her eyes and around her mouth that should not have been there yet. She was thirty-six.

"What did he do?"

"Stole a bunch of fireworks. Him and that Justin he hangs around with. Stole them a week ago, the cop said, but I guess they just caught him today."

"Fireworks," Asa said.

"It was that Justin, Asa. He's a bad influence."

"Davy is not influenceable. Besides, I'm sure it was his idea. He loves fireworks," Asa said. "And stealing," he added.

"You better go get him. I told him you would, I can't go to the jail. My nerves can't take it, Asa."

"Your nerves," Asa said. "What, are you low on Xanax? Maybe my nerves can't take it either. I'm tired, Tina." He sat forward on the couch, rubbed his forehead slow and hard. "I've been thinking. Nothing between us has turned out like I thought it would."

She was not listening. "And tomorrow you need to do something about your mama. She's driving me crazy, keeps seeing Universal Studios Monsters every which way. Under beds, in closets. She's going to have to be put somewhere."

"Do you ever listen? I'm tired, Tina. Tired of all this. Davy's out all hours with all these red-haired and blue-haired girls with tattoos and no morals, and now he's stealing. My mother's senile. And you. You cheat on me and don't even try to slip around. You take all these prescriptions. This is not a marriage. I don't know what this is."

"Go get Davy. We can talk later. Besides, nobody said life was supposed to be easy."

"I never asked for easy. I never even thought easy was an option. I was only aiming for normal." She still was not listening, had already turned to something in the kitchen, opening cabinet doors. Asa stood and stared at Tina for half a minute. She did not look at him. He caught the back of his neck with his right hand and squeezed the tightening muscles, breathed deeply and walked out.

On the way to get Davy he thought about the kind of life he'd once envisioned for himself. A wife who cooked, who made iced tea and wore dresses once in a while. Tina didn't own a dress, didn't cook, might not even be home at suppertime. Or at bedtime. She wasn't quiet when she staggered in at two in the morning, didn't take a washcloth to the strong smelling aftershave.

He'd met her in a pool hall, she'd beat him in a game. When she sank the eight ball, she walked straight and put up her cue, said, "I'm going home. Do you want to come?" More than his own desire for a woman, some neediness in her gray eyes had led him to say yes. And somehow that one moment had led to this one here on this highway, here with this feeling that something had to give, that he could not go on like this much longer.

Coming back from the police station Davy said he aimed to kill Justin for getting them caught. "The fool," he said. "Offering free bottle rockets to every person he knows. Giving fountains to girls. Girls that wasn't even that pretty. I'll strangle him for being so stupid."

Asa could only hope he didn't mean it. Knew that he might. Asa was tired, exhausted, much too weary to prevent a killing among friends.

"Daddy?" Davy said when they pulled into the driveway, but Asa didn't answer. After Davy got out, he drove away.

When Asa woke up the next morning he wasn't sure where he was. He lay there until his mind cleared, and he remembered. He got off the waterbed and walked around the tidy house examining things. The log walls, bookshelves stuffed with books, the Persian cats named Flannery and Hemingway asleep on the carpet. He stepped into a doorway and saw Zoey in the kitchen making coffee, her honey-colored hair hanging loose down her back. "Hey," he said.

"Good morning. Come have coffee with me before the girls wake up."

"It feels strange to wake up here," he said.

"That's because you always rushed off. Before. You'll get used to it." She smiled at him. She was very thin and green-eyed, and attractive. She was pretty when she smiled. "I can't believe you're here," she said. "I tried for a month to talk you into leaving her."

This was true. He had met her two months ago in the garage where he worked. She'd come in for an oil change before setting off to a book festival. There had been a big heap of foreign language books on her passenger seat. Asa thought maybe Russian. He was not sure that Tina could read English, at least he never saw her doing it.

"Well, I'm here," he said, but he didn't feel especially happy about it this morning. He'd been sleeping with Zoey for a month now. He'd changed a church sign on the way home after that first night. It had originally said GOD WANTS FULL CUSTODY, NOT JUST VISITS ON WEEKENDS. He'd made it read: DOGS SUE TWENTY JUSTIFIED TOADS, NOT COWS.

Zoey got into his head. When he found himself thinking about her, there was definitely something there, but he still didn't know what. Maybe she was just different from Tina. She wanted to be a great Southern novelist. She talked of books and poems and music. She had no television, just shelves and shelves of books. She was ten years younger than he was, but very sure of herself.

He kissed her cheek now. "I've got to get to work," he said. "I'll see you around six." It rattled Asa some to hear those words coming out of his mouth, sounding like it was so natural.

"I'll have dinner ready," she said. So natural.

It wasn't really time to go to work yet, so he drove around for a while on the back roads, thinking. He wondered what would happen to his family now that he was gone. Almost without realizing it he pulled onto a church parking lot. He reached the notepad out of his glove box and sat studying the words on the sign. LIFE IS NOT SPINNING MADLY OUT OF CONTROL, YOURE JUST ON GODS HOLY POTTERS WHEEL, the sign said. On his notepad, he unscrambled the letters, making new words, crossing them out, trying another. He could do it almost absentmindedly. He had been doing this for years now. He was the Signchanger. There had been newspaper articles wondering who he was, letters to the editor damning his soul to hell. He'd changed his first sign the year his mother moved in with them, the year Davy started school. The year Tina got really out of hand. He looked down at the notepad, at the unconnected words formed there. JELLY DOUGHNUT, he had written. DESPAIR. FUTILITY. "No, not that," he said aloud, scratching them out.

He kept rearranging, remembering while he worked a time when

Davy was in first grade and had come home telling Tina of a movie he'd watched at school. The bad guy had carried his life in a glass vial, and if it broke, he would die. Tina told Asa about it that night in bed, laughing. "Imagine," she said. "I'd drop my vial on concrete, or leave it on a store counter like I do the checkbook. I'd throw it in the clothes dryer by mistake. But you'd be immortal, Asa. You'd keep your life safe and sealed off in its little glass container." She snuggled against him and said, again, "Imagine. Just imagine if life was that fragile. Breakable as glass." He was quiet, thinking, and by the time Asa turned to her and said, "Tina, honey, it *is* that fragile," she was asleep.

He lay awake awhile thinking how a heart could stop in a second and simply not start back. Once over breakfast Asa's mother had lectured on the importance of leading a Christian life. "You have to live life preparing to die," she said, "so when you die you go to Heaven."

"Ha, not me," Davy had said. "*I'm* not going to die."

That night long ago as Tina slept he thought of her and Davy and his mother and himself, and he knew that he was accountable for not just his own, but three other vials of life. When he fell asleep he was picturing the vials, each marked with a name, clear glass filled with amber fluid, delicate and terribly heavy. He would have to guard them fiercely even as they weighed him down, carry them with great caution every step of the way. He had taken them on willingly, even asked for them. They were his.

Now all these years later he was choosing the one vial marked Asa, all he could handle. The others he'd set back down. It seemed to him that he should feel lightened, freer. He did not.

He shook his head, tried to clear it, focused on the letters before him. Finally he got out, dragged his ladder from the truck, and began taking down the letters. JOLLY FOUL MOUTHED LEPRECHAUNS TWIRL AND SING ON NOISY TIN ROOFTOPS, it said when he was done. This morning, risking the daylight, he didn't even smile. He just dropped the leftover letters into his toolbox and got back into the truck.

Tina found him at work that day. He'd known she would. "I can't believe you left us," she said. He was changing a tire, and he got up and led her to the office and shut the door. "I never thought you'd leave us," she said. She was trembling and her hair was uncombed, her clothes wrinkled.

"I'm sorry," he said. "I just couldn't stay. I can't come back."

"I can stop the drugs, Asa. I haven't taken anything today. I'll stop everything."

"It's the drugs, the men, Davy, my mother. It's everything. It's built up till I can't stand it."

"I'll stop the men too," she said, but he'd heard that before. Once in a fight, when she'd said she'd keep away from other men, Asa had told her she was not capable of stopping. "There's not a twelve-step program on how to stop fucking random men, Tina."

"Asa?" she said now. "I'll stop everything. Come home, please, I'll cook for you."

"You don't know how to cook," he said. "It's too late. I have to stay away for a while."

As quickly as that Tina gave it up. "You're staying with her, I guess. The lady who wants to be a writer."

He didn't answer.

"I know about her, Asa. I've known. I just didn't have the right to say anything."

"I have to get back to work. Tell Davy I love him and I'll be in touch. And my mother. I'm not sure what to do about her?"

"Leave her. I'll take care of it." Which surprised him, because Tina and his mother had hated each other from the first time they met. Even now, on bad days, when Tina came into a room, Mildred's mouth would pull itself into a tight line, and Tina's eyes would get a fierce, defiant light in them. She had always flaunted her wild behavior to Mildred when any other woman would have hidden it.

"Fine," he said. "We both know she's got to be in Columbia Pines, somewhere she'll be watched after. You've got the checkbook. I'll keep money in the account for you."

"Okay," she said. But, without warning she went off on another tack. The drugs, he thought. Now he saw that she was crying. "I can't believe this is happening," she said. "It's just, Asa, I don't think I can do it without you. Live, I mean. Without you."

He told her just to go, to please go, and finally she went, her small shoulders hunched. She looked beaten, defeated, and it seemed to Asa this might take and hold for some time. That night Zoey brought beer home, Rolling Rock, in sparkly green bottles. "Why not just get Budweiser?" he asked her. "It's just as good and a lot cheaper."

"I like this better. Why? What's wrong with it?"

"Seems this beer is bought to say look at me I'm a fashionable beer drinker. It's trendy. I just want a cold beer."

"Why, Asa," she said, and he saw that he had hurt her.

"I'm sorry," he said. "It's been a long day, Zoey. That's all." It was Friday. They stayed home all weekend. Her twin girls stayed in their bedroom reading most of the time, and Zoey read one book after another. *How to Sell Your First Novel. The Art of Dialogue. Prose in Five Easy Lessons.* Yet he never saw her write. Why didn't she just do it, he wondered. He found himself watching her as she went about the house. She kept watching him, too. Every time he looked up from his newspaper, she would smile at him. It made him nervous. He wished for a television, just for the background noise. He got up and put a Bob Dylan record on and she looked up at him. "What?" he said. "You like Bob Dylan."

"It's fine. I was just enjoying the quiet," she said. She went back to reading her book. Asa was restless, he wandered around the house. He found her wedding picture on the wall in the hallway and studied it, looking at Zoey's face first. She appeared calm and unruffled, not the least bit unnerved by the fact that she was entering into a marriage. Even then, less than twenty, she'd been poised and self-assured. But her husband, why, he looked like a child. A kid not much older than Davy, all tricked out in a tuxedo with his hair clumsily smoothed down, his eyes bright and shining. He never stood a chance. Defeated before he was even through the starting gate. Asa felt vaguely sorry for him.

"What's Tom like?" he asked her in bed that night.

"Hmm. Like. I don't know. He has a lot of surface knowledge, but there's nothing beneath it. I thought he was so smart when we met. I was working in a bookstore, and he used to come in and buy books all the time, but he must have been decorating with them."

"Nothing wrong with that. Likely he was just coming in to see you," Asa said.

"Well. Anyway. I guess I thought marriage was going to pass me by, like slumber parties and roller skating had. So I jumped at the chance. He was so immature, though. When the girls were born he should've grown up some, but he never did. Still hasn't. When he visits them he romps around on the floor with them as if they were puppies. The girls don't know quite what to make of him."

Asa could see how that would be true. The girls were very serious, especially for eight-year-olds.

"It's good for them to play," he said. "They're little kids, Zoey. They should have fun."

"They do have fun. They go to soccer. They play piano and read." She sounded annoyed, and Asa left it alone. Who was he to give parenting advice, anyway? The girls might grow up lacking social skills, but most likely they would never end up stealing fireworks.

"I don't understand why you picked me," he said.

"Don't be silly," Zoey said.

"No, really. I don't get it. I'm way older, and I don't read much. What got you interested?" He was propped up on an elbow now, his big rough hand resting on her thin white arm.

She smiled at him; her cheeks dimpled, and he thought how different, even beautiful she was when she smiled. "You're good-looking," she said. "And you're a real grownup. Go to sleep, Asa. I'm tired, it's late." She turned over and was asleep so fast that Asa was envious. She slipped into slumber as easily and capably as she did everything else. A real grownup, he thought. Somehow he didn't get the appeal of that. It didn't seem like such a wonderful thing.

A nagging dull feeling had begun to plague Asa by the time he'd been there three weeks, and one night when Zoey slept and he lay wakeful it became plain that he was homesick. He looked at Zoey, pale and serene, no doubt dreaming elaborate artistic dreams in a foreign language, and wondered what exactly he had gotten himself into. It came to him that he missed his house. He missed his beat-up recliner and his rough-and-tumble old orange cat. That cat had been around since Davy was six. Davy had for some reason named the cat Blue. He missed watching sports with Davy and just listening to him tell of his adventures. The boy had always had a wry and clever sense of humor that Asa enjoyed. He missed hearing Tina sing country songs off key while she washed the dishes. He felt stifled, and he sighed, getting out of bed. He would not sleep tonight, no use trying. He dressed silently then went out to his old truck.

He got in and rolled the windows down; the air felt hot and still even this late at night. Somehow July had given way to August. He hadn't changed any signs since that first day at Zoey's, but now he felt like doing it again. He didn't know what that might mean, decided it didn't really matter. He drove to find a sign, trying not to think too much. He came to a rickety Church of Christ that had taken to quoting hymns. HE WALKS WITH ME AND HE TALKS WITH ME, their sign said. Asa fooled around with it until he came up with HEMAN HAD DIET MILKSHAKES, which he was fairly proud of. Down the road a piece, the Pentecostal Church sign said EXPOSURE TO THE SON PREVENTS BURNING. Asa's mind was slowing down tonight, and it took him forever to change it to REX PRESSURES ONE BUTTER PIG TOO.

He felt gloomy. He drove a little faster, taking a turn and fading too far out on the high side close to the shoulder, but the adrenaline at least gave him a little energy. He drove on out to one more church and almost without thinking switched the letters around. When he stood back and looked at it he saw that he had changed DON'T MAKE GOD ANGRY, ALWAYS KEEP HIM NEAR to DANG ME, TAKE A ROPE AND HANG ME. He blinked, surprised. Wasn't that from some old song he used to know? He thought the next line was, hang me from the highest tree. Well. He knew how that guy must have felt.

When he pulled out of the parking lot and headed back to Zoey's house something about the way the trees and the dirt road looked in the moonlight made him think of his childhood, of the shack he'd been raised in, of the tiny church where his father had preached. His father had been a giant half-crazed man, had handled snakes during his sermons. There has to be a Heaven, Asa, his father had told him once when Asa voiced doubts. There has to be a Heaven because if *this* is all we got, why, we got nothing. And ever since then Asa had been trying to prove him wrong, even though his father had died before Asa left home.

"Ah, damn it all," he said now, thoughts crowding in on him.

It was two in the morning when he got back to Zoey's, but she was up waiting for him. "Your wife called," she said. "Asa, your mother had a heart attack. She's dead."

Asa sat down on the couch. "Jesus," he said. "She wasn't but sixty-eight." Zoey sat next to him and squeezed his hand, but he didn't squeeze back. "I'll wake the girls," she said. "We should go to the hospital. They'll soon be taking her away, I suppose."

Asa looked at her, into her serious green eyes. "Wait," he said. "Just wait. I don't want you to go."

She was hurt, he saw, but all she said was that that was all right, that she would wait here. He took both her hands in his then. "I'm not coming back," he said.

"You're going back to her?"

"I didn't say that."

"Asa. She's crazy, they're all crazy. You don't belong with them. You're normal."

"Zoey, I just got back from driving around changing church signs." Zoey didn't seem to hear him, but most likely she just wasn't interested. Really, she didn't have a shred of simple human curiosity.

When she did speak what she said was, "They're thieves and addicts, Asa." He dropped her hands and stood up.

"Well," he said, "That may be. But at least they don't name their damned cats after writers."

At the hospital no one was in his mother's room. He stood over her feeling only a vague sorrow and forming no words in his mind that would do for a eulogy. She had been a background player in his childhood, shrinking away from his father, who was always center stage, always a little dangerous. She seldom spoke above a whisper. Then after she'd come to live with them it had just been too late for a connection to form.

When he went out into the hallway he saw that Tina was there. She looked ragged, thrown together. A man with a build like a football player stood next to her. "Where's Davy?" Asa asked her.

"He's out with friends. This is Roger," she said. "He was at the house when she had the heart attack. He drove us."

"Oh," Asa said. "Well. Has the funeral home been called?"

"Yes. I waited a while, thinking I'd hear from you. But I knew what to tell them. She left all the directions, how she wanted it done. It was in her Bible. I called and it's taken care of."

"Good. See you around, Tina. Roger." He couldn't get out of there fast enough. There didn't seem to be enough air in the hospital. The fluorescent lights were too bright. The corridors were long and green-tiled, and he kept making wrong turns. When he finally got outside, it was a relief just to breathe without an aftertaste of disinfectant on his tongue.

He started the truck and drove away from the hospital, thinking only of how long this night had been. He drove on, the night air blowing in on him. At the edge of town a nondenominational church with a well-lighted sign stood back from the road near a copse of trees, and Asa stopped there. He didn't bother to read the sign. He took the letters down and mixed them with the extras from his toolbox, selecting the ones he needed.

He placed letters surely, without faltering, until he was done. DON'T THINK TWICE, IT'S ALL RIGHT, the sign said.

He sat in the truck for a while and looked out at the night. The highway was straight and black and gleaming in the moonlight. There was no telling where it led to, it might take him anywhere at all, but from here it looked like it went on forever.

Succubus

Les Standiford

"I'm going home," Beth shouted from the bathroom.

I was lying on the bed, staring up at the ceiling. A water stain had spread out a pale brown outline of Italy. Where Rome should have been, where we were, a chunk of plaster had fallen away, exposing splintered lath and a tiny crevice that led into darkness.

I wondered if she meant it. She wasn't one to make threats. And maybe it would be for the best. Maybe I'd made a mistake, asking her along. I'd also begun to think of earthquakes, of the catacombs that laced the ground beneath the hotel where our tour had put up.

The phone rang then, and the door to the bathroom flew open. She had one towel wrapped around her middle, the other turban-fashion on her head. It made her look exotic.

"You're going to get that, aren't you," she said. It wasn't really a question.

I hesitated. There was a flush in her cheeks. I could barely see her freckles. "If I don't, they'll just come to the door," I said.

"We don't have to answer," she said. I nodded my head, but I wasn't agreeing with her. The ringing of the phone stopped and left a silence in the room. She let the towel slip toward the top of her breasts and cocked her hip at me. "Who's more important?" she said. She could be forgiving. She gave me the smile that offered everything.

"That's not fair," I said.

The phone began to ring again. "Fair doesn't enter into it," she said.

I threw up my hands. "It's my job," I said.

"Then why did you bring me with you," she said, quietly. She pulled her towel up and disappeared into the bathroom.

"That's a dumb question," I called as the door slammed. It was our honeymoon, after all.

Every summer for five years, I had traveled around Europe as an escort for groups of college students, most of them women. The pay was minimal, but it wasn't exactly like work. And I'd been hammering on a dissertation in Art History all the while. The trips gave me access to museums I'd never see otherwise, gave me the sense that I was making progress, that someday I'd finish.

I'd met Beth the previous fall, at an exhibition lecture in Boston. Rossetti, Hunt, Millais: The Pre-Raphaelites. My dissertation subject. The last, doomed, moral ground of art. She taught painting to schoolchildren.

She'd been standing in front of Millet's "Angelus," the sentimental rendering of a peasant couple pausing from their labors in the field, offering an evening prayer.

"Isn't it peaceful?" she said, turning to me.

Green eyes, a spray of freckles, all that dark red hair pulled back, spilling onto her shoulders. I glanced back at the painting. "It was a simpler time," I said, shrugging.

"Do you think life was ever simple?" she said. Her smile. That unflinching gaze. She knew me.

The rest of the story is familiar: I asked her to lunch; we began to date; before long, I moved in. She taught, I kept grinding on the book.

She'd come home excited, trailing bright sheets of fourth-grade watercolors—"Look at this, Jack. You could eat that chunk of blue." I'd listen to her and imagine facing my committee, waving my arms, imploring: "Just feel these colors! Take a bite of the ultramarine down there in the corner." But it took me out of the swamp of moralism for a while. She was good for me.

When summer came, I wavered: stay home, finish the degree, be with this woman. On the other hand, there was Europe: intrigue, adventure, freedom. In the end, I tried to have it all. I'd proposed, and here we were, in Rome, on the ropes.

The phone was still ringing, a notch louder, it seemed. I rolled over, the bed shuddering beneath me like land ready to give way. The phone was a relic, with a fabric cord and a ring that vibrated the nightstand.

"Yes," I said, picking up. I expected one of the students. We'd only been checked in half an hour. There was bound to be something:

someone's toilet not flushing, the wrong number of beds in a room, something dead in a drawer. I was glad that Beth was in the bathroom. It had been the constant complaining that had done her in.

She was still upset about last night, in Naples. I'd promised her dinner by ourselves at a place overlooking the harbor. One of the local guides had told me about it. There was an American cruiser moored far out in the bay. The ship's lights glowed through the summer haze as if all of Sorrento floated there.

Beth had charmed the waiters with her easy smile and pidgin Spanish. Her hair glistened in the candlelight. They love red hair in Naples. I'd felt happy, even smug.

We were halfway through the pasta course when I got the call. One of the boys had been arrested for shoplifting. I was at the stationhouse until midnight.

"Professore," the phone brought me back. It was the voice of the concierge, quivering with anger. "We are missing a key."

I considered it a moment. The older hotels where we'd been staying tended to have just one key for a room. You were to leave it at the desk when you went out. One of the students had probably gone off with it, stranding a roommate outside. We'd been in Europe nearly a month, but our group was a slow study.

Of course, there were other reasons the keys disappeared. They tended to be huge things, fastened to ornate tassels or chained to tooled brass fobs the size of doorknobs. They looked suitable for opening palace gates, and the students favored them as souvenirs. We'd had to hold our departure from Stresa, waiting for one of the boys to "remember" slipping his key into his luggage.

As problems went, this was minor. And though I knew how Beth felt, it was my job to take care of it. I was an escort. An arrangements man. There to make things run smoothly. As one of my colleagues in the escort trade put it, "We're the Metamucil of this screwed-up outfit."

"Don't worry," I told the concierge. "The key will turn up. I guarantee it." The last was a phrase I'd found useful. The hotels disparaged the morals of American students, but if I vouched for the Huns, the management would sit tight.

"You do not understand," he said. "I must have the key now. It is an e-mer-gen-cie." I could sense him jabbing his chin with every syllable.

"Look," I said, "let me talk to whoever it is. They can just wait until the roommate gets back…"

"It is not one of your students," he said, incensed. "It is another guest. He and his wife are locked in their room and they cannot get out."

I looked across the room to the heavy door plate. Sure enough, another relic. No lock switch. A massive brass slab with a lever handle and a keyhole. If the door were locked from the outside, you'd be stuck.

"Please, professore," the concierge was shouting. "The key!" I heard the murky sounds of plumbing from the bathroom, of Beth banging things about. "I'm coming down," I told him. And fled.

"The key was taken from the outer door," the concierge said, confirming what I'd thought. "The cylinder was turned, and then the key was removed." He said it the way you'd say 'stuck the knife into the priest and twisted!'

I nodded. "I've done that," I said. The concierge gave me a look. "Left my key in the door, I mean." He turned away. We were standing under the hotel's entrance canopy so that he could oversee the efforts of a workman who was raising a ladder against the granite facade of the place. A thin Italian man in a suit and his heavy-set wife were standing at the railing of a tiny second-story balcony, staring uncertainly at the ladder as it scraped up toward them.

"The gentleman has an important engagement," the concierge continued.

"Doesn't anyone have a master key?" I asked.

I'd been so naïve that he refused even to shake his head. "We could break the lock," he said, grudgingly, "but it would be very expensive."

I nodded. He meant that there were no conceivable circumstances under which the lock would be broken.

By now, the Italian man was helping his wife over the balcony. A young man in kitchen whites stood a few steps down the ladder, steadying her great ass with one hand, clinging desperately to a rung with the other. He had his head averted as if God hovered just above him, calling down his judgments. The workman holding the foot of the ladder craned his neck, trying to get a better look up the woman's dress. Her husband glared at his watch and shook his head.

"I tried every room on the way down," I said. "But you know how it is. They hit the streets right away."

The ladder shifted slightly on the railing and the woman cried out. The husband steadied the ladder and shouted angrily down at her in Italian. Several pedestrians had stopped to watch and nearby traffic had slowed. A chorus of horns sprang up from vehicles farther up the boulevard. There's not much patience on the Via Veneto.

The concierge glared at me, then looked away. "It is outrageous," he hissed.

"You can't be sure it was one of my students," I said. He had thinning hair slicked back on his pasty dome, carmine lips, and a weak chin that he used in sighting down at me. I knew what the students were capable of, but I was getting tired.

He spun back upon me. "You have been in my hotel an hour. Who else would it be?"

I imagined hitting him, but the thought passed on. It was hardly the thing an arrangements man could get away with. I turned. The Italian woman stood on the sidewalk, patting her chest with a hankie, watching as her husband made his own way down. She didn't seem anxious about the outcome.

"If one of the kids has the key, you'll get it back," I said to the concierge, but he was already on his way to placate the Italians.

I found the bar in a corner of the vast lobby. It was cool, and gloomy, like the rest of the place, and suitably far from the front desk. I'd thought about going straight back to the room, but the thought of Beth waiting with her "what now" expression stopped me. Worse yet, I might find her actually packing. Instead of commiseration, I'd have problems squared. No, a drink was the ticket.

The bar was done up in white Naugahyde, with some tall ice-cream chairs for stools, and a big round mirror behind, the liquors arranged across its face. There was some dim yellow light that trailed up the mirror from a hidden source and a thin man in a white jacket silhouetted against it, his arms folded.

I thought the bartender was watching me approach, but when I got closer, I realized he had his dark eyes fixed on something behind me. I turned then, and understood. It was Leah.

She was sitting at a small table just inside the entrance, her dark blond hair pulled back severely and slung in a long braid across her shoulder. She was wearing a black cocktail dress, one stockinged leg crossed atop the other. She was smoking, ignoring the gaze of the bartender, toying with her glass. I had a fact sheet for everyone of the tour members. It said she was only twenty-one, but that's the trouble with statistics.

She cut her glance at me. "Are we drinking this afternoon?"

She motioned to a chair. I sat down.

I sat there for a minute, letting my anger burn away. I could hear Leah's cigarette hiss. The bartender showed no sign of movement. I had started to signal him, when she put her hand on my arm.

"Have some of this," she said. There was a heavy green bottle in an ice bucket nearby, and an extra glass on the table.

She reached to pour for me, left the bottle on the table, and slid the glass my way.

"It's Asti," she said, waving at the bottle as if to apologize.

She glanced about the deserted bar. "Fellini would like it here," she said.

I nodded and sipped. The fact sheet told me Leah's mother lived in Hilton Head. Her father listed an address in Manhattan. She'd attended more than one of the sister schools.

"Looks like you were expecting somebody," I said finally, raising the glass.

"You," she nodded. She stared at me, expressionless.

I gave her my arrangements man's chuckle. There wasn't much

agreement on the escort's code of ethics, but fooling with the customers was doom on everyone's list. People so far away from home, most for the first time, are basically insecure. They count on you for the maintenance of their comfort as they journey through alien lands. Give twenty-five of them the idea you're sleeping with one of their number, and terrible feelings are spawned.

"You can spot it right away," a local guide from Paris told me once. "You step on the bus and no one smiles, no one talks, no one asks a question." She opened her great French eyes wide. "And oh, how much they complain."

She was right, of course. They become a sullen, defensive crew, impossible to guide through the territories with ease and grace. It is an arrangements man's nightmare. And still, it happens.

I downed my glass. "Looks like you're headed out somewhere," I said.

Leah gave me her stare, her aquamarine eyes slightly crossed in appraisal. It was the same look which had set all eight of the fraternity boys with us into endless torments of lust. "Why don't we cut out the bullshit and talk like two people," she said. There was no malice in her voice. No wonder all the girls hated her.

I reached for the bottle and poured my glass full. "Sure," I said. "What would you like to talk about?"

She smiled then, a rare act for her. She had not been sullen, but neither had she been friendly. She'd been with us from Amsterdam to Munich, to Zermatt, to Venice, to Athens, to Florence, to Pompeii, to Rome, interested enough in everything, excited not at all.

I'd seen her modeling a full-length mink one night in a shop on Mykonos. I'd been passing by on the narrow cobbled street and glanced in the open door as she stood before a mirror, clutching the lapels at her throat, coolly assessing her image. Another tour girl stood nearby, watching mournfully. The coat so suited Leah, even the eager shopkeepers were speechless.

She will look like that all her life, I thought.

"Where's your wife?" she asked.

I finished my drink. "In the room," I said. "I had to come down to deal with a problem." I hesitated, then gave in. "She's getting a little tired of hearing about these things."

Leah nodded. "Those people on the ladder," she said. "Weren't they a pair." I didn't ask her how she knew about it.

She sat back and recrossed her legs. It seemed to take a long time. She lit another cigarette and pushed the pack toward me. "You haven't been together very long, have you?"

I shook my head and lit a cigarette. I hadn't smoked in nearly a year, since I'd moved in with Beth. The smoke seemed to explode inside my head, and I felt my balance waver.

She blew a ribbon of smoke toward the dark ceiling. "Jesus Christ, I think I'd die if my husband brought me along on something like this."

My head was still reeling. "You're married?" I asked.

She shook her head, amused. "Of course not. I meant if I were married." She laughed. "All these people and their needs," she said, drawing out the last word.

I shrugged. "It seemed better than leaving her, five weeks together on the Continent."

She raised her eyebrows. "I'm sure."

"Plus I get to squeeze in some work on my dissertation."

She nodded as if she knew all about it. "You've been at it a while."

I nodded.

"How come it's taking you so long?"

I glanced at the bartender, who didn't bother to look away. Finally, I turned back to her. "If I knew," I said, "I'd be finished now."

It got a faint smile from her, but she was shaking her head at the same time. "Some honeymoon," she said.

"Hey, it's not like we haven't had fun, or anything."

"Travel is so broadening," she said, deadpan.

She thought for a moment, then trained that gaze on me. "I know what your book needs."

"You do?" I said. I knew it was time to get out.

She nodded, her lips parted.

I felt the wine now. I turned. The bartender was still standing motionless before the yellow orb of the mirror. "I'd like a gin, with ice," I called, my throat thick. After a moment, he bowed, and I heard the clatter of glass. Then, something soft dropped to the floor beneath our table and Leah's bare foot was on my thigh.

I was staring out the window of Leah's room over an endless vista of rooftops, listing antennae, and laundry. The sun was going down in a great boiling of red. There was a set of nail marks across my chest, across one shoulder. Would Beth be gone by now, I wondered. The city looked to be in flames.

"You've got a nice butt," I heard her say. I knew she was propped up in bed, watching me. She would be lit with the harsh glow from the sky.

"What happened to your roommate, anyway?" I had turned in profile, but I wasn't going to look at her. Studying art, you get to know the old stories. I had a long pull from the bottle we'd carried up.

"She's upstairs, screwing her way through the Southeastern Conference."

I nodded. "I'm thinking this was not such a good idea." How had it happened? I asked myself, staring at the bottle.

"Get a grip," she said. "I'm no gossip." I heard the sound of a match popping.

"That's not what's worrying me," I said. I traced the shadow of a bird's flight across the dying light. I thought I saw a larger shape swooping down upon it.

"Don't you get tired, taking care of everybody else?" she said.

I thought about it a moment. "No," I said, staring out. "I do other people well."

She laughed, but it sounded angry.

"By the way," she said, finally, "I've got that key."

I turned. I was hoping I'd misunderstood, but I knew better. What story had Ulysses given Penelope, I was wondering. 'I tied myself to the mast, sweetheart, but it still didn't do any good.'

"What key?" I asked

The light angled across her perfect breasts. Her face was in shadow.

Where her hair trailed down into the light, it seemed ablaze.

"What key?" I repeated.

"It's on the dresser," she said.

I stared. There was a key there. I pushed away from the window and, as I did, I felt a tremor sweep quietly through the building.

I went to pick up the key. It was for a room on the second floor. We were somewhere on six. "How did you get this?" I asked. I thought of the trapped Italians. Of Beth. Gone most likely, gone for good. A siren wailed somewhere in the distance. I felt very tired.

"You figure it out," she said.

She laughed again, a harsh, biting sound. The sun tipped over and, abruptly, the light was gone from the room. It was stifling with the windows open, and still, I was freezing. However she'd gotten it, I didn't want to know.

I reached down in the darkness for my clothes. "I have to be going now," I said.

"Ciao," she said, as I went out. I did not recognize the voice.

When I got back to the room, I found Beth asleep across the bed, still in her robe. Her lips were parted and her hair was fanned out darkly as if she'd collapsed there. I could see the deep bruise high up on her thigh where she'd stumbled against a chair arm on the bus.

Her bag had been pulled out from the closet, but whether it was half-unpacked or the other way around, I couldn't tell. I was groggy. I thought of Millet's painting, of those trusting peasants praying in their field at nightfall. I imagined a mushroom cloud erupting on the horizon behind them.

I went into the bathroom, cleared some of Beth's things from the ledge above the sink, brushed my teeth, and shaved.

I paused before the mirror. It is possible I spoke to the image there. I was a student of art. I was an arrangements man. I had married. Nothing seemed to cohere.

I wanted peace. And still I heard Leah's voice, faintly mocking, "I know what your book needs." There was a groan from the walls, and the floor seemed to shift beneath my feet, as if the ancient hotel had sagged another notch toward all the history beneath it.

The glass in the mirror was cloudy and did not clear when I wiped it. I turned on Beth's hair dryer and aimed it at the glass, but I couldn't get rid of the haze. I set the dryer aside, finished the shave by touch, and drew a bath in the huge tub that gripped the tile floor with the claws of a sphinx.

I filled the tub until I was nearly floating, the water at my ears, lapping the edges. Still, I wanted more of the hot, and I was leaning forward for the knob, when I heard the sound behind me. At first I thought it was Beth, awake at last, and I wondered what I was going to say to her.

I was just turning around when it began. For an instant, I thought the tub was shaking, that the hotel was finally crashing down, but then I realized that it was my own body and not the tub at all. Every one of my muscles had gone rigid. My mouth was frozen open, and I heard myself uttering little gasps. I was paralyzed, unable to breathe, unable to cry out. It was as if an enormous hand had clamped down on me and was shaking me violently in the water. I'd cleaned a fish that way, once, over the side of a boat.

The muscles along my spine began to contract, pulling my head back, deeper into the water. I still held to the sides of the tub with my hands, but they were useless, fused to the thick porcelain steel. I willed my arms to pull me up, but there was no response. My vision sparkled, flashed to darkness, then came back again.

I was still bucking, my head going under, when I saw the electrical cord. It snaked down from the socket above the sink mirror and plunged into the water of the tub, near my shoulder. Water was pouring up my nose now, burning, choking me. Yet my mind raced along, unimpaired. The sound I'd heard was something falling.

Then I realized. The hair dryer. Of course. I'd shoved it aside myself, shaving, too close to the edge. It must have turned on as it fell. I could feel the thing now, edging down my chest, my stomach, gliding along like some creature beyond nightmare. "It has a switch for European use, sir." I could remember the clerk who sold it to us. Helpful, helpful, helpful.

My head was all the way under now, my eyes locked open, the light above the sink shattering into dancing planes of light. I felt the dryer balance on the shelf of my groin momentarily, then my body convulsed, and it slid on over into the deep. My head was vibrating against the bottom of the tub. My fingers had begun to quake. A shadow fell across my eyes. How the one in charge dies, I was thinking…and that is when everything stopped.

There was a moment of utter quiet, of peace, of time suspended. This was how she'd find me, like that poor bastard we'd seen in Pompeii, a fossil of volcanic ash just trying to do something simple like get out of bed. I wondered what he'd been up to the night before it happened.

I imagined the three artists watching from the shadows of the bedroom, pointing at Beth, at me, discussing the composition, the light, the moral implications of the scene. They have arranged it all, I thought. I'd have laughed if I could.

And then, I felt feeling return to my hands, to my feet. A tingling at first, then a buzz, a fire in my lungs.

I burst out of the water gasping, the cord still draped over my shoulder. I glanced up in panic, but saw that I was safe. The plug had separated from the socket near the light. The dryer swirled in the eddies at the foot of the tub.

At first, I wondered if Beth had rescued me, but the place was eerily quiet. It took me a moment to realize: the dryer's own weight had pulled the plug out as it slid down to the bottom of the tub. Or so it must have been.

I heaved myself over the edge and lay gasping on the cool tiles of the floor. When I had finally caught my breath, I wrapped myself in a towel and staggered into the bedroom.

Beth stirred when I sat down on the bed next to her. Her eyes flickered open, stared blankly, then began to focus. She pushed herself up on one elbow. "God," she said, groggy. "Are we still here?"

I nodded. I wasn't sure I could speak. There was a series of dots pressed into one side of her face from the pattern of the spread. She was lovely.

She raised her hand against the light flooding in from the bathroom. She squinted at me, and this time there was concern in her voice. "What happened?"

I thought for a moment. I saw her eyes tracing the marks on my shoulder. We could hear the water draining from the tub. "Nothing," I said, "Just some guy and his wife couldn't get out of their room."

She nodded, her eyes clouding. She stood up from the bed, began putting things into her bag.

"Hey. It didn't have anything to do with us," I said.

She examined a pair of socks, tossed them at me. "I meant it when I said I was going. This is crazy."

"I know," I said. "It's no honeymoon."

"It's no honeymoon," she said. She laughed, but didn't mean it. She glanced at the open door of the bathroom, then back at me.

"You can't have everything, Jack."

"I don't want everything," I told her.

She looked at me squarely. "At least be honest with yourself."

Then the phone began to ring. Beth glanced at it, went back to her packing. It gave me a moment. I was an arrangements man. An expert at smoothing things over. In that light, the thing with the hair dryer was a gift, a happy accident. Tell her I almost died, she might forget the rest.

There was an ancient print on the wall above the phone stand. Fuseli. Darkness at the fringes, bright flesh at the center. A demon crouched on his lady's breast. The incubus leered out at me. I could feel the silk clutched in his hairy toes, the pulsing in his veins. You're with me, he nodded. We'll eat your artists up.

The phone rang on.

"Aren't you going to get it?" Beth said, over her shoulder.

I hesitated. She pulled on a shift and hoisted her bag. The artists hovered in the shadows, disgusted with me, ready to pack it in, head back to their own century. And who could blame them, after all?

The phone had shifted to some higher key. This was life, imitating art. I'd studied art. Life was another matter.

I reached out suddenly and yanked on the phone cord. It was strong, but it was old. On the second try, it snapped, sending a little burst of plaster up from the wall. The Fuseli print crashed down behind the bed.

"What are you doing?" Beth said.

"Let them work out their own problems," I said, and meant it.

She stared at me, uncertain. After a moment, she put her bag down. I took her hand and told her everything. It was time for that. I prayed she'd lean my way.

My Heroes Have Always Been Grill Cooks
Ruminations on William Price Fox's *Southern Fried*

John T. Edge

Y ou know just the sort of fellow I'm talking about. He's almost tall. Rawboned and rangy. Wears a mustard-stained, short-sleeve shirt and a shiny pair of double-knit slacks. A paper skiff rides atop a tangle of thinning hair. Eye sockets ringed in black, irises shot through with a spider web of red.

He's on the backside of forty and sliding fast. Showed up for work one day a while back way too hungover even to slice onions, and now his left thumb is flat where it should be round. Years of scooping up rashers of bacon with his bare hands have left the tips of his fingers capped with calluses, as if sealed in thin jackets of paraffin.

He earns his keep walking the salted duckboards at the local greasy spoon. If he weren't working the grill, he'd be a diesel mechanic, maybe a taxi driver. And I'll argue with you until I'm blue in the face that he's somebody worth knowing.

I owe my love of the grill—and my admiration of grill cooks—to two men: my father and William Price Fox.

Both were born into the Depression. Both grew up in the same hard-scrabble neighborhood of clapboard homes set just south of the state-house in Columbia, South Carolina. My father was a lifelong civil servant, a federal probation and parole officer. Fox, after turns as a bellhop, golf caddy, schoolteacher and salesman, settled into the writing life. Though the two knew one another, they were never close friends. "I ran with a pretty rough crowd back then," my father told me once. "Billy Fox never had much to do with us roustabouts."

By the age of five, maybe six, I was clambering up onto a stool alongside my father at the local Waffle House, straining to get a better look at our burgers as they sputtered and spat on a flattop grill. I couldn't understand how the cook juggled all those orders, how he could flip a meat patty with the spatula in his right hand while cracking two eggs in his left. My father seemed to share the fascination and was happy to stay perched on his stool, sipping coffee long after the meal was over, so that I could drink in the scene. By the time I was eight, I had plotted out two potential career paths: archeologist and grill cook. Daddy told me that they were both honorable professions.

Fox came later, say when I was about ten or twelve. He had hit it big in 1962—the year of my birth—with his first collection of short stories, *Southern Fried*, a khaki-colored paperback peddled in drugstore spinner racks for a buck and a quarter. Released by Gold Medal Books, publisher of such pulp noir favorites as *The Woman with Claws* and *Park Avenue Slut*, *Southern Fried* sold more than 300,000 copies in five years. Upon its release, the work was heralded as a modern comic classic, populated with baseball pitchers who can't throw straight unless they've got a snoot full and politicians who hold their audience in such thrall that, when they pause for effect, you can "hear a grasshopper fart."

But what has stuck with me since my first reading is the title story. Simply put, it's the best piece of food writing I've ever had the pleasure to peruse. I knew that before I knew what food writing was. Now you might argue that, by all rights, the short story *Southern Fried* should be understood within the context of other comedic writing about the South, say that of George Washington Harris or Mark Twain, and that it's only incidentally about food. And I would tell you that you're flat wrong.

Here's the essence of the story: Out at Holly Yates's drive-in, Preacher Watts works the grill. He's a strong and dignified black man of indeterminate age, the kind of fellow press reports once referred to as a "pillar of the Negro community." His face is creased by a razor welt that looks "like someone had laid a ruler from the tip of his left ear to the edge of his chin and carefully followed it." When we meet Watts, he's reading a lot of Kant and studying to be a minister. The unnamed narrator of the story, a white boy of sixteen or so, is his assistant.

Fleetwood Driggers is the soda jerk, a callow malcontent at perhaps the zenith of his young life. He is not, however, without his admirers. Indeed, he has the reputation of wielding the fastest ice cream scoop in town. It helps that he looks the part. "His face was long and thin like a greyhound's," writes Fox, "and his ears were smoothed down at the sides of his head like he'd been raised at top speed or in a high wind." Problem is, he's lacking in what a man of his father's generation might call intestinal fortitude. When asked to help out in the kitchen, Driggers invariably feigns heatstroke and claims to see a monkey rise up from the rows of sizzling hamburgers.

The tension in the story turns on life in the kitchen. One summer night, after the first service of a weeklong tent revival lets out, hordes of hungry worshippers descend upon the drive-in. The narrator sets the scene:

> All eight of the three-basket Fry-O-Laters were full and going, the big grill was packed solid with hamburgers, and every broiler had four steaks with the fat hissing and flashing. Preach kept saying, "Don't rush boy. Don't fight 'em. I got everything under control. Just fry…You see an empty space on the grill, fill her up. I keep track. Don't worry." And then he'd laugh. "If we get in real trouble, we can always get ole Fleetwood back here to help us."
>
> But I was worried anyhow. The ten curb boys were screaming at the windows and slamming on the order bell, the four waitresses up front were pounding on the partition glass and Holly was chewing his cigar and shouting, "Get it out, get it out. Come on, Preach, get it out…"

Preacher Watts gets the food out that night—and every night thereafter—while Driggers falters under pressure and generally shows his ass. The other shoe drops late in the week when, at the close of a long shift, Driggers saunters back into the kitchen, plants his rear end on the sandwich board, pulls his feet alongside, and says to Watts, "What if I said I wanted eggs and bacon and I wanted you to fix them for me?"

Instead of slugging the soda jerk, Watts challenges him to a duel of sorts: Two chocolate sundaes, four strawberry sodas, eighteen small Cokes, and seven banana splits. Fastest time wins. Driggers has more to lose than Watts, for Holly Yates has made it clear that he too has grown weary of the young Turk. If anyone can best him at the fountain, Driggers is out of a job.

Watts wins handily, by moving low and slow. "No elbows or knees or pivots," writes Fox, "just wrists and hands and head." Driggers exits shamefaced. And as the drama comes to a close, Preacher Watts and his young protégé are pondering whether to tell Yates about the contest. Dawn is breaking as the narrator brings the story home:

> We were both tired now. It was going to be a long hot day and it would be hard to sleep. I knew Preach was thinking about Immanuel Kant and now I wished I had listened to him when he explained Kant's philosophy to me. I spoke in a strangled voice. "What would old Mr. Kant say about a thing like this? What would he say to do about a bastard like Fleetwood Driggers?"
>
> Preacher turned and smiled. His face lit up like a banana split. "How you know that was what I was thinking about? Boy, you're getting smarter every day. I was just figuring what he would say about a situation like this and I believe I got me an answer."
>
> I jumped in. "He'd say ram it to him."
>
> Preach looked serious, "No he wouldn't say that. But I know exactly what he would say, though...I suspect he'd rub his little beard and then he'd say, 'Let him sweat.'"

So perhaps you now understand why my heroes have always been grill cooks.

With *Southern Fried*, Fox introduced this young, bourgeois boy to an old, black prole of a hero. He bestowed nobility upon a benighted trade. Fox stood convention on its head and accomplished what I think only the best food writing comes close to doing. He used burgers and fries as an entrée to pondering what William Faulkner termed life's verities: race, class, the big stuff. Fox got me to thinking at an early age and, in a way that I still don't fully comprehend, set me on my way.

As for my father, he made sure I got up close and personal. He put me on a swivel stool in clear sight of the flattop griddle and indulged my fascination. His lessons were simple. Over bacon and eggs, patty melts and milkshakes, he brought Fox's prose to life, teaching me the value of honest work, the fraternity of man, the way of the grill.

Thanks, gentlemen.

Orphans

Donald Hays

I see him in the waiting crowd at the Moscow airport. Richard. It's odd how he seems both familiar and strange. The dentist in rough, workman's clothes. He's already seen me, and his tanned face beams. I'm touched by that. Walking toward him, I find myself moved by everything, by the whole of the life we've shared. I'm surprised at myself. Maybe I'm already feeling a kind of grief for what I haven't yet lost.

He takes me in his arms. He kisses me. "I've missed you," he says. "I love you."

He holds me at arm's length now, a hand on each of my shoulders, and, tears in his eyes, he's looking at me as if at some just discovered—or rediscovered—marvel. "Look at you," he says. "Ann. I prayed for this"— he shakes his head at the wonder of it—"and now you're here."

I reach down and grasp the handle of my carry-on bag. It's the kind that has little wheels on it. When I look up at him again now I see a haunted, long-faced man, the fanatic face of self-denial, sainthood, and terror.

I know I'm being unfair. Let it go, I tell myself. Here you are, in Moscow, where you never thought you'd be. Why not make the best of it? See St. Basil's, picnic in Gorky Park, make the Red Square rounds.

But it's not to be. Tomorrow is the long-awaited Sunday of the dedication ceremonies at the church orphanage Richard's been working on. He begins telling me about it. Then, seeing my disappointment, he apologizes. He promises we'll spend some time together back here in Moscow before we fly home. We can't miss the dedication and reopening, though. It means everything to him. Now we've got just time enough to catch the night train to Belgorod. He hopes I understand.

We take a cab to the Kursk Station. Richard does have the driver take us to the center and then drive slowly along the Moscow River opposite the Kremlin and Red Square and the great cathedrals, St. Basil's and Assumption. You can see them clearly from here, he tells me. It's the best view you can get from a car. After we pass the center, we cross the river and turn right and east, and ten minutes later we're at the station.

As soon as we're out of the cab, the homeless, dirty, and deformed clutch at us, pleading for money. Children circle us like hyenas, yapping, grabbing at me and at the suitcase I pull along behind me. A blind woman holds up a filthy, stoic baby and, through the slack, black gap of her mouth, beseeches me in Russian. She presses the baby against my chest and says, "She die here. You take. Save life. One thousand dollar."

Richard forces himself between me and the woman with the baby, then says something to the woman in Russian, but she keeps pressing forward, keeps offering the baby to me, keeps lowering the price. Not until we reach the steps leading up into the station does the woman fall back. All the homeless fall back. And then I see why. Grim, uniformed policemen, submachine guns across their chests, guard the entrance. One of the children, a boy—a teenager, I think, though you can't read time on such a face—comes too close to the entrance, and a policeman steps toward him, raises the rifle, and says something. The boy slinks back into the crowd. On his face I see an animal patience, a resignation more frightening than rage. It's the same expression the baby wore.

Inside the station, everything is for sale everywhere—T-shirts and toilet paper, computer software and video games, running shoes and jogging suits, Rasputin posters and Red Army uniforms, cigarettes and samovars, cheap vodka and broken icons. Earnest men hand out Christian pamphlets. Others, equally earnest, just as evangelical, brandish guidebooks to the Moscow night—sex shows, brothels, escort services, a night at the Luxor. I walk briskly, forthrightly past them all, without looking at any of them, but Richard lags behind, stopping now and then to say something in Berlitz Russian to one or another of the panders we pass. I go on to the platform and wait for him there.

It's still fifteen minutes to departure time, but the train's already there, so we find our car, climb on, and make our way to our compartment. The car is crowded, rank with the smell of sausage, onions, and sweat, thick with the smoke of charcoal and cheap tobacco. Our compartment is jammed. Two men, already drunk, are in our seats. They're smoking harsh, hand-rolled cigarettes and sharing a bottle of what looks like vodka, some clear liquor.

Trouble, I think. But when Richard shows them his ticket and mine, the drunks get up and leave. They stagger past me and lumber down the passageway toward the next car. Richard lifts my bag and slides it onto the overhead rack. We sit down. The other people in the compartment—three middle-aged men in bad suits and a weary-looking woman with a baby in her lap—eye us warily, sullenly.

After we have sat there for a moment or two, Richard starts talking about the man he mentioned in his letter. Valentin Vinogradov. It turns out he owns the orphanage. In fact, he owns several orphanages in central Russia, several others close to St. Petersburg. Soon after Gorbachev's fall, Vinogradov left the University of Moscow and opened a Mercedes dealership. Then he took over a television station. Then it was more car dealerships, more television stations. After that he branched out into computers, pharmaceuticals, oil, coal, hotels. There are all kinds of rumors—that he owns brothels and escort services, that he owns Anastasia Connections, which arranges "romance tours" of Moscow and St. Petersburg for Western businessmen shopping for wives. Lately, saying that he's doing it for humanitarian reasons, Vinogradov's been buying orphanages. And it is true, Richard says, that Vinogradov improves conditions in the orphanages he buys. They're cleaner, better staffed, better equipped. There's more and better medicine. The children are healthier. But the price of a child keeps going up. Vinogradov keeps insisting he'll have to raise the price to $100,000 for the next group.

Richard shakes his head. "Sometimes I think we've struck a bargain with evil itself," he says. His gaze seems to turn inward. He says nothing for several seconds. Then he says, "But still, the children...you saw the one back there...some of them would have no place, if he hadn't bought the orphanages. Vinogradov, I mean." He nods at this. "Lots of children dead." He closes his eyes, opens them. He seems to be having an argument with himself, one he must have been having over and over again. "I don't know," he says. He shakes his head. "Sometimes I just don't know."

The train lurches forward and begins to pull out of the station. Richard keeps talking, telling me that he and Dolph need to separate themselves from Vinogradov but can't bring themselves to abandon the children already at the orphanage. He goes on and on.

I'm very, very tired. I rest my head against his shoulder and close my eyes.

The train gains speed. I'm in Russia, I think. I'm entering the night. My mind surrenders to the rhythm of the wheels. *Vinogradov. Vinogradov.* It quickens and quickens. *Vinogradov. Vinogradov.* It reaches speed and steadies. *Vinogradov. Vinogradov.*

I'm the one the paramedics brought back from the dead, the one who had the quintuple bypass surgery. But it was Richard, my husband of twenty years, a fifty-year-old Tulsa dentist in the pink of health, who renounced alcohol, became a vegetarian, started walking five miles before dawn every morning, and dedicated his life to Christ. Nearly every day he had lunch with Dolph Holloway, the pasty-faced assistant pastor of University Lutheran, a mushy man with the soft earnest eyes of a child molester. They ate the tofu-and-lemongrass special at Suzy Wong's Rice Bowl. They didn't laugh. They didn't speak in any way of pleasure. They talked earnestly, man to man. What would Jesus do? they asked each other. There was no sex, no sake, no cigar.

Simple, really, the inevitable progression—*memento mori*, fear in a handful of dust, the horrifying recognition that you've pissed your life away minding your manners and paying your bills, and then, well, for a man with any spine at all, it would be fast cars and hired women. But not Richard. Instead of getting a mistress and a Miata, Richard began getting right with God. Now he's gone gaga over the idea of the life of service.

Not me.

I've taught high school history for eighteen years. I'm on sick leave this semester. I can go back in the fall if I want to. I know the subject. I know the kids. I can handle a class. American History Survey or Western Civ. AP or remedial. My students learn what they're supposed to learn—and sometimes more. They do well on the standardized tests. My own life of service, in other words. But what good does it do? It is as it has always been. The intelligent learn in spite of us. The ignorant breed and multiply.

I was sick of it. I wanted something else.

Then, just when I'd about decided to leave him anyway, Richard came home from his office and told me he'd decided to "suspend" his practice. "I'd like to work with children," he said.

I was standing at the kitchen counter. I had pine nuts, fresh basil leaves, olive oil, a peeled and quartered tomato, and Parmesan cheese in the blender. I was thinking, *Damn, I'd like a cigarette.*

A pan of water was heating on the range. I gave it a look. It wasn't boiling yet. Children. "I don't want to hear about it."

I accepted being childless years ago—a scarred uterus—and had come to see it as a blessing, actually. Sure, there was a time Richard and I talked of other ways: test-tube babies, surrogate mothers. I decided against any of that. I didn't want to be one of those women who, to gratify her desire for offspring, was willing to hire a battery of lab technicians and an illegal alien with an unscarred uterus. Still, the desire wouldn't go away. We started thinking about adopting. Koreans, Rumanians, Russians, children of the ravaged countries, they were easy enough to get, if you had a little patience and a lot of money. It went on for maybe a year. We filled out forms and suffered through several interviews with an adoption agency that worked with overseas orphanages. But finally I came to my senses. I didn't need a child to be a woman. Anyway, I had the kids at school. Year after year. Class after class. More than enough to cure anyone of the childbearing urge.

For a while after that, Richard kept at me to change my mind. And he never completely gave up on it, not really. Anytime he thought I might be vulnerable, he'd start in again. We had so much to offer. We could save a child's life. And the child would do so much for us, would make our lives, our marriage, complete. But then he'd wear out and shut up and settle back into the routine that got us through our days. Weeks, even months, might go by before he mentioned children, orphans, adoption again.

Or that's the way it was until about six months ago. It had been ten years, mind you, since Id gotten past the idea of having children. But I'd had the heart attack and the surgery just three weeks earlier and I wasn't myself. It was evening, and I was lying there feeling all barren and bleak, a futile, beside-the-point woman. Richard came in carrying my supper on a tray. Skinless chicken breast, steamed broccoli, brown rice, sliced cucumbers, skim milk. The heart-happy, Sugar Busters platter. Just looking at it made me want to skip the meal and have a cigarette. Instead, I made the mistake of telling Richard what I'd been thinking. About my life, about not having children.

Well, of course, he went right after that. He held my hand, told me he loved me, he'd learned to be satisfied, happy, without children, with just me. But, sure, he'd admit it, he'd always wanted a child, children even, maybe. Anyway, he kept petting me and soothing me and talking about these Russian orphans Dolph Holloway had told him about. I listened and smiled and nodded and—I admit it—I felt the tug of temptation. By the next morning, though, it was gone. I was over it. But not Richard. He never let it go after that evening. To make it worse, he had it all tangled up with the idea of serving God.

Christ, somebody give me a smoke.

Then, there it was, a fine evening near the end of May. I'd opened all the windows. The air was sweet with spring. I was ready to live. But there before me was this lugubrious pilgrim. The dentist who'd given himself to God, grain, and the life of service. I pushed the PUREE button on the blender.

Richard kept talking to me as I prepared the pesto, the pasta, the salad. But I kept stopping him. I told him to pour us each a glass of chardonnay. He poured me one. He'd be having mineral water.

We sat down to eat, and Richard, as he'd been doing since Thanksgiving, bowed his head and closed his eyes. His little prayer of thanks. He'd have liked me to hold his hand and join in, but I wouldn't. I'm a short-time woman with a spliced heart—I want to live while I can. But Richard? It's not life he wants. He just wants not to die. A world of difference. I want what's here. He wants what's not.

While his head was still down, I rolled pasta onto my fork, brought it to my mouth, and ate. I sipped my wine. I looked across the table at him. He was still at it. Taking his time with grace tonight.

I went back to the pasta.

"Ann," he said, "I've wasted my life."

I stopped, my loaded fork halfway between plate and mouth, and stared at him. He was leaning over his plate, all round-eyed earnestness. He looked as if he'd just experienced some great revelation he was eager to share. He got that look three or four times a day. Good news for modern man.

"Nothing in the Beatitudes about dentists being blessed?"

"Please," he said. "I'm serious." He was the picture of frustrated piety.

"Yes," I said. "Unfortunately."

Resolution began, predictably, to reclaim his face. "But it's true, Ann," he said. "I can't deny it any longer." He nodded emphatically. "I've wasted my life."

He looked down at his pasta, gathered himself. I could feel him forming the words he wanted to say. "I'm serious about leaving the practice." He looked up. There was hope in his eyes, optimism, as if this might be just the thing to turn me around, point me toward the light. "For six months, at least. And I've got a year, if I need it. If I'm not back in the practice by then, it's Ben's. We've settled on a price that's fair to everyone. So"—he gave me a look—"the first of June, I'm through." He held up a hand. "We'll be fine. Financially, I mean. You'll be set for life. No matter what. I made sure of that."

Set for life. "I see," I said. "Repudiated that den of iniquity, have you? The dental clinic?"

"I was living as if I'd live forever," he said, sweeping his left hand toward me, dragging his sleeve across the pasta. "As if there were no such thing as death."

I laid my fork across my pasta, leaned back in my chair, and stared at him. The truth was, I didn't care what he did. Just give me my money and be gone. "Sure," I said. "We're going to die, and soon, you and I. Me, any heartbeat could be my last. So you're right, Richard. Of course. What I want to do with whatever time I have left is hang around with Lutherans. Make life seem to last longer by boring myself blind. Make death, when it comes, be a mercy."

A week went by, then part of another, it's June, and bang! Richard was off to Russia—some town called Belgorod—to work in an orphanage. Suited me. In April and May, he said, he'd made the calls and the connections and filled out the forms and gotten a visa for himself and, just in case, one for me, though I told him at the time there was no chance of my winding up in Russia. He and Dolph Holloway have flown food and clothes and medical supplies to the orphanage. They plan to rebuild a church on the grounds there and arrange for a dozen barren Oklahoma Lutherans—the six couples are going there with them—to adopt Russian orphans.

I was glad he was gone. Maybe a sentence among the suffering Russians will cure him. If not, then, well, he could just stay there in his paradise of eternal winter and redemptive suffering. I was getting my strength back. I still had a little life I'd like to enjoy while my heart was still beating. I had money. I didn't have to work. I was free. I told myself I'd start looking around.

But more weeks went by—two, three, four—and I didn't do anything except go to the club, do my prescribed exercises, and come home. I was afraid I'd do something that would change everything so much I wouldn't know what to do next. I hated that part of me, timid, suburban, but it remained. Then one Friday I got this letter:

> Dear Ann,
> God's grace is indeed boundless.
> There have been some problems and delays with the adoptions. The people at the orphanage have treated us all right, and I don't think any of this is their fault. There's a man named Valentin Vinogradov who seems to be in charge of everything. Apparently he owns several orphanages. Dolph says that under the Communists he was a chemistry professor at Moscow University. He's

obviously a sophisticated man. He dresses well and speaks good English, and he seems sympathetic to both the orphans and the prospective parents, but he always finds a way to ask for more money. And he always wants the money in cash. Dolph has tried to make it clear to him that he's not getting any more. Counting everything—fees, gifts, bribes, everything—the price each of our couples will be paying for a baby comes to over $60,000. I think Dolph has finally convinced Vinogradov that if he asks for more, we'll go home and start over and look to other sources if we have to. Anyway, he's stopped asking for more money, but he's still insisting on cash. So Dolph is flying to Germany with our six couples. They'll get the cash through a bank there and then fly back to Moscow on a chartered plane. They're going to hire armed guards, too. Six couples, so that's at least $360,000 in cash they'll be carrying through the airport and into Moscow. Still, what else can they do?

Anyway, I'm waiting here in Belgorod. You should see the place that will soon be our church here. It was a church until the Revolution, and then it was a cannery, but it has been empty since just a few months after the fall of Communism. And it must have been in really bad shape even then. It had a solid foundation, though, and stone walls. We have a carpenter and stonemason who have been helping us refurbish the walls and put up a new roof these last couple of weeks. There are twelve teenage boys and girls from the orphanage, and they've been working with us, too, doing what I do—mixing hod, carrying stone, the brute labor. They're great, the children are. Good workers and so appreciative of everything we're doing. Anyway, the walls are sound now, and we've laid the beams and joists for a new roof, and already you can just stand here and see what God can do with something when we give Him the chance.

I've set up a kind of dental clinic here. In the evenings I work on the children's teeth. Fillings, mostly. Though I've pulled quite a few teeth I could have saved if we had the proper equipment. We have to make do with what God has given us.

Well, I won't go on. It's my prayer that you'll be here in a couple of weeks and see the church and the children for yourself. (Remember, you need to come on the day specified on your visa.) I'm more certain than ever that this is what God wants me to do. This is my work on earth. It would all be perfect if you were here with me. You and the all of God are everything to me, Ann. That's the truth.

Pray for me, my darling wife. I will pray for you.

I love you.

Richard

Three days later he called to remind me that if I wanted to come to Russia I needed to get there exactly a week from then. That was the day my visa specified. He'd made reservations for me. Would I please come? He needed me. I told him I would. But I had no such intention. I was just wanting to get him off the phone.

It wasn't until I was lying in bed that night trying to understand myself that I decided, sure, Russia. Why not? At least it's not Oklahoma. Something might actually happen to me in Russia.

It's nearly dawn when we get off the train in Belgorod. A sluggish rain comes down. The few other passengers who get off there are met by someone, friend or family, and led to a waiting car. Others pause briefly just outside the door, then lower their heads and trudge off into the rain. The night absorbs them. There are no cabs. I stand beside Richard beneath the station's arched entryway, my luggage between us. Despite the rain, the air stinks of sulfur. The lights are few and dim. Slick, empty streets recede into a ruined Russian town.

Richard looks at his watch. "The train was on time," he says. "It's usually late." He turns to me and nods. "They'll be here."

And a few minutes later, they are. A black van emerges from the night and pulls up to the station. "Vinogradov," Richard says, and I am roused, curious.

I hurry through the rain to the van. A wiry, dark-haired adolescent steps out of the passenger side, slides the side door open for us, takes my bag, and places it inside. His quick eyes dart here and there. He seems at once obsequious and insolent. "Alexey," Richard says. The young man nods at him. "Is very good to see you wife," Alexey says. "Is beautiful woman. No?" He all but bows and scrapes as he speaks. A voice from inside the van says, "He wouldn't sleep. He wanted to be the first to ride in the van. I decided it was easier just to let him come with me." It's certainly not the voice of Valentin Vinogradov. It's American, a voice from Oklahoma. Dolph Holloway. Richard gestures for me to enter the van. I climb in. He steps in behind me, and Alexey slides the door to.

As we drive away, Dolph Holloway and Richard begin talking about Vinogradov. He had the van delivered to the orphanage just that very afternoon. He's planning to attend the rededication tomorrow.

I sleep until almost noon the next day. After I bathe and dress and eat some bread and cheese from the cafeteria, Richard shows me around the orphanage, and we walk the grounds for a while together. He wants me to understand how much all this means to him. He wants me to share his new purpose. I listen, paying half-attention. I tell him I'm still too tired, too jet-lagged, to think. I eat more of the bread and a little stew for supper and go to bed almost immediately after that. It's still a couple of hours before sunset. Richard tries to talk to me when we're in bed, but I feign sleep. After a while, he slips out of bed and leaves the room. I lie there, curled against myself in the bed, until the light is gone. I think I'll rise and walk alone into the darkness. Maybe the night air will make me feel alive again. But I don't move, and the thought passes, and soon I'm asleep again. Richard lets me sleep until about half an hour before time for the dedication ceremony the next morning. I dress and go to the ceremony without having breakfast.

When Richard and I enter the chapel, the first person I notice is Valentin Vinogradov. I'm sure it's him. It can't be anyone else. He's surrounded by his entourage—bodyguards, confidants, and a gorgeous racehorse blonde. He's tall, himself, a broad-shouldered, barrel-chested man of maybe fifty. Thick silver hair, ice-blue eyes. He's wearing a white summer suit, linen, apparently, a soft blue tie. Very expensive.

A woman begins playing the piano softly. At the front of the chapel there is only a simple wooden altar—a low table really—and behind that a pulpit. The orphanage choir stands behind the pulpit and below a mural of John baptizing Jesus in the River Jordan. A door opens in the wall to the choir's right, and Dolph Holloway enters the sanctuary and walks to the pulpit. He's wearing a gray suit. A soft man in a sad suit, I think. An old woman in a nurse's uniform follows him and stands next to the pulpit. Both of them have Bibles in their hands. Dolph Holloway opens his and begins reading. "But Jesus called unto him and said, 'Suffer little children to come unto me, and forbid them not: for of such is the kingdom of God.'" And then the old woman reads it in Russian. They go on, back and forth like that for a while. Then Dolph Holloway and the old nurse leave the pulpit, walk to the first pew, and sit down. One of the orphans in the choir—it's Alexey, but seconds go by before I recognize him, he looks younger and cleaner today—steps forward and turns around to face the rest of the choir. The pianist begins playing, the boy director lifts his arms and moves the choir to song. They sing "Amazing Grace" in Russian.

Dolph Holloway returns to the pulpit and delivers the dedication sermon—a history of the orphanage and the chapel, an offering of thanks to the donors and workers who made the restorations and improvements possible, an optimistic vision of the future—made interminable by his pausing after every two or three sentences while the old nurse translates them into Russian. Then the choir sings again. Another hymn, I'm sure, though this time I don't recognize the melody. Dolph Holloway asks Richard to say a prayer of benediction. As Richard prays, his voice, soft and clear, is shaded by a just discernible, not quite servile shyness. An orphan's voice.

When it's over and we're outside the church, I watch the others, exchanging greetings, convivial smiles. Sun-washed, all of them, easy in the light. Standing at the edge of the crowd, the mingling human forms, I feel myself fading, drifting, losing all sense of identity. I turn away and look into the distance behind the church and the orphanage—orchards and hayfields and, beyond that, dark woods retreating into the horizon.

"Are you all right?"

I stare down at my arms and see that I'm shivering. I keep looking until, after what seems a long moment, the shivering stops and my body comes back to me.

Only then do I turn my face to the source of the voice. A man. Valentin Vinogradov. Still I don't respond to him. I turn back toward the others and look for Richard. I don't see him at first, then notice him talking to Dolph Holloway and several of the Oklahoma Lutherans. His back is to me. I look at Valentin Vinogradov again. I think I see both concern and calculation on his face. I don't know what to say to him. I want him to go away. I turn my face away from him and see the tall blonde, standing, her back to me, at the edge of the crowd some ten or fifteen yards away. She's smoking a long cigarette in a sleek black holder. Alexey is beside her, talking to her. She seems to be paying him no attention. With bored eyes, she's looking back at the church.

Valentin Vinogradov touches my forearm. "Madam?" he says.

"I'm all right," I say. "Please. I just lost myself for a minute. The sun, I guess. I don't know."

He smiles, and, with that, he's all male confidence. "You must be careful here," he says.

"Here?"

"It is very easy to lose yourself in Russia."

"I see." I look again, and there's Richard, still bright-faced among Oklahoma Christians and Belgorod orphans. I shift my gaze and there are Alexey and the blonde. She's still smoking. He's still talking. He looks as if he might be propositioning her. She looks as if he's not yet mentioned a price that interests her.

"Your husband," Valentin Vinogradov says. I turn back to him. "He is one who has lost himself here. But he has found God, I am told." He raises a brow. "A good exchange, you think?"

"I didn't mean that," I tell him. "I just got dizzy for a minute. That's all."

He removes a pack of cigarettes from his shirt pocket. Marlboros, the bright red pack. He takes one from the pack, which he returns to the pocket. He removes a silver lighter from his jacket's right front pocket. He lights the Marlboro. He exhales. The luxurious breath, pure pleasure. Self-indulgence itself. Sin and the wages of sin. My knees go weak with want.

He stares at me, then tilts his head back as if to get another perspective. Then he nods. "Sorry," he says. He takes the pack from his pocket again and offers me a cigarette. I feel reappraised, upgraded. He's interested. No, more than that. He wants me. I can tell. Sure, I know, he has the racehorse blonde. But he's used to her, tired of her, she's bought and paid for, jaded, bored, a plutocratic perquisite. Otherwise he wouldn't be looking at me. I'm forty, and even when young I'd have been no match for the blonde. I know that. But to Vinogradov I'm new and, as the wife of Richard the Good, Richard the Pure, especially enticing. I know that, too.

"Yes," I say. "Thank you. Please."

I take the Marlboro. I will not resign myself to the pious lung and the wholesome heart. As he's giving me a light, Vinogradov says, "It is very good to see this. You Americans, sometimes it is sad. So careful with life. You do not seem to know that you will die anyway."

I straighten, look at him, a promise in my eyes. I inhale deeply, and there it is—the forbidden breath, the thrill of smoke against the lungs, the taste of darkness. I can feel the beating of my heart. Anything can happen now. I am alive again.

THE SAINT OF BROKEN OBJECTS

Beth Ann Fennelly and Tom Franklin

In Lloyd's twenty-sixth year, he became clumsy. He'd just made Level III Manager, and they'd bought their first house, a Queen Anne in a safe neighborhood with good schools. First, he shattered the smoke detector swatting a gypsy moth with the broom. Then, stripping wallpaper with a putty knife, he pushed too hard and gouged the plaster, revealing the dark, tender underskin. It surprised his wife, because she had always been the one to chip glasses, nick her underarm with a Lady Bic, back over the mailbox. Now, as the spackle hardened in the dining room, he frowned as he oversnipped the conical shrub by the rose trellis. Later he fell off the roof.

Because his family had a history of brain tumors, Molly took him to a specialist, a Dr. Moss, who never stopped talking—how little we know of the brain, its mysteries, machinations, its dark convolutions. "For instance," he said, "this one guy, about your age—"

Molly clenched Lloyd's fingers.

"Outta nowhere," Dr. Moss said, "he starts getting hairy. In his ears, on his back, even his palms. Understand, this was a guy who'd had trouble growing a mustache. But now he has a five o'clock shadow by noon."

"What was it?" Lloyd asked. "A tumor?"

"Of course it was. It's always a tumor."

"What about Lloyd?" Molly asked.

"You?" Moss angled his computer screen toward them. "You got nothing."

That night, in quiet celebration, a wardrobe box for a table, Lloyd spilled his champagne on Molly's late grandmother's just-unrolled Turkish carpet.

"Maybe it's this," Molly said. "Maybe, subconsciously—"

"You're going to tell me I don't really want the house, so I'm being passive-aggressive."

"I'm just saying—"

"Well, don't."

Years to come, he broke windows, mirrors, ships in bottles, their daughter's kitten's spine, an antique crystal chandelier, a church pew, the binding of a first-edition *Alice in Wonderland,* the lid of a piano. He broke a blunderbuss at a silent auction. He broke tennis racquets, fishing rods, luggage, a globe, his collarbone, an MRI machine.

Certainly there were moments when he wasn't clumsy, but these were not the moments he remembered. What he remembered was the skein of accidents, the stubs, the stumbles, the small explosions, the near misses, all of them exhilarating.

If, in the Far East on business, he tried to conjure Molly, her round face surfaced with a look of perpetual alarm, her voice a shrill yelp of warning. She never adjusted to his mishaps, as she called them, questioning his finger, for instance, which had slipped and forwarded the wrong email to the wrong people, costing him the vice-presidency in the firm where, over the years, he'd broken thirteen briefcases, twenty-one pairs of eyeglasses, fifty-nine umbrellas, and occasionally the heart of Molly, who never learned to embrace the uncertainty.

Lloyd did, and grew to see his clumsiness as a kind of gift. To take a thing and use it showed failure of imagination. He took a thing and read its fault-lines, knew five ways it would break for him. When his great-grandchildren visited, they came gravely to his wheelchair, and when they left there were two toys in their hands where there had been one. He had blessed them. By now Dr. Moss had died, and Molly had died, and two of their children and even one of their grandsons. But Lloyd, Lloyd wasn't tired. How could he let his trembling hands fall empty to his sides? How could he leave the world before it was broken?

DIALOGUE OF MEN AND BOYS

David Wright

Your intercom buzzes and Martha's voice tells you that you have a phone call on line one. You're expecting a call from your wife, but Martha warns, "It's another reporter."

Shit.

"Did you tell him I was in?" you say.

"I told him I didn't know if you were at your desk or not," she says. "But he's calling from France. He's very insistent."

From France, huh? To Kylee. It's like you've done something great or something. Like it was third and one on the thirty-three, and you broke it and took it all the way and scored the points that put the other team away.

"France?"

You remember the time it was third and one on the thirty-three and you did break it: you broke the linebacker's arm tackle—you can't remember his name—and outran the safety—his name was Jonathan Menson—to the flag, the only safety you ever outran to any flag. That touchdown beat SMU.

KUDOS FOR PHLEBAN OF HORNED FROGS, you remember that headline as you say, "I'll take the call."

You think about how hard it is to believe that your memory still slips so easily back into the glories from twenty-one years gone and forty-two pounds ago. But this call has nothing to do with that. This call ain't about kudos but about court martial.

"Hello, Coach Phleban?"

"This is Phleban."

"My name is Jeff Walker, I'm a journalist for *Le Sport* in Paris, France."

You'd expected an accent slick like motor oil, but this guy sounds like he's from Toledo. "Jeff Walker?" you say.

"Yes, sir."

"You sound like you're calling from next door."

"Yes, well, actually I'm calling from Kansas City."

"Kansas City?"

"I'm covering the World Series."

The lucky shit, you think. If he's really at the Series, that is. "What was the name of that magazine?"

"*Le Sport.*" He's enunciated it like you would a long word for a twelve-year-old kid, slowly, so that the kid sees each of the letters in his head and so sees the word. Hell, you ain't stupid. It's the same damned word in English. And that ain't what you were asking.

"From France, did you say?"

"Yes, it's a French weekly. Sort of the equivalent of our *Sporting News.*"

"But you're American?"

"Yes, sir. I cover American sports for the magazine." He finally gets your meaning. "For the past five years, I have, yes. I moved to France to work for the *International Herald-Tribune*, then started writing two years ago for *Le Sport.*"

Lucky shit, you think. When he says the title of his magazine, he says the French so nice you hear a different person.

You goad him: "And the French want to know about football?" You know what he really wants to talk about.

"Mostly I cover basketball, and track and field," he says. "But sometimes I do special features…"

"About football?"

"About football," he says, "yes. Or baseball. Once about professional wrestling."

Wrestling, huh? That's what Danny Farino did, when the Steelers cut him, after he'd injured himself for the third time in the first three weeks of the season. 'Dandy Danny Sweetlove,' he called himself. Became the Professional Wrestling Federation World Champion. Professional wrestling. That ain't a sport, it's paid exhibitionism.

"Coach Phleban, I'd like to talk to you about Richard Adamson."

Ricky. Lil Rick.

You know that this is why he called, but the sound of Rick's name spoken aloud still startles you. "Richard Adamson."

"Yes, sir," you hear.

You've told this story before. Parts here and there, what others wanted said. They made you tell it: to clear the air, to clear the name of Texas high school football, and of the high school. Gave bits and pieces to *S.I.* and to the *Dallas Morning News* and to every rag that ever draped a newsstand. But nobody ever wanted the whole picture, just the little parts that meant nothing by themselves. Pieces like: what a handsome kid he was—a preacher's son, the youngest one, and Mom, head of the PTA—and bright, as sharp as a mosquito's pecker—but a nice kid, too. Then *S.I.* and the *Morning News* took what suited them and made him into something he never was. Richard Adamson was never just those things. He was Lil Rick.

"Coach Phleban?"

You hear that syrupy sympathy in this guy's voice. He's taken your silence for mourning when, in fact, it's been a time of passing judgment. You're thinking that you don't care where this guy's from—Paris, Peoria, or Timbuktu—you ain't got to talk to him. You're thinking that you've already done your time, you've talked to *S.I.* and to the *Morning News*, and all the hubbub has died down now. Folks can support their local high school team on Friday nights again. It's safe to go back to their Supporters Club seats and their "Go kill 'em!" cheers. It was just a freak accident. A one-in-a-million thing. The sport still builds character in young men, it's still the best way to keep them off the streets, off drugs, off this, off that...

"Coach Phleban?"

"What's the point, Mister—" You only remember Jeff.

"Walker."

"What's the point, Mister Walker?"

"The point is an article, Coach Phleban. An article about injuries in sports, about the hazards of amateur athletics."

He ain't injured, you want to say. Lil Rick never got injured. Well-coached players rarely do.

"You know, I been a football coach for twenty-one years," you say, "and I never experienced nothing like this before." You're just forty-two years old. "Ever."

"You're one of the relatively few who has, sir." Like it puts you in some elite club or something. "It's a story that needs to be told. And I want balance in my article. I've talked to doctors and trainers, and to the people who keep the statistics on such things, and I've talked to injured athletes. Now, I want to talk about tragedy…"

"Tragedy?"

"Yes, sir."

"But why me?"

"Because of Richard Adamson, sir," he says.

Lil Rick.

You say, "It does, you know."

"Sir?"

"It does build character." You remember the bad taste that having to play on the same team with Danny Farino for four years has left in your craw. "Did you ever play football, Walker?"

"Well, yes," he says, "until the ninth grade, I mean," and he sounds embarrassed, like you caught him with his pecker in his hand.

"Makes men of boys," you tell him. "Football makes men out of boys. What kind of men those boys become depends on other things. But football takes them from there to here."

"Can I quote you, Coach?"

"No," you say.

"Sir?" You hear frustration in Jeff Walker's voice.

"No," you say. You ain't agreed to do nothing yet. "I don't think you understand. Kylee's a town of twelve thousand. A cactus land. Dirt and oil derricks. Did you know that, Mr. Walker?"

"No, sir."

"Well, it is," you say. "Still, we get eight thousand people come to every home game." You think you hear him scribbling on the other end. "Stadium only seats six and a half. We got fifteen hundred people every other Friday night standing shoulder-to-shoulder, ringed around the field to watch a high school football game. Do you understand the magnitude of that?"

Jeff Walker doesn't say anything.

"These boys live something most grown men never know."

He stays quiet—his silence, such a deliberate disguise.

You say: "Listen, I won't disparage the sport, Walker. I don't care what French readers want to read."

"Don't worry about that," he says, "I'm not asking you to do that."

"If you misquote me, I'll sue you, I'll sue the whole goddamn country for libel if you misquote me." As if you could read French.

"Don't worry," he says. "I'll send you an advance copy of the issue, you can have someone from the school translate it and verify." Jeff Walker takes a breath. "So, Coach Phleban, tell me, what was—"

"Not now," you say.

"Sir?"

"You can call me back tomorrow if you want, but I won't interview now."

The quiet on the line screams his frustration, but you don't care. This is your show. "What time can I schedule to reach you?"

"After lunch. One thirty."

"I believe Kansas and Texas are in the same time zone," he mumbles to himself. You know they are, but you say nothing. You can almost hear him scribbling your name into a time slot in some fancy, thick pocket calendar. "Thank you, Coach," he says. "I'll talk to you tomorrow…"

But you just hung up. Not because you're angry—you ain't—but because you're in control, and Jeff Walker's got to understand that. You won't be made to give any more of those pieces that don't mean a goddamn thing by themselves. That's all the other articles were: a heap of broken-up images, crumbs that all together didn't even make a single slice of bread.

The shriek of the intercom startles you. You press the 'Speak' button to silence it. "Yes."

Martha's voice asks, "More leeches about Ricky Adamson?"

"More leeches," you confirm.

"I'm sorry, Coach Phleban, but he was calling from France and…"

France. Right. "It's okay, Martha. You were just doing what I hired you to do," you say, but you add, "Listen, if anyone else calls this afternoon, I'm away from my desk."

"I understand." Her voice is still apologetic.

"Thank you, Martha." And you flip off the intercom before she can say anything else.

No, Mr. Walker, you think. This time, you, Cody Phleban, will make the big picture you want made. This'll be your interview. And Ricky's. Not the *Morning News*'s. Not *S.I.*'s. And not *Le Sport*'s.

Like: You could have told *S.I.* about your TD against SMU. Or about the blocks against Joe Greene at North Texas State, big hits that opened boulevards for Farino to run through. Those pieces show something, they give some idea of who you are. Not "Coach C. Phleban, of Kiley, Texas"—three lines in a feature on fatal injuries in football: your name just once, and Rick's only twice, and they put "Richard" but no picture of the smiling kid that was Rick. They painted a false picture that they wanted seen. Class President. A preacher's son. The All-American Boy that he wasn't.

Rick was something else. Something more. Just as you were more than just "C. Phleban." You were Cody Phleban, the "Bruiser from Kylee," like in the twenty-year-old news clipping under the glass on your desktop. Or "Division 2A Coach of the Year" Phleban—the trophy stares at you across the width of your desk. You're the man who made a bi-district championship team out of too many too small and too slow country kids and who discovered among them a long spider-like boy— PineMan—and formed him into a future third-round draft pick of the NFL. The man who made men out of boys. Not just some high school coach from small-town Texas who didn't have a first name, just an initial, who never left his home town or the sport he loved, and who, in three lines and a misspelled name (it's Kylee!), just watched while the sixteen-year-old All-American Boy died on his football field—the boy's father in the stands and eight thousand screaming fans—from his brains all mashed to mush inside his head after a helmet-on-helmet collision.

Tomorrow, you—Bruising Cody Phleban, the Division 2A Coach of the Year—will put the pieces together. Not Jeff Walker.

This is nearly the only time you work up a sweat anymore, and you do it on your back and by not doing much at all, and you ain't even in your own bed. You think about how pretty she is. So blonde. All hair. She's just twenty. The sort of girl you would have married when you were twenty, at TCU. Maybe the sort of girl you did marry.

But you just fuck Martha, though. Y'all don't hardly talk much. Nor do anything else really. It's better this way. You talk with your wife. With her, talk, sometimes dinner out, is enough now. Your house is a home.

Martha says, "You been thinking about Ricky, haven't you?"

You roll over onto your side, content to just lie there, the small of your back against her hip. "Yeah, some," you say, to answer her question mostly, so she'll drop it and not say anything else. "News guy from France wants to talk about it."

"France," she says. Her voice carries dreams.

"He's not talking about coming over here or going over there or nothing like that. He just wants to talk. Over the phone."

"Ricky was a good kid," Martha says.

"Kid" sounds weird coming from Martha's mouth. She's hardly older than Ricky was. She's lying on her back, and she takes her hands from her stomach and like a clicking motor pat-pat-pats her hair back into place when it's not moved an inch from where it was. She says, "He reminded me of my brother, when he was in school."

You remember her brother, Marty Sostriss, and he wasn't nothing like Lil Rick. He graduated the same year as PineMan did, five years before, and Pine was the only man on that team.

Marty was just…ordinary. Played tight end. Worked hard, real hard at practices. You let him play because he worked so hard, and because he had pretty good size, and because you figured he wouldn't hurt your team by making mistakes. But you watched him cry one day and wished he'd never set foot on your football field.

It was third down, you sent in Marty's play—a safe pass in that situation—but the safety from Levelland closed real quick and separated

Marty from the football. A good hit. Clean, but vicious. One even the opposing coach has got to respect. You try to get your kids to do the same. You weren't even going to say nothing to Marty when he came off the field about dropping that ball, but Marty didn't get up after the hit. He just lay there on the ground on his back like a sack of grain, like yesterday's laundry, clutching his face-bar in his hands. Ah shit, you thought—the same thought you thought any time you saw one of yours stay on the ground.

You remember jogging out, pushing through the players crowded around to get to him, past the safety who'd kissed him. But when you knelt down over him, wasn't a damn thing wrong. Not his ribs or his shoulder. Not an ankle, not a knee. He was just lying there, eyes clenched and crying, in front of God, his teammates, eight thousand fans, and the boy who'd put him on his back in the first damn place.

You wanted to yank him by his face-bar, slap him silly or plant your shoe in his hind parts. You wanted to say, "Get your ass up! You get up and get that boy that got you!" But you just knelt there on one knee, leaning over that crying Marty Sostriss, not knowing what to say. When he finally unclenched his eyes and seemed to settle, you remember trying to pierce his tears with your glare, remember telling him, "You get the hell off my football field." You remember standing and turning and walking back to the sideline.

Martha says, "You want to talk to that guy about Ricky, don't you?" Her voice sounds more manly right now than Marty's ever did. "I know you," she says, "and I can tell you do."

You don't say anything. Just lie there, quiet.

"I think it'd be good for you, Cody"—You're startled not to hear "Coach Phleban," although she never calls you that like this—"I think it'd be good to just get it out, to just get it off your chest."

This is when things like this get sticky. When she wants to be something more for you, something else. But she can't be that, you've told her all along. It's getting sticky, and you don't know what to say.

Martha had been lying on her back, both breasts standing straight up, but now you see she's shifted onto her side, facing you, and her breasts angle toward the sheets. "Remember that one practice this year," she says, "when the Johnson kid broke his leg?"

Martha called the ambulance before you even got back inside the field house to tell her to. "Yeah," you say. "So?"

"You had them do that drill…"

"Shotgun Alley." A meat drill. Your favorite. Requires sacrifice, reckless abandon. Gets you fired up and gets kids fired up, slapping helmets, slapping asses…

"Yeah, that one," she says. "I remember just knowing, Cody. Just knowing. I was too far to see the drill much less hear a 'pop' or anything." You remember the "pop," when a thick bone snaps clean. "I remember, all I could see was your cap and gray T in that muddle of helmets. And I could see your arms swinging, gesticulating-like, getting them boys going. It was like…excitement all around you, an aura, like when we make love. And all of a sudden, it was all gone. All the excitement. Everything. It all got focused, all that energy, on one spot I couldn't see in the middle of all those helmets. And I just knew."

She twists her body up and sits Indian-style, holding a pillow over herself, her knee grazing the flesh of your flank. "It reminded me of that time Marty's senior year when he got hurt. Maybe you don't remember?" You say nothing. "It was before I worked for you. I wasn't nothing but a sophomore still. But I watched you, Friday nights. And when Marty got hurt, I watched the way you went to him and helped him off the field. All that passion about the game, and compassion for those kids. It was like that with Ricky." She reaches her hand onto your chest—her hand, her voice, all trembling with tenderness. "When Ricky went down, I saw something in you on the sideline fall, too."

"I got to go, Martha." You swing your legs around and off the bed, feel the weight of your belly roll flaccid onto your thighs.

Then there's Martha's hand on your back. "Marty always loved you for what you did for him," she says.

"I got to go."

"They all do."

You don't hear any of the rest. Maybe she says nothing. You dress

quickly, remarking every bit of loose flesh that'd once been tight, and you
go.

It's one thirty and the phone hasn't yet rung. You busy your hands by
shuffling some loose-leaf memos around on the desk.

One thirty-three. PineMan, on one knee and leaning on his Seattle
Seahawks helmet, peers down at you over the "Coach of the Year" trophy
from his framed place on the wall opposite your desk.

One thirty-six and still nothing.

At one forty, the panel of buttons on the bottom of the telephone
lights up just as you hear a muffled ringing through the closed door of
your office. Even when you expect it, the sudden scream of the intercom
is so shrill it startles you.

"Jeff Walker on line one," Martha's voice informs you.

"Who's that?" you say.

"Jeff Walker," she says. "The reporter from France."

He's calling from Kansas City, you think. "Thanks, Martha." From
the World Series.

You stare at the phone, wait an instant before answering. Then
another. The red light lighting the button that designates line one blinks
in rhythm, measuring every second and every dime you're making Jeff
Walker pay before you let him look at this picture. And he's got to pay,
for the look. If he wants to see, you can make the picture for him, but he's
got to pay. You can't afford to carry others anymore. This one owes you.
He's got to write it right, to paint the right picture, or you won't let him
write it at all.

At one forty-four, you pick up the receiver. "Hello. This is Phleban."

"Coach Phleban, this is Jeff Walker." You don't respond. "From
France. We spoke yesterday."

"Yes. Of course."

"I'd like to thank you for agreeing to interview…"

"Yes."

"…and to start off by asking you a few questions about yourself."

"Sure."

"You've been in coaching for twenty-one years, is that right?"

"Yes. Twenty-one."

"Always at the high school level?"

You maintain that professional distance. "No. I started as an assistant at Texas Christian, where I played college ball."

"You played for TCU?" The slowed rhythm of his speaking tells you he's scribbling that piece in his notes. "When?"

"From '65 to '68. I wasn't ever drafted by the pros," you add, but you don't know why.

"What position did you play?"

"I was a fullback." Then, two hundred five pounds of rock and pumping iron for more; now you can't keep under two-fifty, and no part of your body could be compared to stone. Except your head, your wife claims.

Always did have a hard head, though. Little talent to speak of. No speed. But lots of heart and a head big on brains and that you could shatter a bottle over. The perfect complement to the fluid grace of Danny Farino, who ran as naturally as a deer. Farino, the speedster from New Jersey, had more athletic ability in the index finger of his left hand than you ever dreamed of having. But Bruising Cody Phleban had the heart and just enough football smarts to make the difference.

You think: That's how a sportswriter would write it. And that's how you tell it to your teams, too: you don't have to have a lot of talent to play football, if you have a lot of heart and some brains. Farino might have made the big plays, but he also made big mistakes. You made the sure plays.

"...I been coaching high school nearly twenty of my twenty-one years," you hear yourself saying. "I only coached at TCU long enough to complete my degree."

"You prefer coaching at the high school level?" Jeff Walker asks. "I mean to say, you prefer working with boys?"

"I like working with them," you say. "At times, I toyed with the idea of returning to college coaching. But I enjoy working with the boys."

Like PineMan: John Wayne Milam. From the bi-district championship team. You look over at him, looking back at you from his framed place on the wall opposite. Milam was a gangly center for the basketball team who mostly took up space on a football field until you made him a six foot six, two hundred sixty pound monster. An All-State Defensive End. Became a four-year starter at Tech because he already knew how to play when he got there, All-Southwest Conference his senior year, and a third-round draft choice of Seattle. You molded Milam into a towering man with a lumberjack's chest and arms like tree trunks. How many coaches had boys they'd chiseled into professional football players? That must mean something.

What happened later—the illegal substances and the suspensions— he must have learned that at college. That wasn't PineMan. A boy's mistake that cost him a career. Let us all down with that crap.

"…to talk about Richard Adamson?" you hear.

Richard Adamson. It sounds so cold like that.

"Yes," you say. "Fine."

"How old was he?"

"Ricky was sixteen."

"Ricky…" He's jotting that down. "He was a junior, is that right?"

"A junior, yes. My starting halfback for two years, and class president…"

Goddamnit, don't give that piece! Not like that. The All-American Boy, Beaver Cleaver in shoulder pads! Lil Rick was more than that. He was real.

Like: We all called him 'Little,' but he was anything but. Ricky lived in the weight room, like you had when you played—he was put together like a statue.

You hear Jeff Walker repeating, "Class president?"

"Yes," you say, and you imagine his manic scribbling over the long lines that link your voices from Kylee to Kansas City—probably as close as you'll ever get to the World Series.

"So he was a popular boy? In school, I mean."

"He was the kind of kid you'd want for a big brother if you were a boy."

Yes, that sounds right. And it's true: Rick had all those things: courage, loyalty, a natural leader. Never had to teach Rick those things.

"...was a man among boys," you hear yourself say. "Weighed one seventy and change when I had him as a freshman." That's your voice talking. "Grew five inches and put on thirty-some-odd pounds of muscle in two years." But the voice, your mouth—all excited—sounds like you don't know who. "And Rick had all kinds of speed. Here was a boy who weighed two hundred plus pounds and ran a four-five forty-yard dash, as a junior..."

Like Farino, Ricky ran as naturally as a deer. PineMan made the pros and you had made PineMan. Rick had made himself. You, Phleban, were teaching him other, better things: football smarts; toughness; to play with reckless abandon like Phleban had played himself. Every nagging little injury would keep Farino on the bench, a trainer massaging something or getting him ice. Phleban—you—didn't want Rick to turn out like that.

Danny Farino was a whore. Even before wrestling. In school, with the coaches, with the alums. Everywhere with everyone. He'd lie like a rug, look a man dead in the eye and call it truth. It was all me-me-me with him. The team was just his stepping stone. When a kid's that good, it can...corrupt. But not Rick. Phleban was making sure of that.

"...boys today have got to lift weights to be competitive..."

And they do. Phleban hadn't touched a weight before he was a freshman at TCU, and if he hadn't started then, he wouldn't have stayed a freshman at TCU for long: he wouldn't have played and they would have taken his scholarship. He learned to live like football was religion and barbells were the Bible. Phleban changed his diet, took supplements—nothing illegal, mind you—and put on thirty pounds of stone in his chest and thighs in six months. Thirty pounds. At nineteen, he became a man, physically, so quickly that his body rebelled. Couldn't hardly handle that much muscle put on that fast. Spring practices were hell. He strained ligaments, pulled a hamstring. But Phleban was tough. Had to know the difference between pain and injury: pain plays mutely on; injury goes home to Kylee, Texas, and hires on at the oil refinery, if they're hiring, or at Hanson's Texaco if they ain't. Phleban came to camp his sophomore year, two hundred five pounds and pissed off. Farino made the coaches kiss his ass, but Phleban administered that blessing on opposing defenders. Reckless abandon. Coaches preached it and Phleban was the Apostle Paul who spread the Good News to the unbelievers. He was the word and the rod, and defensive players were all heathens.

"...Lil Rick did things I never could. Like he ran for two hundred eighty-two yards against Ouachita City after spraining his ankle in the first quarter. Set a 2A record that day. Had a picture of him and his dad hugging after the game on the front page of the paper..."

Never anything flashy, like Farino. Hardly ever see "Phleban" mentioned in the paper. Never once made the national press. But effective. He was the "Coach's Choice Player of the Week" versus North Texas State as a junior—for those big blocks on Joe Greene—and his last season, against Oklahoma State and again against SMU. Given the "Most Conscientious" award his senior year.

"...I was talking to recruiters nearly every day, from all over. Hawaii even called. His daddy got a kick when I told him that..."

The coaches kept Phleban on in the program, hired him as a graduate assistant. The Special Teams Coach. That was no handout: all that time in the weight room; studying film; all that aggression, the reckless abandon...

"That wasn't it, though," you hear yourself say, "it wasn't like that. It was. It wasn't a big hit, you know. Big hits are heard. Even in film sessions, when all you hear is the projector's buzz and the clicking of sixteen-millimeter film, you hear a big hit by the reaction on the screen of all the players around it. All movement freezes, helmets turn toward it. Teammates react to it, jump up and down. The other side slumps their heads. But with Rick...I mean, I went back and I looked at the film. Wasn't nothing. This boy came at him, at Lil Rick, and Lil Rick bent to block him. There wasn't no big hit at all. Nobody turned. Nobody reacted. The other boy wasn't even knocked backwards. But Ricky collapsed and just laid there like yesterday's laundry. I didn't even go out on the field at first, when it happened. I just—It was just—"

"Coach Phleban"—you hear Jeff Walker's voice—"Coach Phleban."

And then it's quiet.

"Coach Phleban, please know that, unfortunately, this isn't so uncommon." You hear some sort of absolution in Jeff Walker's voice, but that wasn't what you were asking for. "Ten to twelve boys die each year on football fields. Mostly high school football fields."

He's missing the goddamn point: you ain't asking his pardon for nothing, a puny punk who couldn't hack it past the ninth grade.

You remember how you made a PineMan of a gangly fifteen-year-old boy. Then you remember that PineMan is a whore. When did Pine learn that?

You say, "You know, his daddy loved that Ricky played football. He did. Talked about it, used it in the pulpit on Sundays. Ricky was the youngest of seven. Six girls and Rick. His dad took most of his afternoons off so he could come out to the field. Sit up in the bleachers. Watch practice. No lie, every single day. He'd watch Ricky run, tear up a defense. In the open field, Rick behaved as the wind behaves. He was unstoppable. After practice was over, after the boys had done their conditioning and sprints—Ricky'd win 'em every time—then Ricky'd go get his stuff, wouldn't even shower, just put his street clothes on and come walking over to his dad, and they'd drive home. Whole world might be in ruins, but they'd be together.

"Well, Monday, the Monday after that Friday, I looked at all those boys, all Ricky's friends. I mean, we'd just got back from the funeral and all. And. Well. Here were all these boys, their necks choked in collars that were too tight, wearing ties, dress shoes on feet didn't hardly ever see nothing but sneakers. I had all those young eyes around me. On me. And I asked them what we should do.

"I told them straight out that we could quit the season. That there wouldn't be no disgrace if those boys didn't want to play anymore. But they all just stared. And they all voted that they wanted to. Go on, you know. Every last one of them. And they, they all do.

"When those boys left to go home and I turned to go to my office, there was Ricky's daddy, sitting up in them bleachers like he always was. The world was in ruins, but there he was. It was like he was waiting for a ghost to come running up and say, 'Okay, Dad, let's go home.' You know? So I looked over at him. And he, he walks over to me. He says, 'He was a good boy, Coach,' and I say, 'Yes, sir. He was.' Then he looks at the ground. Back up at me. And I'm steady looking him in his eyes, eyes I wouldn't dare meet in my worst dreams but I'm steady looking, because I. Well. Because I was.

"And then he says to me, 'God's will is sometimes strange,' and I say, 'Sir?' It was me should have been consoling him. But he says, 'It wasn't your fault, Coach.' He repeated it, you know. He said, 'You mustn't believe it was your fault.' And I. Said nothing. He said, 'Now he's somewhere better.' He said that. And, well..."

Shit. You don't even know what happened to Marty Sostriss. He might be manning the pumps at the Texaco for all you know.

"Well."

It took you twenty-some years to learn what a boy found out in the flash and extinction of a single second, of a soft hit. It took you twenty-some-odd years to see what you should have seen before you ever set to teach it. Lil Rick, lying there, showed you.

But then the silence is burdensome, a highlighter highlighting too many things you didn't say, a light exposing pieces you don't know how to put together so the picture looks right.

"Thank you, Coach Phleban," Jeff Walker says, "for taking the time to talk to me."

He says, "I think I have plenty of material for a good story. And I want to reiterate that this is not going to be a football-bashing thing. I've seen some of the other articles, and that's not my intention."

"This will be a human interest piece," he says.

Then he says, "I'll be back in France next Monday. You should be receiving a copy of the article within two weeks or so."

"Yeah, all right, Mr. Walker," you say finally. "Sure."

"Let me know what you think."

You say nothing.

Hell. You can't even read French.

LOMAX'S TRIALS

Joe Formichella

Willie "Shoe" Lomax stands bent over at the waist, staring in toward home plate. It's a perfect day for baseball, the time of year, down in southern Alabama, where it's warm enough for short sleeves, warm enough to break out a sweat as the day moves into evening, but not so hot that he's baking out there, the heat radiating back up from hard-packed red dirt that was forged into a baseball diamond just a few years ago. Shoe was a teenager then, just another gangly kid from the neighborhood who couldn't seem to keep meat on his bones, learning how to pitch a baseball. Now in his early twenties, he's only *old* by baseball standards. He doesn't feel old. And he doesn't feel cheated, even though he knows that all those scouts behind the backstop didn't come to see him, even though it wasn't but a year or so since the manager of that San Francisco Giants farm club said Shoe was pro material already, said he was as good as Koufax, the next Warren Spahn, if only he weren't colored.

Shoe is wrong. The scouts are looking at him, as he stands on the mound, scratching at the dirt with the cleat of his right shoe, conditioning the box. He rolls the ball around in his left hand, perched back behind his hip, away from the batter, callused fingertips brushing against the seams, fingertips that can almost see the red catgut. He's fully warmed up now. He can feel the hot blood pulsing through the shoulder and forearm of his powerful left arm, through the long muscles of his legs. Sweat has taken the itch out of the woolen shirt on his back. He's poised to really start pitching now.

What's it going to be? the batter thinks to himself.

Shoe had already taken him through the sequence a couple of times, showing Amos nothing but breaking stuff. He'd started him with his roach ball, a nasty slider that disappeared as it broke over the plate. Shoe didn't name the pitch. He wouldn't do that. The other guys on the team, the talkers, guys like the Candyman, or Sleepy, who'd taught him most of what he knows about pitching, they liked to name pitches, said *everyone* names their pitches, just like Satch.

After Amos swings himself in a circle at that one, Shoe gives him the deuce, his Monroe curve ball, named after the roller coaster out at Monroe park that Shoe had never even *seen*. And then the kidney bean, his fork ball.

"Why do they call it a fork ball, Mr. Sleepy?" he'd asked when he was learning the pitch.

"'Cause it breaks into hitters, bites into their wheelhouse, and they damn near hurt themselves trying to swing with their hands up under their chins like this."

From his post deep in center field, captain Robert Emanuel, Jr., no doubt recognizes the grip Shoe settles on and comes sprinting in toward the mound calling for time, calling to his pitcher, "Shoe!" before he can wind up.

"Shoe," he says when he gets to the mound, "They're trying to *sign* Otis. Throw him something he can hit!"

The man who put this team, the Prichard Mohawks, together, the Chief, Jesse Norwood, joins them on the mound.

"Willie," he says, "Show Amos some gas. Give him a chance," he says, patting the young man on the back.

"Yes, sir, Mr. Jesse." That's all Shoe needs by way of direction.

He shifts the ball in his hands again, rears back and fires a bullet toward the plate. Amos smacks it down the left field line. Then he wallops another one, harder, and farther, down the opposite baseline. Once he finds his groove, Amos can handle Shoe's breaking stuff, and it isn't long before he's putting everything into play, running the bases leaving those scouts gawking at their stopwatches, signing his contract, headed for an All-Star stint in the show.

In later years, after he's retired as one of the most popular Kansas City Royals ever, second only to Brett probably, Amos Otis will freely admit there were players back in Mobile that were better than he was, even if he won't quite remember how many times he swung and missed against Shoe that day, as if ballplayers ever forget their numbers.

Emanuel says he reminds him though. Anytime Amos is back in town for another award or as a guest at some gala event, Emanuel says he tells him, "Don't you be coming around here all uppity," he says. "You wouldn't have made it but for me!" And then he laughs, laughs easily, genuinely, at the memory, without any hint of bitterness, even though he's another of the players who, had they been anywhere else, or had they been white, most certainly would have made it to the show, too.

"It's *true*," James Harris swears, true that for every Aaron or McCovey that made it to the big leagues, made it to the Hall of Fame in Cooperstown, there were at least a handful of guys back on the sandlots of Mobile better than they were. "Aaron says so in *his* book. And I *know* Billy's older brothers were better than he was."

Billy as in Billy Williams, another Hall of Famer, the man who stole headlines from Ernie Banks, Mr. Cub.

Harris *would* know though. He managed, at one time in their young careers, all three of them, Aaron, McCovey, and Williams, along with countless other prospects with raw, dazzling baseball talent. But he doesn't want to talk about them, at least not yet. He wants to talk about another Hall of Fame baseball player from Mobile enshrined in Cooperstown.

He sits slouched against a stack of pillows on an overstuffed couch in the den of his tidy, single-story brick home. He's wearing an "Elect Sam Jones" T-shirt over yellow Bermuda shorts. Red-striped tube socks cover most of the rest of his gangly legs. There's a white hand towel draped over his left shoulder, to dab at the sweat that will bead up on his forehead when he mows his postage stamp of a lawn later in the afternoon. Harris will rinse the towel in cold water from the outside spigot and drape it around his neck, cooling his blood as he mows, slowly, on aching legs.

He raises his chin a little defiantly, though, and says, "I had the privilege of hitting one out on the big man once," of his days in the old Southern Negro League.

"The big man?"

"Leroy."

"Paige?"

"Took him downtown," he says, savoring those last two syllables. He has to shift his position regularly, rearranges the pillows to try and find the right compression to ease the ache in his back just a little, long enough to finish his sentence, long enough to finish a story, though the stories never seem to cease. They just flow, one into another, seemingly without context, except for the game, and Harris is a living history of Mobile baseball, as far as you could possibly get from a textbook, just names, and stories, and more stories. He adds, "Oh, Leroy could bring that ball. He could *bring* it."

Dizzy Dean once said of Paige's fastball, as proof that Satchel was the best pitcher *he'd* ever seen, "My fastball looks like a change of pace alongside that little bullet old Satchel shoots up to the plate."

"You know how he always promised to strike out the first nine hitters he faced?" Harris adds. "I seen him do it," chuckling.

It's sometimes hard to tell if Harris is speaking anything like verifiable fact, or merely offering up a taste of that other compendium of baseball history, its folklore. It doesn't really matter, least of all to Harris, who goes on to tell a story of how he outwitted the great Josh Gibson once, who together with Paige, was billed as the greatest battery in the history of the game; how from his position as catcher he coaxed a young knuckleballer into striking Gibson out, as if to suggest he was at least as good a ball player as those two legends. And he probably was.

"Oh, we knew we could play," he says, of himself and his contemporaries. "We knew we could play."

Harris's rise in the Negro leagues of the early decades of the twentieth century had already passed its zenith by 1946, the year Jackie Robinson was signed by Branch Rickey and the Brooklyn Dodgers, *The Great Experiment*. He knows that at thirty he wasn't going to catch anyone's eye. They were looking for models, young phenomenal studs with steely tempers and explosive skills. "I probably wouldn't have put up with the crap he did," he says. "Still, we knew we could play."

And they knew that if they had been anywhere else almost, in Kansas City, or Memphis, it might have been them. It *could* have been them, though that's not what they thought at the time, according to Harris. "At the time, it was the greatest thing that could have happened. You wouldn't *believe* how much your chest can swell overnight," he says, puffing himself up, before coughing, and laughing, and rearranging those pillows again.

"Too many years behind the plate," he says of the sore back that keeps him shifting on the couch. In the same sentence he'll say that anyone who wants to play catcher ought to be put in a straitjacket, and that it's the only position to play if you really want to learn the game. And then he'll chuckle some more, for his own damn sake, which he's earned.

He isn't slowed much by his age, approaching eighty, or his back, though he gets a little frustrated trying to come up with some of the names. He spends most of fifteen minutes, shifting, standing and pacing, pawing through one box after another of old articles and pictures stashed around the place, trying to remember the name of the second baseman from the 1947 Mobile Bears, league champions that year, having chewed on the irony that despite the Bears being a Brooklyn farm club, and despite their success, Harris can never remember any Brooklyn scouts hanging around Mobile before 1947. "Now why was that?" he asks, as if to suggest that some executive fifty years ago clearly wasn't doing his job, and should have been fired.

When he does remember a player, calling his name, "Wasiak, Stan Wasiak," it takes him another minute to remember *why* he needed to remember him.

Wasiak went on to become the winningest manager in minor league baseball history, and Harris's point was that he remembers, on into the '50s as a player/manager, beating some of Wasiak's teams, and then he grins, and winks, letting you fill in the rest.

Asked if they were playing integrated games that early in the south, "They were in Mobile," he says, without elaborating, in a way that makes you think he's got lots of other secrets he'll tell in his own way, his own time.

When asked when he stopped playing, he explodes, "Stopped! I *still* play."

"Really?"

"Every night," he says, and pauses. "Every night I'm running the bases, chasing down foul balls. Gets so I can't hardly make it down the stairs in the morning," he finishes, laughing so hard that you fear he's going to choke, and when you stand to get him a glass of water, or something, he waves you off. He wants to talk about the time as a child he saw Babe Ruth hit a home run completely out of old Hartwell Field in Mobile in 1924. "From the colored section out beyond the right field fence it went clean over our heads, across the lot, into the railyard and landed in a moving freight car. I don't think it *ever* stopped."

"Nineteen fifty-seven was the year," Bill Dillard says. That's the year Harris took him, Ralph Taylor, and Willie McCovey across the state line to Jasmine, Mississippi, for a tryout before San Francisco Giants coaches. Attending the same tryout as those three teenaged black players were about thirty-five white ballplayers from the region. But Dillard and Taylor and McCovey didn't work out against the white players. They didn't even try out the same day on the same field. Their tryout was the next day, after the scouts and coaches had seen all the other talent, on a field in the other part of town.

Dillard sits in a booth by the window of the McDonald's in downtown Mobile. He cradles his cup of coffee in both hands, like it's an egg, as an infielder would. "Everyone *knew* they were only going to sign one of us, if they signed any at all. Me, I could catch most anything I could get to, and knock down a lot of other stuff. I played a busy third base," he says, crouching even now, in his seat. "And Taylor could throw hard, real hard. But you should have seen Stretch swat that ball. He had those long arms and legs so that they couldn't get anything by him. And by the time he finished uncoiling everything, like a clock burst open, that ball would be out of the park, into the woods, Mr. Green hollering, 'Find me that ball!' to all the little kids that'd come out to watch. And Willie stood there at the plate for the longest time just a-swatting and grinning at those boys scurrying around out there. You should have seen him."

They signed Willie McCovey that day. "It was a September day, a fall day. You could feel the greatness," Dillard says, closing his eyes and slowly shaking his head.

Every baseball season begins for the young player with hopefulness. *Maybe this is the year I get signed.* Nineteen fifty-seven had begun with more hope than any preceding year for black baseball players, for all blacks. In January the federal government had gone to a high school in Little Rock, Arkansas, and enforced the edicts of *Brown v. Board of Education*, edicts that otherwise were not making many inroads in the South.

A year and a half later Willie McCovey would make his major league debut, going four for four, and never look back, finally stopping more than five hundred home runs later.

Dillard, almost twenty years old, went on to play college ball at one of the state's black schools. He'd started playing for Harris when he was sixteen, back in 1953. He made a dollar a game, five if they went out of state. Still in high school, Dillard, couldn't collect any money. Harris had to hold it for him, and it paid his way to school. He would have gone on scholarship, certainly, if there had been such things available to those athletic departments. Most black schools didn't have room in their budget for athletic scholarships.

Things changed. Grambling University granted Mobilian Jimmy Knight a baseball scholarship in the mid-'60s. When he was a junior, the team went to the college World Series, and he went on to play in the Oakland Athletics system for a while. At the beginning of the decade Lomax had been accepted to the school, on the personal recommendation of Jesse Norwood to the legendary Eddie Robinson, but they couldn't scrape together enough money to pay his way so he stayed in Prichard, stayed with the Mohawks.

Far removed from Little Rock, Arkansas, or Topeka, Kansas, for that matter, Lomax started playing with the Mohawks in 1957, their first year. He was just fifteen, not yet full grown, not nearly aware of what he could do with a baseball. It wouldn't take long. Willie "Sleepy" Burns, the elder statesman of the team, the player with the most experience and knowledge of the game, provided most of Lomax's tutelage.

Sleepy didn't have to formally instruct those around him in order to teach. All they had to do was listen to his nonstop chatter. He could play any position on the field, and play it well. He knew how to play the position, at least, and that's where the learning started, how from his first-base position he would take up after a runner, calling to everyone else, "Did you see how he hit the inside of the bag with his right foot?" circling back around and repeating the maneuver once the runner had stopped and time was called. Sleepy was constant motion and constant dialogue, in practices *or* in games. He was anything *but* somnambulant, though everyone says he got his nickname for other reasons. From deep in the hole at shortstop he'd shift the rest of the infield based on the batter's stance in the box, "Watch the front foot, where it's pointed, where it lands after practice swings." In the outfield he'd shift players based on the pitcher's grip on the ball, and from the bench he'd call pitches shortly after they left the pitcher's grasp from the rotation of the ball. All the Mohawks, most of the rest of them just as young as Lomax, all they had to do was listen to Sleepy.

From time to time, as Shoe tells it, Sleepy would interrupt his general discourse and give Lomax some specialized instruction. Able to see the pitching gem in the rough young boy, he taught him how to throw a breaking ball, a fork ball, said that with a fork ball and a standard hook, "Managers won't know *who* to send up to the plate."

Sleepy groomed him well enough for Lomax to find himself a starting pitcher against high school graduates and college players while he was still just fifteen. He didn't even own a pair of cleats, he was so raw, and had to borrow his uncle's, Albert Lomax, one of the three founders of the team. The shoes were not an exact fit, though, and every once in a while, if Lomax got really wound up, a shoe would come flying out of the whirl of dust. Sleepy would hustle in from whatever position he happened to be occupying, talking, "Now *that's* what I call follow through. Did y'all see that? Oh, Shoe, they don't know *what* to do about you now," retrieving Lomax's errant cleat.

"Yes, sir, that's how it started," Shoe says now, of *his* nickname, sitting stately, regally, almost, in the middle of a couch in a reception room off of the main sanctuary of the New Light Baptist Church where he is the minister, the Reverend W. L. Lomax.

Sadly, though Shoe would never say so, they didn't know what to do about him. Scouts were already talking about him before he graduated Blount High School. His best chance to make it, most everyone agrees, was in 1962. Early that year a scout for the Chicago White Sox, out of Birmingham, called *him*. Said he wanted to sign Shoe. He was going to come watch a game, and then return another time with some front office people to ink the deal. They made a date, and the scout came down to Prichard the next time Shoe pitched, against a team from Shreveport, Louisiana.

"Now we knew this team," Shoe says. "We knew that those first six hitters were tough, but once we got by them it was easier. "

"You'd played them before?"

"That's right. And we had a scouting report."

"A scouting report for a semi-pro team? How'd you manage that?"

"Mr. Jesse took care of that."

Sleepy played catcher that day, and under his guidance, Shoe struck out four of those first six batters. That was pretty much all the scout needed to see, and he left before the game was complete, a 3–2 victory for the Mohawks and Shoe Lomax. He said he'd be back in five days, Shoe's next scheduled start.

"So what happened?"

"I couldn't make the start. Day before the game I got a fishbone stuck in my mouth and had to be hospitalized," he says, and shrugs.

That scout never did make that second visit to Prichard, though the White Sox extended an invitation to Shoe to attend a training camp in Orlando, Florida, the following year. Shoe's not even sure exactly what happened there. He was there with four other blacks and seventy-five to a hundred white players. He remembers a Cleveland scout took him aside and had him throw against some hulking thunder-stick. Shoe didn't know who it was. Might have been Killibrew. Shoe threw a couple of fast balls, ninety-five, ninety-six miles an hour. Sure enough, the slugger pounded them out of the yard. And then the scout told Shoe to throw some breaking pitches, which went untouched.

"They signed the bat," Shoe says matter-of-factly.

Cleon Jones, who would make his debut with the Mets that summer, called Shoe upon his return home and offered encouragement, saying he was certain Shoe would make it.

Cleon had reason to be so optimistic. He had tried out for the Mohawks team that Shoe was becoming a star pitcher for and couldn't make it.

"Yes, that's correct," Shoe says, with a befuddling equanimity. Like Harris before him, he knew he could play, he *had* to know he was the equal of any of those other guys leaving Mobile and moving through the minor league franchises of those big league clubs. Everybody said so. John Lee Colvin and Lionel Pugh, who'd been signed off of the Mohawks, they told him they hadn't seen any pitchers nearly as good as Shoe.

And Cleon? "I pitched against him once in high school." Cleon attended rival Mobile County High. "The first time he comes to the plate I says to myself, I'm going to strike Cleon out. I wanted to do it in three pitches, but it took four. I started him off with a curve ball, when I knew he'd be looking for my heat. Then I showed him the kidney bean, which looks a little like a fast ball at first. So he moves up and over the plate, looking for more breaking stuff and trying to reach it early. He hadn't even swung yet, but I knew he was dangerous. We all knew of each other. So I finally show him my fast ball, but up and in, backing him away from the plate. So he's ready now. He's seen everything. He's pounding and windmilling and snorting up there, so I rear back and throw him a pitch I don't think he knew I had, a change-up. He was way out in front of it and couldn't hold back. I struck him out, everyone on the Blount side cheering, Shoe! Shoe!

"Yes, sir, I sure won that battle. He *did* hit a home run off me the next time up," he adds, slyly, laughing to himself. "But I sure won that battle."

And that seems enough, to have played the game, to have fought those battles, and won his share. Willie "Shoe" Lomax remembers the battles, remembers the victories, and he remembers plenty of near misses. He remembers taking a no-hitter into the ninth inning against the

Theodore Bobcats, and he remembers that trip to Montevallo, Alabama, to play against San Francisco's AA farm club out of Knoxville, where he was told he was already big league material, except for the color of his skin. He knew his only real chance had come back in 1962, and he'd missed it. By the time he'd visited Montevallo, both Cleon and Tommie Agee, born five days and less than a mile apart, were already roaming the outfield of brand-new Shea Stadium for the New York Mets. And Amos Otis, who would, in a few short years, complete the starting outfield for the World Champion Miracle Mets, was already erasing all the batting records back in Mobile, his ticket just waiting to be punched. Shoe's chance had come, and gone.

It's just like Mr. Jesse had told them, which, again, was all the direction he needed. "The door's going to open, but it won't stay open. Your job is twofold: Be ready to step through the door, and hold it open as long as you can for whoever else you can get through."

Shoe had done his job. He'd been ready. And even if he suffered that momentary lapse, he helped A. O. through the door as well. And Amos knows it.

"When he comes back home he shakes my hand, hugs my neck, says he wouldn't have made it without me."

That's enough for Shoe. He admits that every once in a while he wonders about the curious working of fate, "I've had some flashbacks," he calls them. But he's not bitter, not bitter at all. "A different door opened for me," he says, "And I thank Mr. Jesse for that."

Shoe is genuinely thankful for his time as a Mohawk, for the lessons he learned about baseball, and especially those lessons he learned about life. The only time he chokes up while recalling those years is when he's telling of a team meeting, the only team meeting he'll mention specifically, the end-of-the-year meeting of 1963. The Mohawks had just been awarded a special civic trophy by the City of Mobile, for their championship baseball year and their community involvement, an award created to recognize the work of the Mohawks. Jesse broke down before the players. Shoe's uncle Albert and Robert Emanuel, Sr., Jesse's partners, started hustling the players out of the clubhouse, before Jesse stopped them, saying, "It's all right, it's all right, it's all right for them to see a man cry, that a man can cry. It's all right." And when they were all settled back in their seats, he told them, "This," hoisting their trophy up, "is the fulfillment of my dream. I hope, I *hope*, that working together, each of you will be able to say the same thing about your life some day."

Lomax sits in the middle of his couch, his large, smooth hands, wrinkled more than callused now, folded in his lap. He looks about him with minimal motion of his head, at the nice furniture, out the window to the neat grounds, and down toward his polished shoes, and says, "I can. I can say that."

He says he has a doctorate of ministry now and spends time traveling as a guest speaker or a panel member, and every once in a while, "Every once in a while," he says, in a cadence you suspect he picked up as a Mohawk, a cadence that lends itself quite naturally to the pulpit, "Every *once* in a while, someone at those conferences from those days recognizes me and will call out, Shoe! Shoe!" he smiles broadly at that memory. "Other folks around me ask what that means, and I usually don't tell them, but man, that brings me all the way back, brings it all back, and that sure is nice."

A Fairhope Alien

Gregory Benford

I remember how Mitchell was putting the moves on some major-league pussy when the news about the aliens came in.

That Mitchell, he stopped in mid-line and cocked his big square head and said kind of whispery, "Double dog damn." Then he went back to the little redhead he had settled onto the stool next to his, way down at the end of the mahogany bar at The Pub.

But I could tell he was distracted. He's the kind of fella always drawn to a touch of weirdness. At Mardi Gras he just loves the confusion, not being able to tell guys from gals, or who's what, the whole thing. Like I say, weirdness.

He left with the redhead before ten, which was pretty quick even for Mitchell. When he's headed for the sheets there isn't much can get in Mitchell's way. But he kept glancing over at the Alphas on the TV. Going out, he gave me the old salute and big smile but I could tell he was thinking off somewhere, not keeping his mind and his hands on the red-head. Which wasn't like him.

Now, Mitchell's been my buddy since the earth's crust cooled off. I can read him pretty well. We graduated high school about the time the dinosaurs started up and we went into farm equipment sales and leasing together, back when there were still a few nickels to make in that game. I've seen Mitchell bare-ass in the woods howling around a campfire, watched him pulling in six-foot tuna off the back of McKenzie's old boat, laughed when he was drunk up to his eyeballs with a big brassy broad on each arm and sportin' a shitass happy grin. For sure I know him better than any of his goddamn two ex-wives or his three kids. None of them'd recognize him on the street, pretty near.

So when the Alphas showed up right here in Fairhope I could tell right away that Mitchell took it funny. These Alphas come in slick as you please, special escort in limos and all. They go down to the wharf, stop at Gambino's, glide down Section and Magnolia holding up traffic, look at the big new Civic Center and library and all, but nobody has a dime's worth of an idea what they're here for.

Neither does the escort. Two suits on every Alpha, dark glasses and shoulder-slung pistols and earplug radios and the like. You could see it plain, the way their tight mouths twitched. They dunno from sour owl shit what to expect next.

For sure nobody thought they'd go into The Pub. Just clank on in, look around, babble that babble to each other, plunk down on those chrome stools.

Then they order up. Mitchell and me, we was at the other end of the bar, along with Sonny, who runs that bookstore around the corner. The Alphas, they are ordering up and putting them down pretty quick. Nobody knows their chemistry but they must like something in gimlets and fireballs and twofers, cause they sure squirt them in quick. Sonny, he goes over and asks them straight out do any of them write, he could take it in any format, typed, CD, whatever, and they ignore the hell out of him, so he leaves.

Pretty soon there's a crowd around them. The suits stand stiff as boards, but the locals ooze around them, curious. The Alphas don't pay any attention. Maybe they're used to it or maybe they don't even know people are there unless they need something. Way they act, you could believe that.

But Mitchell, he keeps eyeing them. Tries to talk to them. They don't pay him no never-mind. Buys one a drink, even, but the Alpha won't touch it.

I could see it got to him. Not the first day maybe or the second. By the third, though, he was acting funny. Studying them. The Alphas would show up at Biscuit King or Julwin's for breakfast, but by afternoon they're back at The Pub. They suck in plenty of the sauce, then blow out of town in those limos with their Men In Black escort.

News people around, crowds waiting to see them, the whole god-damn shooting match. Made Fairhope hell to get around in.

I was gone three days to Birmingham on a commission job with International Harvester, so I didn't see what started him on it. I come into town all busted out from chasing tail in Birmingham, and first thing you know, phone rings and Mitchell wants help.

"I'm in that beat-up shack back of Leroy's TV," he said.

"That place's no bigger'n a coffin and smells worse."

"They spruced it up since Briggs run that poker game in here."

"So who you pokin' there now?"

"Fred, your dick fell off, your IQ would be zero."

"That happen, what'd I need to think for?"

"Get your dumb ass over here."

So I did, over to the shack on Satsuma. I walk in on Mitchell in a chair, this brunette working on him. First I figured she was from over Bessie's, giving him a manicure with her kit all spread out. Turns out she's a makeup gal from clear over to New Orleans. Works Mardi Gras and like that.

Only she's not making Mitchell up to be a devil or in blackface or anything. This is serious. She's painting shellac all over him. He's already got a crust on him like dried mud in a hog wallow, only it's orange.

"Christ on a crutch," is all I can say.

"Mix me a bourbon and branch." Mitchell's voice comes out muffled by all these pink pancake-size wattles on his throat, like some kind of rooster.

So I do. Only he doesn't like it, so he gets up and makes his own. "Got to add a twist sometimes," he says.

Mitchell was always picky about drinks. He used to make coffee for the boys, morning after a big carouse, and it had to be Columbian and ground just so and done up in this tricky filter rig he made himself out of tin sheeting.

That's how he was with this makeup girl, too. She layered on ridges of swarthy gum all down his arms, then shaped it with little whittling tools. She was sweating in that firebox shack. Mitchell was too under all the makeup.

I'm wondering what the hell, and Mitchell says, "Go take a squint, see if they're in The Pub yet."

So I'm catching on. Mitchell's always had something working on the side, see, but he takes his time about letting on. Kind of subtle, too. When Mr. Tang moved into Fairhope with his factory, Mitchell was real respectful and polite and called him Poon for a year before that Tang caught on.

As I go out the shack and down the alley I see why he used that place. I angle across Simpson's parking lot and down by those big air conditioners and pop out on Ivy right next to The Pub. That way, none of the suits can see you coming. Slip in the side door and sure as God's got a beard, there's three Alphas. Got a crowd around them but the room is dead quiet. People just looking and wondering and the aliens drinking like there was nobody there but them.

I'd heard that plenty of fastlane operators were trying to get information out of Alphas, seeing as they got all this technology. We didn't even see them coming, that's how good their stuff is.

First thing anybody knew, they were bellying up to Venus, this other planet out there. Covered in clouds, it was. Then the Alphas start to work on her. First thing you know, you can see those volcanoes and valleys.

Anybody who can clear up muggy air like that inside a week, you got to pay attention. Turned out that was just cleaning off the work bench. Next they spun a kind of magnetic rod, rammed it in at the pole, clean down into the core of the whole damn planet. Easy as sticking an ice pick through an apple. Only the ice pick was hollow and they sucked the liquid metal out of there. Up the rod like it was a straw, and out into space. To make those metal city kind of things, huge and all.

That's when people started getting really afraid. And some others got really interested. The way they figured, any little scrappy thing you got from an Alpha might just be a billion-buck trick.

That's the scoop I heard on CNN coming down from Birmingham, anyway. Now here was the whole circus in Fairhope, big as life and twice as ugly. Snoops with those directional microphones. Cameras in the backs of vans, shooting out through dark windows. Guys in three-piece suits kind of casual slouched against the bar and trying to get an Alpha to notice them.

So back I go. Mitchell is getting some inflated bags stuck on him by the makeup girl. Bags all over his back and chest and neck even. He's all the Alpha colors now, from Georgia clay red here to sky blue there.

"Three of 'em sucking it up in there," I said.

"Holy shit, let's go," Mitchell croaks back at me. The girl had fitted him out with this voice box thing, made him sound like a frog at the bottom of a rain barrel.

The girl pats him all over with that fine, rusty dust the Alphas are always shedding. She straightens the pouches so you can hardly see that his arms are too short for an Alpha.

"Let's make tracks," Mitchell says, and proceeds to do just that. Alpha tracks, fat and seven-toed.

We go across the parking lot, so the escorts can't see. In a minute we're in The Pub. The other Alphas don't take any notice of Mitchell, but all the people do. They move out of the way fast, and we parade in, me a little behind so it'll seem like I'm just a tourist. Mitchell's got the Alpha shuffle down just right, to my eye.

Bold as brass, he sits down. The suits look at each other, dunno what to do. Long moment passes. But they buy it, that Mitchell's one of them.

The Alphas still don't notice him. Bartender asks and Mitchell orders, making a kind of slithery noise.

He slurps down two drinks before anything happens. An Alpha makes a gesture with that nose thing of theirs and Mitchell does, too. Then there's some more gesturing and they talk like wet things moving inside a bag.

I sit and listen, but I can't make sense out of any of it. Mitchell seems to know what he's doing. He keeps it up for maybe five more minutes. I can see it's wearing on him. He gives me the signal.

I clear some space for him so he can get back up—that crap he's wearing weighs real considerable. He gets up smooth and shuffles some and then we're out the door. Free and clean. We got back to the shack before we let go with the whooping and hollering.

We pull it off four more times in the next three weeks. Each time the Alphas take more notice of Mitchell. Hard to know what they think of him. The girl comes over from New Orleans and does him up, getting better each time. I keep an ear open for word on the street and it's all good.

Or seems so to me, anyway. Everybody thinks Mitchell's the real thing. Course that's people talking, not Alphas. After the fourth time I couldn't hold back any more. "You got some money angle on this, right?"

"Money?"

"What I want to know is, how you going to get anything out of them?"

"I'm not in for money."

"You figure maybe you can get one of those little tool kits they carry? They don't look hooked on real firm or anything."

Mitchell grinned. "Wouldn't try that, I was you. Fella in Cincinnati went to lift one, came up an arm short."

"Then what the hell you in for?"

Mitchell gave me this funny look. "'Cause it's *them*."

I blinked. "So goddamn what?"

"You don't get it, Fred. Thing about aliens is, they're *alien*."

In his eyes there's this look. Like he was seeing something different, something important, something way bigger than Fairhope.

I couldn't make any more sense out of what he said after that. That's when I realized. Mitchell just wanted to be close to them, was all.

That pretty well took the wind out of my sails. I'd figured Mitchell was on to something for sure. I went with him one more time, that's all. And a few days later I heard from the guys at Vernon's Barber Shop that the same Alpha was coming back to The Pub every day, just sitting and waiting for more Alphas to come in, and hanging out with them when they did.

It went that way for a while and I was feeling pretty sour about it. I went on a carouse with the Perlotti brothers and had me a pretty fair time. Next morning I was lying in bed with a head that barely fit in the room and in walks Mitchell. "Heard you maybe needed some revivin' from last night."

He was grinning and I was glad to see him even if he did waste a slab of my time. We'd do little things like that for each other sometimes, bring a fella a drink or a hundred-dollar bill when he was down and could sure use it. So I crawled up out of bed and pulled on some jeans and went into the kitchen.

Mitchell was filling a pot and popping open one of his Columbian coffee packs. I got some cups and we watched the water boil without saying anything. That's when it happened.

Mitchell was fooling with the coffee and I was still pretty bleary-eyed, so I'm not sure just exactly what I saw. Mitchell was stirring the coffee and he turned to me. "Ummm. Smell those enzymes."

He said it perfectly natural and I wouldn't have taken much notice of the funny word. I looked it up later at the library and it's a chemical term, I forget what it means. Now, Mitchell would never have said something like that. He barely knew a rock from a rat. And I wouldn't have given it any mind, except that just then his arm stuck a little farther out of his denim work shirt. He has big arms and thick wrists. As the shirt sleeve slid up I saw the skin and curly hair and then something else.

At first I thought it was leather. Then it seemed like cloth, real old fabric, wrinkled and coarse. Mitchell turned farther and looked at me and that's when I heard the sound of him moving. It was like dry leaves rustling. Old and blowing in a wind. In the next second I caught a whiff of it and the worst smell I ever knew came swarming up into my head and I finally really saw what the thing next to me was.

I don't want to describe that. It sent me banging back against the plywood wall of the kitchen and then out the door. The smell stayed with me somehow even in the open. I was off into the pines way back of my place before I knew it. Running, running, and it felt good to put space between me and them. I cut east and crossed the Greeno road, nearly got turned to road kill by a Peterbilt truck.

I had the shakes for hours. Made myself circle around for three miles, hiding in the live oaks, jumping at shadows. Got to my sister's place. They were having a fish fry, bass and mullet and perch and flounder, and I couldn't eat a thing. Didn't tell her anything about it but I think she might of guessed. I was pale and woozy. Played like I was hung over, was all, but she didn't buy it.

I got my truck and went off to Pensacola for a week. There was maybe some work there, but it didn't pan out, and I hadn't gone for that anyway.

I didn't go back into my place for another week. And I was real careful when I did.

It was all picked up, neat as you please. Not a sign. Mitchell was a fine man but he would never have done that.

I stood in the kitchen and tried to work out what had happened, how it had been. Couldn't. There was that one second when I saw straight into whatever was there and was being Mitchell, and that was all.

He had tried to blend in with them. And I'd helped him. So in some way maybe this was the reverse. Or a payback, kind of. Or maybe a signal or something. No way to tell.

Only, you know what I think? I figure there isn't any Mitchell any more. There's something else.

Now, could be there's still some Mitchell in there, only he can't get out. Or maybe that thing's Alpha for sure. I guess it could be something in between. Only thing I know is, it isn't anything I ever want to know.

Maybe it's something I *can't* know. Thing about aliens is, they're alien.

They say that one Alpha still hangs out at The Pub. I haven't been to check. I don't even walk down that part of town any more.

BASEBALL DREAMS

Charles Ghigna

In memory of Jack Marsh, second baseman, Yale University, 1943

Before the bayonet replaced the bat,
Jack Marsh played second base for Yale;
his spikes anchored into the April clay,
his eyes set deep against the setting sun.

The scouts all knew his numbers well,
had studied his sure hands that flew
like hungry gulls above the grass;
but Uncle Sam had scouted too,

had chosen first the team to play
the season's final game of '44,
had issued him another uniform
to wear into the face of winter moon

that shone upon a snowy plain
where players played a deadly game,
where strikes were thrown with each grenade
and high-pitched echoes linger still,

beyond the burned out foreign fields
and boyhood dreams of bunts and steals,
young Jack Marsh is rounding third,
and sliding, sliding safely home.

The Bowman's Hand

Charles Ghigna

A 15-year-old athlete died of cardiac arrest from a high
school friend's punch in the chest during a classroom "cuss
game" popular with students. Witnesses said he complimented his
opponent on the "good hit," then died. —*The Birmingham News*

The game over, the target rests on the ground;
but the heavy hand of the standing boy
will carry the weight of this dark moment

into the bull's-eye of memory, into the
corners of every swollen night.
This is the hand that will open and close

too many times before it sleeps,
before it catches that first star,
shines it bright within its praying palm,

puts it back into the black heaven of boyhood.
This is the hand that will shade the eyes
that study the sky for a cloudless past,

the hand that will grip and hold
the burning weight of growing old.
This is the hand that will not rest in peace,

that will not heal the broken arrow,
that will not lose its quiver;
the hand that will shake inside

the hand of too many smiling strangers.
This is the hand that will caress a sleeping son
named after his father's brave young friend,

after the one untouched by time,
untouched by the sharpness of age,
by the point of a pointless game.

Last Days of the Dog-Men

Brad Watson

When I was a boy my family always had hunting dogs, always bird dogs, once a couple of blueticks, and for six years anywhere from six to fifteen beagles. But we never really got to where we liked to eat rabbit, and we tired of the club politics of hunting deer, so we penned up the beagles, added two black Labs, and figured we'd do a little duck.

Those were raucous days around the house, the big pen in the back with the beagles squawling, up on their hind legs against the fence, making noises like someone was cutting their tails off. It was their way. At night when I crept out into the yard they fell silent, their white necks exposed to the moon, their soft round eyes upon me. They made small, disturbed, guttural sounds like chickens.

Neighbors finally sent the old man to municipal court charged with something like disturbing the peace, and since my mother swore that anyway she'd never fry another rabbit—they looked like little bloody babies once skinned, she said—he farmed out the beagles and spent his Saturdays visiting this dog or that, out to Uncle Spurgeon's to see Jimbo, the best runner of the pack. Or out to Bud's rambling shack, where Bud lived with old Patsy and Balls, the breeder. They hollered like nuclear warning sirens when the old man drove up in his Ford.

After that he went into decline. He liked the Labs but never took much interest, they being already a hollow race of dog, the official dog of the middle class. He let them lounge around the porch under the ceiling fan and lope around the yard and the neighborhood, aimless loafers, and took to watching war movies on TV in his room, wandering through the house speaking to us like we were neighbors to hail, engage in small talk, and bid farewell. He was a man who had literally abandoned the hunt. He was of the generation that had moved to the city. He was no longer a man who lived among dogs.

It wasn't long after that I moved out anyway, and got married to live with Lois in a dogless suburban house, a quiet world that seemed unanchored somehow, half inhabited, pale and blank, as if it would one day dissolve to fog, lines blurring, and seep away into air, as indeed it would. We bought a telescope and spent some nights in the yard tracking the cold lights of the stars and planets, looking for patterns, never suspecting that there were the awful bloody secrets of the ancient human heart and that every generation must flesh them out anew. Humans are aware of very little, it seems to me, the artificial brainy side of life, the worries and bills and the mechanisms of jobs, the doltish psychologies we've placed over our lives like a stencil. A dog keeps his life simple and unadorned. He is who he is, and his only task is to assert this. If he desires the company of another dog, or if he wishes to mate, things can get a little complex. But the ways of settling such things are established and do not change. And when they are settled and he is home from his wandering he may have a flickering moment, a sort of Pickett's Charge across the synaptic field toward reflection. But the moment passes. And when it passes it leaves him with a vague disquietude, a clear nose that on a good night could smell the lingering presence of men on the moon, and the rest of the day ahead of him like a canyon.

Which is how I've tried to view the days I've spent here in this old farmhouse where I'm staying with my friend Harold in the country. I'm on extended leave of absence from the *Journal*. But it's no good. It's impossible to bring that sort of order and clarity to a normal human life.

The farmhouse is a wreck floating on the edge of a big untended pasture where the only activities are the occasional squadron of flaring birds dropping from sight into the tall grass, and the creation of random geometric paths the nose-down dogs make tracking the birds. The back porch has a grand view of the field, and when weather permits we sit on the porch and smoke cigarettes and sip coffee in the mornings, beer in the afternoons, often good Scotch at night. At midday, there's horseshoes.

There's also Phelan Holt, a mastiff of a man, whom Harold met at the Blind Horse Bar and Grill and allowed to rent a room in the house's far corner. We don't see a great deal of Phelan, who came down here from

Ohio to teach poetry at the women's college. He once played linebacker for a small college in the Midwest, and then took his violent imagination to the page and published a book of poems about the big subjects: God, creation, the confusion of the animals, and the bloody concoction of love. He pads along a shiny path he's made through the dust to the kitchen for food and drink, and then pads back, and occasionally comes out to the porch to drink bourbon and to give us brief, elliptical lectures on the likes of Isaac Babel, Rilke, and Cervantes, gently smoking a joint which he does not share. In spite of his erudition, thick, balding Phelan is very much a moody old dog. He lives alone with others, leaves to conduct his business, speaks very little, eats moderately, and is generally inscrutable.

One day Harold proposed to spend the afternoon fishing for bream. We got into the truck and drove through a couple of pastures and down an old logging road through a patch of woods to a narrow cove that spread out into the broad sunlit surface of a lake. The sun played on thin, rippling lines that spread from the small heads of snapping turtles and water moccasins moving now and then like sticks in a current.

Harold pulled a johnboat from the willows and rowed us out. We fished the middle, dropping our baits over what Harold said was the old streambed, where a current of cooler water ran through down deep. The water was a dark coppery stain, like thin coffee. We began to pull up a few bluegill and crappie, and Phelan watched them burst from the water, broad, flat gold and silver, and curl at the end of the line, their eyes huge. They flopped crazily at the bottom of the boat, drowning in the thin air. Phelan set down his pole and nipped at a half-pint of bourbon he'd pulled from his pocket.

"Kill it," he said, looking away from my bluegill. "I can't stand to watch it struggling for air." His eyes followed the tiny heads of moccasins moving silently across the surface, turtles lumbering onto half-submerged logs. "Those things will eat your fish right off the stringer," he said. He drank from the little bottle again and then in his best old-fashioned pedagogical manner said, "Do we merely project the presence of evil upon God's creatures, in which case we are inherently evil and the story of the garden a ruse, or is evil absolute?"

From his knapsack he produced a pistol, a Browning .22 semiautomatic that looked like a German Luger, and set it on his lap. He pulled out a sandwich and ate it slowly. Then he shucked a round into the gun's chamber and sighted down on one of the turtles and fired, the sharp report flashing off the water into the trees. What looked like a puff of smoke spiffed from the turtle's back, and it tumbled from the log. "It's off a little to the right," he said. He aimed at a moccasin head crossing at the opposite bank and fired. The water jumped in front of the snake, which stopped, and Phelan quickly tore up the water where the head was with three quick shots. The snake disappeared. Silence, in the wake of the loud, hard crack of the pistol, came back to our ears in shock waves over the water. "Hard to tell if you've hit them when they're swimming," he said, looking down the length of the barrel as if for flaws, lifting his hooded eyes to survey the water's surface for more prey.

Harold himself is sort of like a garment drawn from the irregular bin: off-center, unique, a little tilted on his axis. If he were a dog, I'd call him an unbrushed collie who carries himself like a chocolate Lab. He has two actual dogs, a big blond hound named Otis and a bird dog named Ike. Like Phelan, Otis is a socialized dog and gets to come into the house to sleep, whereas Ike must stay outside on the porch. At first I could not understand why Otis received this privilege and Ike did not, but in time I began to see.

Every evening after supper when he is home, Harold gets up from the table and lets in Otis, who sits beside the table and looks at Harold, watching Harold's hands. Harold's hands pinching off a last bite of corn-bread and nibbling on it, Harold's hands pulling a Camel cigarette out of the pack, Harold's hands twiddling with the matches. And soon, as if he isn't really thinking of it, in the middle of talking about something else and not even seeming to plan to do it, Harold will pick up a piece of meat scrap and let it hover over the plate for a minute, talking, and you'll see Otis get alert and begin to quiver almost unnoticeably. And then Harold will look at Otis and maybe say, "Otis, stay." And Otis's eyes will cut just for a second to Harold's and then snatch back to the meat scrap, maybe having to chomp his jaws together to suck saliva, his eyes glued to the meat scrap. And then Harold will gently lower the meat scrap onto the top of Otis's nose and then slowly take away his hand, saying, "Stay. Stay. Stay. Otis. Stay." Crooning it real softly. And Otis with his eyes crossed looking at the meat scrap on his nose, quivering almost unnoticeably and not daring to move, and then Harold leans back and takes another Camel out of the pack, and if Otis slowly moves just an eighth of an inch, saying, "Otis. Stay." And then lighting the cigarette and then looking at Otis for a second and then saying, "All right, Otis." And quicker than you can see it Otis has not so much tossed the scrap up in the air as he has removed his nose from its position, the meat scrap suspended, and before it can begin to respond to gravity Otis has snatched it into his mouth and swallowed it and is looking at Harold's hands again with the same look as if nothing has happened between them at all and he is hoping for his first scrap.

This is the test, Harold says. If you balance the meat scrap, and in a moment of grace manage to eat the meat scrap, you are in. If you drop the meat scrap and eat it off the floor, well, you're no better than a dog. Out you go.

But the thing I was going to tell at first is about Ike, about how when Otis gets let in and Ike doesn't, Ike starts barking outside the door, big woofing barks, loud complaints, thinking (Harold says), Why is he letting in Otis and not me? Let me IN. IN. And he continues his barking for some couple of minutes or so, and then, without your really being able to put your finger on just how it happens, the bark begins to change, not so much a complaint as a demand, I am IKE, let me IN, because what is lost, you see, is the memory of Otis having been let in first and that being the reason for complaint. And from there he goes to his more common generic statement, voiced simply because Ike is Ike and needs no reason for saying it, I am IKE, and then it changes in a more noticeable way, just IKE, as he loses contact with his ego, soon just Ike!, tapering off, and in a minute it's just a bark every now and then, just a normal call into the void the way dogs do, yelling HEY every now and then and seeing if anyone responds across the pasture, HEY, and then you hear Ike circle and drop himself onto the porch floorboards just outside the kitchen door. And this, Harold says, is a product of Ike's consciousness, that before he can even finish barking, Ike has forgotten what he's barking about, so he just lies down and goes to sleep. And this, Harold says, as if the meat scrap test needs corroboration, is why Ike can't sleep indoors and Otis can.

The other day, Harold sat in a chair in front of his bedroom window, leaned back, and put his feet on the sill, and the whole window, frame and all, fell out into the weeds with a crash. I helped him seal the hole with polyethylene sheeting and duct tape, and now there's a filtered effect to the light in the room that's quite nice on cool late afternoons.

There are clothes in the closets here, we don't know who they belong to. The front room and the dark attic are crammed with junk. Old space heaters in a pile in one corner, a big wooden canoe (cracked) with paddles, a set of barbells made from truck axles and wheel rims, a seamstress dummy with nipples painted on the breasts, some great old cane fly rods not too limber any more, a big Motorola radio, a rope ladder, a box of *Life* magazines, and a big stack of yellow newspapers from Mobile. And lots of other junk too numerous to name.

All four corners of the house slant toward the center, the back of the foyer being the floor's lowest point. You put a golf ball on the floor at any point in the house, and it'll roll its way eventually, bumping lazily into baseboards and doors and discarded shoes and maybe a baseball mitt or a rolled-up rug slumped against the wall, to that low spot in the tall, empty foyer, where there's a power-line spool heaped with wadded old clothes like someone getting ready for a yard sale cleaned out some dresser drawers and disappeared. The doors all misfit their frames, and on gusty mornings I have awakened to the dry tick and skid of dead leaves rolling under the gap at the bottom of the front door and into the foyer, rolling through the rooms like little tumbleweeds, to collect in the kitchen, where then in ones and twos and little groups they skitter out the open door to the backyard and on and out across the field. It's a pleasant way to wake up, really. Sometimes I hang my head over the side of the big bed I use, the one with four rough-barked cedar logs for posts and which Harold said the mice used before I moved in, and I'll see this big old skink with pink spots on his slick black hide hunting along the crevice between the baseboard and the floor. His head disappears into the crevice, and he draws it out again chewing something, his long lipless jaws chomping down.

The house doors haven't seen a working lock in thirty or forty years. Harold never really thinks about security, though the bums walking on the road to Florida pass by here all the time and probably used this as a motel before Harold found it out here abandoned on his family's land and became an expatriate from town because, he says, he never again wants to live anywhere he can't step out onto the back porch and take a piss day or night.

The night I showed up looking for shelter I just opened up the front door because no one answered and I didn't know if Harold was way in the back of the big old house (he was) or what. I entered the foyer, and first I heard a clicking sound and Otis came around the corner on his toes, claws tapping, his tail high, with a low growl. And then Harold walked in behind him, his trusty old .38 in his hand. He sleeps with it on a bookshelf not far from his bed, the one cheap bullet he owns next to the gun if it hasn't rolled off onto the floor.

The night that Phelan arrived to stay, fell through the door onto his back, and lay there looking up into the shadows of the high old foyer, Otis came clicking in and approached him slowly, hackles raised, lips curling fluidly against his old teeth, until his nose was just over Phelan's. And then he jumped back barking savagely when Phelan burst out like some slurring old thespian. "There plucking at his throat a great black beast shaped like a hound, 'The Hound,' cried Holmes, 'Great Heavens! half animal half demon, its eyes aglow its muzzles and hackles and dewlap outlined in flickering flame.'"

"Phelan," Harold said, "meet Otis."

"Cerberus, you mean," Phelan said, "my twelfth labor." He raised his arms and spread his fingers before his eyes. "I have only my hands."

How Harold came to be alone is this: Sophia, a surveyor for the highway department, fixed her sights on Harold and took advantage of his ways by drinking with him till two a.m. and then offering to drive him home, where she would put him to bed and ride him like a cowgirl. She told me this herself one night, and asked me to feel of her thighs, which were hard and bulging as an ice skater's under her jeans. "I'm strong," she whispered in my ear, cocking an eyebrow.

One evening, after she'd left, Harold stumbled out onto the porch where I sat smoking, bummed a cigarette, braced an arm against a porch post, and stood there taking a long piss out into the yard. He didn't say anything. He was naked. His hair was like a sheaf of windblown wheat against the moonlight coming down on the field and cutting a clean line of light along the edge of the porch. His pale body blue in that light. He kept standing there, his stream arcing out into the yard, sprayed to the east in the wind, breathing through his nose and smoking the cigarette with the smoke whipping away. There was a storm trying to blow in. I didn't have to say anything. You always know when you're close to out of control.

Sophia left paraphernalia around for Harold's fiancée, Westley, to find. Pairs of panties under the bed, a silky camisole slumped like a prostitute between two starched dress shirts in Harold's closet, a vial of fingernail polish in the silverware tray. It wasn't long before Westley walked out of the bathroom one day with a black brassiere, saying, "What's this thing doing hanging on the commode handle?" And it was pretty much over between Westley and Harold after that.

I must say that Sophia, who resembled a greyhound with her long nose and close-set eyes and her tremendous thighs, is the bridge between Harold's story and mine.

Because at first I wasn't cheating on Lois. Things had become distant in the way they do after a marriage struggles through passionate possessive love and into the heartbreak of languishing love, before the vague incestuous love of the long-together. I got home one night when Lois and I were still together, heard something scramble on the living-room floor, and looked over to see this trembling thing shaped like a drawn bow, long needle-nose face looking at me as if over reading glasses, nose down, eyes up, cowed. He was aging. I eased over to him and pulled back ever so softly when as I reached my hand over he showed just a speck of white tooth along his black lip.

"I read that story in the *Journal* about them, and what happens to them when they can't race any more," she said. She'd simply called up the dog track, gone out to a kennel, and taken her pick.

She said since he was getting old, maybe he wouldn't be too hard to control, and besides, she thought maybe I missed having a dog. It was an attempt, I guess, to make a connection. Or it was the administration of an opiate. I don't really know.

To exercise Spike, the retired greyhound, and to encourage a friend-ship between him and me, Lois had the two of us, man and dog, take up jogging. We'd go to the high school track, and Spike loved it. He'd trot about on the football field, snuffling here and there. Once he surprised and caught a real rabbit and tore it to pieces. It must have brought back memories of his training days. You wouldn't think a racing dog could be like a pet dog, foolish and simple and friendly. But Spike was okay. We were pals. And then, after all the weeks it took Spike and me to get back into shape, and after the incidental way in which my affair with Imelda down the street began out of our meeting and jogging together around the otherwise empty track, after weeks of capping our jog with a romp on the foam-rubber pole vault mattress just beyond the goalposts, Lois bicy-cled down to get me one night and rode silently up as Imelda and I lay naked except for our jogging shoes on the pole vault mattress, cooling down, Spike curled up at our feet. As she glided to a stop on the bicycle, Spike raised his head and wagged his tail. Seeing his true innocence, I felt a heavy knot form in my chest. When Lois just as silently turned the bicycle and pedaled away, Spike rose, stretched, and followed her home. Imelda and I hadn't moved.

"Oh, shit," Imelda said. "Well, I guess it's all over."

Imelda merely meant our affair, since her husband was a Navy den-tist on a cruise in the Mediterranean, which had put Imelda temporarily in her parents' hometown, temporarily writing features for the *Journal*, and temporarily having an affair with me. It was Imelda's story on grey-hounds that Lois had seen. It was Imelda who said she wanted to meet Spike, and it was I who knew exactly how this would go and gave in to the inexorable flow of it, combining our passive wills toward this very moment. And it was I who had to go home to Lois now that my marriage was ruined.

Imelda left, and I lay there a while looking up at the stars. It was early October, and straight up I could see the bright clusters of Perseus, Cassiopeia, Cepheus, Cygnus, and off to the right broad Hercules, in his flexing stance. I remembered how Lois and I used to make up constellations: there's my boss, she'd say, scratching his balls. There's Reagan's brain, she'd say. Where? The dim one? Where? That was the joke. Looking up at night usually made me feel as big as the sky, but now I felt like I was floating among them and lost. I got up and started the walk home. There was a little chill in the air, and the drying sweat tightened my skin. I smelled Imelda on my hands and wafting up from my shorts.

The door was unlocked. The lamp was on in the corner of the living room. The nightlight was on in the hallway. I took off my running shoes and walked quietly down the hallway to the bedroom. I could see in the dim light that Lois was in bed, either asleep or pretending to be, facing the wall, her back to the doorway, the covers pulled up to her ears. She was still.

From my side of the bed, Spike watched me sleepily, stretched out, his head resting on his paws. I don't imagine I'd have had the courage to climb into bed and beg forgiveness, anyway. But seeing Spike already there made things clearer, and I crept back out to the den and onto the couch. I curled up beneath a small lap blanket and only then exhaled, breathing very carefully.

When I awoke stiff and guilty the next morning, Lois and Spike were gone. Some time around mid-afternoon, she came home alone. She was wearing a pair of my old torn jeans and a baggy flannel shirt and a Braves cap pulled down over her eyes. We didn't speak. I went out into the garage and cleaned out junk that had been there for a couple of years, hauled it off to the dump in the truck, then came in and showered. I smelled something delicious cooking in the kitchen. When I'd dressed and come out of the bedroom, the house was lighted only be a soft flickering from the dining room. Lois sat at her end of the table alone, eating. She paid me no attention as I stood in the doorway.

"Lois," I said. "Where's Spike?"

She cut a piece of pork roast and chewed for a moment. Her hair was wet and combed straight back off her forehead. She wore eye makeup, bringing out the depth and what I have only a few times truly recognized as the astonishing beauty of her deep green eyes. Her polished nails glistened in the candlelight.

The table was set with our good china and silver and a very nice meal. She seemed like someone I'd only now just met, whom I'd walked in on by her own design. She looked at me, and my heart sank, and the knot that had formed in my chest the night before began to dissolve into sorrow.

"He was getting pretty old," she said. She took a sip of wine, which was an expensive bottle we'd saved for a special occasion. "I had him put to sleep."

I'm surprised at how often dogs make the news. There was the one about the dog elected mayor of a town in California. And another about a dog that could play the piano, I believe he was a schnauzer. More often, though, they're involved in criminal cases—dog bitings, dog pack attacks on children. I've seen several stories about dogs who shoot their masters. There was one of these in the stack of old *Mobile Registers* in the front room. "Dog Shoots, Kills Master," the headline read. Way back in '59. How could you not read a story like that. The man carried his shotguns in his car. He stopped to talk to his relative on the road and let the dogs run. When his relative walked on, the man called his dogs. One of them jumped into the back seat and hit the trigger on a gun, which discharged and struck him "below the stomach," the article said. The man hollered to his relative, "I'm shot!" and fell over in the ditch.

There was another article called "Death Row Dog," about a dog that had killed so many cats in his neighborhood that a judge sentenced him to death. And another one sentenced to be moved to the country or die, just because he barked so much. There was another one like that just this year, about a condemned biter that won a last-minute reprieve. I'm told in medieval times animals were regularly put on trial, with witnesses and testimony and so forth. But it is relatively rare today.

One story, my favorite, was headlined "Dog Lady Claims Close Encounter." It was about an old woman who lived alone with about forty-two dogs. Strays were drawn to her house, whereupon they disappeared from the streets forever. At night, when sirens passed on the streets of the town, a great howling rose from inside her walls. Then one day, the dogs' barking kept on and on, raising a racket like they'd never done before. It went on all day, all that night, and was still going on the next day. People passing the house on the sidewalk heard things slamming against the doors, saw dog claws scratching at the windowpanes, teeth gnawing at the sashes. Finally, the police broke in. Dogs burst through the open door never to be seen again. Trembling skeletons, who wouldn't eat their own kind, crouched in the corners, behind chairs. Dog shit everywhere, the stench was awful. They found dead dogs in the basement freezer, little shit dogs whole and bigger ones cut up into parts. Police started looking around for the woman's gnawed-up corpse, but she was nowhere to be found.

At first they thought the starving dogs had eaten her up: clothes, skin, hair, muscle, and bone. But then, four days later, some hunters found her wandering naked out by a reservoir, all scratched up, disoriented.

She'd been abducted, she said, and described tall creatures with the heads of dogs, who licked her hands and sniffed her privates.

"They took me away in their ship," she said. "On the dog star, it's them that owns us. These here," she said, sweeping her arm about to indicate Earth, "they ain't nothing compared to them dogs."

On a warm afternoon in November, a beautiful breezy Indian summer day, the wind steered Lois somehow in her Volkswagen up to the house.

She'd been driving around. I got a couple of beers from the fridge and we sat back sipping them, not talking. Then we sat there looking at each other for a little while. We drank a couple more beers. A rosy sun ticked down behind the old grove on the far side of the field and light softened, began to blue. The dogs' tails moved like periscopes through the tall grass.

"Want to walk?" I said.

"Okay."

The dogs trotted up as we climbed through the barbed-wire fence, then bounded ahead, leaping like deer over stands of grass. Lois stopped out in the middle of the field and slipped her hands in the pockets of my jeans.

"I missed you," she said. She shook her head. "I sure as hell didn't want to."

"Well," I said. "I know." Anger over Spike rose in me then, but I held my tongue. "I missed you, too," I said. She looked at me with anger and desire.

We knelt down. I rolled in the grass, flattening a little bed. We attacked each other. Kissing her, I felt like I wanted to eat her alive. I took big soft bites of her breasts, which were heavy and smooth. She gripped my waist with her nails, pulled hard at me, kicked my ass with her heels, bit my shoulders, and pulled my hair so hard I cried out. After we'd caught our breath, she pushed me off of her like a sack of feed corn.

We lay on our backs. The sky was empty. It was all we could see, with the grass so high around us. We didn't talk for a while, and then Lois began to tell me what had happened at the vet's. She told me how she'd held Spike while the vet gave him the injection.

"I guess he just thought he was getting more shots," she said. "Like when I first took him in."

She said Spike was so good, he didn't fight it. He looked at her when she placed her hands on him to hold him down. He was frightened, and didn't wag his tail. And she was already starting to cry, she said. The vet asked her if she was sure this was what she wanted to do. She nodded her head. He gave Spike the shot.

She was crying as she told me this.

"He laid down his head and closed his eyes," she said. "And then, with my hands on him like that, I tried to pull him back to me. Back to us." She said, No, Spike, don't go. She pleaded with him not to die. The vet was upset and said some words to her and left the room in anger, left her alone in her grief. And when it was over, she had a sense of not knowing where she was for a moment. Sitting on the floor in there alone with the strong smell of flea killer and antiseptic, and the white of the floor and walls and the stainless steel of the examination table where Spike had died and where he lay now, and in that moment he was everything she had ever loved.

She drained the beer can, wiping her eyes. She took a deep breath and let it out slowly. "I just wanted to hurt you. I didn't realize how much it would hurt me."

She shook her head.

"And now I can't forgive you," she said. "Or me."

In the old days when Harold was still with Westley and I was still with Lois, Harold had thrown big cookout parties. He had a pit we'd dug for slow-cooking whole pigs, a brick grill for chickens, and a smoker made from an old oil drum. So one crisp evening late in bird season, to reestablish some of the old joy of life, Harold set up another one and a lot of our old friends and acquaintances came. Then Phelan showed up, drunk, with the head of a pig he'd bought at the slaughterhouse. He'd heard you could buy the head of a pig, and after an afternoon at the Blind Horse he thought it would be interesting to bring one to the barbecue. He insisted on putting it into the smoker, so it would have made a scene to stop him. Every half hour or so, he opened the lid with a flourish and checked the head. The pig's eyelids shrank and opened halfway, the eyes turned translucent. Its hide leaked beaded moisture and turned a doughy pale. People lost their appetites. Many became quiet and left. "I'm sorry," Phelan stood on the porch and announced as they left, stood there like Marc Antony in Shakespeare. "No need to go. I've come to bury this pig, not to eat him."

Finally Harold took the pig's head from the smoker and threw it out onto the far edge of the yard, and Phelan stood over it a minute, reciting some lines from Tennyson. Ike and Otis went sniffing up, sniffing, their eyes like brown marbles. They backed off and sat just outside of the porch light and watched the pig's head steaming in the grass as if it had dropped screaming through the atmosphere and plopped into the yard, an alien thing, now cooling, a new part of the landscape, a new mystery evolving, a new thing in the world, there whenever they rounded the corner, still there, stinking and mute, until Harold buried it out in the field. After that we pretty much kept to ourselves.

We passed our winter boarded up in the house, the cracks beneath doors and around windows and in the walls stuffed with old horse blankets and newspaper and wads of clothing falling apart at the seams, the space heaters hissing in the tall-ceilinged rooms. We went out for whiskey and dry goods and meat, occasionally stopped by the Blind Horse of an early afternoon, but spent our evenings at home. We wrote letters to those we loved and missed and planned spring reunions when possible. Harold's once-illicit lover, Sophia the surveyor, came by a few times. I wrote Lois, but received no reply. I wrote to my editor at the *Journal* and asked to return in the late spring, but it may be that I should move on.

It is March just now, when the ancients sacrificed young dogs and men to the crop and mixed the blood with the corn. Harold is thinking of planting some beans. We've scattered the astonished heads of bream in the soil, mourning doves in their beautiful lidded repose. The blood of the birds and the fishes, and the seeds of the harvest. I found the skin of our resident chicken snake, shed and left on the hearth. He's getting ready to move outside. The days are warming, and though it's still cool in the evenings, we stay out late in the backyard, sipping Harold's Famous Grouse to stay warm, trying in our hearts to restore a little order to the world. I'm hoping to be out here at least until midnight, when Canis Major finally descends in the west, having traveled of an evening across the southern horizon. It rises up before sunset and glows bright above the pastures at dusk, big bright Sirius the first star in the sky, to wish upon for a fruitful planting. It stirs me to look up at them, all of them, not just this one, stirs me beyond my own enormous sense of personal disappointment. And Harold, in his cups, calls Otis over and strikes a pose: "Orion, the hunter," he says, "and his Big Dog." Otis, looking up at him, strikes the pose, too: Is there something out there? Will we hunt? Harold holds the pose, and Otis trots out into the field, restless, snuffling. I can feel the earth turning beneath us, rolling beneath the stars. Looking up, I lose my balance and fall back flat in the grass.

If the Grouse lasts we'll stay out till dawn, when the stellar dog and hunter are off tracing the histories of other worlds, the cold distant fig-ures of the hero Perseus and his love Andromeda fading in the morning glow into nothing.

And then we will stumble into the falling-down house and to our beds. And all our dreams will roll toward the low point in the center of the house and pool there together, mingling in the drafts under the doors with last year's crumbling leaves and the creeping skinks and the dreams of the dogs, who must dream of the chase, the hunt, of bitches in heat, the mingling of old spoors with their own musty odors. And deep in sleep they dream of space travel, of dancing on their hind legs, of being men with the heads and muzzles of dogs, of sleeping in beds with sheets, of driving cars, of taking their fur coats off each night and making love face to face. Or cooking their food. And Harold and I dream of days of following the backs of men's knees, and faint trails in the soil, the overpowering odors of all our kin, our pasts, every mistake as strong as sulfur, our victories lingering traces here and there. The house is disintegrating into dust. The end of all of this is near.

Just yesterday Harold went into the kitchen for coffee and found the chicken snake curled around the warm pot. Otis went wild. Harold whooped. The screams of Sophia the surveyor rang high and clear and regular, and in my half-sleep I could only imagine the source of this dissonance filling the air. Oh, slay me and scatter my parts in the field. The house was hell. And Ike, too, baying—out on the porch—full-lunged, without memory or sense, with only the barking of Otis to clue his continuing: already lost within his own actions, forgetting his last conscious needs.

My Life Is a Country Song

Cassandra King

Would you believe me if I told you that Garth Brooks was partly to blame for my life falling apart? Garth and Clint Black both. You'll think I'm crazy, but I swear it's the truth. I like Clint better than Garth, though that's pure heresy to Bud. He likes Clint okay, but says Garth is much more authentic. Garth's great, don't get me wrong, he just doesn't have the range Clint does. My favorite song of Clint's is "Loving Blind." I get chill-bumps the way he sings, "I been loving blind, so sure there was something I could find."

Anyway, the whole thing started with me and Bud carrying on like that about Clint and Garth. But it ended with Bud leaving me for Shirley Faye Tate, breaking my heart into little pieces, like glass beneath the heel of his boot.

Remember, I met Bud at the Rhinestone Rodeo the time I was taking line dancing. When I two-stepped into his arms and looked up into those eyes of his, I was a goner. My concentration was shot the rest of the night. I tripped on the Vine and lost count on the Toosh-Coosh. You know that all the women had been talking about Bud Baxter ever since he moved into town—Annette was the one who said he looked just like George Strait. *She's right. Nothing but a phony George Strait look-alike*, I thought when I first saw Bud and his black cowboy hat across the dark dance floor. I thought that until I looked into those sleepy blue eyes of Bud's. George's are brown.

Bud swept me off my feet. He wouldn't dance with anyone else, had Annette and them glaring daggers at me. Bud and me went to Shoney's for strawberry pie after the Rodeo closed, and we've been an item ever since. I found out he was with the construction company building that new mall out towards Wicksburg, and that he was originally from Americus, Georgia. You might know some of his people over there—his uncle J. D. owns that big body shop.

Bud's real name is Buford Baxter, Jr., but he's been called Bud all his life. Within three months of first looking into those baby-blue eyes at the Rhinestone Rodeo, I became Mrs. Buford James Baxter.

Things started to go wrong on our wedding day, things that should have warned me. Since I didn't have a big wedding the first time, I wanted this to be an event to remember. I wish you could have been there—everybody said it was a beautiful wedding, in spite of everything. Surely you remember our wedding. It was the one written up in *The Dothan Eagle* where they messed up the preacher's name, reversing it— somebody even sent it in to the *Reader's Digest*. Reverend Dick Small, it was supposed to be.

But that wasn't all. The ceremony was held at the Freewill Baptist Church, and we had the reception at the Rhinestone Rodeo since it held such fond memories. The Wiregrass Gourmet catered it, and we had buffalo wings, nacho dip, cheese straws, things like that. Beer for the men and pink champagne for the ladies, and Shoney's strawberry pies along with the wedding cake. Bud drank so much he passed out before we even cut the pies, and Kyle and some of the other guys dragged him out to the backseat of my car. I ended up driving to Gulf Shores for our honeymoon while he snored away.

Actually our first fuss was before the wedding. I wanted my cousin Brenda to sing a Clint song, but Bud insisted we get Kyle Willis, who sings at the Rodeo. He wanted Garth's "Somewhere Other Than the Night," but I refused. Imagine folks sitting there in church—my church!—while Kyle sang about somewhere other than the night in front of the preacher and the deacons. We compromised with Brenda and Kyle singing a duet, Wynona's "Love Can Build a Bridge." After Brother Small pronounced us man and wife, Kyle and Brenda sang as we walked down the aisle, out of the church. My idea. I liked the symbolism of us going out as though walking over a bridge, from one life to the next. As Bud and me walked down the aisle, I was puzzled by the expressions on the faces of the congregation. That's because I couldn't see Aunt Lola, sitting up front, next to Mama and Daddy. Wynona's her favorite, so she stood up and sang along with Brenda and Kyle, big as you please. By the time we got out the door, the congregation was laughing out loud. I should have known. All that was a bad sign.

Even so, I would never have dreamed of Bud leaving me for Shirley Faye Tate, would you? *Shirley Faye Tate?* In high school we called her Shirley Faye Tits. If her brain was even half the size of her boobs, things might have turned out different for her. You know that soldier from Fort Rucker she married, the day after graduation? Couple of years later he left her, her with one in her lap and another on the way. They were living in Fort Dix, New Jersey. Near his people, but they were Catholics and Shirley Faye was Holiness, so they didn't recognize the marriage. They did give her enough money to get the Amtrak home. She moved back in with her family till she married Don Jenkins. Damned if he didn't beat her up so bad she ended up in Southeast General. Folks say she stayed in the psych ward a month after her brothers half-killed Don. Ended up with Shirley Faye's mama keeping her kids so that Shirley Faye could go to George C. Wallace Junior College this side of Dothan. She took some classes and then had a stroke of luck—she got hired in their admissions office and now runs their night program, her with not much more education than me.

That's where she and Bud met. I remember the night Bud came in from his classes and told me about an old classmate of mine who had registered him. At first I couldn't remember Shirley Faye, since she was two years behind me, and I'd been out of high school nearly twenty years. Finally I said, "Oh, yeah, I know her—Shirley Faye Tits," and didn't think anymore about it.

Bud's a pipefitter. He went to the trade school in Americus to learn how. Naturally he loves to get with his beer-drinking buddies and make dirty remarks about having to grab hold of his pipe and fit it in a little hole, stuff like that. After we married, Bud decided he wanted to better himself, that pipefitting was not how he wanted to spend his life. I was glad, because Bud is union, and they can send him anywhere there's a job. Before he came to Dothan he worked several months in Tampa, Florida.

I got sidetracked, but you have to know all this to understand how my life got so messed up. You know about my first husband and how sorry he was, but it was different with Bud. I thought he loved me, I really did. He told me he'd never loved anyone like he loved me. He'd been married twice, both times to girls he was raised with in Americus, one of them a Miss Georgia who placed third in the Miss America pageant. Funny thing, I remembered her from the pageant, though it was 1978, quite a while back. Reason I remember is all of us sitting around watching almost died laughing when Miss Georgia was introduced as Miss Edie Pye, from Americus. Imagine a girl being stuck with a name like that! Who would have thought me and Edie Pye would be connected in some way, her being Bud's first wife? Small world.

Anyway, Bud wanted to go back to school and take computers. He wanted to better himself, as I was saying, and to get us into our own home. I was all for that, so I didn't say a word when he started going nights to George C., though I did have to cut back on the tanning booth and aerobics classes so we could afford it. And to think I gave up a fit, tanned body so that Bud could leave me for Shirley Faye! No one has ever said life was fair, right? I mean, I've always wanted to go to college myself, but I'll be forty in a few years. Oh, I forgot to tell you that Bud's four years younger than me, which may be part of the problem. Mama told me not to marry a younger man, that men who marry a woman that much older are looking for a mother, not a wife. I've never listened to Mama, but this time it seems she was right. Now I think all Bud wanted from me was my biscuits and sausage gravy every morning, and someone to snuggle up to at night. We didn't even make love that much, which surprised me, him with those bedroom eyes that promised so much. Of course, I had no idea that he was fitting his pipe elsewhere.

Here's the way it happened: After a few weeks of classes, Bud came in later than usual. I'd already gotten Scottie down for the night, though he cried because Bud wasn't there. Scottie's crazy about Bud, took right to him. Scottie's taking to Bud was one of the other ways Bud swept me off my feet. Every time he came over when we were dating, he brought me chocolate-covered peanuts and Scottie a little model car, and they'd huddle on the floor, putting it together with cement glue.

Anyhow, Bud came in about midnight, no chocolate-covered

peanuts this time, and he told me that him and some folks in his class went to the Rodeo to get a beer, and that he lost track of time. He took off his hat and rolled those sexy blue eyes my way.

"You remember me telling you about your classmate, girl named Shirley Faye? I found out she's about as crazy about Garth as I am. We got Kyle to sing a Garth medley. Man, you should have been there."

And dumb me, I didn't suspect a thing, like why Shirley Faye was at the Rodeo with them. "If Kyle can do Garth for you he can do Clint for me," I hooted. "I've asked and asked, but no. Claims he doesn't take requests." If only I'd been more tuned in to the real issue instead of carrying on because Kyle, like Bud, favored Garth over Clint!

After that night, Bud would come in later and later following his class, half-drunk, claiming him and some guys went for a beer to the Rodeo and got to talking computers. Now, this part is kind of embarrassing, but I've got to tell you so you'll understand how it all happened. Bud and me had only been married a few months, but we hadn't done anything in two weeks. You can't tell me that's normal for a newly married couple, even one our age. Another week went by, and I decided I'd had enough. I didn't marry a George Strait look-alike so I could cuddle every night. I could have bought a teddy bear, saved a lot of trouble. When Bud came in half-drunk again and fell into the bed, I was ready to trounce him.

"Bud!" I poked him in the ribs, hard. "We need to have a little talk."

He groaned and pulled the pillow over his head. "Leave me alone, Janeen. You know I get up at five."

"Why stay out past midnight, then?" I pulled the pillow off his face, and he opened a bleary blue eye.

"Damnit, Janeen—leave me alone, you hear?"

I waited until he dozed again, blowing his beer breath into my face. Then I slipped my nightgown off and straddled him.

"Bud," I said, shaking him awake, "it's been almost three weeks."

His eyes flew open. "Jesus, Janeen—what the hell are you doing?"

"What does it look like?"

Bud groaned, grabbed me real hard, and flipped us so that he was straddling me. He'd never let me stay on top, not with that male ego of his.

I found out that night that Bud, in spite of looking so young and innocent, was like all men I've ever known, and that he could lie with the best of them. "Sugar baby," he whispered afterwards, looking right into my eyes, "we hadn't made love lately because I've been worn out, working so hard days and going to classes every night. But I'm going to make it up to you, I promise."

And fool that I am, I let him sweet-talk me into believing him, and we cuddled up to sleep. The next morning, I made biscuits and sausage gravy for breakfast.

We were okay for a while, but one night things came to a head, so to speak. I'd gotten Mama to come over and stay with Scottie so I could go to the Rhinestone Rodeo and surprise Bud, but I ended up being the one surprised.

When I pulled up in the parking lot at the Rodeo, I spotted Bud's pickup right off. I sat for a minute because the radio was playing Clint singing "Loving Blind." Last time I'd heard it was before me and Bud married, and we'd slow-danced so close that we couldn't wait to get off the dance floor and into the bed. I'll tell you this part if you promise not to tell anybody. I'd die if anyone found out, because it might get back to Mama or Scottie. Truth is, me and Bud didn't make it that far. We did it in his pickup, in the parking lot, like a couple of teenagers. That was before we married. Afterwards—well, you know. Things just aren't the same, are they?

Clint finished his song; I turned off the ignition and was reaching for my purse when the door to the Rodeo swung open. You might remember, it's shaped like a saloon door in the old West. And out came Bud. Just seeing him made my heart beat faster, he looked so good. I watched him adjust his cowboy hat with one hand then reach back to hold the door open for someone with the other. At first I couldn't take in what I was seeing. It looked like Bud was pulling someone out the door, and in a way, he was. Pulling someone out, that is. He was holding hands with a girl, kind of pulling on her. I watched as they proceeded to walk hand in hand to Bud's truck, not three pickups down from where I was parked. And I swear, it was Shirley Faye Tate! I admit I didn't recognize her at first, she'd toned herself down so much. She still has big hair, but it was shorter. And she has put on weight. She reminded me of that black-headed woman who plays Suzanne on *Designing Women.*

You know me well enough to know what I did. Oh, sure, I cried like everything, but that was later. Right then I jumped out of my car and stormed up to Bud's truck. He was cranking up and Shirley Faye was snuggled under him, those big boobs in that tight white satin blouse pressed right against him. Fortunately the window was open so I didn't have to yell so loud. "Bud Baxter, you two-timing son-of-a-bitch, what do you think you're doing with Shirley Faye Tits?"

I didn't think it was loud, but my yelling caused a commotion. Folks began to stick their heads over the top of the swinging doors, trying to see what was going on. Bud didn't even have the gumption to stick around. Soon as he saw it was me yelling, he took off like a bat out of hell, tires squealing. Last thing I saw was Shirley Faye's black-penciled eyes, big as a possum's, looking at me through the back window of the truck.

You know how Mama is. Of course, she had to say I told you so. "Looks like you'd know better, Janeen," she said, standing over me while I cried myself to sleep that night. "Looks like you'd have better sense by now. Men treat women just like linoleum, laying them one day and expecting to walk over them the next."

I was at work when Bud came and moved his stuff out, moved into Shirley Faye's place at the Dothan Deluxe Duplexes. He left a model airplane for Scottie and a box of chocolates for me. Plain old chocolates, cheap, from Walgreen's. I threw them in the garbage. I guess Shirley Faye is getting my peanuts now. The thought made me so mad I threw Bud's Garth tapes, which he'd left in a stack by the door, in the garbage, too. Guess he'd been planning on coming back for them later. I never wanted to hear Garth again, because I never could without thinking about Bud.

It wasn't a month later before I heard that Bud had gotten himself thrown out, too. Of the Rodeo. Annette told me he'd gotten drunk and got in a fight with Sonny Pettus. Annette said Sonny kept cutting in on Bud and Shirley Faye slow-dancing, and Bud had cleaned his greens. Annette couldn't understand why I cried when she told me this. She kept saying, "Bud's all right, hon—he busted his hand on Sonny's face is all." I couldn't stop crying long enough to explain it was the image of Bud and Shirley Faye dancing to "Love Can Build a Bridge" that tore me all to pieces.

Finally, it came to this: instead of my usual country music station, I started to listen to classical music on public radio. I didn't care what song was playing—it didn't have to be Clint or Garth—it got so *everything* I heard reminded me of Bud, and I'd start crying. I bet you I cried a river that month Bud was gone. My life was so messed up I didn't know what to do. Only thing I knew was to start listening to classical music since it broke my heart to hear sad lyrics, and I never could stomach Easy Listening. I tuned in to WTSU, public radio from the campus of Troy State University.

You're not going to believe what happened next. You will think I'm crazy for sure when I tell you.

I started out listening to WTSU while I drove to work every morning. Soon as the school bus took Scottie away, I'd head to downtown Dothan, going into Dr. Day's office like I'd been doing for the past twenty years. Before I realized it, I was beating my fingers on the steering wheel, keeping time to Bach's Concerto No. 3 in D Major. Next, I talked Dr. Day into putting me in charge of the music he played while he drilled teeth, which wasn't hard to do since he'd gotten good and tired of me crying every time a sad song came on the piped-in music. Soon Dr. Day was drilling to Beethoven's sonatas and I was scheduling appointments to the serenades of Schubert.

Come to think of it, it was Dr. Day who said I ought to take the Music Appreciation class at George C. I was scared to because I might run into Shirley Faye at registration, but Dr. Day said it wasn't taught at night anyhow, that it was part of their continuing studies program and I could probably take a class during my lunch hour. Sure enough, I did, and did my life ever change! It was nothing short of miraculous.

I was at home when it happened, listening to the Brahms Third Symphony, which is so soothing. I'd been using it to lull Scottie to sleep instead of his usual Ninja Turtles video. He'd quit asking about Bud in the last few weeks. Bud had called a few times, I guess wanting to talk about a divorce, but I'd hung up soon as I heard his voice. Then I just let the answering machine pick up. It about broke my heart anytime I heard Bud's voice. First he'd try to get me to pick up, then he'd start in on Scottie. "I know y'all are there," he'd say, and me and Scottie would look at each other and shake our heads, because Bud always sounded drunk as a coot.

Anyhow, like I was telling you, I was about to go to bed and Brahms was playing on the stereo. I'd gotten a CD player because the sound was so much better. Since I'd been taking that course, I knew things to listen out for, things like clean, well-balanced orchestrations, which sound so much better on a CD.

I was looking over George C.'s winter schedule. Dr. Day had surprised me by saying if I'd go back to school and take radiology, his wife would hire me in a New York minute at Southeast General. She runs the radiology department there. Dr. Day said he'd work around my schedule if I'd go back to school. I liked my class I was taking now so much I was excited about the idea of taking radiology and bettering myself.

Who should show up with me in my ugly flannel nightgown and Oil of Olay on my face but Bud? He about knocked the door down. I didn't want him to wake up Scottie so I let him in.

At first he wouldn't say much. He hemmed and hawed around, saying he came over to get his tapes. I wasn't going to tell him that I threw Garth in the garbage can. Then he asked for a beer. I didn't think he'd been drinking, but I wasn't taking any chances. I told him that I didn't have one but I'd fix him a cup of coffee. It was when we was sitting on the couch drinking our Maxwell House that it happened.

"Janeen?" Bud started out, not looking at me, hanging his head low; "You know that song of Clint's, 'Loving Blind'?"

I nodded. How could he have forgotten so soon what used to be my favorite song of all times?

"That's the way I've been lately," he continued. "I made the biggest mistake of my life when I left you for Shirley Faye Tate. I don't know what came over me. I don't blame you if you never want to see me again."

My throat tightened and tears stung my eyes. I looked quickly away from those sad blue eyes of his. I wouldn't let myself be taken in by a man like him again, no sir. Mama was right. The way to make a fortune was to buy a man for what he was worth and sell him for what he thought he was worth.

Bud looked up and this time his eyes held mine. "I miss you and Scottie so much, Janeen. I've been the biggest damn fool in the world."

I jumped to my feet, and to keep from looking into those eyes that were breaking my heart, I went to the stereo. "I got a new CD player," I told him, feeling like an idiot because I couldn't think of anything else to say. I inserted a CD blindly, making a big fuss over fiddling with the knobs, getting the sound just right.

"I see you did," Bud said. "But I've gotten so I can't take country music, it breaks me up so bad. I reckon I'd better go now, or I'll be making a fool out of myself, crying like a baby." He stood up and got his cowboy hat, fixing to leave.

"I'm the same way," I told him, adjusting the volume when the soft strains of Chopin's Nocturne No. 2 filled the air.

Bud hung his head. "Tell you the truth, it doesn't have to be country music to make me feel bad. That Opus 9 of Chopin's—it just tears me up."

I stared at him, frozen in place by the stereo. Finally I managed to open my mouth. "Bud! I can't believe that *you* know Chopin."

Bud shrugged. "I don't let on, but I listen to a little Chopin sometimes. My favorite composer is Bach."

Bach, Chopin, my favorites. I couldn't believe my ears. "But—I thought—I mean, Garth is your favorite—"

"Yeah. I still like him best. Especially to dance by. Remember when we danced to "If Tomorrow Never Comes"? I'll never hear it that I don't think of that moonlit night, at the Rodeo. Though I don't believe I can ever go back there."

"Because you got kicked out for fighting?" I asked him.

"Because I made such a fool out of myself. I wish there was some way you could find it in your heart to forgive me. But I understand if you can't."

"Scottie sure misses you," I said, not looking at him, though I felt his eyes on me.

"What about you, Janeen?"

Neither one of us said anything for a while. Chopin floated in the air like smoke from a winter fire. I sighed finally and looked at Bud, full in the face for the first time in a long time. He looked at me.

"I don't know, Bud. We'll have to see. Why don't we have another cup of coffee and just listen to the music for a while? How about that?"

Bud nodded. "All right. If you'll play something that's not so damned depressing."

So we got our coffee cups and sat down to Mozart, talking on and on, late into the night, waiting for the next movement to begin.

SPECKLED TROUT

Ron Rash

Lanny came upon the pot plants while fishing Caney Creek. It was a Saturday, and after helping his father sucker tobacco all morning, he'd had the truck and the rest of the afternoon and evening for himself. He'd changed into his fishing clothes and driven the three miles of dirt road to the French Broad. He drove fast, the rod and reel clattering side to side in the truck bed and clouds of red dust rising in his wake like dirt devils. He had the windows down and if the radio worked he would have had it blasting. The driver's license in his billfold was six months old but only in the last month had his daddy let him drive the truck by himself.

He parked by the bridge and walked upriver toward where Caney Creek entered. Afternoon sunlight slanted over Brushy Mountain and tinged the water the color of cured tobacco. A big fish leaped in the shallows but Lanny's spinning rod was broken down, and even if it hadn't been, he would not have bothered to make a cast. There was nothing in the river he could sell, only stocked rainbows and browns, knottyheads, and catfish. The men who fished the river were mostly old men, men who would stay in one place for hours, motionless as the stumps and rocks they sat on. Lanny liked to keep moving, and he fished where even the younger fishermen wouldn't go.

In forty minutes he was half a mile up Caney Creek, the spinning rod still broken down. There were trout in the lower section where browns and rainbows had worked their way up from the river, and Old Man Jenkins would not buy them. The gorge narrowed to a thirty-foot wall of water and rock, below it the deepest pool on the creek. This was the place where everyone else turned back. He waded through waist-high water to reach the left side of the waterfall, then began climbing, using juts and fissures in the rock for leverage and resting places. When he got to the top he put the rod together and tied a gold Panther Martin on the line.

The only fish this far up were what fishing magazines called brook trout, though Lanny had never heard Old Man Jenkins or anyone else call them anything other than speckled trout. Jenkins swore they tasted better than any brown or rainbow and paid Lanny fifty cents apiece no matter how small they were. Old Man Jenkins ate them head and all, like sardines.

Mountain laurel slapped against Lanny's face and arms, and he scraped his hands and elbows climbing straight up rocks there was no other way around. The only path was water now. He thought of his daddy back at the farmhouse and smiled to himself. The old man had told him never to fish a place like this alone, because a broken leg or a rattlesnake bite could get you stone-dead before anyone found you. That was near about the only kind of talk he got any more from the old man, Lanny thought to himself as he tested his knot, always being lectured about something—how fast he drove, who he hung out with—like he was eight years old instead of sixteen, like the old man himself hadn't raised all sorts of hell when he was young.

The only places with enough water to hold fish were the pools, some no bigger than a wash bucket. Lanny flicked the spinner into the pools, and in every third or fourth one a small, orange-finned trout came flopping out onto the bank, the spinner's treble hook snagged in its mouth. Lanny would slap the speckle's head against a rock and feel the fish shudder in his hand and die. If he missed a strike, he cast again into the same pool. Unlike brown and rainbows, the speckles would hit twice, occasionally even three times. Old Man Jenkins had told Lanny when he was a boy most every stream in the county was thick with speckles, but they'd been too easy caught and soon enough fished out, which was why now you had to go to the back of beyond to find them.

He already had eight fish in his creel when he passed the No Trespassing sign nailed in an oak tree. The sign was scabbed with rust like the ten-year-old car tag on his granddaddy's barn, and he paid no more attention to the sign than he had when he'd first seen it a month ago. He knew he was on Toomey land, and he knew the stories. How Linwood Toomey had once used his thumb to gouge a man's eye out in a bar fight and another time opened a man's face from ear to mouth with a broken beer bottle. Stories about events Lanny's daddy had witnessed before, as his daddy put it, he'd got straight with the Lord. But Lanny had heard other things. About how Linwood Toomey and his son were too lazy and hard-drinking to hold steady jobs. Too lazy and drunk to walk the quarter-mile from their farmhouse to the creek to look for trespassers, too, Lanny told himself.

He waded on upstream, going farther than he'd ever been. He caught more speckles, and soon ten dollars' worth bulged in his creel. Enough money for gas, maybe even a couple of bootleg beers, he told himself, and though it wasn't near the money he'd been making at the Pay Lo bagging groceries, at least he could do this alone and not have to deal with some old bitch of a store manager with nothing better to do than watch his every move, then fire him just because he was late a few times.

He came to where the creek forked, and that was where he saw a sudden high greening a few yards above him on the left. He left the water and climbed the bank to make sure it was what he thought it was.

The plants were staked like tomatoes and set in rows the same way as tobacco or corn. He knew they were worth money, a lot of money, because Lanny knew how much his friend Travis paid for an ounce of pot, and this wasn't just ounces but maybe pounds.

He heard something behind him and turned, ready to drop the rod and reel and make a run for it. On the other side of the creek a gray squirrel scrambled up a blackjack oak. He told himself there was no reason to get all jumpy, that nobody would have seen him coming up the creek.

He let his eyes scan what lay beyond the plants. He didn't see any-thing moving, not even a cow or chicken. Nothing but some open ground and then a stand of trees. He rubbed a pot leaf between his finger and thumb, and it felt like money to him, more money than he'd make even at the Pay Lo. He looked around one more time before he took the knife from its sheath and cut down five plants.

That was the easy part. Dragging the stalks a mile down the creek was a lot harder, especially while trying to keep the leaves from being stripped off. When he got to the river he hid the plants in the underbrush and walked the trail to make sure no one was fishing. Then he carried the plants to the road edge, stashed them in the ditch, and got the truck. He emptied the creel into the ditch, the trout stiff and glaze-eyed. He wouldn't be delivering Old Man Jenkins any speckles this evening.

Lanny drove back home with the stalks hidden under willow branches and potato sacks. He planned to stay only long enough to get a shower and put on some clean clothes, but as he walked through the front room his father looked up from the TV.

"We ain't ate yet."

"I'll get something in town," Lanny said.

"No, your momma's fixin' supper right now, and she's set the table for three."

"I ain't got time. Travis is expecting me."

"You can make time, boy. Or I might take a notion to go somewhere in that truck myself this evening."

It was seven-thirty before Lanny drove into the Hardee's parking lot and parked beside Travis's battered Camaro. He got out of the truck and walked over to Travis's window.

"You ain't going to believe what I got in back of the truck."

Travis grinned.

"It ain't that old prune-faced bitch that fired you, is it?"

"No, this is worth something."

Travis got out of the Camaro and walked around to the truck bed with Lanny. Lanny looked around to see if anyone was watching, then pulled back enough of a sack so Travis could see one of the stalks.

"I got five of 'em."

"Holy shit. Where'd that come from?"

"Found it when I was fishing."

Travis pulled the sack back farther.

"I need to start doing my fishing with you. It's clear I been going to the wrong places."

A car pulled up to the drive-through and Travis pulled the sack over the plant.

"What you planning to do with it?"

"Sell it, if I can figure out who'll buy it."

"Leonard would buy it, I bet."

"He don't know me though. I ain't one of his pot-heads."

"Well, I am," Travis said. "Let me lock my car and we'll go pay him a visit."

"How about we go over to Dink's first and get some beer."

"Leonard's got beer. His is cheaper and it ain't piss-warm like what we got at Dink's last time."

They drove out of Marshall, following 221 toward Mars Hill.

"You in for a treat, meeting Leonard," Travis said. "They ain't another like him, leastways in this county."

"I heard tell he was a lawyer once."

"Naw, he just went to law school a few months. They kicked his ass out because he was stoned all the time."

After a mile they turned off the blacktop and onto a dirt road. On both sides of the road what had once been pasture was now thick with blackjack oak and broomsedge. They passed a deserted farmhouse and turned onto another road no better than a logging trail, trees on both sides now.

The woods opened into a small meadow, at the center a battered green-and-white trailer, its windows painted black. On one side of the trailer a satellite dish sprouted like an enormous mushroom, on the other side a Jeep Cherokee, its back fender crumpled. Two Dobermans scrambled out from under the trailer, barking as they ran toward the truck. They leaped at Lanny's window, their claws raking the passenger door as he quickly rolled up the window.

The trailer door opened, and a man with a gray ponytail and wearing only a pair of khaki shorts stepped onto the cinderblock steps. He yelled at the dogs, and when that did no good, he came out to the truck and kicked at them until they slunk back from where they had emerged.

Lanny looked at a man who wasn't any taller than himself and looked to outweigh him only because of a stomach that sagged over the front of his shorts like a half-deflated balloon.

"That's Leonard?"

"Yeh. The one and only."

Leonard walked over to Travis's window.

"I got nothing but beer and a few nickel bags. Supplies are going to be low until people start to harvest."

"Well, we likely come at a good time then." Travis turned to Lanny. "Let's show Leonard what you done brought him."

Lanny got out and pulled back the branches and potato sacks.

"Where'd you get that from?" Leonard said.

"Found it," Lanny said.

"Found it, did you. And you figured finders keepers."

"Yeah," said Lanny.

Leonard let his fingers brush some of the leaves.

"Looks like you dragged it through every briar patch and laurel slick between here and the county line."

"There's plenty of leaves left on it," Travis said.

"What you give me for it?" Lanny said.

Leonard lifted each stalk, looking at it the same way Lanny had seen buyers look at tobacco.

"Fifty dollars."

"You trying to cheat me," Lanny said. "I'll find somebody else to buy it."

As soon as he spoke Lanny wished he hadn't, because he'd heard from more than one person that Leonard Hamby was a man you didn't want to get on the wrong side of. He was about to say that he reckoned fifty dollars would be fine but Leonard spoke first.

"You may have an exalted view of your entrepreneurial abilities," Leonard said.

Lanny didn't understand all the words but he understood the tone. It was smartass, but it wasn't angry.

"I'll give you sixty dollars, and I'll double that if you bring me some that doesn't look like it's been run through a hay baler. Plus I got some cold beers inside. My treat."

"Okay," Lanny said, surprised at Leonard but more surprised at himself, how tough he'd sounded. He tried not to smile as he thought how when he got back to Marshall he'd be able to tell his friends he'd called Leonard Hamby a cheater to his face and Leonard hadn't done a damn thing about it but offer more money and free beer.

Leonard took a money clip from his front pocket and peeled off three twenties and handed them to Lanny. Leonard nodded toward the meadow's far corner.

"Put them over there next to my tomatoes. Then come inside if you got a notion to."

Lanny and Travis carried the plants through the knee-high grass and laid them next to the tomatoes. As they approached the trailer Lanny watched where the Dobermans had vanished under the trailer. He didn't lift his eyes until he reached the steps.

Inside, it took Lanny's vision a few moments to adjust, because the only light came from a TV screen. Strings of unlit Christmas lights ran across the walls and over door eaves like bad wiring. A dusty-looking couch slouched against the back wall. In the corner Leonard sat in a fake-leather recliner patched with black electrician's tape. Except for a stereo system, the rest of the room was shelves filled with books and CDs. Music was playing, music that didn't have any guitars or words.

"Have a seat," Leonard said, and nodded at the couch.

A woman stood in the foyer between the living room and kitchen. She was a tall, bony woman, and the cut-off jeans and halter top she wore had little flesh to hold them up. She'd gotten a bad sunburn and there were pink patches on her skin where she'd peeled. To Lanny she mostly looked wormy and mangy, like some stray dog around a garbage dump. Except for her eyes. They were a deep blue, like a jaybird's feathers. If you could just keep looking into her eyes, she'd be a pretty woman, Lanny told himself.

"How about getting these boys a couple of beers, Wendy," Leonard said.

"Get them your ownself," the woman said and disappeared into the back of the trailer.

Leonard shook his head but said nothing as he got up. He brought back two long-neck Budweisers and a sandwich bag filled with pot and some wrapping papers.

He handed the beers to Travis and Lanny and sat down. Lanny was thirsty, and he drank quickly as he watched Leonard carefully shake some pot out of the baggie and onto the paper. Leonard licked the cigarette paper and twisted it at both ends, then lit it.

The orange tip brightened as Leonard drew the smoke in. He handed the joint to Travis, who drew on it as well and handed it back.

"What about your buddy?"

"He don't smoke pot. Scared his daddy would find out and beat the tar out of him."

"That ain't so," Lanny said. "I just like a beer buzz better."

Lanny lifted the bottle to his lips and drank until the bottle was empty.

"I'd like me another one."

"Quite the drinker, aren't you," Leonard said. "Just make sure you don't overdo it. I don't want you passed out and pissing on my couch."

"I ain't gonna piss on your couch."

Leonard took another drag of the joint and passed it back to Travis.

"They're in the refrigerator," Leonard said. "You can get one easy as I can."

Lanny stood up and for a moment he felt off plumb, maybe because he'd drunk the beer so fast. When the world steadied he got the beer and sat back down on the couch. He looked at the TV, some kind of Western but without the sound on he couldn't tell what was happening. He drank the second beer quick as the first as Travis and Leonard finished smoking the pot.

Travis had his eyes closed.

"Man, I'm feeling good," Travis said.

Lanny studied the man who sat in the recliner, trying to figure out what it was that made Leonard Hamby a man you didn't want to mess with. Leonard looked soft, Lanny thought, white and soft like bread dough. Just because a man had a couple of mean dogs didn't make him such a badass, he told himself. He thought about his own daddy and Linwood Toomey, big men you could look at and tell right away were badasses, or, like his daddy, once had been. Lanny wondered if anyone would ever call him a badass and wished again that he didn't take after his mother, who was short and thin-boned.

"What's this shit you're listening to, Leonard," Lanny said.

"It's called 'Appalachian Spring.' It's by Copland."

"Ain't never heard of them."

Leonard looked amused.

"Are you sure? They used to be the warm-up act for Lynyrd Skynyrd."

"I don't believe that."

"No matter. Copland is an acquired taste, and I don't anticipate your listening to a classical music station any time in the future."

Lanny knew Leonard was putting him down, talking over him like he was stupid, and it made him think of his teachers at the high school, teachers that used smartass words against him when he gave them trouble because they were too old and scared to try anything else. He got up and made his way to the refrigerator, damned if he was going to ask permission. He got the beer out and opened the top but didn't go back to the couch. He went down the hallway to find the bathroom.

The bedroom door was open, and he could see the woman sitting up in the bed reading a magazine. He pissed and then walked into the bedroom and sat down on the bed.

The woman laid down the magazine.

"What do you want?"

Lanny grinned.

"What you offering?"

Even buzzed up with beer he knew it was a stupid thing to say. It seemed to him that ever since he'd got to Leonard's his mouth had been a faucet he couldn't shut off.

The woman's blue eyes stared at him like he was nothing more than a sack of shit somebody had dumped on her bed.

"I ain't offering you anything," she said. "Even if I was, a little peckerhead like you wouldn't know what to do with it."

The woman looked toward the door.

"Leonard," she shouted.

Leonard appeared at the doorway.

"It's past time to get your Cub Scout meeting over."

Leonard nodded at Lanny.

"I believe you boys have overstayed your welcome."

"I was getting ready to leave anyhow," Lanny said. As he got up, the beer slipped from his hand and spilled on the bed.

"Nothing but a little peckerhead," the woman said.

In a few moments he and Travis were outside. The evening sun glowed in the treetop like a snagged orange balloon. The first lightning bugs rode over the grass as though carried on an invisible current.

"You get more plants, come again," Leonard said and closed the trailer door.

Lanny went back the next Saturday, two burlap sacks stuffed into his belt. After he'd been fired from the Pay Lo, he'd about given up hope of earning enough money for his own truck, but now things had changed. Now he had what was pretty damn near a money tree, and all he had to do was get its leaves to Leonard Hamby. He climbed up the waterfall, the trip up easier without a creel and rod. Once he passed the No Trespassing sign, he moved slower, quieter. I bet Linwood Toomey didn't even plant it, Lanny told himself. I bet it was somebody who figured the Toomeys were too sorry to notice pot was growing on their land.

When he came close to where the plants were, he crawled up the bank, slowly raising his head like a soldier in a trench. He scanned the tree line across the field and saw no one. He told himself that even if someone hid in the trees, they could never get across the field to catch him before he was long gone down the creek.

Lanny cut the stalks just below the last leaves. Six plants filled the sacks. He thought about cutting more, taking what he had to the truck and coming back to get the rest, but he figured that was too risky. He made his way back down the creek. He didn't see anyone on the river trail, but if he had, he'd have said it was poke shoots in the sacks if they'd asked.

When he drove up to the trailer, Leonard was watering the tomatoes with a hose. Leonard cut off the water and herded the Dobermans away from the truck. Lanny got out of the truck and walked around to the truck bed.

"How come you grow your own tomatoes but not your own pot?"

"Because I'm a low-risk kind of guy. Since they've started using the planes and helicopters, it's gotten too chancy unless you have a place way back in some hollow."

One of the Dobermans growled from beneath the trailer but did not show its face.

"Where's your partner?"

"I don't need no partner," Lanny said. He lifted the sacks from the truck bed and emptied them onto the ground between him and Leonard.

"That's one hundred and twenty dollars' worth," Lanny said.

Leonard stepped closer and studied the plants.

"Fair is fair," Leonard said and pulled a money clip from his pocket. He handed Lanny five twenty-dollar bills and four fives.

Lanny crumpled the bills in his fist and stuffed them into his pocket, but he did not get back in the truck.

"What?" Leonard finally said.

"I figured you to ask me in for a beer."

"I don't think so. I don't much want to play host this afternoon."

"You don't think I'm good enough to set foot in that roachy old trailer of yours."

Leonard looked at Lanny and smiled.

"Boy, you remind me of a banty rooster, strutting around not afraid of anything, puffing your feathers out anytime anyone looks at you wrong. You think you're a genuine, hardcore badass, don't you?"

"I ain't afraid of you, if that's what you're getting at. If your own woman ain't scared of you, why should I be."

Leonard looked at the money clip in his hand. He tilted it in his hand until the sun caught the metal and a bright flash hit Lanny in the face. Lanny jerked his head away from the glare.

Leonard laughed and put the money clip back in his pocket.

"After the world has its way with you a few years, it'll knock some of the strut out of you. If you live that long."

"I ain't wanting your advice," Lanny said. "I just want some beer."

Leonard went into the trailer and brought out a six-pack of cans.

"Here," he said. "A farewell present. Don't bother to come around here anymore."

"What if I get you some more plants?"

"I don't think you better try to do that. Whoever's pot that is will be harvesting in the next few days. You best not be anywhere near when they're doing it either."

"What if I do get more?"

"Same price, but if you want any beer you best be willing to pay bootleg price like your buddies."

The next day, as soon as Sunday lunch was finished, he put on jeans and a T-shirt and tennis shoes and headed toward the French Broad. The day was hot and humid, and the only people on the river were a man and two boys swimming near the far bank. By the time he reached the creek his T-shirt was sweat-soaked and sweat stung his eyes.

Upstream the trees blocked out most of the sun and the cold water he splashed on his face and waded through cooled him. At the waterfall, an otter slid into the pool. Lanny watched its body surge through the water, straight and sleek as a torpedo, before disappearing under the far bank. He wondered how much an otter pelt was worth and figured come winter it might be worth finding out. He knelt and cupped his hand, the pool's water so cold it hurt his teeth.

He climbed the left side of the falls, then made his way upstream until he got to the No Trespassing sign. If someone waited for him, Lanny believed that by now the person would have figured out he'd come up the creek, so he stepped up on the right bank and climbed the ridge into the woods. He followed the sound of water until he figured he'd gone far enough and came down the slope slow and quiet, stopping every few yards to listen. When he got to the creek, he looked upstream and down before crossing.

The plants were still there. He pulled the sacks from his belt and walked toward the first plant, his eyes on the trees across the field.

The ground gave slightly beneath his right foot. He did not hear the spring click. What he heard was the sound of bone shattering. Pain raced like a flame up his leg to consume his whole body.

When he came to, he was on the ground, his face inches from a pot plant. This ain't nothing but a bad dream, he told himself, thinking that if he believed it hard enough it might become true. He used his forearm to lift his head enough to look at the leg and the leg twisted slightly and the pain hit him like a fist. The world turned deep-blue, and he thought he was going to pass out again, but in a few moments the pain eased a little.

He looked at his foot and immediately wished he hadn't. The trap's jaws clenched around his leg just above the ankle. Blood soaked the tennis shoe red, and the leg angled back on itself in a way that made bile surge up from his stomach. Don't look at it anymore until you have to, he told himself and laid his head back on the ground.

His face looked toward the sun now, and he guessed it was still early afternoon. Maybe it ain't that bad, he told himself. Maybe if I just lay here a while it'll ease up some, and I can get the trap off. He lay as still as possible, breathing long shallow breaths, trying to think about something else. He remembered what Old Man Jenkins had said about how one man could pretty much fish out a stream of speckled trout by himself if he took a notion to. Lanny wondered how many speckled trout he'd be able to catch out of Caney Creek before they were all gone. He wondered if after he did he'd be able to find another way-back trickle of water that held them.

He must have passed out again, because when he opened his eyes the sun hovered just above the tree line. When he tested the leg, pain flamed up every bit as fierce as before. He wondered how late it would be tonight before his parents would get worried and how long it would take after that before someone found his truck and got people searching. Tomorrow at the earliest, he told himself, and even then they'd search the river before looking anywhere else.

He lifted his head a few inches and shouted toward the woods. No one called back, and he imagined Linwood Toomey and his son passed-out drunk in their farmhouse. Being so close to the ground muffled his voice, so he used a forearm to raise himself a little higher and called again.

I'm going to have to sit up, he told himself, and just the thought of doing so made the bile rise again in his throat. He took deep breaths and used both arms to lift himself into a sitting position. The pain smashed against his body again but just as quickly eased. The world began draining itself of color until everything around him seemed shaded with gray. He leaned back on the ground, sweat popping out on his face and arms like blisters.

Everything seemed farther away, the sky and trees and plants, as though he were being lowered into a well. He shivered and wondered why he hadn't brought a sweatshirt with him.

Two men came out of the woods. They walked toward him with no more hurry or concern than men come to check their tobacco for cut-worms. Lanny knew the big man in front was Linwood Toomey, and the man trailing him his son. He could not remember the son's name but had seen him in town a few times. What he remembered was that the son had been away from the county for nearly a decade and that some said he'd been in the Marines and others said prison. The younger man wore a dirty white T-shirt and jeans, the older, blue coveralls with no shirt underneath. Grease coated their hands and arms.

They stood above him but did not speak. Linwood Toomey took a rag from his back pocket and rubbed his hands and wrists. Lanny wondered if they weren't there at all, were nothing but some imagining the hurting caused.

"My leg's broke," Lanny said, figuring if they spoke back they must be real.

"I reckon it is," Linwood Toomey said. "I reckon it's near about cut clear off."

The younger man spoke. "What we going to do?"

Linwood Toomey did not answer the question, but eased himself onto the ground beside the boy. They were almost eye level now.

"Who's your people?"

"My daddy's James Burgess. My momma was Ruthie Candler before she got married."

Linwood Toomey smiled.

"I know who your daddy is. Me and him used to drink some together, but that was back when he was sowing his wild oats. I'm still sowing mine, but I switched from oats. Found something that pays more."

Linwood Toomey stuffed the rag in his back pocket.

"You found it too."

"I reckon I need me a doctor," Lanny said. He was feeling better now, knowing Linwood Toomey was there beside him. His leg didn't hurt nearly as much now as it had before, and he told himself he could probably walk on it if he had to once Linwood Toomey got the trap off.

"What we going to do?" the son said again.

The older man looked up.

"We're going to do what needs to be done."

Linwood Toomey looked back at Lanny. He spoke slowly and his voice was soft.

"Coming back up here a second time took some guts, son. Even if I'd have figured out you was the one done it I'd have let it go, just for the feistiness of your doing such a thing. But coming back up here a third time was downright foolish, and greedy. You're old enough to know better."

"I'm sorry," Lanny said.

Linwood Toomey reached out his hand and gently brushed some of the dirt off Lanny's face.

"I know you are, son."

Lanny liked the way Linwood Toomey spoke. The words were soothing, like rain on a tin roof. He was forgetting something, something important he needed to tell Linwood Toomey. Then he remembered.

"I reckon we best get on to the doctor, Mr. Toomey."

"There's no rush, son," Linwood Toomey said. "The doctor won't do nothing but finish cutting that lower leg off. We got to harvest these plants first. What if we was to take you down to the hospital and the law started wondering why we'd set a bear trap. They might figure there's something up here we wanted to keep folks from poking around and finding."

Linwood Toomey's words had started to blur and swirl in Lanny's mind. They were hard to hold in place long enough to make sense. But what he did understand was that Linwood Toomey's words weren't said in a smartass way like Leonard Hamby's or Lanny's teachers or spoken like he was still a child the way his parents did. Lanny wanted to explain to Linwood Toomey how much he appreciated that, but to do so would mean having several sentences of words to pull apart from one another, and right now that was just too many. He tried to think of a small string of words he might untangle.

Linwood Toomey took a flat glass bottle from his back pocket and uncapped it.

"Here, son," he said, holding the bottle to Lanny's lips.

Lanny gagged slightly but kept most of the whiskey down. He tried to remember what had brought him this far up the creek. Linwood Toomey pressed the bottle to his lips again.

"Take another big swallow," he said. "It'll cut the pain while you're waiting."

Lanny did as he was told and felt the whiskey spread down into his belly. It felt warm and soothing, like an extra quilt on a cold night. Lanny thought of something he could say in just a few words.

"You reckon you could get that trap off my foot?"

"Sure," Linwood Toomey said. He slid over a few feet to reach the trap, then looked up at his son.

"Step on that lever, Hubert, and I'll get his leg out."

The pain rose up Lanny's leg again but it seemed less a part of him now. It seemed to him Linwood Toomey's words had soothed the bad hurting away.

"That's got it," Linwood Toomey said.

"Now what?" the son said.

"Go call Edgar and tell him we'll be bringing the plants sooner than we thought," Linwood Toomey said. "Bring back them machetes and we'll get this done."

The younger man walked toward the house.

"The whiskey help that leg some?" Linwood Toomey asked.

"Yes, sir," Lanny mumbled, his eyes now closed. Even though Linwood Toomey was beside him, the man seemed to be drifting away along with the pain.

Linwood Toomey said something else, but each word was like a balloon slipped free from his grasp. Then there was silence except for the gurgle of the creek, and he remembered it was the speckled trout that had brought him here. He thought of how you could not see the orange fins and red flank spots but only the dark backs in the rippling water, and how it was only when they lay gasping on the green bank moss that you realized how bright and pretty they were.

Panama

Suzanne Kingsbury

anama, 1986. Panama before the invasion. Panama with moist heat and women in bars giving the American Army hand jobs beneath unlit tables holding bottles of whiskey and packs of cigarettes and a lady's used-up lipstick tube.

August storms rage off the beaten Caribbean coasts and the soldiers dress in white *Miami Vice* suits and take taxicabs into the city. You can rent a hotel room with TV and room service and hot water for twenty American dollars a night. There you share eight balls with a General's wife, have her until you are spent, and in the morning drag yourself to base to do calisthenics with three hundred other American men between the ages of 17 and 30 with crew cuts and jungle fatigues and weapons at their shoulders and black boots on their feet and name tags on their shirts' left-hand corners and set jaws and no smiles and bodies firm and muscles obedient.

A black Sergeant heads the platoon and calls you Flames. He says, Get your goddamn hair cut, Flames, or I'll waste your ass. You ever had your ass wasted by a poor boy from Alabama who made his way to Sergeant not for nothing?

In 102-degree heat you shake your head and say, No, Sarge. Beyond you is the jungle where you simulate war and where you sneak smokes behind banana trees and eat dehydrated meals out of brown plastic pouches.

They take you to the Costa Rica highlands to teach you warfare. You carry an M16 with a grenade launcher across your body and follow the hand signals of squad leaders and sleep on the brown earth with your rucksack beneath you and the dome of star and sky above you.

Near dawn you are tear-gassed until you choke and your eyes spit teary fire and you hold your nose and roll on the ground away from the invisible, poison, which leaks through your skin and enters your breath as air.

You are a redheaded high school drop-out turned paratrooper from Bristol, Tennessee. You are an Irish Catholic turned Baptist from when your mother found the Lord.

Before you entered the Army you read great novels like *Black Beauty* and *Treasure Island* while heat blasted out a vent in your room in February. You masturbated for the first time just five years ago in a North Carolina wood in October when your father left you alone to try to push the deer westward. Your hot, young sperm spurted like nippled milk onto the wet, colored leaves of autumn. Your rifle lay just an arm's length away.

On Sundays you attended church with your mother where you sang songs with the other Baptists. You loved your mother's wide girth and large bosom, fell asleep to the way she rocked you back and forth when you had the winter flu, your arms around her warm, soft belly. You hugged her as if you were an infant though you were old enough to get a learner's permit and to know how to love a woman and shoot a pistol. You ran cross-country track for your high school and rode a dirt bike in the muddied course behind your house and boxed at the neighborhood ring and listened to the Beatles' White Album in your room with a girl with sandy brown hair and full lips and green eyes. You kissed her until your groin ached and pulsed, but that is all you did.

Then you saw a film in school about how the Army wanted you and you caught glimpses of men parachuting out of planes and your parents got divorced and your father loved drink and another woman.

One day in late April, your drafting teacher told you if you had to daydream instead of paying attention, you should walk out the school doors forever. Quite suddenly you joined the Army, existing on the hot training bases of Fort Benning for eight weeks and then finding yourself in a southern, Spanish-speaking country learning to defend the nation, which birthed you.

In Panama you do not think of your past life. It is as if that world were someone else's and the memories enter only the black hollows of your mind when you are in bars in Panama City where the lights are dim and the women are dark and eyeshadowed. Their tight jeans show the pleats of their femininity and the roundness of their bottoms. Thewhiskey slips easily down your throat and you get fat lips and swollen eye-lids and cut hands and cracked jaws and busted ribs from bar room brawls when soldiers from the U.S. military butt the bottoms of full beer bottles against

Panamanian men's foreheads. These American boys haul the men over their shoulders, throw them across tables and left hook their cheeks and headlock their necks in the crooks of their elbows.

The girls scream and the bartenders blow whistles and the crooked cops come with batons and pistols and sharp Spanish words.

You disperse to back alleys and parking lots and roads crowded with streetlamps and people and litter. You lick blood from your mouth and feel the tender bruises on your face and talk with your friends in clipped, happy tunes about the battle and how you won by a landslide and did you see that dude's right eye and I think I broke his arm and that guy in the corner next to the cigarette machine might be dead or else in for a long black sleep.

The night is bold in its heat and the sky is clear and the base waits with whores at the front gate eager to be signed in and to love who might be there with the folds of their womanhood flung open and their eyes wide to the ceiling and to you, on top of them, pumping and sweating for sweet mercy.

Back in your hometown, your father throws pints of whiskey down his throat, hunts deer in any season and saves his money for a 1986 Heritage Softail Harley-Davidson, which he buys straight off the floor in Nashville. On Father's Day he rides up the interstate in a studded half-helmet to the Laconia bike rally where he tells cops to fuck off during a riot in which two of his buddies are killed. You called these men uncle. One was Stitch Herald, your best cousin's father. Your dad gets his teeth caved in by a billy club at this riot. You hear of this in letters from your mother.

While you are in Panama, you do not write your father a single letter. You drive around the country in a flat green deuce and a half that has your name and rank on the side of it. You drive through the northern Panamanian countryside and jerk off at the sight of the girls on the side of the road in bright cotton cloths that cling to their bodies. They are laughing and they carry straw baskets in their arms and babies and bread. Their hair is brown and long down their backs, and their skin is so smooth it makes you think about the wild, silky loveliness inside of them. They wave to you. They do not know yet to despise Americans, they do not know yet to hate.

Twelve months into your stay there, you fall in love with one of them. She has high cheekbones and eyes like onyx stones and straight, white teeth and an easy smile. She lives in a small hut with a dirt floor and has seven brothers and a sister and a mother who speaks no English.

Her father yells and drink cervezas, too many, and she speaks to you soft, when she speaks, her English thick with Spanish. Her smell is sweet and reminds you of something in childhood. You damn near kill yourself trying to put your finger on it, but you cannot recall what it might be. At night when you close your eyes you remember that smell. It eases you to sleep. When you are with her, she loves you warm with noises so low and tender you run your finger down her face in the dark to see that she isn't crying. She is not.

During days on base you learn when, how and in what situation you are to use your weapon.

One evening during firing practice, thirteen men are lined up in fox-holes thirty meters from the target and directly behind them in a second row, thirteen other men lie in prone position with their weapons cocked. From the command tower a voice booms over the loudspeaker shouting, Ready on left, ready on right, all clear.

The day is dusking, the sun sliding down the sky in strips of magenta and purple and fierce gold, making long, slender shadows before you while you stand on the sidelines with your hands on your hips and a mortar tube beside you.

Next to you boys your age just like you stand also in green fatigues, watching the shooting men and the targets and the sky's darkening and lis-tening to the loudspeaker saying for the men in the front row to fire at will.

As if in slow motion, you see the silhouette of one body from the second row come up simultaneously with the first row. This soldier rises with his M16 locked and loaded and his eye on the sight and the man directly in front of him lies down in a heap like laundry, with three jerks of his body and blood spurting from him.

The cry of the unmeaning murderer lifts up the dayless sky. A mad rush of a helicopter comes with its buttressing sound like an M60 firing. The great gaffs of its wind billow hair and shirt and pant legs and grass.

In the mess hall at dinner you find out it was Jorge Guevero, a Puerto Rican man, who did not know English very well. He fired from the second row and killed Patrick Kelly, a white boy from Philadelphia.

Jorge did not understand that it was the front men who were to shoot, he thought it was an order for the second row to fire, and he killed the man dead at fifty-foot range in less than one second.

You will never see Jorge again. You look for him at mess hall and card table and morning exercise and shower. He is not spoken of. His ready laugh and his bright, flowery civilian shirts and his curly black and oiled hair, will be lost to Panama and to you and to the American Army, forever.

You go on leave, home for Christmas, where it is cold. Crusty brown snow covers the ground. For the eighteen days you are there, you are not able to get yourself warm.

Your grandmother wipes her eyes with her handkerchief when she sees you. She gives you homemade, crocheted pictures with Home Sweet Home on them in green and white, and she gives you a box of food to bring back containing Jiffy peanut butter and Lipton's chicken and rice soup and Jolly Green Giant green beans and corn in cans that tastes like baby food. She kisses your cheeks and holds your face and says your name and hugs you so hard the breath comes out of you.

You sleep on your mother's couch with drool dripping from your lips and when you are awake, you watch reruns of Westerns and Elvis movies.

Your father gives you a twenty when you go to see him on Christmas Eve. He is watching *It's a Wonderful Life* with a Scotch between his thighs and a beer in his hand and a cigarette wasting itself in the glass ashtray next to him.

Thanks Pop, you say.

He barely looks at you. His eyes are watery and his mouth is wet and all his body is loose and forgetful with drink.

Finally, you say, Well, see you later, and you go home to put on your suit for Christmas Eve service at the Baptist church so you can see someone, your mother, happy for an hour.

On the deserted red-eye flight home you enter a Panamanian girl beneath the thin blanket with the airline's name stamped on it. Your legs hit the seat belts and the armrests and the tray table on the seat in front of you.

When you come back to base, the boys in the battalion who went on leave look clean-shaven and less tired and there is a bounce to their steps. Their eyes shine and they say to you, Hey Flames! How the fuck are ya? They talk about their mother's home cooking and their high school girl-friends' tight pussies and how really stoked they are not to be home in the goddamn boring town of so-and-so.

You go to the girl you left behind. You do not tell her about your grandmother or your father or midnight service or the girl on the plane because she looks too beautiful and you want to hold her. Her hair smells of oranges. You want to lose yourself in the softness of her skin, in that scent you cannot name.

But her eyes are downcast and sad, and she says to you, I have something to tell you.

You have met her outside a bar in Panama City where a band is playing American music. They sing, *If You Think I'm Sexy and You Want My Body* with a Spanish accent.

She tells you she did not want to say this to you, but she must now that she has seen you. She crosses herself as they do in church, and then she says, I was pregnant, and I aborted.

When she says it, you do not let yourself comprehend the words. Instead you hear her accent. You think before Christmas you would not have heard her accent, but now you hear it clear. It is as if you had started all over in Panama again, with an accent sounding like that. Her hands clasp one another as if in prayer, and she looks up to you with her mouth quivering. Then you hear what she has just said. You go to her and hold her, and hate yourself for hoping no one from the base walks by. You do not understand how you could be hard for her at a time like this, and you hope she does not feel it.

You say, Why? Why did you do it while I was gone? It seems unfair to you, and you want to know how she could go and do this while you were watching reruns from your mother's couch, how she could go on without you.

She says, Because I could not tell you. You would not have wanted me. You would have thought I was trying to trick you.

You tell her you wouldn't have thought such a thing. You say you are horrified she would believe something like that. You stroke her silky hair and say, We could have gotten married, you could have come back home with me. We could have lived at the base together.

But she shakes her head and says, You wouldn't have. Now that it is over you say that but, no. She says the word no again and again like a cadence. Your neck goes wet with her tears. You say, It's okay, shh, it's all right. This you think you must have learned long ago because it comes out naturally now, from deep inside the recesses of where your first memories are. Behind the black of your closed lids, with her heart beating against your chest and her small fingers clutching the sides of your shirt, something bright and flicking comes like a struck match, split second in the jungle. You are not sure, but you think it is relief.

The next day you are sent to the Major's office because your hair isn't in regulation. It is too long, should be shaven on the sides and leveled at the top.

He calls you Private. You call him Sir. You call him Sir over and over even while you are saying no. You call him Sir when you rip your beret in front of him and tell him you will never wear your hair like a goddamn Nazi. You answer, Yes, Sir! when he says you are a no good Irish pussy-licker bitch and to get out of his office before he puts his boot in the crack of your ass.

Later, you sit on your bed sweating under your groin and armpits. Even the tops of your hands sweat, and your teeth chatter, and you think you might mess your pants. You don't know what could have come over you to speak to him like that, and you wonder again and again who you are without the Army. You think of home and the thought makes bile rise in your throat and you think, What next?

Then, like magic, they transfer you to another base fourteen miles out from the first base with a whole new crew of men and new generals' wives to make love to, and their battalion won't care about the length of your hair.

You still see the girl but now only privately in hotel rooms in the afternoon and in restaurants tucked into the walls of Panama City, in small cafés and on cloistered beaches. You touch her without so much desire as tenderness. You hold her but you do not make love to her and sometimes she cries in your arms at the loss of the life in her womb and speaks soft Spanish words you believe to be religious.

A new Battalion Commander comes to base. You enter the concrete lecture hall for the first meeting with him, your boots stamping in time with the 300 other soldiers who are part of the headquarters, alpha, bravo, charlie and delta companies in the 187th battalion on a day when the sun is kicking your ass, it is a hot, blazing piece of blinding fire, it is an open, burning wound in the sky lying heavy on your chest, taking your breath away and pulling the sweat from your pores in fountains down your belly and back and thigh, making your body slippery like the finest Chinese silk from the market in the inners of Panama City next to where the shoeshine boy slicks your leathers for a dime.

In this heat the new Commander speaks to you in motivational tones about why you are here and what great service you are giving your country and how you are doing what must be done to preserve democracy in the great United States of America.

His head is waxed bald and shines pink in the overhead lights. He is grim-faced and square-shouldered and speaks in a voice as if God had entered his body and were using the microphone to give his message. He says he has been in every conflict since the Vietnam War and would be proud to bring you and your men into battle. He tells you Mr. President Ronald Reagan is a great man and has picked the country up and given it the strength and power to eliminate communism and charge democracy forward into the next century.

You know back home Reagan is smiling and waving and forgetting. He is the same president who has said the U.S. can win a limited nuclear war and you understand, somewhere in the marrow of who you are, this cannot be true. The booming voice of the man before you speaks of possible dissension in the hot country that holds you, this country where you have loved a woman who has lost your child, and which has allowed you to smoke its cigarettes, drink its whiskey, swim in its ocean, tear up its jungles with gunfire, and grow hate like a sore and bulging muscle.

You stand from your seat and make your body flat against the chairs in the row in front of you so you can exit. Your Sergeant leans over with his fierce eyes and his urgent voice and whispers, Where are you going, Private? What in hell do you think you're doing?

You say, I'm not listening to any bullshit about an invasion. This sir doesn't know a bull crack from his own crack, and I'm not taking it.

Your Sergeant points to your empty seat and says, Sit down or else you won't be able to sit down once I get through with you.

You sit, not because of your Sergeant's threat, but because you know you are a hypocrite, that the same Army you wish to walk away from is making it possible for you to be here, in this country in Central America, where the cocaine is cheap and the women's thighs fall apart to your American maleness, your food is paid for, and your laundry is done. The United States government is making your life easy while pumping up the military as if it were a twelve-gauge shotgun ready for the aggressive and hostile cry of an arriving enemy.

It is your birthday and you wish for the girl to celebrate with you. You want her to dance with you and drink with you, her dark, beautiful body alongside yours.

You ask her to come to a bar on the west side of the canal where the lights are colored and twirling and cutting up the floor with silver diamond-shaped halos.

She arrives, wearing a white linen dress passed down from a neighbor's daughter, and she holds your hand. The men are drunk and the women are laughing and she dances beside you with her body pressed to yours and her lips grazing your ear.

You hold her waist and the men from the base look on and smile and nod and pat your back. She is happy for the first time in months. She drinks glasses of beer and you see her smoke a cigarette. She sits tight beside you, smiling, with her hands in your lap, tapping her fingers to the music.

Just before midnight, hours ahead of when you intend to be home, you bring her outside and put her in a blue taxicab. She has her father's orders to be home early, and you do not want her to be in trouble on account of you.

You tell the taxi driver where she is to go. A card encased in plastic on the dash says: Carlos Juevo, Taxi Cab Driver.

You pay him in advance and he looks you in the eye and says to you that he will drive carefully. Don't worry mister. You kiss her mouth and ask her, Are you all right?

The color is high on her cheeks and her eyes are heavy lidded and she nods her head yes.

When they drive away you note the number on the license plate and then you walk back in the bar with its pounding bass and easy women.

Carlos Juevo will rape the girl that night in the backseat of his taxicab, her legs spread to his insistent knees, his hot breath on her neck, her cries muted and futile, the liquid from his penis splattering onto the ripped vinyl and glistening the rugged floor.

Meanwhile the meter ticks and the moon shades itself behind gloomy clouds and for one moment the world outside goes silent.

She tells you this two days later in her dirt yard where chickens squabble and steal corn from one another with their eager beaks. She tells you with spilled words and unnatural jerks of her body and vacant eyes. It seems a Lucifer has come to inhabit her frame. You believe perhaps one has.

You search for his taxicab for days and one evening you find him at a corner bar off of J Street drinking a can of beer. You do not make yourself known to him but you begin to follow him. His face is the first thing you think of when you wake up at dawn and it is the last thing you remember before you fall to sleep at night. Every free moment you have is spent rehearsing this man's life: where he goes and when he does it, and what routes he takes home and with each new moment you hate more the vein and water and flesh and bone which make him man. You have learned a culture of violence through basic training and simulated war exercises and know the ways and workings of weapons and now you will use it to put your mind at ease.

One day at dawn, in front of the house you now know to be his, you watch from a broken hedge as he parks his car in a small alley. The day is perfectly still with no dogs barking nor early morning chatter nor the sound of any doors opening or planes' engines overhead. You sidle up to the window of his car where he sits with an unlit cigarette in his mouth and an almost struck match in his hand.

You say, Excuse me, sir.

He turns to look at you. You slide a newly bought .22 caliber pistol from the inside of your denim shirt and shoot the man at point blank range in the forehead.

Blood spurts before you in thick, membered globs and covers the inside of his vehicle. His body shudders violently and twitches and trembles. His hands and legs and arms quake in a way you have not seen limbs nor parts of body shake before.

You do not shoot again.

He falls sideways onto his passenger's seat, his eyes staring like unseeing stones at nothing at all.

You back away, fast, without running, without looking back.

Your world goes into a deaf man's vertigo. You do not remember the walk home, the throwing of the weapon into a brown river in back of the neighborhood where he once lived. That river feeds the canal that flows into the huge expanse of ocean spanning the entire eastern side of Panama.

You do not remember how you made it to her house that afternoon. You will always remember how her face looked when you told her. It does not register relief but a shocked visage of terror. Her eyes do not see you but through you, her body rigid as one's is in death. She says for you to go away and not come back. When you try to go to her, she kicks at you and screams. From a side street, one hundred yards away, her brother sees her flailing limbs and hears her cries. He runs to her and takes her away by the waist and shakes his fist at you and says words in Spanish you have never heard before.

The police somehow and for some reason hide the killing of this man and the media does not speak of it and hard as you look for news of Carlos Juevo's death, none arrives.

A cold numbness overtakes you. You are able to think of nothing save his murdered body and the look of the girl when you told her what you had done. The images of this man and the girl you love come to you intermingled during shower and mess hall and morning march and guard duty. Their faces reveal themselves in the expressions of your fellow soldiers, on the dusty streets of the countryside, and in the swish of palm leaves rubbing together like fans of canvas.

At night the dreaming images of him and of her rise up to you and you wake to the hushed, breathing battalion, your body a pool of sweat, your heart beating hard against your chest.

You do not go to her house again. Instead you send messages there and letters by postal service. You hear nothing from her. Through the streets of Panama City, you strain your eyes to look for her. She does not appear.

Finally she writes you a letter. She says she loves you but she cannot see you anymore. In her curved script she tells you that you both have secrets to behold and they are not for the telling and each should be alone in his silence.

You understand she is lost to you. The pain rises in your chest so your breathing is labored. You sit on the side of your bed with your head in your hands for hours and tell yourself what you must do to survive. You are a master now at discipline and you must train yourself not to think of her or of him or of anything. You speak to yourself of justice and fairness and good and evil, and then you speak to yourself of nothing at all. You get up and walk out your door. The soldiered battalion waits for you.

Through your days you do again what you did before. You drink whiskey and run like hell and fight when there is need to, you go to bed with whores and shoot your weapon and eat your food packs and sleep on the hard ground and wake to the light of day and curse yourself the thoughts and images and memories which wish to plague you.

This next December you will not go on leave. You are twenty days short of going home and Christmas finds you sitting on a deserted beach with a soldier from the Midwest. The sun is hot and the sand is white and the water is green. There is no one on the beach except the two of you. Your bodies are tight and muscled. Your instincts for fight and survival are like an animal's. You know how to follow orders and handle loaded artillery and jump out of planes with a parachute and gear in the middle of the night over the ocean. You know how to exist on no sleep and endure heat and yell to your drill Sergeant Yes sir! in unison with three-hundred other men.

You sit and watch the water arrive and recede and this boy admits to you he misses home. He describes the silvered green in the flat expanse of cornfields behind his house in Iowa and the breaded smellof his mother's kitchen. He remembers aloud swimming in copper creeks in summer. As he talks, you close your eyes and think of the green beans from your grandmother and the twenty from your father, of the base with its scrubbed linoleum floors smelling of ammonia. You realize you are not sure where your home is.

You allow yourself to think of the girl. You try to remember the feel of her hair and the smell of her skin. That scent. Though you concentrate until black spots show like pinpoints on the golden of your lids, you cannot remember it. You open your eyes to the boy beside you, drawing circles in the sand with a broken branch. You want to ask him about the scent of her, but it is something you do not know how to speak of, so you say nothing.

You and this boy strip naked. He is crying silent tears that slip down his cheeks as if he did not realize they were there. You have not seen a man cry before and you try not to look at him, though something in you wants to go to him as you did to the girl when she was so sad.

The two of you swim in the ocean, the kiwi-colored water running through your cut hair like a heavy liquid wind. Even under water the boy looks lonesome, and you find yourself reaching to touch his hip bone. The instant your callused fingers graze his smooth, unclad skin, a panic washes over you. The boy's flesh is as any others. It is the flesh of the general's wife you made love to. It is the girl on the plane you entered last Christmas, the made-up whores at the gates of the battalion, your grand-mother crying into your neck, your mother rocking you when you were a small boy, and it is the girl you loved and lost. This boy's flesh is also that of the man's, broken apart before you in a car at dawn.

You realize you can no longer love someone as you once did. You cannot submerge yourself without guilt in the warmth of someone else's arms. You will never be drowned in another, devoid of appetite. Because you cannot do this, rage has become you, ruinous and hungry.

Your limbs go limp with what you know to be fear, ascending like a gull in the body without room for flight. A lithe, skilled swimmer only moments before, now your arms flail frantically, and you swallow salty gulps of sea water.

You crawl to shore on your knees and tuck your head into your body, rocking back and forth on the scalding sand. Vaguely you hear the desperatesound of the boy beside you asking, Are you all right, should I get help? The ringing in your ears is louder than his voice. The hot welt of tears is relentless and your breath swells with weeping. You cry into your belly, which in the dark of your womb-like position is frightening to you, as if it were not your body at all but a black hole, empty as a waiting tomb.

Beneath you sand blares in fierce reflection, beside you waves slap and recede in repetition, behind you land rises in curved grandeur, and above you the unrelenting sun shines, religious in its omnipresence.

You dress while he stands watching. Your civilian clothes are heaped on your boots and they are hot and sweatridden and grimy. Your boots are Army issue jungle boots of black leather and canvas and you tie up the laces without looking at the boy. You turn and stare at his barefeet and tell him, If you follow me I will beat you until you can't speak and I will leave you here for the buzzards.

You walk down the beach. It curves inland at a rock formation and you enter a small path into the jungle. The air is fetid and hot and tricolored birds call to one another at the sound of your footsteps, and you walk deeper. The sun filters in patterns between the gridwork foliage above you and dragonflies mate in the air and cutter ants make rivers of moving objects at your feet and you continue.

You walk until dark falls and then you find a village in a clearing of mahogany and laurel trees where dwellings made of straw and mud gather together in a circle around a small courtyard.

The inhabitants are sitting around a fire and the smell of meat rises to greet you. They look stunned to see you, their slanted eyes widen and the girls touch their hair and the men's brows furrow. One girl of unde-termined grade-school age walks forward and takes your hand.

You find yourself sitting on a rotted log at the edge of the fire being fed by women dressed in shawls and patched dresses and bare feet. The men offer you seco, which travels hot down your throat and makes the world around you swim in green night-darkened majesty.

That night you lie on cloth bedding in a strange hut. The noises of the jungle filter through the open air windows and sound like people talking and faucets dripping and music.

You close your eyes and remember the Lt. Colonel telling you of the man from Florida, who walked off a field exercise in Costa Rica, took his clothes from his body while he went, one armhole at a time. One pant leg. Naked and AWOL. He disappeared through the sallow dawn heat into the jungle, never to return.

A Best Seller's Pursuit of Technology
Or, How My State-of-the-Art Printer Almost Ended My Publishing Career...

W. E. B. Griffin

A photograph survives of the Christmas when I got my first typewriter. A bourgeois mob scene, in emulation—conscious or otherwise—of the photos of the royal family. My father's parents, sitting down, surrounded by the four sons and their wives, the maiden aunts, and the grown cousins. And down in front, two adorable blond-haired boys in sailor suits, one six, the other five.

On the male faces is evidence that they had already sipped deeply at the wassail cup, and on the female faces, disapproval, anger, and strained smiles.

The six-year-old was me. I had been on my good behavior for what seemed an eternity, the reward for which was supposed to be a typewriter. God only knows why I wanted one, but it was important to me. What I took from the box looked like a typewriter. But then I saw that the keys were phony, printed on tin—clearly not state-of-the-art. To make the infernal device operate, it would be necessary to turn a wheel until the desired letter appeared at an arrow, and then press the arrow. Only then would a character appear on paper.

"Aren't you going to thank Aunt Elsie for the typewriter?"

"No."

"What?"

"It's not a typewriter. It's a piece of $%^#."

Absolute silence, followed by The Court talking all at once.

"Where did you learn that word?"

"Who has she been permitting that child to associate with?"

"It's not at all funny, Dad. I don't know what's the matter with you."

"Billy said a dirty word. Billy is a bad boy!"

This last from Cousin Bozo, whereupon I threw the typewriter at him. There was a little blood, and a lot of parental screaming. They took the typewriter away from me and gave it to Bozo to teach me a lesson.

I got my first real typewriter three years later. It was a portable and came in a genuine simulated leather carrying case. When I opened the case, I found real keys, a red-and-black ribbon, and a pamphlet entitled *Touch Typing Made Easy*.

With my index finger I typed out my name, in both big and little letters, and then again in red. Who needed *Touch Typing Made Easy*?

By the time I got to high school, I could type forty-five words a minute on the portable. That was my sole intellectual accomplishment. I was having trouble with everything else, and especially with English. My teacher suspected I was retarded. Not only did the difference between a verb and a noun completely elude me, but I was absolutely unable to diagram a four-word sentence.

I desperately needed an A, and thought I saw a sure way to get one: the announced objective of Typing I was to teach its students to type fifteen words per minute.

Smugly, I sat down at a shiny new Royal office machine, prepared to dazzle one and all with my blazing forty-five words per minute. When I looked at the keys, they were all blank.

My mother had great difficulty in understanding how I could flunk typing. "Why, you've been burning up your own typewriter since you were a little boy!"

My high school career ended with me knowing no more about how to diagram a sentence or how to type without looking at the keys than I had known when I began.

I was seventeen when I bought my first typewriter with my own money. It was a second-hand Hermes Baby, and when I saw it in a shop window on the Place de l'Opéra, in Paris, I knew I absolutely had to have it. I bought it on the spot, even though that meant abandoning my purpose for being on the Place de l'Opéra in the first place. The U.S. Army had taken great pains to warn me that wicked ladies hung around the Place de l'Opéra just waiting for a chance to drag innocent young American soldiers into whiskey-soaked immorality.

The Baby was that beautiful. It was about three inches thick and a masterpiece of Swiss workmanship. It was unbelievably light. And it was rugged.

I had it with me in Korea, where I was an Army combat correspondent. It survived The Punchbowl and Heartbreak Ridge. But in the Iron Triangle, Sergeant Jack Miller drove over it with his Jeep. I sent it to my wife at the time, who was in Vienna, Austria, and she had the Swiss repair it.

I still have it. The only trouble I've had with it since was when my son said he wanted to borrow it and take it to school. His mother heard me tell him I'd break both his arms if he so much as opened it up, and for some reason this upset her.

I wrote my first novel on the typewriter from my office at Fort Rucker, Alabama. I took it home at night and brought it back in the morning. If they'd caught me at it, I was going to tell them I was testing security, but they never did, which obviously proves something about the Hire-A-Cops they had at the gates.

When I sold my first novel, I kept $79.99 out of my $1,000 advance and threw the rest as a bone to the creditors howling at my door. Sears sold me a rebuilt Underwood for the $79.99. It came with a free book, *EZ Touch Typing*, but by then of course it was too late for that.

The distinguished writer William Bradford Huie, who had been my childhood hero (and still is, come to think of it), was kind enough to let a one-novel novelist come to see him. His Hartselle, Alabama, office was equipped with not one but three IBM typewriters. He was working on *The Americanization of Emily* at the time, and had parts of it in each of the typewriters.

With the check for my fourth novel, I bought my first new typewriter. If an IBM was good enough for William Bradford Huie, it was good enough for me. It was delivered by four men who obviously bought their clothes the same place FBI agents do and wanted to see with their own eyes somebody who wanted a flaming red typewriter.

Somewhere between fifty and sixty books came out of that machine. I typed a draft, then my wife at the time typed a new copy of that, then I worked on it, and she typed the final version. Our kids grew up thinking there was another holiday, like Labor Day, and that it came whenever Mommy staggered out of the office crying, "Thank God that's over!"

I still have the red IBM, but it is in honorable retirement, put to pasture by something called a word processor.

The first one of these I ever saw was in novelist and fire-breather Ed Corley's house in Pass Christian, Mississippi. The author of *Air Force One* and a dozen other heavy novels had in his youth been with a carnival, where he learned to blow flames ten feet. He used to come to see us, but after he nearly incinerated a waitress in a local watering hole, he was given to understand by the authorities that even my small Alabama town has its limits, and we had to go see him.

Ed's word processor was a Lanier No Problem. There was a typewriter keyboard, but no carriage. The carriage had been converted to what looked like a small black-and-white television.

When one typed, the words appeared on the television screen. It was possible to make corrections and shift paragraphs around and do whatever was necessary to make it perfect. Then it could be "memorized," and, once memorized, it could be called forth on demand in perpetuity. It would also drive the keyless typewriter to type, at a rate of a hundred words per minute.

The key to all this wizardry, Ed explained, was the Random Access Memory, or RAM, and his miracle of modern technology had 64,000 bytes in its RAM, about enough for a long chapter. There were also little floppy plastic disks in square plastic covers, cleverly dubbed "floppy disks." Each of these could be stuck into a slot, where the No Problem would cause it to store 360,000 bytes or, as the cognoscenti put it, "360K." They cost only $5.95 each.

"Zut alors!" Ed cried. "Could anything be easier and more simple? If you had one, your wife would never have to type a manuscript again!"

On our way home, my then wife, who normally would rather leap into the clutches of the Devil and all his wicked works than buy anything on an E Z Payment Plan, suddenly asked, "Do you think we could get one of those things on the Never-Never?"

We bought a No Problem on the Never-Never, and she never typed a manuscript again. The No Problem was everything it was supposed to be, and a lot of books went through it.

Then Lanier came up with a new machine. It was a state-of-the-art word processor and would do, they said, everything the No Problem would do, but faster and better.

It was an awesome machine. It had 256K RAM (I now knew what that meant) and for only the price of a small cabin cruiser extra it could be equipped with a "hard disk." A hard disk, I was told, could store 10 million bytes—several large book manuscripts at once.

Unfortunately, the machine became a New Problem Lanier, so smart that it really thought for itself. One of the things it decided on its own was that it was a qualified literary critic. It automatically went through my immortal prose in the RAM and erased the material that did not meet its high literary standards. A word here, a sentence there, some-times a whole chapter.

It could not be reasoned with, although a platoon of Lanier engineers really gave it the old school try. Finally, a van arrived in the dark of night, and Lanier hauled it off for "study." I hope they ran over it with the van.

To replace it, the friendly folks at Baldwin Computer & Software sold me a computer. It came with a dot matrix printer.

Shortly afterward, the editor-in-chief of G. P. Putnam's Sons, my publisher, a gentleman of impeccable erudition and deep cultural attain-ments, called.

"What did you type this [expletive deleted] manuscript with?" he said. "A [expletive deleted] rake?"

"My dear fellow, it's clear that you are unfamiliar with the latest trend in technology. The manuscript was printed on a dot matrix printer."

"Matrix, schmatrix," he cleverly replied. "All I know is I can't read it. You send me another stack of [expletive deleted] chicken tracks like this—a word of friendly advice I'm sure you will accept in the spirit with which it is offered—and you'll be back to parking cars for a [expletive deleted] living."

I moved quickly to better printer technology.

And on to better computers, because I could not resist the siren call of "faster, faster, more features."

The first of these, I remember, was a Sperry. My reasoning here was that if Sperry could manufacture navigation equipment guiding airplanes across continents and oceans, they ought to be able to handle something like a computer with ease.

And it was an amazing device.

Its 5-inch floppy disks stored 1.2 million bytes per floppy, which I now knew was properly referred to as 1.2 meg (for megabytes). The hard disk had a capacity of more than 40 meg (40 million bytes). The Perfect Writer version 2.2 word processing software could in six seconds flat check the spelling of a page of my semi-immortal prose against the Random House Dictionary. In another sixty seconds it could analyze my literary efforts and compare, say, two pages thereof against accepted academic standards and announce with great certainty that its 4,134 characters, 950 words, 30 paragraphs, and 94 sentences indicated that ninth-graders should have no trouble understanding it, according to the Modified Automated Readability Index. According to the Modified Coleman-Liau Formula, it was comprehensible to the average eighth-grader.

I was always personally prone to go along with the Coleman-Liau folks: you will recall that I flunked ninth-grade English.

All of that is now behind me, in what now seems like the dark ages of computer-assisted literary effort.

Much of this piece was written on what the techies at Hewlett-Packard assure me is the absolute state of the art in notebook computer technology.

And it is an amazing device. Its hard drive stores 50 gigabytes, which means there is plenty of room to hold the complete typescripts of all the books I ever wrote on a computer, starting with the Sperry and Perfect Writer 2.2, plus (and I find this really amazing) all the data necessary to keep the Internal Revenue Service off my back.

It came with the latest version of Mr. Bill Gates's Microsoft Word. And this is a truly impressive program. If I type "teh" or "sotp" when I meant to type "the" and "stop," the corrections are made automatically.

For a two-fingered typist such as myself, this is really helpful.

Also, when I am writing about characters with complicated names—for example, Karl-Heinz von und zu Dichterberger in my *Honor Bound* series of novels—I only have to type it correctly once, punch the appropriate keys, and thereafter by simply typing "khd" there it is: "Karl-Heinz von und zu Dichterberger" wherever and whenever I want it, perfectly spelled, capitalized, and hyphenated.

Word, of course, comes with a grammar-checking program that cleverly underlines my grammatical errors in color on the screen and even offers friendly suggestions. So far as I'm concerned the real proof of Mr. Gates's genius and compassion for this customer is that the program also comes with a control allowing one to turn the grammar checker off.

I'm an old man now, and the last thing I need is a machine telling me that I don't know any more about grammar and sentence structure than I did in the ninth grade.

I'm reasonably convinced that I now have the best "typewriter" known to man. But last night, surfing the net, I read about a new program that's supposed to be faster, faster and have more features than anything to date. I'm going to check into this, of course.

Escape by Zebra

Jack Pendarvis

You remember Tom Sawyer. Well, he's fat and forty now, rich, as you might expect, off his own cunning and other people's work—but he hasn't had an adventure in thirty years. Things are changing, though: On a routine business trip to Philadelphia from his South Carolina rice planta-tion, Tom and his private railroad car are waylaid by scoundrels and aban-doned on the tracks, where they are the cause of the wreck of a circus train. Who should save Tom from the wrath of the injured circus people but his long-lost brother Sid?

Though presumed a casualty of a certain War, the hellish atrocities of which a particular segment of the book-buying public simply adores to relive over hot cocoa and a muffin, Sid has in fact been capering about in a sideshow for fifteen years, since misplacing his bottom half under circumstances that he shall begin to relate forthwith.

A hippocampus grazed by a tree. Tom's mind gave it that name, for he had never seen a zebra. Burdened as he was by half-again another man, he mounted the creature as quickly as he could, grabbed its mane in both hands and dug into its flanks. It bleated mournfully, but it ran. Tom clung as tightly to its neck as Sid to his. Sid told Tom things in his ear, and Tom repeated them, soothing things Sid had learned from the trainer, magic words, and soon enough the animal was under control, outpacing the coterie of angry circus folk.

A good breeze cooled Tom's brow, chilled the sweat laid on him by exertion and fear.

"Look!" said Sid.

The great golden bulbs of a lion's eyes rose from the dark weeds at the edge of the forest. He did not give chase, but returned his attention to the dark shape—what?—lying in the briars at his feet.

"We'll catch the train yet!" Tom shouted. He guided the zebra along the track.

"Thank God you came to take me from that place!" Sid said. "It's often I've thought of Aunt Polly and Mary and you."

"Aunt Polly's poor heart give out when you was presumed dead, I am grieved to tell you. Now as for Cousin Mary, you might have found her well cared for in my own household—"

"I rejoice to hear it!"

"—up until last winter, when she passed from this life on account of a spinsterhood-related malady."

"Dear Mary and Aunt Polly, merciful Jesus! I am amazed at all of this, though it is much as I had feared. Why God should have chosen to call them, however, when He might have just as easy had an errant wagon wheel sever your spine or an escaped bedlamite take a goodly chunk out of you with a hatchet..."

"And I reckon He could've had me et alive by dogs. Don't forget that!"

"Er, I mean only to express my wonderment that you still look the same, Tom, your good fortune, that is, that time has not seen fit to push you through its mighty sausage-grinder as it has apparently taken the trouble to do for the rest of us. Must be the first occasion that you ain't had the bulk of the attention! Though I will say it is more wonderful still to see that beardless boy's face on a figure of such...heft. Jesus, how long has it been?"

"Fifteen years, I think! But how is it that you're alive? How came you to this—situation?"

"You mean to ask how I came to be what they call a human oddity."

"What? Why such a thing had never occurred to me. But as long as you bring it up, there is nothing behind us and nothing before—I can hardly think of a better time for a story."

"Well, you recall I marched off with General Price's Missouri State Guard like the Good Dutiful Boy I always was, and I don't know who looked sadder to see me go, Aunt Polly or dear Mary. Myself, I reckon I was more excited than anything else, but I would have been as sad as they, could I have but seen just a little ways into the future! And I don't even mean the usual slaughter.

"I'm thinking just of mites and bedbugs, I'm thinking of the bad drinking water that give me the fiercest burning runs you'd ever want to wish on your worst enemy, black burning water shooting out my bung-hole, I was almost twenty-two, by far the old man of the bunch, and I'm thinking of fourteen-year-old boys hunching in the bushes, shitting their breeches, brown recluse spiders biting their peckers, and that was our first night out I mean to tell you, and I could yet see Mary and Aunt Polly and all them wailing women in calico disappearing in the kicked-up dust.

"'Course, you weren't there with Mary and them to see me off, you were too busy doing your secret work, your secret plans for Dixie, much more important than a raggedy-ass foot soldier, and I admired you, Tom, I did, even though I reckon, looking back, your secret plans didn't work none too well, but it did seem a poorly thing to me that you couldn't take two minutes to see me off, and I admit I got to thinking bad things about you.

"I got to thinking maybe you were doing what you always done, getting somebody else to whitewash the fence, and maybe I grew a mite revengeful, but don't worry about that right now, big brother. Let's speak of cheerier things, like the Battle of Pea Ridge.

"Oh, that was an ecumenical battle, Tom! We had us the queer creatures known as Texans, we had us the Cajuns, we had us the Cherokee and Choctaw and Creek and God-knows-what-all straight up out of the Indian Territory, and never did I feel so at peace with the brotherhood of mankind as when we was all killing Yankees together!

"It looked marvelous good for us, not least because Pap was amongst us always, taking his licks just so in the thick of the battle. General Price, you know—all us boys called him Pap on account of his obliging nature—he made us feel that we couldn't lose, so bravely he fought, such encouraging words he shouted as to what the other regiments were up to.

"We held the ridge, Tom! We held Pea Ridge, the very spot they named the battle for! They shot us for it must have been an hour, and we shot them right back. There was dirty snow full of twigs and everybody fell down and died in it.

"Well, sir, we skirmished on and off till we were losing the light. The snow turned blue, and the blood turned black on the snow. And old Pap had had just about enough. He shouts out the order: 'Press on, boys! Press on! We'll push them blue devils off the field or die in the attempt, but by God we'll press on!' I was there to hear him! And he sent a scrawny messenger boy, must have been all of twelve years old, to run and tell all the other commanders of all the other regiments to press on. Press on! A full assault! And did that Missouri farm lad with an Adam's apple big as a persimmon, did he take off like ball lightning? No sir, he stands there like he has three silver legs and says 'Have ye any terbacky, General?'

"Well Pap lays his hand on the hilt of his sword, and by God I'm thinking I'm about to witness a summary execution. But Pap, he just laughs. He laughs and he says 'Who has a plug of weed for this brave boy?' Your foolish brother pipes up with 'I have about half a plug, sir.'

"Here's Pap: 'Well, give it him, soldier, so's we can get this damned battle won.'

"And that's how Sid Sawyer done his part for the glorious cause. Off goes Little Johnny Peckerwood to spread the word with the last of my flat 'backer and a little raw bacon I was saving besides.

"Anyhow, Pap's orders. We come at them blue bastards from every side, Cherokee screaming like panthers, longhaired Louisiana swamp devils hollering in their mother tongue, and here comes the contingent of freckly-faced Missouri shitkickers down the ridge, pushing them back with bombshell and musket ball, back till they was lost to sight in the thick white trees of the woods.

"You was always famous for your fancies, Tom. Now try to fancy. We been running, shooting, sneaking, and getting shot at for a day and a half and now it's time to take a rest, of sorts. There's a big long line of us camped out in the open field on the edge of the forest, hunkering down for the night, and I'm starving and dead tired but it ain't no easy trick to sleep when the woods are most likely crawling with Yankees just waiting for you to go to sleep, and besides, every time I'd shut my eyes I'd see your face all shiny like a moon and you were grinning or laughing, only it weren't as if you were mocking me, no, you were plumb encouraging, benevolent, but somehow it still rankled me, now wasn't that unsporting?

"Because I knowed you was at your big oak desk with the lion's-claw feet, drawing up billets of sale and writing up great sheaves of contracts and incidentally hefting great pursefuls of money, all for the love of Dixie, Tom, and I should've been thanking you for it.

"But here I am straying again from my tale.

"Let's skip ahead to first light. There's a mist on the ground and a mist at the edge of the timber. And as the sun began to burn the white mist off the white woods, somebody give a shout and we could see the shadowy Yankees standing there in a row and more Yankees coming from the woods quiet as you please, and soon they formed a battery and stood stock still and us just standing there watching them, and then we all just stood there watching each other. And just when we had stood there so long that I thought I might start laughing, and then a Yank might start laughing, and then we all might laugh a while and turn around and go our separate ways—that's when the firing commenced.

"First it was just the small arms, crack crack crack, they give us a little, we give them a little back. Then we perceived they were moving in on our right, they weren't near so scattered nor so scared as we had thought, and I reckon there was a little touch of panic. A young officer on horseback, a Confederate officer, mind you, was aiming at an advancing Yank when his pony misstepped and he hit me full in both legs. Well, sir, down I tumbled and though I didn't know it at the time the shot had knocked one of my family jewels clean off in the bargain.

"My young officer must have been a fine cadet, for he reacted with cool compassion. In no time my wounds were tightly bound in strips of good gray flannel torn from his own splendid uniform, and he had tossed me upon the back of his horse where we rode much as you and I are riding this zebra tonight, with the exceptions that I had legs and he was shooting Yankee foot soldiers easy as woodchucks and I was full of the applejack he had poured down my throat from a silver flask. Now I cannot explain one thing except to simply say it. My spirit soon rose out of my flesh and I looked down on the scene as a hawk might look down on it.

"I saw the dots of gray and blue scurrying like warring ants, the horses like grasshoppers, puffs of cannon smoke that looked as harmless as dandelion tufts scattering in the wind, I saw the dark tops of trees and more and more tiny little Yankees running out from the cover of the woods.

"It struck me strong, Tom, while I was floating up there, what a marvel it was that I was in the heat of the action, good clean Sid, while dirty old Tom, the rascal, was most likely in a silk robe sipping gunpowder tea over the sunlit morning paper.

"But not such a marvel, really. While I was eating all my greens and picking tomatoes in the garden and chopping wood and shelling peas and all my childish chores I was preparing for battle, Tom, I was training up my heart in the ways of fortitude only I didn't exactly know it—I was readying myself for the hard work of adventure, laying a foundation as the Good Book says, while you were building your house on sand.

"All your playacting at pirates and robbers, your mock adventures, they served no purpose but to divorce you bit by bit from the world of human people till you were not fit for any job, save perhaps that of going on the stage, or concerning yourself, as you did, with the getting of money, which is more of an idea than an object, represented on earth by a gold coin, yes, but not contained in so gross a thing—no, more a Prince of the Air, and thus a fitting companion to an airy boy like yourself."

"And all this you reasoned out while suspended in the ether over the battlefield," Tom said.

Sid laughed wildly.

"That and more, dear brother! More than you might believe! Until I was pulled rapidly backward as if through a black vortex in the sky and the roaring blackness overcame me, and for a long time I could neither see nor hear nor entertain any thought, good nor ill, for my heart had stopped beating and I was dead."

Just an Old Cur

Michael Morris

I n the ten months after Darlene found the fake gold earring in Baker's truck, she managed to permanently lose a bottle of hairspray and a vanity table full of expensive makeup. She also lost her husband. What she found was twenty-three pounds and the ability to make herself disappear.

On that day, D-Day her daughter, Donna Gayle, called it, Darlene stood in front of the pickup, clutching the cheap earring. Against a backdrop of dead love bugs plastered to the hood of Baker's truck, she held the heart-shaped jewelry out for inspection. Maybe Donna Gayle had accidentally dropped it, Darlene thought. Or maybe it belonged to Mavis. Baker often asked the housekeeper to vacuum his truck. It had fallen off during a cleaning frenzy, Darlene concluded.

As Darlene twirled the earring between two fingers, her shoulders slumped. Donna Gayle would not be caught dead in something so tacky, and Mavis didn't take to any kind of jewelry, expensive or otherwise. In fact, Mavis would usually reprimand Donna Gayle for her flashy appearance and put a load of clothes in the washer all at the same time. When all her imaginings began to make Darlene's migraine act up, she promptly took the earring inside and hid it in the garbage. She buried the ugly thoughts right next to an empty can with flakes of tuna clinging to the metal.

And then the earring was forgotten. Just like the hair appointments, the Garden Club meetings and the weekly luncheons with her friends— the Montavio Mafia they called themselves. They all were forgotten, one by one, after Baker left his note. The note telling her that he was not happy and that in all his fifty-eight years he had never known anyone like Lisa Shelling. Lisa, the twenty-nine-year-old engineer Baker had met at one of his construction sites.

Two weeks after finding the earring Darlene arrived home in a good mood after spending the morning at Salon Two-Twenty-One. Good hair color had more than once made Darlene's day. She spotted the legal pad on the kitchen island and expected a note about an unplanned job and what time Baker would be home. But what she read there came to define misery for her. Baker's tiny, first-grader penmanship wrote away her life. And by the next week, the excuses for why Baker did not come home faded faster than her hair color.

Darlene washed her hair eight times in a row trying to fade the blond highlights. The vanity table covered with cosmetic bottles was the next attack. With one fast swipe of the arm, anti-aging creams and perfume tumbled into the black garbage bag. That night marked the first time Darlene slept curled up in the bedroom window seat.

Darlene flinched when the doorbell rang in the middle of the day. Mavis greeted someone at the door and Darlene sat on the edge of her powder-pink window seat straining to hear the voices downstairs. She pictured Mavis mumbling and wiping her broad brown hands on the dishtowel. She inched closer to the edge of the window seat and her heart began to thump harder. Was it that lawyer again? Darlene wondered. Mavis would put him off. Twice before, Mavis had explained to him that Darlene was not up to visitors. When the man coughed to clear his voice and spoke, Darlene breathed again. Ernest Bennett. The man who had once inspired her with his Sunday morning messages, now coming to check on the lamb strayed from his flock.

When she heard the front door squeak and the car crank, Darlene focused once again on the oak trees outside her bedroom window. If the tail had not been wagging, Darlene might've missed her second visitor. A hound the color of rust was cautiously sniffing around the bed of petunias.

From the corner of her eye Darlene saw Mavis's wide hips blocking the bedroom door. "Looks like we have more company," Darlene said.

"No, the preacher done left."

"No, no," Darlene quickly said and pointed out the window. "Down there."

The mama dog's nipples sagged inches above the concrete surrounding the swimming pool. Sharp ribs lined her sides, spotted with patches of missing fur.

"Old mangy cur," Mavis said.

"Well, she looks like a hound to me," Darlene said and tucked a wiry strand of gray hair behind her ear.

Mavis leaned her head back and howled. "Child, don't you know a cur dog? That dog ain't no account for nothing but eating a biscuit. And she ain't worth that." Mavis studied Darlene's face, began to laugh, threw her hands up in the air and then abruptly disappeared down the stairs. Darlene was thankful that her laughing grew dimmer with each step Mavis made towards the kitchen, but even the slam of the skillet hitting the stove couldn't drown her out completely. The laughter pounded down hard on Darlene's head until finally she stuck her fingers deep inside her ears.

After lunch Mavis loaded the plates into the dishwasher and kept one eye on Darlene. "I don't see no sense wasting good chicken on some old mangy cur," Mavis said.

"Now, Mavis." Darlene placed sliced-up chicken on a paper towel. "For just as you've done to the least of these…"

"Oh, no, you don't." Mavis stood as tall as the live oaks that guarded the backyard. "Don't you go using the words of sweet Jesus to justify feeding some old dog."

Darlene pretended not to hear her and pulled the patio door open. A breeze stirred in the oak leaves outside. The dog bowed her head and moved backwards away from the patio. With the nervousness of a flower girl, Darlene carried the paper towel filled with chicken. She hadn't made it three steps before the cur ran off in a blur of rust. The flash was so sudden that it reminded Darlene of the way the greyhounds came out of the starting gates. The same greyhounds Baker used to place bets on every Saturday down at the racetrack, and once he'd asked her to go. Her mama's words of caution rang out in her mind. *You can get a man to take the trash out, but you will never take the trash out of a trashy man.* She quickly set the paper towel down and rushed back inside.

Mavis was sitting at the kitchen table shelling peas, just like she did every Tuesday after a trip to the Farmer's Market. The opening piano notes from "The Young And The Restless" chimed from the television at the spot where Baker's Mr. Coffee coffeemaker had once been. Darlene wiped her hands on the sides of her jeans and tried to make it to the sink without being noticed. "Oh, I see you done give up," Mavis said without looking away from the TV screen. "Mind yourself or you'll have your blue jeans greasier than the inside of my skillet."

Once Mavis had left for the day, Darlene ventured back outside to prune the roses. She hadn't made it to the third bush when the snap of a twig caused her to stop. The rust-colored dog stepped forward and then slunk sideways. The body twitched, and the head bobbed. When Darlene's eyes locked on the deep-set sockets, she caught her breath. Though the dog's brown eyes seemed empty and removed from anything with a heartbeat, there was a softness there, an unspeakable softness. Words from the poem she had recited decades ago during the Miss Watermelon beauty pageant floated across her mind. That night she had stood right in front of the oblong silver microphone dressed in the evening gown her mama had picked out and told the town that the eyes were windows to the soul.

The dog turned her head like she wanted to run but only crossed her paws in some sort of fear dance. A faint whimper finally emerged. A plea for help, Darlene decided. She took one step forward. The dog skirted to the left and tucked her head again. Before Darlene managed another step, the portable phone began to ring. The piercing sound made them jump at the same time. Before the third ring, the hound tucked her scrawny tail and fled for a thicket of pines.

When she answered the phone, Darlene tried her best to sound aggravated. The voice on the other end of the phone was Baker's and was far raspier than usual. Darlene remembered the high pollen count reported by the weatherman before the afternoon stories. Baker always was the world's worst for allergies. Some things you just know about a person after living with him for thirty-one years, Darlene decided.

"Has Sam called you about signing the papers?"

Darlene started to hang up. She had missed the last appointment with their lawyer and wasn't sure what was included in the divorce papers.

"Darlene, you still there?"

She rolled her eyes and flung the pruning scissors deep into the grass. "Yes."

"Now you need to go on and sign the papers. You're getting half the business, most of the land, the house. I'm doing right by you. It's for your own good to go on and sign."

"Well, I just...I forgot to meet with Sam is all. You know, I just—"

"Listen. We're meeting this Friday. Two o'clock in Sam's office. I want you to write this down and put it up on the refrigerator. You hear now, two o'clock."

Darlene held the receiver away from her ear, and liked the way Baker's voice suddenly became weak and hard to understand. Being talked to like a child was almost worse than being left for a younger woman.

"Can't we just sign the papers out here at the house?" Darlene repeated the question twice before she got a response. Baker exhaled long and deep. She pictured the phone receiver rubbing up against the goatee he now sported.

"Hell no, you can't sign them at the house. Now, it won't kill you to crank up that car and drive to town."

"For your beeswax the car is driven," Darlene said. She stopped short of saying that Mavis drove the car regularly up to Winn-Dixie and to pay bills.

"Just write it down. Friday at two o'clock." Before he hung up, Darlene heard a voice in the background say something about a bid for a hospital.

She focused back on the dots of red in the rose garden. Scissors clipped dead ends in a fast forward motion. With each swipe, Darlene's anger grew. He wouldn't have a pot to piss in if it wasn't for me, she thought and wiped a trail of sweat from her forehead. She could recite her early sacrifices as easily as the beauty pageant poem. Quitting classes at North Florida Junior College to work for Baker's start-up business as the bookkeeper, secretary, blueprint copier, and occasional tool dispenser.

As the jobs and business grew, their lifestyle had become fancier. She could walk around her home and rattle off tokens from the construction firm's prosperity. The swimming pool, thanks to an elementary school in Valdosta. The Mercedes, thanks to a new strip mall in Tallahassee. But the two-carat diamond pendant tucked inside the drawer of her jewelry box was thanks to Baker's new love interest. A gift she gave to herself the week after Baker left his note.

You shouldn't study on the past, Mavis repeatedly warned her. But as usual the reprimand came to mind too late. The July sun poured down on her hair. She touched the side of her head and wondered if she had that disease that Lucinda Jacob's grandson had. The one that causes water to gather on the brain. Dots of pink and red began to swing carelessly in circles before her eyes. When she stumbled backwards, she snatched a rose bloom free from its branch.

She landed on the ground with crushed petals in her palm, listening to a roar like locusts. Sound of orchestrated chaos. Her buttocks ached from the fall and she was certain a bruise would appear. A bruise only she would see. The tears fell easily. Stop doing this, Darlene ordered. As usual, the tears paid no mind. They continued to warm her face, and she pulled her knees close to her chest until she gave in and tucked her head.

She first thought the brush against her hand, hard as leather that had been left out in the rain, was Mavis's touch. Darlene flinched and looked up in time to see the rust-colored dog shyly step away. The eyes still held fear, but when Darlene reached out, the tail began to wag. The dog skidded sideways and whined before seeming to gather its courage and lurch forward to lick Darlene's hand a second time.

"Do you know how much Winn-Dixie charges for a dog collar and leash?" Mavis asked with the grocery list in hand. "I can get one after my doctor's appointment. Get it down at Wal-Mart for half the price."

Darlene licked vanilla icing from the spoon and smiled. "No, go ahead and get it this morning, Mavis."

Mavis shook her head and mumbled in a war-like chant. Darlene watched her drive away in the Mercedes and persuaded herself not to let Mavis know that the dog collar and leash weren't really for Sashi, Donna Gayle's prized poodle. Nor would she tell Mavis that she had enticed Cupcake, the secret name she had given the rust-colored hound, into eating icing from her hand. Certainly she would not let Mavis know that at night she had been letting Cupcake sleep in the laundry room. A secret Darlene kept covered by vacuuming dog hair from the room each morning. No, Darlene thought, Mavis had no use for a cur down on her luck.

The phone rang. Baker's raspy voice clipped Darlene's nerves right down to the quick. "You remember about our meeting this afternoon? Now I bet you didn't even write it down like I told—"

"I said I'd be there," Darlene snapped and slammed down the receiver.

Mavis returned with bags of groceries and hadn't yet finished unpacking them when Darlene began rounding her up. "You go on now. That doctor might see you early if you're there waiting," Darlene said guiding Mavis's elbow to the door.

By the eleventh attempt with the leash, Cupcake no longer dug her toe-nails into the grass. She trotted alongside Darlene and hung her long tongue out. "Attagirl," Darlene said.

Cupcake waited in the laundry room while Darlene put on the pantsuit that Donna Gayle had bought for her months ago. Clipping price tags from the outfit, Darlene felt silly for not wearing the designer label in the first place. The new Reeboks, bought when Donna Gayle was still trying to talk her into taking that yoga class, now sat on top of the dresser like special-occasion slippers. Darlene even brushed her hair and for old times' sake pinched her cheeks.

During the walk to town Cupcake tried to dance a jig, jumping and twirling whenever a car or semi-truck passed along the highway. Darlene kept a tight rein. The spotless shoes pounded through the ditch of beggar weeds. She pictured Donna Gayle smiling in approval of the lime-green pantsuit, but then suddenly biting her lip as she looked down at the shiny white tennis shoes. The rose tucked behind Darlene's ear would send Donna Gayle over the edge.

By the time Darlene and Cupcake reached their destination, Montavio, Florida, was bustling with lunchtime traffic. Cupcake trotted with her nipples dangling inches above the hot sidewalk and water dripping from her tongue. Cars drove slowly past while people craned their necks and little children pressed their faces against the windows. Red, white, and blue plastic flags left over from the Fourth of July celebration hung from the streetlights.

Walking towards the courthouse, Darlene thought of the year she accepted Baker's marriage proposal. The same year she was named Watermelon Queen and rode, waving to the crowd from the green-and-red float made of papier-mâché, around Montavio's town circle. Darlene gave in to the impulse and cupped her hand and waved at the cars backed up along Main Street. Sadie Simpson, Miss Congeniality in the 1967 Miss Watermelon pageant and founder of the Montavio Mafia, rolled down her car window. "Darlene, honey, is anything the matter?" Darlene blew Sadie a kiss and marched past the bakery window lined with giggling children and on towards Frankie's Flower Shop. Frankie Putnall stood at the glass door staring with his mouth wide open. Darlene remembered how his bony hand had brushed against her breast as he presented a bouquet of red roses for her to cradle on parade day. "Pretty roses for a pretty young lady," he had whispered in a spray of musty breath. Before Cupcake could drag her away, Darlene halfway turned and shot the old man a bird.

She continued the pilgrimage past the courthouse circle filled with admiring spectators and on towards the historic district. A shingle reading Dirksen and Pratt, Attorneys at Law, dangled from a black lamppost in front of the old home that had been remodeled into an office. Walking up the porch steps she saw Baker through the tall window. His chin dropped as he rubbed the gray goatee. Cupcake jumped the steps two at a time and wagged her tail when she entered the air-conditioned building.

Darlene spotted her reflection in the mirror over the fireplace. Her hair was matted and rings of underarm sweat had spread into giant circles. She smiled as widely as she had the day she was named Watermelon Queen and rubbed her escort's head. "Cupcake, these gentlemen would like to wish us Happy Independence Day." Darlene's calf brushed against the dog's shoulder, and, patting her hair, she added, "And now where's that proclamation for me to sign?"

GATLINBURG

Silas House

T he two brothers start out by driving around town, taking long sips from a pint of bourbon. They talk and savor the warmth of the Jim Beam, which spreads out through their bodies like blood, smoking cigarettes and rolling down the windows just enough for the cold air to sizzle in and the smoke to be sucked out.

They finish the pint before they have even reached the edge of town and decide to drive on down to the state line for more. The heater blows hot air and the radio gives a constant stream of songs, made incoherent by static. Dusk has turned the world into a gray, shadowy place. Yesterday's snow lies in glowing stripes against the darkening mountainsides. There is black ice in places along the highway, and each time they feel their tires slide beneath them they laugh and slap the dashboard.

"Let's take the old road," Justin says. He is still young enough to enjoy driving. He keeps one hand on the steering wheel and the other on the ball of the gearshift, which vibrates softly with the whine of the motor. "We got four-wheel drive if the roads get too bad."

"I ain't got nothing to do," Bradley says, and shrugs. He is two years older than Justin but he looks much more. His face tells his story. Each line is a battle, a struggle. Justin looks at his brother for a long moment and realizes that Bradley's troubles are on constant display. Even his eyes seem black and reflect something lost, staring inward instead of out. He had always been the sort of person who hushed a room when he entered, his presence was so big and beautiful. When they were younger, Justin had envied him, but had never been jealous. He had been too proud of his brother for that. But now, Bradley hushes the room with his hardness, his face square in every way, and even when he smiles his forehead is scowling. Now women look at him because they want to know more. They long to smooth the hard edges of his face and learn what it is he keeps silent.

Just over the Tennessee border there stands a small cinder-block building with a large sign reading First Chance Package Store. Neon signs crowd the windows. Over the door hangs a plastic banner: *Celebrate the Bicentennial with Pabst Blue Ribbon,* and Justin thinks that the year won't really feel like the bicentennial until summer. One corner of the banner flaps in the wind rushing down the valley. Icicles cling to the overhang, and perfectly round drops have frozen at their tips.

"Come in with me," Justin says. He leaves the truck running and jumps out. Immediately his words appear on the air in plumes of white. "Been forever since we was in here together."

The walls of the liquor store are stacked high and close with cases of beer on two sides and a wall of glass-doored refrigerators on another. Two space heaters struggle to warm the place. One of them is off balance, causing the elements to pop in an off-key rhythm, as if drops of water were being thrown onto them. A radio near the cash register is playing Donna Fargo. Justin sings along quietly to "I'm the Happiest Girl in the Whole USA." The cashier is watching a basketball game on a little black-and-white television with the volume turned down. He hasn't looked up since they entered. Usually there is a big crew of men in here, leaning on the counter and drinking 24-ounce cans of Budweiser, tilting the pinball machine, or looking through the copies of *Hustler* sold from behind the counter. But the snow has driven them all away.

"Just get a fifth of Beam and let's get out of here," Bradley says. "That ought to do us a while."

Justin picks up a half-gallon instead and grins maniacally, widening his eyes. "How about a handle instead? It's on me," he says, and takes two quarts of Pepsi from the cooler. "We don't get together much."

Bradley looks at a stand of peanuts and Nabs and shuffles his feet while Justin pays the man, who keeps cutting his eyes back to the silent game.

"Colder'n hell in here," Bradley says and shoves his hands into his coat pockets. "Don't see how you stand it."

The cashier takes the bills from Justin. A waterlogged toothpick is clenched between his teeth. His hands look as if he has just changed the oil in his car. "Got to do what you got to do," he says after a long time.

When they go back outside, it has begun to snow again. The snow drifts down like chunks of sky, impossibly slow. The sky is a living thing now, low and black. Dusk still stands gray and solid, taking its time to stretch out. The mountains seem more rounded in the oncoming darkness. Justin has lived in the hills all his life and knows that once night comes they will seem bigger and closer.

The cab of the truck is so hot it's smothering. They sit there for a moment, the engine idling softly—a comforting sound, like their mother humming when she washes the dishes. Justin turns off the wipers so they can watch the snowflakes land on the windshield, then unscrews the bourbon and takes a bubbling pull. He wipes his mouth on his sleeve and lets out an exaggerated "ahh."

"Let's not go home," he says, and hands the heavy bottle to Bradley by the handle. "Let's keep right on driving."

"It's bound to get bad, Justin," Bradley says, but there is a smile in his voice. "We keep driving on these old curvy-ass roads and we'll land in the ditch. A four-by-four ain't worth nothing on ice."

Justin eyes the road as if looking for a sign as to what he should do. Pulling out of the parking lot to the right will take them back home. To the left are curves in the road and things they do not know by heart. He has not done anything on the spur of the moment in years, since before Bradley left for the war, since before Justin married Emma. Everything was different before the wedding, before the war.

"Let's just drive on down to Gatlinburg. We'll get us a room and set up all night, drinking." He taps the gas, but still does not put the truck into gear. The snow begins to fall faster, coming down the valley like white quilts flapping on a clothesline.

"You're the one with a woman at home," Bradley says.

"That don't mean I have to set at the house every minute of the day."

"You ought not worry a pregnant woman, though, buddy," Bradley says. "That's red."

Justin pictures Emma. She is lying on her side on the bed, a feather pillow tucked between her legs as she studies the baby-naming book she got at the Health Department. She smells like coconut lotion, which she rubs on every night when she gets out of the tub. Her hair is wet and combed straight back. He likes to put his face against her belly this time of night, when juices swirl and dance within. Her skin is stretched so tight that it feels like a rubber ball when he runs his hand over her stomach, but is still soft against his face. Every night they sit up and she reads names out of the book to him, and sometimes they come up with names on their own. She wants to name the baby Harper if it is a girl, after this writer who wrote her favorite book, but he just laughs when she mentions that. She also has a book of poems by Robert Frost and she makes Justin get down to her belly and read from it just before they go to sleep. He feels stupid doing it, but he likes it, too. It makes him feel like a father. It seems like something a good daddy would do.

"One night away from me won't kill her," he says and watches the image of his wife dissolve on the windshield.

"Hell, I don't have nobody to answer to. I don't want you all getting into it over me, though."

"If she gets mad over me wanting to be with my brother one night, I don't need her no way." Justin waits to see approval on Bradley's face. He has always needed to be certain of it. "Come on, let's do it."

"Go on, then, but don't blame me when you get put in the dog-house."

Justin doesn't reply. The square muscle in his jaw flexes tightly but he puts the truck in gear. He pulls out onto the narrow highway and heads south. The big mountains have dashed any hope of picking up a radio station so he shoves in an eight-track tape of Creedence Clearwater Revival. They sing along loudly to "Lodi."

Justin wants to go to Gatlinburg, wants to tear down whatever has come between them. There is a barrier there, although he does not know what it is, nor did he notice it being built. Before, they were always closest when they were drinking. Sharing the half-gallon of whiskey might tear down a row or two of bricks.

When they were in high school, everyone called them "the twins." They didn't look anything alike, but they were always together. On the rare occasions when they went out alone, people seemed taken aback.

"Where's your shadow?" someone was sure to ask. They shared the same body language. They laughed identically, ran their hands back through their hair with the same deliberate motion. They hooked their thumbs in their belt loops and leaned against a wall and held their cigarettes the same way. As they walked down the road side by side, there were four legs in perfect stride, four arms that pushed in unison against the air with each step. They sounded so much alike on the phone that even their mother couldn't tell their voices apart.

But then Bradley went to Vietnam and Justin got married, and soon people stopped asking where the other was. The war and the wedding seemed to set them out on different roads, to walk them off to become different people. It seemed to Justin that in one year he lost his brother. What they had was back down that road and there was nothing for them up ahead.

Bradley was the last boy in Crow County to be drafted. The war ended six months after he arrived over there but as soon as he stepped off the train Justin knew, could see from where he stood on the platform that Bradley had been gone long enough. Bradley's face was different, and the way he held his body had changed. His eyes, once shiny and alive, were dull as the worst grade of coal. Justin stood there for a moment before going to meet his brother and thought: *He's become a man, and I haven't.* Bradley had been there, in Vietnam, in the war, on the battlefield. Justin had spent those weeks in front of the television, hearing what it was like from Walter Cronkite. His brother had been there and he had been in the living room.

"How long's it take to get to Gatlinburg from here, anyway?" Bradley says, when the song goes off. "I ain't been down there in ages."

"About an hour is all." Before Justin can say more another song comes on and they both begin to sing again. They know the words to every song on this CCR tape. They used to drive around like this every weekend, singing along with John Fogerty, hollering to people as they cruised Main Street and parked at the football field to lie on the hood of the car, their backs flat against the windshield. This same tape playing while they studied the stars or flirted with girls or got drunk.

Bradley is sitting with his arm extended out across the back of the seat, and each time they hit a bump or go around a curve, his thumb is a solid presence on Justin's arm. Justin likes having him so close. He loves how Bradley has done this without even thinking about it, how he has touched him without even being aware of it. Growing up they always slept in the same bed, and they would wake up with their arms intertwined. It was something Justin never even thought about until Bradley went off to war.

The snow shows no sign of letting up. They travel a while through small hills and rolling fields but eventually the mountains begin to rise high again. The night is incredibly black, so dark that it seems possible daylight may never emerge again. They do not meet many cars, and the houses along the road are dimly lit with no sign of people anywhere.

Just when Justin thinks that the world has ended, they enter Gatlinburg.

Gatlinburg is the kind of place where people go for three-day vacations and spend a whole year's savings. There are lots of cars and well-lit motels, close to the road. People walk the sidewalks with their shoulders made big and square by well-padded coats. Women hold onto men's arms and place their feet carefully on icy sidewalks as they peer into shop windows. The Christmas lights are still up, even though it is February, and they seem perfectly in place as the snow twirls down like confetti on a big city parade.

There are plenty of people here, but the snow has kept more from coming. This resort town is usually packed. But each motel bears a glowing red sign: Vacancy. They have arrived just in time, since Justin is beginning to feel a little drunk. He sees a motel called the Roaring Fork Inn and since the name appeals to him, he pulls the truck into its parking lot.

The heater in the motel room is running full-blast. The room is so hot that the air seems damp. Bradley rushes over to the sliding glass doors and shoves them open as if he cannot breathe. Cold air invades the room and snowflakes swirl down to melt on the yellow shag carpet as soon as they hit. Below the balcony rushes a wild creek that seems to steam over the frozen rocks. The sound of running water fills the room along with the chilling air.

On the balcony there is a half-foot of snow, but Bradley strides out onto it like a baron intent on looking out over his vast lands. He pulls off his coat and unlatches the top button of his jeans. He strips off his flannel shirt and throws it back into the room. He stands there in his T-shirt and Levi's, arms stretched wide. He leans his head back and catches some snowflakes on his tongue.

"Are you that drunk?" Justin asks, laughing.

"It feels good. I love the cold," Bradley says. "I used to love summertime, but since I went overseas I can't stand the heat."

Justin is busy setting up their drinks. He finds a couple of plastic cups in the bathroom and takes the bucket to fill it with ice. He pours a little pitcher full of water and sets this all up on the low dresser. He is still wearing his coat, which is the one he has to wear at work. On the left side of his chest there is a small oval patch: *Ashland Oil—Justin*. The slanted, cursive letters seem odd for a gas station uniform.

"Won't you pull that big coat off and stay a while?" Bradley says. He is leaning on the metal railing now, peering out at the town. "There's a creek."

"I hear it," Justin says. He has poured them each a drink and stands near the door holding them out as if he expects Bradley to take both. "Come in now, and let's get apeshit wild drunk."

Bradley is looking out at the line of cars that has formed on the road leading out of town. Their red taillights glow like a row of square eyes. The storm is brewing and people are leaving, afraid of being snowbound.

"I never could understand why people up home always come down here on vacation," Bradley says. "Live all their lives in the hills, and when they get time off from work, they head right back down into them. Don't make no sense."

"I guess it's the closest place to home that's worth going to," Justin says, and thinks about this more than he wants. He knows why people back home come to Gatlinburg—it is somewhere different from home that looks like home. There are mountains here, black and crooked, and they don't feel like strangers when they walk the streets. That's why everybody they know comes to Gatlinburg: they are sure it will not change them and that it will never change itself.

"Matter of fact, what're me and you doing here?" Bradley asks.

"We're here to drink this whiskey. Close that door now, I said. I've got us one poured," Justin says. He sits on the bed and bounces a little to test its firmness. "Anyhow, we'll have to be passed out to sleep on these hard-ass mattresses."

Bradley finally comes in, but he leaves the doors open. The room is getting cold now, but Justin doesn't say anything because he likes the sound of the creek too much. It reminds him of home. In the summer, he and Emma sleep with the windows open so they can hear Free Creek splashing by.

"You better be calling that little wife of yours and telling her where we at," Bradley says and flops onto the bed opposite Justin. The snowflakes in his hair haven't melted yet.

Justin lights a cigarette, taking his time in such a way to suggest that he is stalling. "Lines are down. Phone lines broke up on the mountain," he says. "That woman told me when I rented the room. She knocked four dollars off the bill, too."

Bradley takes a drink long enough to empty his cup. "It's wrong of you to worry her and her pregnant, now Justin. Maybe we ought to just head back out. They'll give our money back."

Justin laughs and starts to mix another drink. "Shit-fire, man, who are you—Daddy?"

"No," Bradley says in a voice that seems unnecessarily loud to Justin. Bradley looks into his cup, then speaks quietly. "I'll never be the man he is."

This is the kind of thing that Justin cannot understand about his brother. It worries him that Bradley can go from laughing and cutting up to funeral home serious in a heartbeat. There are times when he says things that end up sounding like they're remembered right out of that Robert Frost book Emma keeps on her nightstand. When this happens,

Justin feels like he doesn't know his brother at all.

Justin doesn't say anything, simply doesn't know how to respond to Bradley's feelings about their father. He has pulled the card table away from the door and placed it between the beds. He places his emptied cup in the middle of the table and pours an inch of liquor. He pulls a quarter from his pocket, bounces it on the table, and the coin leaps in a silver arc to land in the cup.

"Drink up," he says. "I told you, I intend to get you wild tonight."

If he focuses his blurred gaze on Bradley too long, the room will start spinning again, so Justin simply closes his eyes and doubles over in laughter. But then he feels like he can't keep his head from bobbing around on his shoulders when he is leaned over, so he rights himself. He is floating above the floor as he moves across the room to open the door and breathe in the cold air. Bradley leans back in his chair with a strange little grin on his face.

They have been talking and laughing about old times together. The drunken girl who told them she had always dreamed of having what she called a "men-ag-a-troy" with the two of them. Fights they were in at the old honky-tonk, parties they had down at the lake, the time they played chicken and the other racer slammed right into the mountain but crawled out of his totaled car without a scratch.

Justin watches the snow—it doesn't seem real to him—and wishes they had a radio. He likes to sing when he is drunk. The television is out, too. Justin hears the song of the creek and feels that this, along with the winter air, has momentarily cleared his head. He pulls the balcony door closed, and there in that silence filling the motel room is the echo of their own voices and their own memories, relived too many times now. Their laughter this night has been frequent, but has also sounded like the kind that is recorded to play during television shows.

Both of them are drunk and don't notice that the snow is a blinding wall now. It makes tiny wet sounds when it hits the glass doors and the single window.

Justin goes into the bathroom and sways to the toilet, spraying the floor and the side of the bathtub. He stares into the mirror, finds nothing in the eyes looking back at him, so he splashes two handfuls of cold water on his face. When he goes back into the room he falls onto the bed and props his chin up on one row of knuckles.

"Tell me what it was like over there," Justin says. The words escape his mouth like little birds that have been flapping against his teeth, trying to get out. They have never talked about the war before.

"Ain't nothing to tell," Bradley says. "Nothing worth telling."

"I know better than that. You was there, and I wasn't. So tell me." Justin can hear that his own speech is slurred.

"Thank God you wasn't."

"I wish to God I had been. You know what that feels like, to have people ask 'When was you overseas?' And I want to lie and say that I was but they already know, just by looking at me. I wasn't the brother that went. They say 'Bradley served, didn't he?'"

"So what. You're two years younger than me."

"But I was nineteen when the war ended. I should've went, too."

Bradley lights a cigarette, takes a drink then gets up and ambles over to the sliding doors and peers out as if there is something interesting to see. After a long while, "Well, you didn't have to go. And that's all there is to it."

"Tell me what it was like, Bradley," Justin says again. He nearly knocks over the table getting off the bed. He tries to catch a cup of whiskey but it falls over and splashes into the overflowing ashtray. It causes a black speckled stream to move in rivulets across the table where it slowly drips off the edge. Justin watches this with fascination for a moment before he walks over to stand very close to Bradley's back, so close he can see his breath moving against a loose fold of Bradley's T-shirt.

Bradley speaks quietly, choosing his words carefully. It is something that everyone has always respected about him. "Don't ask me about the war no more, Justin."

"Used to you told me everything."

"I don't know what to tell you it felt like, damnit. It's not something

I can explain to make you feel better about yourself."

"It was hard for me is all, knowing you was over there."

Bradley turned around but didn't look at Justin. Instead, he bowed his head like he was studying his own hands. "You don't know what hard is, man."

"I feel like you became a man and I didn't."

Bradley goes back to the bed and picks up the quarter. He runs his thumb over it as if it were a valuable thing. "That's stupid," he says. "A stupid thing to grieve over with all the real trouble in the world."

Justin pours himself a shot of bourbon and throws back his head. He looks at Bradley as if he expected his brother to say more, not even wiping away the whiskey, so that it shines on his lips.

Bradley shakes his head, exasperated. "You're the one married, ain't you?" he says. "Got a baby coming. Think about that."

Justin thinks of his wedding day. He got married while Bradley was over there. When he stood in front of the preacher and Emma said her vows, he was wondering where Bradley was, picturing him in the jungle. He imagined big leaves and rain that fell in straight silver lines.

"You don't know what it felt like," Justin says, watching the room shift and move. "That's all."

"We have that in common then. Because you sure as hell don't know what it felt like for me."

"But I'm your brother," Justin says.

"Ain't there something that you want just for yourself, that you don't want anybody else in the world to know?"

"I don't love her," Justin says, not knowing if this is the truth or not. For some reason this is what he wants to say.

"Don't love her?" Bradley says now, sounding just like their father.

Justin looks away to let know Bradley that he doesn't intend to say more about this. He doesn't say how sometimes he wishes that he lived with Bradley instead of Emma. She doesn't know him at all. Doesn't know what is on his mind just by the expression on his face. She hates it when he turns the radio on too loud; says she can't hear the words of the song for him singing along. She doesn't like to be snuggled up, can't stand his leg being thrown over hers at night. When she touches him, it feels like a thing she has thought over first. Her movements seem rehearsed to him. She cannot tolerate a silence to rise between them, and jabbers on about senseless things when one arrives. Sometimes her words are a blurred string of sounds to him; birdcall is often more coherent.

"I just can't stand that we're not close like we used to be," Justin says. "We go days without talking and you live just up the road."

"Shit, buddy. I'm up your house three times a week. I know Emma gets sick of looking at me."

"But it ain't the same. It's not like it used to be," Justin says, and all at once he thinks he might cry. He thinks if he does, though, he will feel cleaned out. He will be washing away something that he cannot find a source for or put a name to.

"We're not the same, Justin," Bradley says. "Look at you. Look at your life. Don't you think I'd give anything for that?"

"I miss the way it used to be. I miss how close we was." Justin knows that if he weren't drunk he would never ever admit this out loud.

"We don't have to go out partying every weekend and live right together to be close, man. You're my brother. No matter if I ever seen you again, you'd always be my best friend. That's the way kin is. Now come on, you're too drunk," he says, and his hand moves out to tap Justin lightly on the cheek. "This kind of talk ain't no fun."

"Yeah," Justin says, although he can't understand where this word has come from. His throat feels like it is closing up and might never release again. "Right."

"Everything changes, little man," Bradley says. He hasn't called Justin this since they were in high school. "That's what it's all about. Things change and you either accept them or they kill you. Knowing that's the only way I got by over there. So don't envy me for having been to war, Justin. Never."

Bradley sets his cup down in such a way that Justin knows the drinking is over. Bradley puts his hands atop his thighs in a finalizing gesture, an act that says he is done for the night.

Justin knows that Bradley is right, but this does little to ease the gnawing at the back of his skull, little to uncurl the fist in his belly. He remembers something his mother always used to say to them. They hardly ever fought once they were teenagers, but when they were small they used to argue over the possession of toys or whose turn it was to help their father with their chores. Often their rows would result in raised voices or an occasional punch to the mouth. When this happened, their mother would squat down right between them. Her skirt would hike up over her big knees, clad in skin-tone pantyhose. She took both of them by the hand and looked first into one's eyes, then the other's. "You all are brothers," she said. "Someday you will be all the other has." He can hear her saying this as if she is whispering in his ear. It is as plain to him as the sound of the helicopter on television, carrying the people out of harm's way, as plain as Emma singing "American Pie" in her slow, mournful way while she takes a bath.

When he thinks of Emma that way, sitting in the tub splashing water up on her swollen breasts while she sings, he feels tangled up inside. He pictures her standing up in the tub, her skin glistening as if oiled. Smiling at him, running her hands over her big belly. "It's our creation together," she said when she told him she was pregnant, and he had put his head on her shoulder and cried from happiness.

"Let's lay down then," Bradley says, and throws the covers back. He shoves a fist into the pillows and runs a hand over the cool sheets as if dusting away dirt.

Justin manages to get up and starts to take off his clothes. As he leans down to pull his pants off his ankles, he falls back onto the bed and sprawls flat. His arms are too heavy to lift. He has a sudden flash of Emma, frantically dialing the phone, calling everyone they know to see if anyone has seen the two brothers. But he's too drunk to take this thought anywhere.

Bradley laughs at him. "You got to take your shoes off first, dumbass." He unlaces Justin's work boots and lets them clomp onto the floor one at a time. He slides the Levi's off and leaves them in a heap beside the bed. He takes hold of Justin's legs and throws them up onto the bed, pulls the covers up to his neck.

"There you go." Bradley snatches off his socks and gets in bed with his brother. "Remember when we was in school, we'd set up all night long talking. We'd talk until we'd finally just fall asleep with words still in our mouths. Mommy'd bang on the wall and holler. Damn, we'd laugh and go on."

Justin snickers, struggling to stay awake. "Yes sir, we did." Even though his eyes are closed he can tell that Bradley has his arms behind his head. He imagines Bradley staring up at the gray shadows moving about the room's ceiling. The room turns round and round. He feels like the bed has levitated and floats above the floor, drifting so slowly that he has to concentrate to notice its movement.

They both lie on their backs and go to sleep. They do not dread tomorrow. They don't think of the snowstorm outside, pecking at the window like wet clots of sugar. Justin dreams of his child, curled up in Emma's womb. They sleep like dead men, their fingers barely touching.

When he wakes up at daylight, Justin imagines for a moment that no time has passed in fifteen years. He expects his mother to holler that breakfast is ready. There has been no war and no Emma and nothing except himself and his brother, asleep in the bed of their youth. Bradley's left elbow points at the ceiling, the back of his hand lying across his face. He always slept like that.

Justin moves to get out of the bed and sees the snow piled up against the glass. He feels the square weight of liquor sitting on his forehead. He smells the motel-room scent and remembers where he is and when it is. He becomes very still and listens. There is nothing but the sound of his brother breathing. A sound he knows by heart. Winter is a silent time, and he is in Gatlinburg, where things never change. He lets his body settle into complete rest, realizing that he has not been so still in ages. He lies there like that for what seems a long time until Bradley finally awakes.

ERNEST

Sidney Thompson

He spent the whole day cashing in his aluminum cans, all thirty-two bags. Two bags each trip on his bike. So he had money, and his bicycle of course, and now a knapsack of Army rations and his toothbrush. He had no intention of staying another night.

It was out of habit and fear that he opened his mother's door to check on her before leaving. He stood there a moment, listening for sleepy breathing, but he could hear nothing. He opened the door wider and walked into the room.

"That you, Carl?"

He paused, as if unsure of his name. "No, it's Ernest."

"Carl?"

"No, Ernest. Go back to sleep." He wished now he hadn't entered her room.

"Ernest?"

"Yes," he answered. "Go on back to sleep."

"Won't you sleep with me?" she asked.

"Not tonight." Ernest backed up, put his hand on the doorknob.

"Please," she said.

Ernest didn't know whether he should turn and run or stay one more night, or stay at least until she fell asleep again.

She giggled. "I promise I won't talk too much. I promise. I'll be real good."

Ernest relaxed his shoulders, giving up, and his knapsack slapped the floor. He stroked his beard. "Sure," he said, unzipping his pants.

"Oh, Carl," she said, "it is you."

"Just don't say nothing."

"I won't say nothing. I won't."

"Shut up, Lucille." He untied his boots and removed his pants. Then he removed his coat and unbuttoned his shirt and threw the shirt on the floor with the coat and pants.

"Carl," she said, "Carl, just tell me what to do, Carl."

Ernest rolled off one of his socks, which made the floor cold to his left foot.

"I've missed you, Carl." Her arms stretched toward him like the stove limbs of a dead animal.

Ernest climbed on the bed, and before he did anything else, he forced the sock into her mouth.

Should he tell her? Before she falls asleep, should he tell her he's leaving, that he has met someone, a little nigger girl named May May who is running away and that he is going with her? Would she understand? But she began to snore, so he eased himself out of bed and dressed.

When he closed her bedroom door, he could see May May's young complexion all about him in the house. He felt her warmth in the black air. And he was suddenly excited, not simply relieved, but excited about escaping the house of his mother. His mother was an idiot by birth, and by birth he was a mother himself.

He went into the kitchen and made a couple of government cheese sandwiches and sat at the small square table beside the window. The curtains, pulled aside, revealed a reflection of the room. He watched as he ate. When he finished the sandwiches, he lowered his head into the sink and drank from the faucet and wiped his beard on his sleeve. He gathered his knapsack on his shoulders, and from the coat rack beside the back door, he took down a green hunting cap, his father's old cap. Pulling it over his head, covering his ears with the flaps, Ernest thought of how Carl had looked when he wore this hat in the woods, with a shotgun across his shoulder. He closed the door behind him as he stepped outside into a cool early morning. The sun wouldn't be up for a couple of hours.

Clouds were moving quickly over the sky like curls of gray hair. There were no shadows, or only faint ones, and everything appeared to be coated with a hazy, almost speckled blackness. Ernest rode his bicycle along a trail of mud from the small wooden house, a leaning silhouette of a house bound by oaks and pines, to the highway, which was no more than a hundred feet away. But the mud was thick and deep, so he stood his weight on the pedals and thrust downward, spinning the wheels of his bicycle slowly but out of the yard. Past the figures of trees, those mangled hands that seemed to touch the low ceiling of sky, trying to clear it, Ernest, grunting, was soon enough on the highway riding toward the opposite side of Byhalia.

Their rendezvous was planned for daybreak. After her father left for work and while her mother still slept, May May would slip out of the trailer, cross their neighbor's cotton field and meet Ernest at the sweet gum tree. And then, off to Holly Springs, Oxford, maybe even as far as Jackson—wherever Ernest's bicycle would take them. All they knew was they were heading south, far away from Byhalia and Memphis, where May May's father worked pressing cardboard.

He pedaled at a slow steady pace, taking almost an hour to reach the dirt road that meandered from 78 into the black section of Byhalia. When he reached the tree and had pulled himself onto the low wide branch both Ernest and May May had often sat upon as they kissed and from which they spied the trailer and her parents and brothers and sisters, he relaxed, let his body melt along the limb's gentle curves, and closed his eyes.

It wasn't the roosters nearby but cars passing on the highway in the distance going to Memphis that woke Ernest just before sunrise. The hum reminded him of his old duties. He watched the cars and trucks pass and suddenly he saw a can fly out of a car. He was glad he was no longer a part of that world. He had vowed when he cashed in his cans the previous day he would never again pick up trash for money.

He looked over the cotton field at the trailer, shivered, and quickly pulled in his warmth, hugging himself. He thought of daybreak and how cold it was. Rubbing his arms, he watched the lighted window of the trailer and May May's father, who eclipsed the strength of the light when he passed in front of it. Now, with the sun climbing into the tree with Ernest, the cotton plants were becoming visible, and tiny cocoons of cloth that somehow remained attached to the dead plants surrendered themselves like flags, still refusing to give up the brittle stems but willing to wave, and by this they were now attached to the wind, being pulled and pulling.

A moment after the trailer's light went out, dust was being turned up on the road, then May May's father and his Fleetwood were out of sight. May May immediately came into view—a thin girl, but she appeared strong and savage as she ran through the cotton field carrying a load on her back and dragging an umbrella.

Ernest dropped from the limb. May May, breathing heavily, was smiling when she collapsed around Ernest. She tilted her face up and stretched her neck, so he bent down and kissed her. She opened her mouth, so he opened his.

"I'm so excited," she said. "We really gonna do it."

"Yep."

"We really doing it. We are." She grabbed his coat. "We are. I can't believe it."

"We better go."

"Yeah," she said, "let's get."

Ernest picked up his bike, and they walked to the road. He steadied the bike between his legs as May May positioned herself on the handlebars.

"What's that for?" He was pointing at the umbrella.

"Case it rains. We can't live like complete animals."

"Well, hang on," he said and pushed off. They wobbled at first and were slow until they reached the highway. There, along the shoulder, they headed southeast toward Holly Springs.

His legs were muscular from bicycling every day when gathering cans, but the extra weight of May May tired him. He'd been pedaling for nearly two hours. Ernest waited for the traffic to pass before braking and helping May May onto her feet. She held her buttocks as she and Ernest quickly stepped down the embankment and up the hill where they hid among the trees lining the highway.

Ernest fell to the ground on a sprinkling of pine needles. He laid his head on his knapsack, watching May May walk deeper into the woods and disappear behind the trunk of a pin oak.

"How much further you think it is, Ernest?"

"Don't know." He wiped the sweat from his eyes and beard. "I hope soon. I'm hungry."

"I never ate Army food before. Good, huh?"

"Good enough."

May May came out from behind the tree, zipping her pants. "Eat if you want," she said. "But I don't want nothing yet."

"We gotta wait," he said. "Can't eat till we get to Holly Springs, or our food'll never last." He reached his arm around May May as she sat beside him. He rested his hand on her bottom, lightly cupping it. She laid her head on his chest and touched the buttons of his jacket.

"Feels good to be out here, don't it?" he said with sudden enthusiasm. "Feels mighty good to be here in the outside, doing what we want. Not hearing garbage from Ma. On the Schwinn. Just me and you." Ernest sat up and held both her arms. "May May," he said, "let's have fun. God-damn, I'm horny!"

"Not now, Ernest. My butt hurts."

"You sure?" He raised his eyebrows and grinned.

She gently pushed him away, and Ernest returned his head to his knapsack.

"You think your momma'll come looking for us?"

"Shit!"

"What about my folks? They might be looking now. They might be out there right now. Maybe we should just travel at night from now on."

"Stop your worrying," he said. "Nobody gonna find us. Nobody even noticing us on that road."

"I can't go back." She rested her head on his chest. "Daddy'd kill me for running off. I just can't go back."

Ernest was looking up at the trees, the meshing of branches of different kinds of trees, at the bits of sky between them.

"Daddy wouldn't think twice about knocking me over. We gonna stick together though, ain't we? We gonna fight back. We fighting back."

"You know, May May," he said, "trees look sick when they don't have leaves."

"You ignoring me?"

"No, but look." Ernest pointed toward a cluster of oak and birch. "Those that ain't pine look sick, don't they?"

She raised her dark eyes. "So?"

"So they're sick. That's all I'm saying."

"You love me?"

"Yep."

She touched his cheek with the back of her fingers and stroked his beard. "You won't let Daddy catch me, will you?"

"Nope." Ernest nestled his head against the knapsack and closed his eyes.

"Ernest?"

"Yeah?"

"What was your daddy like?"

"Nothing special."

"Did he hit you?"

"No. He never hit me."

"Threaten to?"

"No."

She stopped stroking his red whiskers and lay still and closed her eyes.

"We hunted," said Ernest. "I carried the food. He carried the gun. But he died."

"You miss him?"

"Ma did. She cried like a damn dog. But me, no, except for how he took care of her. I miss that."

"You was twelve, right?"

"Ten."

"I wish Daddy died when I was ten."

"Me, too," he said.

"I wish he died and Momma had no time to watch over me and tell me things to do. But I guess at first I'd feel guilty for wishing and being glad of such. Probably be natural, wouldn't it? Be natural for me to miss him some. I probably'd cry outta habit at first. Huh, Ernest?"

"There ain't no habit unless you want it." He looked at May May who had already opened her eyes and was looking into his. "After Pa died, at the funeral, people told me, 'Don't cry' and 'He's in the Good Place' and 'Everything'll work out.' So I didn't cry. I didn't worry. I left like nothing happened. And nothing did."

"You're so strong, Ernest." She squeezed his biceps. "I wish I could forget."

"We better get going. Come on," he said, pushing to his feet. "I'm tired of resting."

Ernest retrieved his bike, and they put on their knapsacks. May May held his hand as they stepped down the hill and up the embankment to the highway.

"Ernest, how long you had this bike?" she asked, looking down at the rusted fender as he began pedaling.

"Couple years."

"Damn, you tore it up in a hurry! Looks older than that."

"It is," he said. "I stole it."

"Ernest, did you?"

"Stole it one night from a nigger."

"I wish you wouldn't say 'nigger.' We don't like to be called that."

"I forget."

They reached Holly Springs two hours later. But the town offered them nothing but stares, so after an hour of checking pay phones for change and finally sitting on a curb in front of a 7-Eleven sharing a Slurpee, they hit the highway once again, hoping Oxford would be the place to settle down for a while.

The two-lane highway to Oxford unnerved May May. She begged Ernest not to ride on the gravel shoulder but farther away from the cars, on the grass, which exhausted him. After half an hour, he was ready to pull over, but when May May saw a sign for Wall Doxey State Park and read it to Ernest, he kept on. They could sleep in the park for the night, maybe break into a vacant cabin. Maybe there would be food in the cabins as well, and they could conserve their own.

But when they arrived there were people scurrying around the cabins, eating on picnic tables, tossing a Frisbee, walking. A couple was necking in a Jeep and listening to loud music. Ernest and May May took a trail to the far edge of the park.

They spread May May's sleeping bag in a small clearing beside the lake, which was off the trail and surrounded with dense undergrowth. The night would be coming soon, and there wasn't much of a chance of anyone hiking this far out in the dark.

Ernest emptied a variety of brown and green packages from a plastic bag. "You want your beef dry or soaked?"

May May took the package from him and turned it in her hand. "This beef?" she asked.

"Yeah. You want it soaked, you can wet it in the pond there a minute or two."

"I ain't putting my food in that water."

"Then we'll both have it dry," he said. "It's better that way. Flaky."

"It ain't enough for us both, is it?" The cooked beef patty was the size of May May's palm.

"This food here'll stay in your system three days. Maybe twice that for you."

She grimaced, picked up the fortified cheese spread and read aloud its directions, "*Knead package before opening.*" She kneaded it, then tossed it aside in exchange for the vacuum-packed crackers. She studied all the bumps and grooves of the plastic wrapper, as though what she held and tilted in her flattened hand so gingerly, so close to her face, was a fossil.

"Where you get this stuff anyway?"

"My neighbor's got a boy in the reserves, and he brought us these meals soldiers eat when they're out in the field. He brought them for Ma and me since we don't have much money, except for what the government gives us." Ernest took the crackers from May May and started opening the packages. "They ain't bad once you get used to it."

Ernest was content with not having to share the beef patty. May May had taken a small corner, but spat it out once it fell apart in her mouth. She did like the beans with tomato sauce. And she ate the brownie. Ernest didn't like brownies.

When they finished their meal, Ernest took his toothbrush from his knapsack and wet it in the pond. May May gathered the wrappers into the original brown bag and set it aside, while he scrubbed his teeth and rinsed and put his brush away. Ernest removed his boots and climbed into the sleeping bag, and she climbed in beside him.

"You think we can stay in Oxford a while?"

"Might could," he said.

"I bet there a lot of cans at Oxford, with the college there."

"It don't matter," he said. "I ain't picking up no more cans."

"Why?" she asked. Collecting cans was how they met.

"I ain't picking up nobody's trash no more."

"So what if it is trash?" she said. "Why you think I got started picking up cans? It was Momma who told me about getting money for them, and that was after I been picking them up. You could say it was instinct for me to clean up somewhere dirty."

"I ain't got no instincts," he said, looking into her eyes. He could see the outline of her face but not the features themselves—the same with her eyes. He knew he was looking at her irises because he could see the white of her eyes reflecting moonlight.

"What we gonna do for money when what we got's spent?"

"I don't know. But I ain't touching no cans."

"Maybe one of us can get a job."

"I don't know." He crossed his arms and turned on his side, looking away from her, into the shifting shadows of the trees. "Just don't talk to me about no job."

She touched his arm. She waited, but he didn't turn, didn't say anything or sigh. She wrapped an arm around his waist. "Ernest," she said, "I'm glad we here together."

For minutes they were quiet, as though they were listening to the sounds of the park or something more faint and distant. Something outside the park.

"You remember what you said to me yesterday?" asked May May. "Remember how you said I was your first girlfriend? Do you?"

"No."

"Ernest? You said you loved your momma, but that I was your first real girlfriend. You said you loved me more than your momma. Remember now?"

"Yeah."

"I gotta say that made me feel special. A twenty-four-year-old man loving for the first time, loving me at fourteen. And me loving for the first time, too. Makes me feel special." She squeezed the hardness of muscle beneath his clothes. Then she counted on her fingers. "In six months, I'll be fifteen."

Ernest counted and thought at first it would be May in six months but then remembered she'd said she had been born in June. She'd told him how she was expected to be born in May, but somehow she arrived late. Her mother called her May May regardless because she'd planned on the name for nine months, already liked it, and didn't like the sound of June June.

"Ernest," she whispered, "what was it like being growed up by a retarded momma?" She patted his stomach. "Can you tell me anything, Ernest?"

"Shut up, May May."

"What?" She pulled her arm away.

"Shut up!" he said. "Damn, you talk. You talk too much. Just shut up a while."

"What? I know you didn't say that, Ernest. I know you ain't talking to *me*. I don't know who you talking to." She sat up, folded her arms. "You must be talking to some Woody the Woodpecker 'round here, but I *know* you ain't talking to *me!*"

Ernest covered his head with the sleeping bag, but he could still hear her. He didn't know what to do. His first impulse was to hit her. His hands were already clenched, but he didn't want to hit her. "I don't know who he think he's talking to," he heard her say, and he put his hands over his ears and shut his eyes. Eventually, it worked.

He felt something between his legs. Then on his belly and crotch. May May's hand was cold as it slipped inside his jeans.

"Sorry I talk too much," she whispered. "I won't talk no more." She kissed his lips and placed herself on top of him.

Ernest had never had a woman on top of him before. She removed his pants and shorts and unbuttoned his coat and shirt. The coldness of her hands dissolved slowly and they were now warm and quick. He did nothing. He didn't have to do anything. He wanted to do everything. May May even moved. "I'll move," she said, and she did.

He could see her face now. The light scattering through the branches landed on her nose and cheeks, shining above him. She made faces he'd never seen her make. He felt pinned. His erection was falling. So he concentrated, looking at the sky, not her face. He didn't want to lose. He grabbed at May May's breasts. But even hanging down they were small. There was a bright white star above her shoulder, and he pretended he was home looking at that star, and he was up and not down. He was looking down. He looked at May May. She was down. He was gaining. She was down and he was moving. I'm up, he thought. I'm up. I'm moving.

When May May stopped moving, she stood up and went to her sack of belongings and wiped herself with tissue. Then she wiped Ernest and kissed him. He was looking at the star. He was struggling with his clothes, fastening them, but he could barely work his muscles. He was weak, looking up at the star through the trees. He closed his eyes. He couldn't look up any more.

Ernest didn't know what time it was when he woke, but he knew it was time. He woke with the thought. He simply knew it was the thing to do and the time to do it. He quietly escaped from the sleeping bag without stirring May May. He pulled on his cap and hung his knapsack on his shoulder. On the ground beside May May's paper sack was her umbrella. Ernest didn't own an umbrella, so he took it. He picked up his bicycle and carried it thirty feet before setting the tires on the trail and straddling it. He was ready to push off when he remembered what he was going home to. There was money there and plenty of food, but his mother was there, with her crazy mouth always blabbering. May May was still young enough to train. Maybe with a little more time she could prove as useful and obedient as his neighbor's coon dog. Maybe she was ready for a good beating.

He turned around and carried the bicycle to the clearing and set it down gently and leaned it back against the tree. He put his knapsack and the umbrella away and shook May May. She jumped.

"What's wrong?" she asked, sitting up.

"Nothing."

"Is it my daddy?"

"I just want to say something."

"What is it, Ernest?"

Ernest sat down on the sleeping bag beside her. "You said you love me."

"With all my heart," she said.

"Then you really saying you gonna do what I say. And what I say is you gonna shut up from now on when I say shut up. Or I will hit you if you don't. And you gonna find a job. Not me. And you ain't gonna make those ugly faces no more when we having fun." He lay down and crossed his arms across his chest. "That's all I want to say. Go on back to sleep."

"What the hell you just say to me?"

"Shut up," said Ernest.

"I done take enough of that talk from my daddy."

"May May, I said shut up." He closed his eyes. He thought he might take a short nap, but May May hammered him in the stomach.

Ernest jumped up. He stood over her, staring at her as if she had lost her mind. She was staring at him likewise.

"You crazier than Ma," he said.

"I can't believe how you done talked to me. I thought we was a team. I thought we was in love."

Sitting thin at his feet and whining, May May didn't seem to Ernest much different than a dog.

"There limits," Ernest said, and he gave May May a little kick in the chin. "Now I done told you I love you. Ain't you got ears?"

May May buried her face in her hands and cried. Ernest had not seen anyone cry so much since his father's funeral. He didn't understand. No one was dead. And he didn't kick her hard. His mother would have already shaken it off and be back to blabbering. A dog would have run off. But May May wasn't going anywhere. She just cried and cried.

"I'm sorry," said Ernest.

May May looked up from her hands. Her entire face was wet, the whites of her eyes bloodshot.

"Really?" she said.

"Yeah."

"You really sorry? You won't do it again?"

"I promise," he said.

May May stood up and hugged him.

"Oh, Ernest, Ernest, I'm sorry, too. From now on I'm gonna shut up when you says shut up just like you want." May May pressed her face against his chest and began to cry again.

"We better get moving," he said. "Almost sunrise."

She turned her head to look up at the sky. "Oxford?"

"Yeah." He bent down for his knapsack. "Get your things together. I'm gonna go take a look, see if it's clear."

"Oh, wait," she said, putting on her shoes, "I wanna go, too."

"Wouldn't be safe. Get your things together. I'll be right back." He picked up her umbrella and raised it in the air like a club. "Case I run into your pa," he said, "I'll kill the bastard."

May May ran to him and kissed him.

"Now go on pack your things," he said, sticking the umbrella in his knapsack. He picked up his bicycle.

"Hurry back," said May May.

Ernest carried his bicycle through the undergrowth until he reached the trail, and once he pushed off he didn't stop. When he reached Holly Springs, he changed highways, but he didn't stop—not until the sun was well above him and he had arrived at the small leaning house, with its blocks sinking into clay.

When he opened the door, his mother tackled him with a firm hug.

"Oh, Carl," she said, "you're back!"

He shoved her aside with his umbrella.

"I knew you was coming back," she said, trying to pick herself off the floor. "I just knew you was coming back. I just knew it, Carl."

"Oh, shut up, Lucille." Ernest closed the door, dropped his knapsack and umbrella, hung his cap on the coat rack, and went into the kitchen. He was thirsty.

BODY PERFECT

Jill Conner Browne

After we got into weightlifting our ownselves in the '80s, me and Tammy would occasionally go to bodybuilding shows—usually because somebody we'd met in the weight room was competing and selling tickets. If you have never been to one of these events—let me encourage you to not only *go*, but buy front-row seats if at all possible for the very next one that comes around—it is *highly* entertaining. I mean, we lift weights ourselves—granted just to try to stave off osteoporosis for as long as possible—but we do enough that we can certainly appreciate the bodies. We know how hard *we* work—and ain't *nobody ever* gonna give us no trophies for our bodies. We are totally in reality on that score. The Next Big Thing is most assuredly *not* going to be "Menopausal Women Gone Wild"—first of all, it's redundant, but more important to the potential viewers would be what they would most likely consider the *threat* of us baring *anything*—the concept of *all* is just too off-putting to really consider for very long.

At any rate, we have achieved that state where the casual observer might comment, "Can you imagine what they would look like if they *didn't* work out?" You get the picture. But to work as hard as we do and still look the way that we do—well, I know what those bodybuilders are doing is pure torture—they *live* at the gym is all I'm saying.

Anyway, what I love about bodybuilding shows is that they are so completely honest. It is totally about Who Has the Best Body, period. They tell you that right up front. They do not pretend it is for the "scholarships." They are as nearly naked as you can possibly get and not be. They are posing in such ways as to show everybody in the farthest reaches of the room as many of their very muscular body parts as possible and to the very best advantage. The audience in turn is expected to clap wildly and yowl with enthusiasm—of which clapping and yowling me and Tammy did more than our share at a show we attended recently. As a matter of fact, when the crowd commenced to standing on their chairs, me and Tammy hopped right up on ours. Actually it's entirely possible that we started that whole thing—but whatever.

The contestants are justifiably proud of their bodies—muscles for days, I'm saying—and the louder the crowd gets, the more enthusiastic the posing gets. These are people with unbelievable bodies who want to show them off to another group of people who really want to see them. As I said, it is totally honest.

At one particularly fine show we attended, we encountered a somewhat jarring note of what seemed to be incongruity, at least to us. As we entered, we were handed a program of the night's events. Taking our seats, we perused the program. About midway through all the gym and protein powder supplement ads, we came to this terribly reproduced full-page black-and-white photo of a young woman. It looked like it had been taken with a disposable camera and copied on the ten-year-old office copier and then copied again for the program. The subject of the photo was standing on a windy beach, facing away from the camera, wearing only a thong bikini bottom. (Let me just say that personally I long for the days when "thong" meant only an inexpensive rubber sandal. Having dedicated every summer of my entire life to trying to keep my swimsuit *out* of my butt, I'm not really in the market for one that is specially designed for that sole purpose. But that's just me.)

So anyway, we came to this bad photo of this girl's butt. Across the top, it said, "Best Wishes." And she signed it, "Keep Striving for Perfection, through Christ—Body Perfect." We had no way of confirming if, in fact, "Body Perfect" was her given name. If so, was it her first and last name or perhaps it was the first and middle? Perhaps her name at birth was something regular but she had it legally changed to suit her current image of herself and if so, I wonder how many years into her life she will be able to maintain it? Might she have to have "Formerly" legally inserted as her middle name to remain appropriate for middle age?

The "through Christ" part really threw us though—it just wasn't the caption we were expecting to read under a girl's nearly nekkid butt in a magazine, y'know? Not that one cannot espouse the teachings of Jesus and wear thongs simultaneously. I am quite certain it's done all the time and we just never thought of it before. It gave us pause. What *were* Billy Graham and Mother Teresa wearing under there? Is there a new movement under way in the church? Do they have a thematic name—"Thongs for Jesus?" "G-Strings for God?" "Christian Butt-cracks?" I can only imagine all those folks who warned against—railed against—*guitars* in the church are preparing a pretty hefty dose of "I told you so" about now.

All I can say is, if it's really catching on—we are totally unprepared, but we will be stepping up our glute workout—just in case.

VENEER

Steve Yarbrough

I t's called the Daily Planet. It's right next to the Tower Theatre, in a
part of Fresno that everyone refers to as the Tower District. Most of
the homes in this part of town are like mine: they were built in the
teens and twenties, they fell into neglect in the fifties and sixties, then in
the seventies and eighties, people like us, folks who either couldn't afford
to buy in the north part of town or couldn't stand the thought of living
in a house that looked just like the ones on both sides of it, moved in and
refurbished.

The Planet is what I think of as an art deco sort of place. There's a
lot of black-and-white tile, mirrors on the walls, some gilded metal here
and there. Until tonight, whenever I've been there, there's been somebody parked behind the baby grand that stands adjacent to the bar. The
pianist is always caressing standards, tunes like "Stardust" and "April in
Paris." He's not here tonight because this is the Fourth of July, and most
folks are in their backyards, cooking hot dogs or burgers and lining up the
bottle rockets.

That's where I would be, too, except that my wife, Irena, and my
daughters are in Prague, visiting Irena's family. In two more weeks I'll
join them. But tonight I'm here with a friend.

The waiter seats us near the front of the restaurant, right next to the
plate-glass window. Irena would never agree to sit here because we'd be
visible from the street, and she fears a shooting. It's not an unreasonable
fear. A few years ago, an eighteen-year-old girl was killed on the sidewalk
outside.

My friend Emily doesn't much like the location of our table either.
"Aren't you afraid," she says, "that somebody'll drive by and see us sitting
here and think we're having an affair?"

Emily has a certain reputation, and she stands what my dad, who
spent most of his life raising cotton in the Mississippi Delta, would have
called a strict-middling chance of attracting attention. She's got on

bright purple skin-tight slacks and a black satin blouse against which her platinum hair sparkles.

"Let them think whatever they want to," I tell her. "We know we're not."

"You're not concerned with appearances, are you?"

"Just reality."

"At a certain point," she says, "the two become one."

I've known her a long time—I recognize the mood. Her father left her mother for another woman when she was seven, the same age as my twin daughters. For a long time her mother dragged her around California, chasing one man after another, getting poorer and drunker and needier.

Emily doesn't like holidays. She owns a lot of stock now in PG&E and runs her own home-decorating business, but holidays make her feel like the outsider she used to be. On holidays she'll tell me that even though I grew up poor, I was always respectable. She'll tell me how easy I had it.

That's what she plans to do now. She takes a sip of merlot and says, "What was the worst Fourth of July you ever endured?"

I try not to take her too seriously. If I take her too seriously, I could ruin a pleasant evening with one of my best friends. "All my Fourth of Julys," I say, "were straight out of Norman Rockwell."

"They would be," she says.

I intend to change the subject, leave it at that.

I intend to, but then a waiter passes by carrying a plate. In the middle of the plate is a small strip steak, surrounded by substances that were never meant to come near it. It looks like there's mango sauce on that plate and something green. Mashed-up kiwi fruit, maybe.

The steak reminds me of something, a story I could tell. Emily loves stories. She has the capacity to lose herself in a narrative. She and I go to suspense movies together—Irena only likes foreign films. At the climactic moments Emily clutches the back of the seat in front of her, gritting her teeth and perspiring. It's hard to pay attention to the movie once you've noticed that she's sitting there beside you taut and bathed in sweat.

The story I've thought of to tell her is one that we both might disappear into.

"Hey," I say, "wait a minute."

"What?"

"You want to hear a true story?"

"Where's it set?"

"Away down south in Dixie."

You can feel her mood starting to break. She tosses her hair, light from the fluorescent bulbs makes it shimmer. "What's it about?"

"The American Dream."

"On the Fourth of July? Jesus," she says. "Why not?"

The house I grew up in stood on sixteenth-section land in Sunflower County. It had started out as a tenant shack—just a couple of rooms, a tin roof, no running water. At some point before I was born, my dad and my grandfather, who died when I was still quite young, added indoor plumbing. That wasn't all they added. Every year or two, a room would be tacked on. For a while the house grew south, toward what we called "the main road," then it began to spread east, in the direction of Beaverdam Creek. The two original rooms were about a foot higher than all the others, except for the last room, the one closest to the creek—it was the highest of them all.

"Hope I don't ever need a wheelchair," Grandma said. "If I do, you just may as well shoot me."

The house featured porches on all four sides—if you could speak of anything so oddly shaped as having sides. At one time or another, three different rooms served as the kitchen. You could enter the bathroom from any one of three directions, a fact that caused my dad no end of anxiety. When he went in there, he'd spend several minutes locking all the doors, double- and triple-checking them.

My wife once said that my dad was a redneck Moses Herzog, and there's much in that description that is apt. Dad was a worried man. Like all farmers, he worried about the weather, but his worries did not stop there.

Basically, I think, he worried because he couldn't figure out why he was what he was. He was a big tall man with a square chin and lots of wavy hair that would never go gray, and his blue eyes were in no way less bright or mischievous than those of Paul Newman. In the Navy he'd scored close to 160 on his IQ test. He'd read Tacitus in translation, he could quote vastly from *Paradise Lost*. Yet when he added everything up and summed himself, what he saw was a man with a small, nondescript wife who slept in a separate bed and shrank at the touch of his hand. He saw a man who had little formal education, who hadn't even graduated from high school, a man who plowed the same furrows his own dad had plowed, who owed his soul to the Bank of Indianola.

He saw a man who lived in our house.

The house worried him. The other people who lived nearby on six-teenth-section land admired it, praising its size, the multiple porches, the unique configuration. ("It's shaped like the Panama Canal Zone," one neighbor said.) But the roof leaked, and the cypress tree on the east side kept sinking its roots into the septic pipes and backing up the toilet, and two or three times each spring Beaverdam Creek flooded—the water got into a couple of the rooms, and the floorboards rotted and had to be replaced.

The main thing wrong with our house, though, was that it was unlike some of the other houses Dad had entered after he became a deacon at Beaverdam Baptist.

Beaverdam Baptist was a country church. For the most part the people who went there were folks like my family—small-time cotton farmers who'd soon be driven under by rising labor costs, the move toward mechanization, and the growing preference for synthetic fab-rics—but quite a few rich people attended that church as well. The one my dad got to know best was another deacon, Tiny Bright.

Tiny was not his real name. His real name was Herbert. People called him Tiny because he weighed about 280 pounds. He owned five thousand acres of the best land in Sunflower County, and he also owned a cotton gin and was a partner in several businesses in Indianola. Most—though not all—of this wealth had been handed down to Tiny Bright by his father.

Despite his success, I've never believed that Tiny Bright was very smart. He once assured a girl of my acquaintance that the capital of Michigan was Milwaukee. Though he'd earned a degree at Mississippi State, his grammar was no better than Grandma's, and Grandma had left school after fifth grade. And things often exploded when he touched them. I once saw him try to air up a basketball at a church picnic—it blew up in his face. I once saw him try to air up the tire on his car, and it blew off the rim. No one else I have ever known was inept enough to make a tire do that.

But Mr. Bright could do two things well. He could make money, and he could sing. He directed the choir at Beaverdam Baptist. He was a baritone who soloed exactly twenty-four times a year, at morning services on the first and third Sundays of each month. Attendance was always high then.

"When Tiny sings 'I come to the garden alone,'" Dad said, "everybody in the congregation wishes they could go to the garden with him.

We didn't go to the garden with Mr. Bright—or Brother Bright, as I called him then—but we did go to his house. We went to his house on June 28, 1970. I can date it so exactly because I had turned twelve the day before.

He invited us over for supper that Sunday after the evening service. He'd insisted we bring Grandma, so it was the four of us and Brother and Sister Bright, and their daughter, who was three or four at the time.

I don't remember too much about the evening. I do remember quite a bit about the house. It was perfectly symmetrical in every way, and it seemed to possess great mass. Also, there were thick white carpets on the floors, several bathrooms, each of which had only one entrance, and lots of gold-plated surfaces—on chandeliers, candlesticks, picture frames, and lamps. A big grandfather clock stood in the corner of the dining room.

"Lovely," Dad kept saying at supper. "This is such a lovely evening, such a lovely home."

I had never heard him use the world *lovely* before. I had never heard anyone use that word before, and I don't think I've heard anyone use it since.

We had salad, baked potatoes, corn on the cob, and ribs, which Brother Bright cooked on a charcoal grill in his backyard. The grill lingered long in Dad's mind. It was probably the only object he saw that night that he could afford to buy.

"That's a fine way to fix meat," he said in the car on the way home. "We're gonna get us one of those. Folks, we're gonna have a cookout on the Fourth of July."

People like Dad did not own grills.

They had never owned grills for the same reason that they could not countenance the idea of an animal—a dog or cat, I mean—living in the house. Animals belonged outside. If animals came inside, it diminished the distance between you—a creature that ought to have a roof over its head—and them. People like Dad, who had to submit bids on their land and their houses every five years, lived with the fear that one day they might not have a roof over their heads. To most people who occupied sixteenth-section land, cooking food outside would have seemed frivolous at best. Some would have said you were tempting fate.

I have often wondered what the grill meant to Dad. This is what I've come to think. I think that when he saw Tiny Bright cooking on the grill, his sense of possibility was altered. He understood that for a man like Tiny Bright, the whole world was home. And having understood that, he made a tremendous leap—a leap of faith. In the car on the way home, he must have decided that if you were willing to embrace Tiny Bright's vision—without knowing the sense of security all Tiny Brights knew—your world and his world might seem less far apart. You could bring a little breath of Tiny Bright into your life.

The Fourth of July fell on a Saturday. Friday afternoon, while Dad was out in the field plowing, Mother and Grandma and I drove to town to buy the grill and various other supplies. Our first stop was the Western Auto.

There were four charcoal grills to choose from. Mr. Cecil Neil, who had run the Western Auto since the day it opened and who probably knew everyone in the south part of Sunflower County by name, extolled the virtues of each grill, so that by the time he'd finished, any rational person would have concluded that no differences existed between the most expensive grill—a big, heavy-looking black thing like Tiny Bright's, with a wooden handle on the top and plastic wheels on the legs—and the cheapest grill, which was only four or five inches deep and made of very thin metal. You couldn't roll it from one place to another because the skimpy little legs lacked wheels.

The cheapest grill had been painted green. "You know what, Mr. Neil?" Mother said. "Seems to me like that little one there's the prettiest."

He was already pulling a flat white box off the shelf behind the display model. "A pretty grill," Mr. Neil said, winking at her, "for a pretty young lady."

Grandma had been busy on the other side of the store, over in the paint section. She met us at the cash register. She was carrying a pint can of latex enamel. From the patch on the label, you could tell that the paint inside was pink.

"I think I'll put a little veneer," she said, "on the coffee table."

I was in college before I had occasion to look up the word *veneer*. I can't remember what the occasion was, but it's probable that I had used the word in a strange way and been corrected by someone. Words frequently got me into trouble. When I was four or five, Mother had bought me a copy of *101 Dalmatians*. Many of my happiest evenings were spent lying beside her, listening to her read it. She read it to me until the pages began to fall loose. Imagine my surprise when, in junior high, I learned from a girl I had a crush on that white dogs with black spots were not called Dallamontarians.

Those many years later, when I looked up the word *veneer*, my heart sank as I read down the list of definitions. Then I came to the last possibility, and after reading it, I dropped my dictionary on the floor and punched the air with my fist in a moment of pure triumph:

a superficial or deceptively attractive appearance or display: GLOSS

You think pink'll look all right on a coffee table?" Grandma asked Mr. Neil.

Mr. Neil said, "Pink will be fine."

Emily says, "You're telling me your grandmother painted the coffee table pink?"

We're on the salads now. The waiter brought them a few minutes ago. The waiter wore a long-sleeved pinstripe shirt, black knee shorts, and a pair of tasseled loafers.

Our salads are potato crêpes rolled in red lettuce leaves, sprinkled with shredded carrots and topped with guacamole.

"She did paint the coffee table pink," I say. "That very night. The evening of July 3, 1970."

"Why?"

"So it would look new for the Fourth of July."

"And this was something she did fairly often."

"She only painted the furniture a few times. Paint was expensive."

"But cheaper than new furniture."

"Cheaper and more colorful."

"And she liked color."

"She loved color. She loved color, and she loved junk. Once when we went to the Smoky Mountains—this was the only real vacation trip we ever took, by the way—she bought a bunch of chalk animals at a souvenir shop in Cherokee. A chalk dog, a chalk fox, a chalk hen, and some chalk chicks. She stood them out in front of the house as decoration. It rained once or twice and they disintegrated. That's the sort of stuff she bought."

Emily lays her hand on my knee. A shiver runs up my thigh.

"So what happened on the Fourth of July?" she says. "What made it so bad?"

I don't exactly lay my hand on top of hers, but I do allow my fingertips to graze her thumb. "I'll tell you," I say, "if you prove you're woman enough to eat those crêpes."

On the evening of July 3, 1970, we slept in a different house. It sounded like the same house—it was raining, and the rain beat down on the tin roof in the same way it always had—but the odor of fresh paint, fresh *pink* paint, filled the air. The house smelled of chemicals, modernity.

Down the hall from my room, in the refrigerator, four T-bone steaks, pink also, lay on top of one another. They had been purchased in the afternoon at Piggly Wiggly. I had eaten steak before, of course, but I had never before eaten *a* steak. A steak was what professional football players always ate in my favorite books, the juvenile novels of *Sports Illustrated* writer Tex Maule. Brad Thomas and Flash Werner and all the other members of Maule's fictitious L.A. Rams—they ate the very same thing that I would eat tomorrow. They sometimes ate it prepared the same way we would prepare ours—on a grill—and usually the grill stood on the balcony of an apartment overlooking the beach in a place like Santa Monica or Malibu.

Tomorrow would be almost like a trip to California. Flooded fields might lie just across the road, chicken droppings might litter the ground, and the closest body of water might be named Beaverdam Creek, but in my imagination I would stand near the Pacific, and while meat sizzled on the nearby grill, I would hear the mighty ocean roar.

"You'll take the steaks out," Dad told Mother, "and do whatever you do to a steak before it's cooked."

"Okay," she said.

"Me, I'll head on out back and start the grill," he said, "and then I've got to go down to the tractor shed and see if I can't figure out what's wrong with the John Deere. And Larry here, well, he's gonna be the chef for today."

Having explained everybody's role, Dad kissed Mother on the top of her head and mussed my hair and left the house.

"What do you do to a steak before you cook it?" I asked Mother.

"I don't know—I never have cooked one."

"Why didn't you say so?"

"That just wouldn't do."

"Why not?"

"Because that's not what your dad wants to hear."

He heard a lot of things he didn't want to hear from other people—

bankers, implement dealers, insurance agents, and the like—and I know he frequently heard one thing he didn't want to hear from Mother. *I'm tired, I don't really feel like it tonight.* She liked to give him good news whenever she could, so if it would make him feel better to think she knew how to prepare a T-bone steak, she was happy enough to say she did. Then maybe she wouldn't have to say yes to something else.

She dumped a lot of salt and pepper on the steaks, and then she decided to throw a little brown sugar on them, too.

"That'll give 'em a little extra flavor," she said.

Grandma said, "If you ask me, them steaks was just a waste of money. For that price, you could have got a whole side of salt meat."

I said, "You can't cook salt meat on a grill."

The waiter comes to clear away our salad plates. I order another bottle of Pilsner Urquell. I ask him if this time he could put the bottle in the freezer for a few minutes before bringing it out. He looks at me with disdain. I feel almost as if he's seen the house I grew up in.

Emily says, "So your mother always said she was too tired?"

"Most of the time."

"How do you know?"

"The walls were thin, and I slept in the room next to theirs."

"Why didn't she want to make love?"

Why didn't she? I wonder. Why would anybody quit wanting to do that?

"She was a Southern Baptist," I tell Emily, knowing full well I'm explaining nothing. "She'd already done what she was supposed to do—you're sitting across the table from living proof of that."

"How did your dad feel about her?"

"He was mad about her."

"Just like you are," Emily says. "Mad about Irena, I mean."

There's an edge to her tone, as there always is when we're alone and my wife's name comes up. Emily has a tendency to think I'm undervalued. She'd be a lot more critical, I believe, if it weren't for my daughters. She says they're the greatest kids she's ever seen, that I'm a lucky man because I get to be their dad.

She says she's lucky because she gets to baby-sit them. One weekend last year, when she was taking care of them so we could go to a concert in San Francisco, we got home to find all three of them in the backyard, taking turns riding a Shetland pony. We were scared Emily had bought the pony for them, but it was only rented for one day.

"Just like I am," I agree. "He was mad about her—to all appearances, anyway. He only lived two weeks longer than she did. People say he grieved himself to death."

"I could see you doing that."

"Not too soon, I hope."

"Not too soon. But one day. Now tell me—what about the steaks?"

"The steaks?" I say. "Dad was mad about them, too."

They must have been at least an inch thick. We'd bought the cheapest grill, but nobody could say we'd skimped on the steaks. When I stabbed the first one with a fork, it felt like it weighed a couple of pounds.

Beneath the grate, the coals glowed red-hot. "How long does it take to cook a steak?" I asked Mother.

She was standing beside me holding the plate. "A long time," she said.

"How long?"

"Two or three hours, I imagine."

"It didn't take Mr. Bright that long to cook those ribs."

"Those were pork," she said. "This is *steak*."

She could hardly stand the thought of eating meat of any kind, she would have lived just fine off tomatoes and black-eyed peas. But the way her voice rose when she pronounced that weighty word—*steak*—assured me that even she was caught up in the spirit of our endeavor, that she held a certain truth to be self-evident: just like Tiny Bright, we were entitled to grill our meat, and on any given day our meat might be better than his.

I threw the first steak on the grate.

Mother said, "Hear that sucker sizzle."

She had never used the word *sucker* in that manner before. All of us, I felt, were pushing our boundaries. We were reimagining ourselves. If you'd told me right then that I might one day see Pikes Peak, I would not have considered it impossible.

I threw another one on. "Two down," I said, "two to go."

"Pitch 'em on there," she said. "Get 'em hot."

In Tex Maule's novels, Brad Thomas was the L.A. Rams' quarterback. Brad came from Texas, a place every bit as much out of the way, I figured, as the place I was now. He'd made it all the way to L.A., and so would I. I picked up my football and went out behind the barn.

For an hour or so I played an imaginary game against the hated San Francisco Forty-Niners. I bent down, barked signals, took the snap from center, and dropped back. Chased from the pocket by panting linemen, I scrambled, dodging a section harrow that tried to trip me up. Over by the pump house, I cocked my arm and fired a bomb.

Once or twice the ball bounced into Dad's watermelon patch, and I had to tromp around in there hunting it, which always made me nervous because you never knew where a cottonmouth might be crawling. Each of those moments I treated as an official's time-out.

I imagined anxious fans in the L.A. Coliseum. *Come on, Brad,* I heard them yell, as I stepped gingerly among the melons, searching for the ball. *Hit Spider on a deep down and out. Come on, come on.*

"Come on!" It was Mother's voice. "Lord, Larry, look!"

I ran toward the barn. When I came around the corner, I saw smoke billowing up from the grill. Mother's hands were clamped to the sides of her head.

For a second I thought she was going to start tearing her hair out.

Grandma was standing there beside her. She shook her head. "People," she said, "wasn't meant to cook outside."

The steaks didn't look much like steaks any more. They were very small. They were small, and they were black. After throwing water on them, we had to pry them off the grate. Part of each steak crumbled. Only the essence remained.

Which, as it turned out, was enough. When Dad came home from the tractor shed and saw how red Mother's eyes were, he said, "What's the matter?"

She said, "We burned the steaks."

Standing on the porch in his dirty khakis, with mud on his boots and an uncertain future, Dad made a decision. He decided to arrange his facial features in a smile. You could argue that it was the equivalent of pink paint on a rickety old table: utterly useless and oddly inappropriate. You could argue that it didn't fool anybody. But the truth is that it did fool someone: Dad himself. He felt that smile there, and he believed in what he felt, just as Grandma believed it when her eyes told her a pink coffee table was a beautiful thing.

"It's the Fourth of July," Dad said. "We planned to have a picnic."

He pulled Mother and me against his chest. He smelled of field dirt. And sweat.

He said, "I like my meat well done."

The Planet pot roast is supposed to be delicious, but the recollection of that meat I ate twenty-five years ago has robbed me of my appetite. Emily doesn't look too tempted either.

I look out the window. In the parking lot across the street, two white cops are talking to a young Hispanic guy whose hair is in a ponytail. He's wearing torn blue jeans, a stained T-shirt. The three of them are standing by a gleaming white Lexus. I know what's about to happen. They'll slap handcuffs on him, bend him over the hood. But just as I start to look away, so that I won't have to watch it, one of the cops puts his hand out. The guy in the T-shirt laughs and slaps the cop's palm, and then the cop laughs and says something, and the guy in the T-shirt unlocks the Lexus and climbs in.

"You ate the steaks?" Emily says.

"Every last bite," I tell her. "Every single one of us pretended it was the best meal we'd ever had. Even Mother ate hers. Later on, she went into the bathroom and got sick."

"That's awful."

"You asked me to tell you about my worst Fourth of July."

"Of course I did. So don't stop now."

"I've got to stop somewhere."

"You can't leave me hanging like that."

"What else do you want to know?"

"Everything."

"Like what?"

"Well, for instance, what about Tiny Bright?"

"What about him?"

"He was your catalyst—your dad wouldn't have bought the grill if it hadn't been for him. Right?"

"Right."

"So what happened to him?"

"Well," I say, "I can tell you if you really want to know."

"You say that like it ought to frighten me."

"If you want me to, I'll tie up all the loose ends. It's up to you."

"I'm game," she says.

So I tell her that the next year, in an effort to increase his cotton acreage without actually buying new land, Tiny Bright—Brother Bright—entered a bid on our portion of the sixteenth-section. I tell her that Brother Bright outbid Dad and that six months later we were living in a trailer out behind Weber's Truckstop, and the house that both Dad and I had grown up in, with all those tacked-on rooms, had mysteriously burned down. The only thing left standing was the chimney.

Her eyes start to fill now. She's probably thinking how my mother must have felt when she had to leave her home, how it must have hurt Dad to leave that house for the last time, to leave that land he'd worked all his life. She's probably wondering if Grandma got to take the pink table with her.

She's probably feeling compassion for the whole troubled world. And why not? It's a world where men run off after other women and leave their wives and little girls behind, where a young girl is murdered outside a tony restaurant. It's a world in which some people spend most of their lives being told no.

She's probably aching for all humankind. But those tear-filled eyes have focused on me.

Her hand squeezes my knee, and my hand squeezes her hand. I think of my own children, on the far side of the Atlantic, sleeping peacefully now in bed beside their mother, not knowing that back home in the New World, where it's still the Fourth of July and their dad has told a story about a dream gone awry, appearance and reality are about to converge.

One Man's Indelible Marks

George Singleton

Braswell needs the job security, so he doesn't speak up at the annual Myrtle Beach sales meeting when the company announces its new plan to expand the product line beyond selling high school rings to rising seniors. He does the math in his head and wonders if a snag in the idea might continue over a twenty-five-year period, until he can officially retire.

"We're still going to offer rings," the president of Oh-Ring says into the microphone, "but we want to get a step up on our bigger and more established competition, you know." Some of the hundred men and women in attendance applaud. Braswell looks up to see Eugene Godfrey, a pious Seventh Day Adventist, walk out of the conference room. "Don't worry. We'll be letting y'all undergo free tattoo lessons taught by professional tattoo artists. Plus, we'll offer free high school tattoo rings for all our salespeople, too. And I shouldn't really bring this up at this time, but think of all the extra money you'll be able to make on the side. You sell the kid our standard ring, *and* you get him for a tattoo ring. Even the dumbest kid will see how he might lose the one but never the other."

Braswell takes his job seriously and sees no reason to eradicate an eighteen-year-old's time-tested rite of passage. He looks out the hotel window and watches a woman stretch the bottom part of her one-piece downward with one hand as she flicks sand out with the other. At least that's what he thinks she's doing

"Here's why we think it'll work," the president says. "We have no control over the economy or the price of gold. There could come a time when graduating seniors and/or their parents just can't afford a $500 high school graduation ring. The price of ink ain't going to fluctuate much. We've done the research, and ink pretty much costs the same always. A hundred-dollar tattoo in 1970 costs a hundred dollars today."

Someone from up front yells, "We can point out that they won't lose a tattoo like they'll lose a ring. We need some kind of graph showing how many people lose their high school rings."

"Jesus. Were you asleep again, Johnson? I already said that, damnit. I'll get back to it," says the president. "Don't you worry. We have some charts and figures on that."

Braswell looks back out the window. As always, the Oh-Ring ring company meets on the first floor of the Adam's Mark, right on the beach, the first week in June—usually the week before students show up to find new temporary loves, then lose their high school rings while body surfing.

Braswell raises his hand. "What about smart kids? There's a law that you have to be eighteen to get a tattoo. What about kids who graduate on time, or have late birthdays, or graduate early?"

The president laughs. "Why do you think we're starting the market test here in South Carolina? On top of that, a tattoo won't take all the same paperwork and planning as a regular ring. A regular graduating class isn't going to be but two, maybe three hundred seniors. We can set up tents practically on graduation night and knock them right out—my people say it won't take twenty minutes to etch an insignia atop the average person's ring finger. With the money we'll save, we can hire enough tattoo artists.

Braswell nods. He thinks about asking a question concerning safety and health hazards, about sterile needles, about parents. He thinks about sending his résumé to Jostens, the big company. "I don't know all the ins and outs of this exciting new development yet, but our vice president of operations, Bodin Adler, is here to quell any reservations you might have."

Braswell's co-workers—most of whom he sees only once a year at the annual convention—chant, "Bo-din, Bowed-out, Bo-din, Bowed-out," which means something, which refers to a liaison that Bodin Adler had with a now-fired Oh-Ring woman a few years back.

Bodin Adler rolls up his shirtsleeve and shows what, from the back row, looks like nothing more than a mandala. "Page High School Class of '76," Bodin says. "Greensboro. See how this might work? We don't have to only do the eighty-dollar tattoos on ring fingers. Listen to this.

I'm privy to this information because my old college roommate now works for the FBI. Pretty soon when we go to write a check or use a credit card, the cashier ain't going to ask for two forms of ID outside of our driver's license. She's going to ask for something a little more permanent. Let me ask you this: how many forgers and counterfeiters are going to go to all the trouble of tattooing themselves to become you? The answer's zero. So. You have your driver's license. And you have your little laminated high school diploma they give you, and you have a tattoo on your finger or elsewhere. No problem with cashing checks."

Braswell raises his hand. He looks peripherally to see if the woman on the beach owns a dog. "How're you going to do this at a drive-through teller at the bank?"

"By this time the banks will have tiny cameras, or lasers that read images. People will just have to stick their finger in some kind of scanner thing, you know, and it'll be approved."

Braswell says, "I don't want to be the skeptic always, but it seems to me that one of the inane traditions of growing up is for a boy to give his ring to a girlfriend when they're going steady. What'll happen now, if everyone gets a tattoo of the ring?"

Braswell's co-workers turn around and look at him. A few nod, but most of them seem irritated, as if they only want out of the meeting in order to buy umbrella-littered drinks at the outdoor tiki bar. Someone says, "Shut up, Braswell. Last year you were mad because we voted for the Fuck option. Get a life, man."

This was true: Braswell had voted against a high school senior's ability to have the word "Fuck" engraved right above his printed high school's name for an additional fee of twenty dollars. Fuck Greenwood High School. Fuck Charlotte Day. Fuck Robert E. Lee, Jefferson Davis, Martin Luther King, George Washington, John C. Calhoun, Thomas Jefferson. Fuck Strom Thurmond Academy.

"I just don't want to see a poor stupid boy cutting off his finger and giving it to his girlfriend. I don't want to see girls walking around the country wearing a boy's blackened, withered finger attached to a necklace."

The president, who has not even turned his head in the direction where Braswell is seated, stands up and looks at his watch. "Our next meeting will be at two o'clock, after lunch. Y'all go on out and I want you to notice how many people have tattoos. This is going to be one of the biggest moves in the history of American entrepreneurship."

Braswell goes back to the room in order to call his wife. He unscrews the top from a fifth bottle of Old Granddad. The hotel operator comes on and says, "Hello, this is Cheryl, Mr. Braswell. How can I help you?"

Braswell pours three fingers into his bathroom glass, no ice. He says, "I'm making a collect call. It'll get charged to my home."

"You have to bring us a credit card or twenty-five dollars cash in order to make a collect phone call, sir."

"It's a collect call. Everywhere in the universe, you make a collect call and it gets charged to your house, or whoever accepts the charge. Go down to a pay phone. Make a collect call. The change you put in trickles back out once the person says he or she accepts."

"I know, sir, but it's hotel policy. You have to pay some money up front for incidentals. You'll get back what's left when you check out."

She sounds to Braswell as if she might have one hand in her pants. "Oh. I just noticed how it says on this piece of cardboard how a collect call costs seventy-five cents." He scans the price sheet. "A local call will cost me a quarter. First off, you could just charge me when I check out. You could say, 'Hey, man, you made a collect call, so we'll have to add three quarters to your bill.' Other than that, why don't I come down there, then, and give you seventy-five cents. Goddamn, it's common sense. And, secondly, I don't know anyone locally. I'm here. If I knew people locally, I'd be staying with them."

"Sir, I would appreciate it if you wouldn't curse. The reason why it's hotel policy is because we don't know how many collect telephone calls you might make. It's not my policy. I just work here. It's hotel policy."

Braswell drinks, places his glass down on the hotel restaurant's menu. "Let me ask you a personal question, Cheryl. Are you a high school graduate?"

"Yes, sir, I am. I graduated from Socastee High."

"How long ago?"

"I graduated in 1998. So two years ago."

Braswell puts her somewhere between twenty and twenty-three. "Do you have a high school ring? Do you have a graduation ring?"

Cheryl pauses. She rings the front desk bell and says, "I'm sorry, sir, but I have to attend to someone checking in."

Braswell laughs. "You rang that little bell yourself. I can tell. You know that we have cameras up here looking down at the front desk, right?" What the hell, he thought.

"If you want to make a collect call then you have to come down here and give us a credit card or twenty-five dollars in cash. Or you can go down on Ocean Drive and try to find a pay phone. If you do the cash option here, we'll reimburse you for what you didn't use up. When you check out. When you leave the hotel."

"I need to call someone," Braswell says. "I guess I have no other options. Do I get interest on the money I take down to you?"

He takes off his tie. He rubs the finger where, he knows, the company will want him to place a tattoo for advertising purposes. Cheryl says, "No."

Braswell doesn't have a credit card. He clipped three of them up a few years earlier, before he even paid what he owed, before he got down below his limit. A gas station attendant took his BP card altogether, and American Express wrote to say that he would have bad credit, et cetera. He stands in the elevator with twenty-five dollars and doesn't make eye contact with people he knows work for the Oh-Ring high school ring company. They all talk of how they're going out tonight, how the tattoo idea might be one of the innovations that will sweep the nation, how the president of Oh-Ring should get a patent, and so on.

He makes a mental note to bring twenty-five hundred pennies with him next year. The elevator door opens and Braswell walks to the desk.

Cheryl stands there as if a Hollywood director might approach her. She's stunning, thinks Braswell: pure and golden and unblemished in any way whatsoever. Airbrushed plain Purity—that's what Braswell sees.

"I'm Alan Braswell from five-twenty-five," he says. "I'm the guy who got pissed off about bringing money down to call," and wonders if he told Cheryl that he needed to call his wife. "I'm the guy who talked to you about making a phone call."

Cheryl nods and smiles without showing her teeth. "I remember you, Mr. Braswell."

In the background Braswell hears the elevator door open again. He hears someone say, "I'm going to count tattoos. I think the president will want this kind of information."

"I have my money up front," Braswell says. "I have it right here." He places a twenty and a five on the faux marble counter. "Here's my money. And as a matter of fact, this might make sense, seeing as I won't really have to pay for anything when I check out—hell, I won't even technically need to check out—seeing as Oh-Ring's paying for everything."

Braswell knows that he's rambling. He doesn't make eye contact with Cheryl. She goes to her computer terminal and smiles, types in the information, slides his money in her direction.

"Five-twenty-five," Braswell says. "I'm in five-twenty-five. Don't forget that I'm in five-twenty-five."

"I've got it in the computer, Mr. Braswell. You can go back up to your room and make a telephone call. Or you can order from room service, you know. We'll get in touch with you if you go over the limit."

Braswell looks as far as he can behind the counter. Cheryl wears a sheer Danskin beneath a miniskirt. "Please tell me that you wouldn't get a tattoo in order to advertise where you went to school."

Cheryl tilts one hip away from him. "We'll call you if you go over the limit, Mr. Braswell."

Braswell backs up two steps. A bellhop comes by to take suitcases from another couple. "I wasn't meaning anything bad," Braswell says to Cheryl. "I swear to God. It's part of my business, evidently."

She holds a chit of some sort. "I'm not stupid, if that's what you're asking. I've graduated from high school, and I'm beginning my sophomore year up in Columbia. I'm studying elementary education, thank you very much, with an emphasis in art. I just work here summers."

Braswell steps forward. He imagines Cheryl down on her knees showing a child how to finger paint, the slit in her short skirt wide open, her hands jacking back and forth like one piston, a smile glistening. He says, "Please tell me you won't get a tattoo."

She lifts up her shirt sleeve. "I already have one. It's a chameleon." Braswell sees only skin. "Oh, it must be camouflaging itself right now," Cheryl says.

Braswell looks up from Cheryl's arm to her face. She shakes her head left to right. He says, "Funny."

"I didn't make that one up by myself. Some writer guy came through one time and told me that one. Or comedian. He was either a writer or a comedian, coming through."

The elevator dings to go up. Braswell looks that way. Cheryl walks out of view.

"They want us to go to tattoo school," Braswell says. "I don't know how to explain this, but we're going from selling regular rings to tattooing rings on people's fingers. Or big emblems on their arms. There'll be a template to follow, but I don't like this idea whatsoever."

"That's a great idea!" Braswell's wife says. "That makes sense!" She's way too excited for Braswell. "Think about it—you won't lose your ring ever."

Braswell says, "I've made it fine to the hotel. That's why I'm calling you. I've made it here fine."

"You won't even have to limit yourself to finger rings. I've always thought about how people could get ear or nose rings outside of regular finger rings. They could get toe rings. Finally there can be some individual expression in the high school ring genre."

Braswell tries not to think about his wife selling herbal soaps daily at a place called Soapy World, how they met in high school, how they went to college, or how he wanted only to take over his father's textile supply company back before the textile industry faltered. He says, "It's not like that at all. It's bad. This is only going to be trouble all the way around."

"Why do you always look at things as if they might end up hurting you, Alan? Why can't you understand that what people ask of you might be beneficial in the long run? Listen, clay pots might take ten thousand years in the rain to dissolve, but they eventually dissolve."

Braswell doesn't know what that means. He hangs up on purpose and will later say that they were accidentally disconnected by the college kid working the front desk.

Downstairs again with Cheryl, Braswell says, "We got disconnected. I called a woman—and she used to be some kind of model, believe it or not—and we got disconnected. I went upstairs, I made the phone call, and we got disconnected."

Cheryl doesn't take her eyes off him. She says, "Y'all got disconnected."

"Uh-huh. That's what I'm saying. We got disconnected."

"Did you call me up? Did you call the operator? Maybe she hung up on you or something. I don't want to make any aspersions or anything."

Braswell thinks, *Aspersions*—who uses those kinds of words these days? Who would cast *aspersions*, and then get a tattoo? He says, "Hey, Cheryl, do you drink those tiki umbrella drinks, by any chance?" He points with his thumb outside.

"No. I don't normally drink much. I'm not legal yet, for one. And I come from a long line of alkies."

"Come on. Let loose. That line about how alcoholics beget alcoholics has been proven fallacious. I read an article about how genes don't really play a part in it, that some pinhead A.A. deacon made the whole thing up. So I'll buy you some tiki drinks on me. When do you get off?"

Cheryl looks behind her to the clock. It's not one-thirty yet. She says, "If you're with the group you say you're with, you have a meeting at two." She looks down at a clipboard. "You have a meeting from two until five."

"I'm not going to that one," Braswell says. "Listen, I'm not irresponsible or anything, I promise. I just don't want to turn into a tattoo artist for the sake of some poor kid remembering where he went to school. Or proving he went to school. Listen. Why are you spending three months inside a hotel lobby? Haven't you ever thought about modeling? I mean, I can't tell with you behind the desk, but you appear to be at least five-ten, and I can't imagine some designer not wanting someone like you to show off his clothes."

"That's very flattering, Mr. Braswell. Thank you for the compliment."

"Technically, I'm not old enough to be your daddy. I mean, if you're twenty, and I'm thirty-eight, that's eighteen years difference. But I didn't lose my virginity until I was right about your age." Braswell keeps eye contact, though he can't figure out why he brought up the subject.

"You look like you're closer to twenty-eight," Cheryl says. She lowers her forehead and raises her eyebrows. "I guess a drink or two might not kill me. Meet me in the bar at three."

Braswell opens his Gideon Bible at random, hoping to find some kind of sign. His finger hits I Samuel 25:18: "Then Abigail made haste, and took two hundred loaves, and two bottles of wine, and five sheep ready dressed, and five measures of parched corn, and an hundred clusters of raisins, and two hundred cakes of figs, and laid them on asses."

He says to no one, "Jesus Christ, now *there's* a good sign. *Laid them on asses.*" Braswell closes the book quickly, before glimpsing a passage about going to Hell. He thinks about re-calling his wife, but knows that Cheryl might bring it up when they meet at three. Braswell looks at his watch. He thinks about returning to the Oh-Ring convention like he's supposed to do.

When the telephone rings at five past two, Braswell waits for the voicemail to pick up. He knows it's either the president or Bodin Adler, wondering what's going on. Once the message light blinks, he hits Message to hear, "Mr. Braswell, this is Cheryl downstairs. I made a mistake. Usually I work from six until three, but they've changed policy and I get off an hour earlier. I'm at the bar now, waiting for you. I hope you didn't change your mind. I'll wait fifteen minutes, and if you don't show up I'll peek inside the conference room. Ciao."

Braswell thinks, *Ciao?* Who the fuck uses *Ciao* as a sign-off in South

Carolina?

He thinks, I should call my wife, but closes the Gideon instead and leaves.

At the tiki bar he finds Cheryl seated at a corner table, away from the bar. He says, "I wasn't in the bathroom or anything. I thought that it was someone in my group calling to ask why I wasn't there."

She says, "I've already ordered you a drink. Not that I'm any kind of prophet or whatever, but you look like the kind of guy who drinks bourbon on the rocks."

"That'll do," Braswell says, though he's gone to mixing bourbon with either water or Coke, ginger ale, or Pepsi.

Cheryl shows her top teeth and props her elbows on the table in a way that squeezes her cleavage together. She says, "You remind me of someone in the movies. You remind me of that guy who always raises his eyebrows and looks scary."

Braswell pulls out a chair next to Cheryl and sits down. He says, "I'm not scary, I promise. I'm confused and stupid most of the time, but not scary."

The barmaid brings two drinks, neither with umbrellas. Cheryl says, "Put these on my tab, Lynnie."

"I'll get them at the end of the night," Braswell says. "The last thing I want you to do is pay for drinks, darling."

Cheryl says, "Now what's all this talk about tattoos, anyway? Tell me about yourself."

Braswell wonders if his death is imminent. He undergoes a flashback that traces every girl or woman he's ever dated. "In my sample case upstairs I have about twenty different high school rings from different places. If you want to pretend that you went to some place besides wherever it was you said you went, let me know. I have a nice woman's ring from John F. Kennedy High School. I have a sample ring from where Madonna went to high school in Detroit, I swear to God."

Cheryl says, "My last boyfriend had a tattoo across his back. It went from shoulder blade to shoulder blade. It was my name, first and last, I swear to God. I broke up with him about a week after it got done, just because I could. From what I understand he's undergoing some painful laser surgeries to erase my name from his back. Sometimes I feel bad about that." Cheryl drinks from a tiny, thin red-and-white straw, a stirrer.

"What's your last name?" Braswell says.

"I don't tell anyone my last name on a first date, but I'll let you in on the fact that it's more than a few syllables. That boy's back got filled up, is what I'm saying."

Braswell looks out the glass door, past the children's pool, past the regular pool, towards the beach. High tide creeps in. A man shades his eyes and looks towards someone sailing on the water. Braswell can only think, Mussolini: that's more than a few syllables.

"My company's about to make a big mistake. I can't hang with them, if you know what I mean. It'd be like being a Democratic senator and being asked to vote against human beings."

Cheryl leans forward. She says, "*Being*. I know what you mean. I can tell you're a good person by how many times you use the word *being*." Braswell drops his miniature napkin on purpose, reaches down, and looks up Cheryl's little skirt. She still wears the Danskin, but he sees the stripe of panties in her crotch and thinks of it as pure womanhood. "I'm surprised you don't wear a wedding band, Mr. Braswell."

"Please call me Alan. Please call me anything besides Mr. Braswell. My friends all call me plain Braswell anyway. I'm surprised I'm not a woman: Bras Well. I wish my name were De-bras-well, get it?"

Cheryl stares through him as if he were a roulette wheel. She says, "You wouldn't know what it's like being brought up in Myrtle Beach, South Carolina, Braswell. You wouldn't know. Every one of my family members has skin cancer. Every man who comes into the hotel wants me to join him in his room. Consider yourself lucky. You can travel around, I'm guessing, sticking plastic rings around people's fingers, trying to figure out their sizes." She sips from her drink again and slants her eyes. "I'm glad you're different."

Braswell rolls his drink between his palms and says, "You wouldn't believe how many people have warts or moles on their ring fingers, though. Especially warts. In some of the pulpwood counties the kids don't even have ring fingers. I had to special-order a graduation bracelet for one boy. I still can't figure out how he keeps the thing up on his nub. The thing cost his father something like fifteen hundred dollars."

Lynnie comes back and says, "Are y'all all right? Who needs another drink?"

Cheryl says, "Lynnie, this is Braswell. He's here with the ring convention."

Lynnie says, "Oh. I've met some of your co-workers. They said something about how they're used to people giving them the finger." Lynnie sits down at the table. Braswell wonders why the women of Myrtle Beach aren't living in Hollywood or New York: Lynnie's got cheekbones that could be carved into another Mount Rushmore.

Braswell says, "My co-workers. You could place their backbones end-to-end and still not have a yardstick. I won't go into the details. They're going to venture into the tattoo trade after this meeting. They're giving up on rings in order to ruin children's dermatology. I won't go into the details."

Lynnie pulls down her top to nipple level and says, "I got this in Florida last Spring Break." Braswell looks at a perfect green-and-red portrait of what appears to be Bill Murray. Lynnie says, "I've always been a fan of Jack Kerouac. I was down in St. Petersburg, and there were a bunch of pictures of him everywhere. I took it as a sign."

"I'm sure Jack Kerouac would be proud to have his face so close to your nipple," Braswell says.

He sees Cheryl slip off one shoe and point her toe straight into Lynnie's lap. "I was," Cheryl says. She rests her toes inside Lynnie's dress, then shudders her leg as if electrocuted. "You sell enough of your rings or whatever, you can afford to watch us all night long, Mr. Braswell."

Two hours later, on the drive home, Braswell thinks about how his wife, Cecelia, volunteers at a nursing home. She paints women's fingernails and gives them makeovers. One woman—like the poor boy without fingers—wanted her nub dipped in red paint so it would look like one giant thumbnail. Braswell's wife complied, then quit going altogether. She told

Braswell that it was nothing but sad seeing a woman walk around with what looked like a bloody unhealing nub.

He drives up 301 thinking up what lies he can tell Cecelia—how he no longer feels driven by fingers, how he detests co-workers, how he had a vision the night before that involved gold insignias. He thinks about Cheryl's foot between Lynnie's legs and wonders when he turned old, when he turned into the kind of man who wouldn't understand tattoos for high school graduation rings.

Braswell wonders what his boss and co-workers there at any of the meetings think without him, or if they've checked with Cheryl's replacement to see if he really left the hotel altogether without even getting change from his incidentals deposit.

Outside of Marion, he pulls off at Colonel Frank's Fireworks and Zoo. Braswell thinks about putting his head on the steering wheel, about looking like one of those lost souls on the road who can't figure out what to do next. He puts the car in Park.

Inside he buys enough smoke bombs to confuse a pack of curs. Braswell picks out a half-dozen hermit crabs for his wife, and a shot glass that reads "If You Can Read This, Then You Need a Double."

The cashier woman says, "Today's the first day we got the aquarium open. Outside we got the tiger and lion. We got some little foxes, you know. We got the Carolina panther outside. But we also got the aquarium now. They's a octopus in there squirts ink if you make sudden move towards it. Every time. Go on up slow and make a sudden move. It'll squirt ink."

She puts Braswell's hermit crabs in a plastic bag and tells him not to let them stay there for more than twenty-four hours. She points out their food and says there's no substitute. Braswell only thinks how he'll never erase "They's a octopus in there squirts ink if you make sudden move towards it" from his head.

"Next month the man's promising to bring us two shark. Man who sold us the aquarium's saying two shark and a manna ray."

They's a octopus in there squirts ink if you make sudden move towards it. Two shark and a manna ray. Braswell takes his bag outside and walks to his car, not thinking about the mileage he could charge Oh-Ring. *They's a octopus in there squirts ink if you make sudden move towards it.*

Braswell starts his car and drives north. He turns the radio off NPR and settles on a station playing—at the time—Lou Reed. Twenty miles down the road he feels safe enough to hit his cruise control button. Then he puts his head back like any driver unworried about his surroundings, the click-clacking of hermit crabs click-clacking behind him, not meaning anything.

Braswell thinks about how he won't be around when the worst things occur, when parents and wives take arms, when scholars figure out the meaning of True Beauty, when their sons and daughters turn their hands over. He drives away from Cheryl, thinking about how everyone in the state, sooner or later, will say how their tattooed graduation rings make them feel like an individual, like a human being unlike anyone else. At the next rest area or roadside zoo he'll climb out of his car, go to the pay phone, and call his wife. He'll say something about how he's on his way home early, how he's never given her due credit, that he's proud of the way she offers people inexpensive products to cleanse themselves properly.

Down in New Orleans

Robert Gatewood

When she opens her eyes they are in a milky light and then out of a door and into the narrow streets, the rain converging with the asphalt and then rising and seething again in an ominous facsimile of woodsmoke, someone's arm about her shoulder and leading her roughly up the curb.

Aroused by the coming night a trembling neon sickle winks down from the Half Moon Bar, carves out of the darkness a diadem of empaneled light beneath which the girl stumbles on in queer rapture. Away from Saint Mary's and down Perdido Street, past a dim square and ranging toward the water she smells in the air the rank evidence of waste and plies her nose violently. As they go the colored lights wash down without cease, assail her feet mercurially. No matter the course, the cold hand that ushers her onward, she watches those lights and those lights only, attempting with a mindless dread to replicate their patterns by her footsteps.

Miles later it seems and someone calls her name. She feels herself leaning toward the voice though she does not speak and is not called for anymore. Only once does she lift her chin from her chest, casting suspiciously about the street where unfinished figures appear to step out of themselves with unseemly swiftness, as if specters emerging from a shared grave to haunt this rainy night.

When she opens her eyes again she is seated on a velvet chair. She swings her back across the supple hairs and feels a pleasant warmth in her chest. There is a candle on the table and she watches it rise and collapse in its rosy, waxen cup. After a while someone takes her hand. She is thinking of something, although she cannot quite say what. Some other touch out of the past, perhaps. She grasps the hand that holds her. Someone says her name again.

She looks up from her lap and her eyes clear and focus on the figure of a woman dressed in a white cellophane gown and with bright scarves falling from her neck. Her black hair is folded into a kind of a hat. She has a dark face that brings to the girl's mind a picture of an African queen she has once seen she does not know when or where. The woman smiles at her. Her teeth are like jewels in the candle's flame. The girl begins to laugh hysterically and then there is another hand upon her, this one on her shoulder, and she twists her ashen throat and looks behind. The man's face is swimming in a translucent pool of darkness and upside down it looks like it could have been the face of some ancient invertebrate from the farthest depths of the sea. She turns in the chair and regards him again, this time more critically, a face she knows and remembers all at once and she says his name and he tells her to listen to the woman. She nods absently and turns back in her chair.

The woman has laid out a series of cards on the table between them and she points them one to the next with a tiny switchblade that goes in and out of the torqued candlelight. As she shifts the cards with the blade she tells the girl without looking up at her that she has the hair of an islander. The long running hair of the wind, she says.

The girl's face lights dimly and she touches her hair with her fingers, then pats it down with the flats of her hands. Oh, she says.

The woman grins at the cards. She looks across the table at her. Pick only three, she says.

The girl leans up in the chair and studies the cards with false sobriety, pressing her finger into one and then pausing a long time before marking out the next. When she has made her final decision the woman glances at her, although this time her smile does not appear jeweled but instead is tight and vaguely sinister. The girl winces and the woman takes her hand again and again she feels calmed and the smile is once more bright and plaintive.

The woman releases her hand. She holds her gaze a moment longer then begins to examine the cards. She flips them onto their backsides with the tip of the knife. The first, the second, the last. There are other faces composed on the cards and they too seem to ponder over the girl with great deliberation from the black flowers of their painted eyes. One is a knight, another a dancing bear. The last is obscure to the girl, a woman's body though with armored breasts and a wand that goes with a multitude of stars from her furred hand. The woman nods at the cards. She taps them with the tip of the switchblade and nods some more. The girl is sitting upright in her chair now and the man is sitting beside her and she looks at him and still she knows his name, that his bedsheets are of an Egyptian cotton the color of topaz.

The girl turns from his stare and regards the woman. She parts her mouth unsurely and casts about the front of the room as if from the undulating bar some abject horror might issue forth and descend upon her. Yes, she says.

All right. Shall I tell you then?

The girl swings her eyes around again and for a moment her face clouds and then she smiles an untroubled smile. She composes her hands on her lap.

Yes, she says, although she is not sure what she herself has asked for. Please. Please tell me.

The woman had been nodding her head and when the girl replies she stops abruptly. Yes, she says. I will tell you. She places her hands together on the table, as if for this girl seated before her she might offer up a prayer. Then she opens her hands and lays the backs of them on the table. There are places within places and it is through these anterior rooms that you move, she says.

The girl leans back in her chair. She watches the fluted light of the candle. Yes, she says.

Who can say is one better than the other, though. I can only tell you that it is into these darker rooms that the winds have carried you.

The girl closes her eyes. She feels her face smiling. She feels too a breeze in her hair and for a while she hears nothing. After a long time she hears the woman's voice on the edge of the wind, or perhaps hears what the wind itself speaks to her from that unseen night. It is a flat, uncadenced voice, as a voice heard through a stone wall. And what the voice speaks is that the path she must now follow is to be a path of her own making or unmaking. Then it is the African queen's voice again and she says that hers is a rare case in which the cards cannot tell but because of the room in which she moves they can only watch from afar. That the door is closed to them because it is not a true door and that the cards hold dominion solely in the world of truth, and in no other world out-side.

Then she tells her not to worry. That hers is not a path untrod. That as with everything in those rooms there are choices uncounted and that it is now up to her to make an inventory of those choices for the choices of that world are a many-folded skirt and within those folds each man each woman is named and that in the fold which is hers there is a path that she will choose for better or worse because the one thing she cannot not do is turn from those choices for they are in fact the fabric of her life to come, and choose she must.

She opens her eyes. The room is very loud. Suddenly there are people moving all about her. Some are dancing. Others stand and laugh. Someone leers down and offers her a cigarette. She takes it without looking up. After a moment it drops from her fingers and falls to the floor. She looks back at the woman, her figure marked wildly by the gut-tered flame out of which she presents herself to the girl in a motley series of unwed objects: The lips, the eye, the blade of the knife.

All time and no time seems to pass when there is that roughness on her shoulder again and she is standing out of the chair, walking back-wards by the man's hand and looking at the woman who has retracted the blade on the knife and is now shuffling the cards with a terrible precision.

Then they are in the street again, the rain still slashing down and erupting in the standing pools of water, the air cool on her face. She makes a pirouette off the curb and spins in the street until his hand catches her up again. This time she flings her arms around his shoulders and presses her breasts into his shirt and kisses him on the mouth.

There are places within places, she whispers hotly in his ear.

He turns his head away and leans and kisses her neck. Then he says: Come on. If you want.

The girl lets her arms fall from his shoulders and she makes another pirouette. Where shall we go, she cries.

The man laughs without pleasure. He comes into the street and stands before her. He removes his hand from his jacket pocket. Just off his chin he holds up a small paper bag. The girl lunges forward and he thrusts the bag above his head and takes her by the waist and pulls her to him and kisses her roughly on the mouth.

Come on, she says. She steps back from his arms. Her face grows serious and she sweeps aside her tangled hair and pats him on the cold white flesh of his cheek. I want.

FLOUNDERING

Ben Erickson

The old man held the floundering light while he and the boy waded through the knee-deep water. The bay was smooth, and the humid summer air hung close and quiet. As the pressurized gas ignited around the fragile ashen mantles, the lamp gave off a constant hiss—the only sound disturbing the night—and its brilliant white light illuminated the water in front of them, magnifying and throwing every feature on the bottom into sharp relief.

They walked slowly, so as not to cloud the already murky water, sliding their feet along to avoid stepping on a buried stingray. Moving the lamp from side to side, the man scanned the water in front of him, searching for the indistinct outline of a flounder lying camouflaged on the bottom. Their luminous beacon attracted a menagerie of small fish that moved when they moved and stopped when they stopped, like a traveling circus of miniature marine performers. Needlefish were also attracted by the light. Shooting through the water like bottle rockets, the slender fish startled the boy from time to time as they collided harmlessly against his bare legs.

The boy gripped the long wooden handle of the gig loosely in his fingers. As they walked he dipped the metal tip underwater, never tiring of watching its single sharp point appear to bend magically in the refracted light. A empty washtub floated behind him, tethered to his belt by a frayed manila rope.

"Have you ever seen a jubilee?" his grandfather asked, without taking his eyes off the water.

"I've heard of them, but I've never seen one," the boy said, chasing a minnow with the tip of the gig.

"Well, this stretch of Mobile Bay is about the only place you'll find them," he told him.

The boy reached down with the gig and touched a crab the size of his hand that was frozen in the light. The point clinked metallically on its hard shell, causing the crab to extend its claws in self-defense as it backed out of the circle of light.

"You really need to live on the bay to see a jubilee, not just visit once in a while during summer vacation," he said, glancing over at the boy. "They don't happen very often, and when they do it's usually late at night after everyone's asleep. Yes sir, they're an amazing thing to behold."

The old man suddenly stopped and pointed at the bottom a few feet in front of them. "Do you see him?" he asked.

Sighting down the bony index finger of his grandfather's outstretched hand, the boy could just make out the dim outline in the sand.

"Ease forward, until you're close enough," he whispered in the boy's ear, as if the fish could hear him through the water.

The boy did as he was told and stood poised to strike.

"Now, do just like we practiced," the voice over his shoulder said. "Remember how the water bends the light, and aim for where he really is, not where your eyes tell you."

The boy calculated the difference between reality and illusion then thrust the gig downward. The bottom in front of him erupted in a cloud of silt, obscuring everything. He held tight to the gig as it vibrated in his hands, pinning his prey to the bottom. Soon the struggling lessened.

"That's it," the old man said. "Now, slide one hand under him."

Still holding the gig firmly with one hand, the boy slid his other one down the handle until he could feel the cold skin of the fish. Sliding his upturned hand beneath it, he felt the hard steel of the gig slip between his outstretched fingers.

"Got it," he said, his mouth barely above water.

"Good. Now, lift him up and put him in the tub."

He cradled the still-quivering flounder into the washtub, then let it slide off the gig. The fish lay gasping in the bottom of the empty tub. Its skin was a mottled patchwork of greens and browns, with both eyes staring up at them from the top of the pancake thin body.

"Nice work," his grandfather said, giving him a congratulatory pat on the shoulder.

They resumed their slow pace through the water. The hissing of the lamp blended with the sound of mosquitoes buzzing around the boy's ear. By now he had grown so used to their high-pitched whine that he didn't even bother waving them away anymore. Another crab appeared at the edge of their ever-changing circle of light, and once more the boy reached out and touched it with his gig. This time there was no answering clink.

"Soft-shell," the old man said. "Best eating around. Pick him up and put him in the tub for me."

"How?" he asked. "I don't have a net."

"You don't need one," his grandfather replied. "Just use your hands."

"But it'll pinch me," the boy said, hiding his free hand behind his back at the mere thought of it.

"He just shed his shell, and the new one hasn't had time to harden yet," he told him. "He couldn't hurt you if he tried."

Reluctantly, the boy reached down into the water and touched the crab with his bare hand, then jerked it back. When there was no reaction, he fished it out and held it up to the light. It looked like any other crab, except that the shell was as pliable as rubber. He touched the claws, and even they bent uselessly.

"Crabs have to shed their shells when they grow too big for them, just like a snake shedding its skin," the old man said. "Trouble is, they're helpless when it happens. So they do it at night in shallow water, where there's less chance they'll be seen. Before long the new shell will harden and their armor will be restored. Put him in there, and I'll cook him when we get back," he said, motioning to the washtub. "You fry them up whole and can eat almost everything."

The boy put the crab in the tub next to the flounder, and they continued wading through the night.

"I can still remember my first jubilee. I couldn't have been but six or seven at the time, not much younger than you are now," his grandfather said, sizing up the boy at his side. "Back then if somebody happened on one, they'd let everyone on the bay know about it. Bells would ring and people would beat pots and pans all up and down the Eastern Shore. Lights would come on in houses, and word would spread like wildfire."

He looked over at the shore, ignoring the glare from the yard lights that now lined the bay and pictured it as it had once been.

"Yes sir, I can still hear them like it was yesterday…"

"Jubileeee!…Jubileeee!"

The disembodied voice ran along the shore calling loudly in the dark, accompanied by the sound of a cooking spoon beating time on a pot. Passing the unlit house, it continued down the narrow strip of sand, growing fainter and fainter until it finally faded out all together.

The sound filtered through the open upstairs window and tickled at the back of the sleeping boy's consciousness. When he had gone to bed, the oppressive heat had caused him to kick off the covers. Now, after midnight, he was huddled in a tight ball against the cool night air. As the house around him began to awaken, he stirred restlessly. Doors opened and muffled voices drifted up the staircase to his room. Softly at first—just a distant tap-tap-tap of the spoon on the pan—then growing louder and louder, the unseen voice approached again in the darkness, as the runner made his return trip down the beach.

"Jubileeee!…Jubileeee!…Jubilee at Point Clear!…Come and get 'em while they's still there!?…Jubileeee!…Jubileeee!"

The boy's eyes opened like released window shades, and in an instant he was wide awake. Rolling out of bed, he looked out the window that faced the bay. In the dim light reflected off the water, he could just make out the receding flash of the pan and the gleam of an unbuttoned white shirt on dark skin. Pulling on his clothes, he opened the door to his room and bounded down the staircase.

His mother was already in the kitchen, piling buckets and croaker sacks on the table. Through the back screen door, he could see his father hooking their old mare to the wagon.

"I'll take them out to him," he said, gathering up the containers.

His mother watched as he struggled to carry more than his small arms could hold. Barely able to see over his burden, he bumped and clanged his way out the back door and down the steps.

His father turned at the sound. "Well, look who's up!" he said. "I guess you heard all that racket on the beach?"

"Can I go? Please!" he asked.

"It's mighty late for a boy your age to be out."

"I'll do everything you tell me. *Please!*" the boy pleaded.

His father eyed him critically. "Well, I wasn't going to wake you," he said, pausing for dramatic effect. "But since you're already up, I suppose so."

A broad grin split the boy's face at the invitation. His father took the armful of containers from him and put them in the back of the wagon. Reaching down, he lifted the boy up onto the seat, then climbed in after him.

His mother appeared at the door with a fruit jar full of iced tea and a paper bag of sandwiches.

"Just in case you men get hungry," she said, handing them up.

"Don't wait up," his father said, giving her a peck on the cheek. "We'll be back by morning. Come on now, Molly," he called to the horse as he slapped the reins.

The mare seemed to sense their excitement and started down the drive at a brisk trot. Turning out onto the main road, they were swallowed up by the night.

Trees and bushes overhung the narrow shell road that paralleled the bay. Even though the boy had traveled it hundreds of times before, the darkness changed everything. Mysterious shadows formed in the dim light from the kerosene lanterns as they swung back and forth on their hooks, inspiring visions of highwaymen or pirates lying in wait around every bend in the winding road. Moving closer to his father's side, he narrowed his eyes until they were reduced to slits he could barely see through. His father whistled a cheerful tune and didn't seem the least bit concerned at their peril, but with every new pair of eyes that stared back at him from the edge of the road, the boy feared the worst. Each time they materialized into the familiar shape of a raccoon or possum, he breathed a small sigh of relief.

Soon they were joined by other wagons, as people from miles around heard the news, and the air was filled with the rumble of wheels on the rough road. When they reached the point of land that jutted out into the bay, the wagons pulled single-file off the main road and down a sandy track that led to the shore.

Lights were on in the hotel that straddled the point, and the balcony facing the bay was lined with guests who had been roused in the middle of the night to witness the unusual spectacle. They leaned out over the porch railings, watching with curiosity as the scene unfolded below. The beach glowed with bonfires and lanterns, and laughter mingled with the chattering of excited voices.

His father stopped the wagon by the side of the road and climbed down. Taking the croaker sacks from the back, he removed one of the lanterns from its hook, and together they walked down to the water's edge.

The pungent smell of the bay was even stronger than usual, and the boy's eyes grew wide as the lantern lit up the shoreline. Flounder, stingrays, and other bottom dwellers of all sizes and shapes flapped help-lessly in the shallow water. There were so many that in places they were piled two or three deep. Crabs crawled over them in an effort to escape, some pulling themselves all the way out of the water in the process. It was almost impossible to set foot in the bay without stepping on something. Looking down the beach, he could see lights scattered for a quarter mile in either direction.

"You've read in the Bible about manna falling from heaven?" his father asked.

"Yes, sir."

"Well, this is manna brought up by the sea."

"What makes them do it, Papa?" he asked, puzzled.

"I guess the powers that be tell them to."

"But there must be a reason?"

"No one knows, son. I guess it's just one of life's little mysteries," he said. "Now hold the light for me while I fill these sacks."

He gathered up more than they could eat, then carried the burlap bags up the beach to the wagon with the boy following behind him. The brackish water of the bay seeped through the porous cloth, leaving a wet trail in the sand. By the time he hoisted the last of the heavy sacks over the side of the wagon, the changing tide had already begun to pull what remained back out into the depths of the bay. Many of the other wagons were leaving, and the hotel guests had long since vanished from their porches to retire for the second time that night.

Taking the paper bag and jar from the seat, they walked over to join the group of men sitting around a bonfire on the beach. Examining their weathered faces in the reflected firelight, the boy recognized them as fishermen, crabbers, and shrimpers who were regulars at his father's store. They would often stop by to chat and spend a hot summer afternoon on the benches and chairs that lined the store's shady porch, accompanied by the popping of the tin roof as it expanded in the sun. Often they would entice his father to join them on fishing trips to try and lure a mighty tarpon from the bay.

The men made a fuss over the boy, rumpling his hair and asking him what he wanted to be when he grew up.

"A fisherman," he replied without hesitation.

They burst into hoots of laughter.

"Well I guess he takes after you, Bill," one of the men said, nudging his father. "You've never been able to leave the fish alone."

The laughter died down, and they found a vacant spot in the circle around the fire. Overhead, the stars twinkled brightly against the dark sky. A flask was passed from hand to hand to take the chill out of the night air, and stories were told as they stared into the dancing flames. Their voices rose and fell in the glow of the flickering embers, then drifted upward, suspended on a cloud of rising smoke.

They told stories about the bay while it lapped against the shore just a few yards away. Over the years their tales had grown and changed in the telling and retelling, until they had been transformed into something else all together.

The boy put his head on his father's lap and listened to the men talk as he looked up at the night sky. If he stared long enough, the tiny points of light above him appeared to move against the vast blackness. Around him, the voices wove in and out of his consciousness.

"So I was out in my boat—you know that little sixteen-footer I had built over at Hawkins yard—checking traps, and it was getting on near dark. I'd just dumped the last one when I heard a boom right behind me as loud as thunder, and a splash soaked me to the skin. Before I could turn around, a wave hit the boat broadside, knocked me clean off my feet. As I picked myself up from the bottom of the boat, I saw something circling around me in the gloom not far away. I could just make out the gray back cutting through the water. Its dorsal fin stuck up at least three feet in the air, and I realized that I was looking into the eyes of the biggest hammerhead shark these parts have ever seen. Before I could decide what to do next, his tail took another swipe at my boat and splintered the transom like kindling. I started taking on water fast and…"

One bright star in particular seemed to pulsate as the boy watched. He imagined it as a lighthouse on some distant shore, guiding the other stars on their way. The sound of the men talking droned on around him.

"It was a slow afternoon, and the fish had long since given up on biting. I must have dozed off, because the next thing I know there's a roaring sound, like I was standing right by a waterfall. When I opened my eyes, the first thing I saw was a dark cloud hovering above me. I sat up in my boat and looked out, and as close as from me to you was a waterspout. Its funnel was black and evil looking, and I could see fish as big as my arm caught in it and sucked up as quick as a cat…"

Out of the corner of his eye, the boy saw a shooting star streak across the sky. He followed its phosphorescent trail until it disappeared as if it had never existed.

"When she stopped dead in the water, I figured my net had hung on a snag. Then, so help me, she started moving backward, picking up speed as she goes. Water began sloshing over the stern as I made my way aft, grabbing a knife as I went. The bay behind me was bubbling and churning like a thing alive. I go to sawing on the port line, and it popped like a piece of piano wire, knocking the knife clean out of my hand. That put all the pressure on the starboard side, and she started heeling over…"

A star low in the western sky far out over the bay attracted the boy's attention. As he watched, it twinkled from red to green and back again. Just like the lights on a ship, he thought, as the soft sounds of the bay lulled him to sleep.

"I guess we was running about ten miles out in the gulf when I saw a line of squalls moving our way. So I told the boys to pull in the lines, and I turned us back toward home. On the way in the wind began to pick up, and the barometer started to drop. We were about halfway there when all hell broke loose. I couldn't see more than fifty feet in front of me, and the wind was blowing so hard that the water was covered in foam. I finally made it to the channel by the grace of my compass and dead reckoning alone. I was about to try and take her through the pass blind when the rain slacked up for a minute, and I could see breakers all the way across it. So I spun the wheel hard about, trying to head back out to sea to ride it out, when a rogue wave come out of nowhere and hit us broadside..."

As the fire burned down, the sky began to lighten in the east. An early morning breeze ruffled the water, sending the smoke swirling across the beach. One by one the men stood up, stretched, and headed for home.

Gently picking up the sleeping boy, his father carried him back to the wagon. When he lifted him up onto the seat, he opened his eyes.

"Where are we?" the boy asked.

"Going home, buddy," his father told him. "I've got to open the store, and you and your mother have fish to clean and crabs to boil."

"Oh," he replied, squinting through sleep-swollen eyes.

Turning the wagon around on the sandy track, his father clicked his tongue, and they headed back down the road toward home. It wasn't the excitement of a night outing that motivated the mare's pace this time, but a vision of the barn with fresh hay in her stall. The rocking of the wagon soon had the boy fast asleep again, nestled against his father's side.

By the time they turned down the lane to the house, the sun had risen and was peeking through the leaves of the live oaks. Opening his eyes, the boy looked around him. The morning breeze played in the branches, causing the limbs to sway. Their rhythmic movement sent flecks of light skittering across the ground in constantly changing patterns, like a shower of shooting stars flung across the night sky.

"Yes sir, that was a long time ago," the old man said, looking toward the distant point of land, its shape outlined by the lights from the hotel. "A lot has changed since then."

"Do you think we'll have a jubilee tonight?" the boy at his side asked, poking his gig at a clump of grass growing on the bottom of the bay.

"No one knows," he said, mirroring his father's words from so long ago. "Like many things in life, they tend to show up when you aren't expecting them and leave long before you're ready for them to go."

"Like me?" the boy asked, looking up at him.

"Yes," his grandfather said with a smile, "and like your grandmother, too."

They walked on in silence.

"Mama says I look like her," the boy said finally.

The old man stopped and searched his face in the lamp's glow, then reached out and brushed his hair back from his forehead.

"Yes, I guess you do at that," he said. "I can see her in your eyes."

The boy looked away self-consciously, pretending to examine the lifeless flounder in the tub.

"I can't remember her," the boy said, guilt filling his voice.

"You were little then," he replied. "Memories fade."

"But you remember the jubilee. You told me everything about it," he said. "I can't even see her face anymore."

"Do you remember how she used to rock you on her lap?"

The boy thought a minute, then nodded.

"What about that time you stepped on a catfish fin, and she bandaged it up and made you her special homemade gumbo?" he asked.

The boy nodded again.

"You remember more than you think you do," his grandfather told him.

"Will I remember you?" the boy asked, a look of concern on his face.

Before the old man could answer, a shooting star streaked across the sky in front of them. For a brief moment, it was brighter than everything else combined.

"You'll remember," the old man said, as the light from the falling star began to fade.

Linda Wahlthal

David Fuller

Linda loved to wrestle, and I was in
love with Linda, so it didn't matter
the stinging pain, my knees bloody,
skinned, and stained bright green.
My stomach straddled, skinny arms pinned
by her round tanned knees, Linda rapped
heartbeats on my sternum. A curled
index finger, the knuckle of punishment
for being weaker or male, or both.
I loved the way her damp hair hung when
she smiled down at me. The more I'd
struggled the harder her pelvis would
press against my chest. Her breath
close enough to swallow.
She smelled of fresh cut grass and
animal musk, like the scent of rabbit's
fur inside a leather glove.
Linda Wahlthal, where are you? Like
most first loves, you moved away too
soon and missed the man I became.
What passion holds you now, that
fifty years have passed?
I'm sustained by memories, no longer
by what I do. And wrestle with a
different foe, but I'd much rather
have lost to you.

The Scrapbook

Frank Turner Hollon

MARTHA ABIGAIL MATTHEWS
FAIRHOPE, ALABAMA

Martha Abigail Matthews died on September 3 at the age of thirty-two after a long and courageous battle with cancer. She was a schoolteacher, a long-distance runner, and the mother of four children.

Survivors include her husband, Mark Matthews; children, Annie, Kevin, Lidia, and Jason; two brothers, Carl Bristol of Topeka, Kansas, and Kevin Bristol of Montgomery, Alabama; mother and father, Lucy and James Bristol of Fairhope; and a twin sister, Maggie Bristol of Long Island, New York.

Visitation will begin Tuesday at 9:00 a.m. at the Fairhope Funeral Home followed by a service at 10:00 a.m. at Pine Forest Cemetery in Silverhill.

There was a black-and-white picture of a smiling lady above the obituary. Jane liked to see the faces of the people who had just died. She liked it, too, when the article explained the manner of death and had some personal note about the deceased.

Jane lived alone. She was fifty-eight years old, divorced, and read the newspaper every day, saving the obituaries for last. She felt she got to know people and their families through reading and rereading the few small paragraphs under each photograph, staring at the face of the person who no longer existed in this life. There was so much to learn reading between the lines, so much in a few words—"the age of thirty-two," "battle with cancer," "four children," "a twin sister."

It was two years earlier when Jane went to her first funeral of a stranger. She had been sipping her morning coffee, reading of the death of a teenage boy in a motorcycle accident. He played shortstop on the high school baseball team and volunteered with the Salvation Army. His entire life was ahead of him. She folded the paper on her lap and decided to attend the funeral.

Jane dressed in her best black dress. She called beforehand to make sure it was an open casket. She waited in the long line stretching out the door of the church and around the corner. No one questioned her as she made her way through the line of grieving family members, nor when she hugged the dead boy's mother, or took the hand of his father. Jane stood for a long time above the casket looking at the face and hands of the teenage boy she had seen in the photograph in the paper. People who sat in their living rooms reading snippets in the newspaper could never really understand. This was much more intimate. She felt she had become part of the family history.

That first experience was good. Jane got the courage to go again, and again. She was there when they buried the dead baby found on the stranger's doorstep. She stood in the rain when they laid to rest the old black man, one hundred and two years old, with sixty-four great-grand-children. Jane was one of only a few white women at the service, but no one said a word.

Jane was careful not to go too often. There was the chance that she would be recognized from another service and questioned about her relationship. She was not aware of any law forbidding uninvited attendance at funerals, but nonetheless, there would be those who would find something wrong about it. It was almost like roaming around another person's home while they were out of town. Jane kept a scrapbook with the obituaries of every funeral she attended.

There weren't really that many funerals Jane wanted to attend, certainly not the boring funerals for those regular people who died of natural causes between sixty-five and eighty years of age. Their obituaries were bland and factual. There was nothing in their few sentences that would make another person want to get dressed up and go out to see them lying dead in a casket. The most interesting fact was almost always omitted, how they died. Jane preferred to know the name of the disease that killed these people, the cause of the fire, the speed of the vehicle, the poison, the caliber of bullet.

The death of young children was the saddest. Not the babies, but the kids three or four years old. Jane could see in the faces of their parents the bewilderment that would grow into bitterness. The bitterness that would fester into anger. The anger that would eat away their marriages. One time, ten months after the funeral of a five-year-old girl who was hit by a car, Jane saw in the newspaper where her father had gone out to the little girl's grave and shot himself in the head. Jane had never had children. The closest she would come to feeling the grief was touching the cold face of the little girl in the open coffin.

One time Jane saw a man in the grocery store that she had met at a funeral. The man was the thirty-five-year-old son of Edward Kellogg. Edward Kellogg had been struck by lightning while fishing in the bay. His body wasn't recovered for several days. It was a closed casket.

The man asked, "Didn't we meet at my father's funeral?"

Jane was frozen in fear. She had never been forced to lie.

"Yes, I believe we did," Jane answered.

"I don't think I ever got your name."

"Jane. Jane Ulrey."

They stood facing each other for a moment in aisle number four in front of the Hamburger Helper. The man seemed anxious to say something. Finally he did.

"My father was a very private man. My mother died when I was a boy."

There was still something he wanted to say.

"Do you mind me asking how you knew my dad?"

Six months after his father's funeral Jane could see tears well up in the young man's eyes. He missed his father very much. Jane reached her hand up and touched the man's face. It was strong. Jane turned and walked away from him, knowing he wouldn't follow. Knowing her silence answered his questions.

It was time to get ready to see Martha Matthews. Her face would be gaunt from her "courageous battle with cancer." She was a runner. A long-distance runner. She would have believed she could beat the disease. The fear of leaving her children behind would have given her the strength every day to believe she could win despite the doctor's words, or the pain, or the sickness in her stomach.

Jane wore the customary black dress. She was always careful not to overdo, not to stand out in the crowd of mourners. She brought a handkerchief and a small black handbag. In the handbag she carried four peppermint candies, one for each of the children Martha Matthews had left behind: Annie, Kevin, Lidia, and Jason. Probably listed in order by their ages, oldest to youngest, with Annie maybe ten years old (Martha was only thirty-two), and Jason at least three years old.

Jane looked forward to seeing Martha's twin sister, Maggie. Surely she would travel down from Long Island, New York. Jane imagined Maggie wondering about her own health. Twins, of the same blood, raised in the same environment, eating the same food, and one grows cancer inside, and the other doesn't? Maggie must be haunted by the thought. She must wonder where inside her own body the first tiny speck of cancer will appear. When will her battle begin?

On the way driving to the funeral home Jane was comforted by the fact that Martha's parents lived in town and had probably been there with her through the illness. She looked forward to seeing their faces and hearing them say, "She's in a better place now. There was so much pain. It's a blessing that it's over."

There were only a few cars parked outside the funeral home. Jane had expected more. She waited for several minutes until another few cars arrived. She walked inside and avoided eye contact. She immediately recognized Martha's twin sister standing at the far end of the room. The older couple next to her probably were the parents.

Jane bypassed the guest book on the table next to a beautiful display of flowers, dark red roses and baby's breath. She headed towards the coffin in the adjoining room. Jane was familiar with the layout of this funeral home. It was her favorite.

Jane walked past the parents and nodded. The father did not turn away. Standing in front of the coffin was a man openly crying. Unlike most men, he made no effort to hide his sadness. Jane believed the man must be the husband of Martha Matthews, Mark. The children were nowhere to be seen. There were only a few other people in the entire room. There was a heaviness Jane could not describe. More than just somber. There was open anger in the room where normally it would have been below the surface.

Jane stood behind Mark Matthews as he cried. He shook his head from side to side and rubbed his eyes. He was lost. Jane turned around to see Martha's mother and father watching her from the door. Mark Matthews stepped aside never knowing anyone was behind him. He found a chair against the wall and sat down. Jane approached the coffin.

Martha Abigail Matthews was a small woman. Her face was different from the picture. Her expression seemed restful at first, but Jane stood over the body long enough to see that the expression was not restful at all. It was the face of a person who hadn't wanted to die. A person who had fought until the last breath, for just one more breath, one more last look at her children. It was the face of an angel who didn't want to go away to heaven because she believed she was already there.

From the chair against the wall a calm voice said, "Who are you?"

Startled, Jane turned to Mark Matthews.

"Who are you?" Mark repeated.

"I'm sorry," Jane said.

They looked at each other a moment. Jane heard people move behind her. Over her shoulder she saw Martha's parents, and Maggie, and two other men, probably Martha's brothers. They had come into the room.

"You don't belong here," Mark said. "I can tell by the way you look at her. You didn't know her."

Mark's voice was flat. There was nowhere for Jane to go.

"You don't belong here," he said. "You don't get to show up at the end and look at my wife and act like you know her." There was a pause before Mark said calmly again, "Who are you?"

Jane looked at Mark's face, his eyes red, his jaw set tight. She turned back to Martha in the coffin. It didn't seem right to be treated this way, she thought. There were peppermints for the children. There was grieving yet to do.

From behind, Jane heard Martha's mother say, "You should leave now."

She turned to see the family. The brothers, Carl and Kevin, looked like their father. Maggie was small like her mother and her sister. They had all grown up in a house together. The girls would have shared a room. The boys were older, probably played sports, they had broad shoulders and honest faces.

There were lots of things Jane wanted to say, but nothing came out. She held her head high and walked past the family of Martha Abigail Matthews. Her legs were weak. When she managed to arrive at her car she was out of breath. At home, after changing clothes, Jane sat down at her kitchen table with the scrapbook. She carefully removed the newspaper obituary and the black-and-white picture of Martha Matthews from the last page. She used a new razor blade to carefully cut the tape. Afterward, looking at the blank page, it was as if she never heard of Martha Abigail Matthews. Jane knew there would be a newspaper tomorrow morning with new names and faces. She would take her chances.

The Seamstress

Suzanne Hudson

"Well, all I can say about that," Mrs. Clark Hogan Wilson announced, "is that Sarah Jo Cooper never had any inkling about how to keep herself a cut above the riff-raff." Mrs. Wilson, "Francie" to her most bosom of friends, lifted a dimpled little hand to brush a puff of parlor-dyed curls back from her forehead, revealing grooved wrinkles born of brow-knitting and, on a typical day, glaring as she sulked. Today, however, she was not sulking, riding instead the crest of an exhilarating wave of self-importance while she engaged in the gossip that nourished her. She stood on a four-by-four raised platform, feeling that much higher than her handmaidens, while a seamstress altered the ball gown she was to wear a week from Friday.

She had just been regaled with the tale of Sarah Jo Cooper, who had left her husband of thirty-two years to ride off into the sunset with a drywall hanger who was renovating the antebellum home said husband had bought for her only a month prior. "Once trash, always trash," Mrs. Wilson said. "I believe I pointed that out to you at Mitzi Stanton's last dinner party if you'll recall. You do recall that?"

"I most certainly do," her most recent best friend, Camilla, Mrs. James Cunningham Dixon, replied, as the seamstress worked at pinning Mrs. Wilson's hem.

The seamstress, Celeste, had observed this cannibalistic friendship over the previous weeks of fittings and alterations as she constructed Mrs. Wilson's Mardi Gras gown. She had noted that Mrs. Dixon was tenacious about doing her duty as a hanger-on, bearing platters of giddy gossip for her mentor to consume. Gifted with an encyclopedic knowledge of maiden names and double first cousins, Mrs. Dixon could sniff out vague ancestral connections to any scandal and find genealogical secrets that would blush a St. Louis streetwalker. She had even prodded Celeste, a deliberately private soul, for personal information, for a family history from which to gain a point of reference. She had been delighted when she discovered that Celeste had grown up with her own maternal third cousin, Martha Sams, in Brannon, Mississippi, south and west of Columbus, immediately seeing that cousin Martha could offer the low-down on Celeste.

In addition to her role as Troubadour of Troubles, Purveyor of Peccadillos, Mrs. Dixon also undertook her task of Flatterer-in-Chief to Mrs. Wilson with an effusive fervor. "You are an excellent judge of character, Francie. It's pure power of perception. You simply *know* people through and through, and I do recall that you pointed that out to me about Sarah Jo Cooper. Saw right clear through her. I swear, you don't miss a beat," she gushed.

Mrs. Wilson picked a piece of lint from the velvet skirt of her gown and flicked it into the air. It dipped and danced like dwarfed confetti. "Of course you also recall that it was at Mitzi's tacky little dinner party," she said. "Do you recall that embarrassing nightmare of a party?"

"Absolutely do," Mrs. Dixon said. "It was right there at that selfsame party that you pointed out to me about Sarah Jo's flawed character. You pointed out to me how cozy she was with the help. How she had her head leaned in to that college boy bartender who—"

"The one in the tiki hut," Mrs. Wilson said. "Do you recall that tacky little tiki hut Mitzi had set up by the pool as an island bar?"

"Well, of course. How could I not? It was the one with the young college boy bartending in it. A medical student, I think."

"It was a Hawaiian luau theme you see, Celeste. A luau is a Hawaiian feast, did you know?" Mrs. Wilson spoke down to the woman at her feet. "All of our parties—well, the very best ones, anyway—they all have a theme. You know, the creation of a tableau, a setting, a dramatic flair."

"My, how elegant." Celeste, the seamstress, pulled another straight pin from her wrist cushion, working with the gold net material bunched at Mrs. Wilson's waist, draped down around the rich, deep-purple velvet gown, the tips of her nimble fingers faintly aware of little rolls of fatty flesh beneath the clingy fabric. "Now, Mrs. Wilson, it's important that you bring those shoes you plan to wear with this when you come for your next fitting. This netting is very tricky to hem and—"

"Yes yes yes," Mrs. Wilson said. "But as I was saying just now, the theme is what makes the party, if you have the flair to make it work. Believe you me, there is nothing more pitiful than a flopped theme."

"Well, you wouldn't know about that, Francie," Mrs. Dixon said, rummaging through an oversized handbag. "I'm telling you, Celeste, there is nothing like one of Francie's parties. They are the best, bar none. You should get to see one before you die, my hand to God. Do you want a LifeSaver?" she held out the roll of candy, its foil wrapper peeled and hanging like tossed serpentine.

"No, thank you," Celeste said. The gold netting was stiff and unwieldy next to the supple purple velvet. "Would you lift your arm, please?"

Mrs. Wilson complied, sending the sprung flesh on the underside of her arm into a series of jiggles. "Like last August. I had an all-black party last August. Not black *people*, you know, but a black décor, like a wake or a funeral, for Hogie's fiftieth birthday party. And he's way older than me, so don't you even think it. Do you recall that party, Camilla?"

"It was only the be-all and end-all of birthday parties," Camilla gushed. Celeste pulled another straight pin from the red satin wrist cushion. Her own husband had not seen fifty, had died instead at twenty-eight, leaving her with four small children, a Singer sewing machine, and an avalanche of debt, estranged from the family that could have helped her.

"And the all-black party was such a hit that on New Year's I had an all-white party, just like those jet-setter folks do. You know, everything white—white food, like sour cream and cream cheese dips, and vanilla cakes and this divine, frothy white wine punch. Oh—and white flowers. You know, floating camellias and such. And white candles—white everything."

"It was nothing short of fabulous, Celeste," said Mrs. Dixon. "Francie throws the best parties of anyone in our circle, and you don't even get into our circle unless you know how to throw a grand party. Well, except for Mitzi Stanton, I guess."

"*Our* circle?" Mrs. Wilson lifted one eyebrow in arch indictment, then she smiled. "At any rate, it is no small feat to be a successful hostess, I am here to tell you. It takes quite a lot of thought and creativity. You can't believe all the little details you have to be mindful of. Just one tiny thing can cause a huge flop."

"My," Celeste said again.

"Right down to the guests," Mrs. Wilson went on. "You have to take care to have a complementary mix of temperaments and a code of dress. Of course, the guests at my white party were all required to wear white, so as not to disturb the theme. You have to be very specific on what to wear. Some people just don't have any finesse. Lord, my arm is tired. Can't I put it down?"

"Yes, ma'am." Celeste drew back and studied the netting she was attempting to drape as per instructions from Mrs. Wilson, who continued pontificating on the art of hostessing a successful party.

"If just one guest breaks the dress code, well, it simply sticks out like a sore thumb. It ruins the larger picture—the canvas, if you will. Anyway, I imagine I have just about done it all, party-theme-wise."

"But whenever we think she's outdone herself, she comes up with a brand-new twist," Mrs. Dixon said. "It's a flair, that's all. It's an inborn talent." She took a compact out of her purse and powdered down her nose. "I declare, I shine like a lighthouse beacon. And I don't have the first idea how to have my hair done for the ball." She scrutinized the stiffly layered flaps of frosty blonde, turning her head at sharp angles. "Good night alive, these highlights are all wrong."

Mrs. Dixon was in the process of moving from a social stratum just beneath that of Mrs. Wilson and into the one Mrs. Wilson presided over, so well-done highlights were of utmost importance. Mrs. Wilson herself was hoping to be elected president of her Mardi Gras society the next time around, poised to launch up to the next social level, the one that every great once in a while pierced the true aristocracy of coastal Alabama.

Mrs. Dixon snapped the compact shut. "I do know one thing, though. Even a magnificent Mardi Gras ball hasn't got much on one of Francie's parties. Go on, Francie, and try to tell Celeste all the themes you've done just this past year," Mrs. Dixon urged.

"Well, let's see," Mrs. Wilson said. "I've done a Roaring Twenties party and a Screen Siren—that's where you come as a movie star. Hogie and I were Liz and Dick. Anyway, a Screen Siren party, a Beach Blanket Bingo party over the bay, a Monaco Casino party at the country club. Gosh, it must be a half dozen. And I'm here to tell the both of you that a Hawaiian luau with a tiki hut bar, a bunch of plastic leis, and Don Ho ukulele music comes a dime a dozen."

"Isn't that the gospel," Mrs. Dixon chimed in. "It's practically one of the commandments: 'Thou shalt not throw a Hawaiian luau.' But then, Mitzi Stanton has nothing near your sense of style, Francie. On top of that, she's a Jew. I don't think they even believe in the Ten Commandments, do they?"

"Yes," the seamstress said. "They do."

"Anyway, that was just fluff about the commandments," Mrs. Dixon said. "My main point was about Francie having oodles of style and Mitzi having not one blessed drop."

"Well, at the risk of seeming big-headed, I certainly won't contradict that," Mrs. Wilson said. "And that is why I was elected parliamentarian and historian of the Merry Makers over Mitzi Stanton. The only reason we let her join in the first place was because her husband is Methodist and the premier auto salesman in Mobile. A Jew and Mardi Gras is oil and water, so she had no business being an officer. The gall. But after that tacky little luau of hers, she might as well have just put a sign on wheels out front of her house saying, 'Mitzi Stanton has no flair whatsoever'. There was no way she could have avoided me beating her in that election."

"It was a landslide, Celeste," Mrs. Dixon said to the seamstress. "It was practically a unanimous mandate."

"Goodness." Celeste walked a slow circle around Mrs. Wilson, studying the fit of the sequined bodice. Mardi Gras sparkles of purple and gold winked promises from the roly-poly pudge of Mrs. Clark Hogan Wilson.

"Oh, absolutely. A landslide," Mrs. Wilson reiterated. "And an honor, of course. A position of leadership, which is where you ought to be if you have flair and a keen sense of style. I mean, the business of the Merry Makers is to have party after party. Leading up to the big party during Mardi Gras, of course. It takes a keen sense of style."

"Well, honey, that is you. That is just you all over," Mrs. Dixon cooed, retrieving an emery board from the handbag and commencing to sand the edges of her fingernails. "I swanee, my nails look like a scrub-woman's." The scritch of the emery board punctuated a short silence before Mrs. Dixon remembered to re-focus on her friend. "Like I say, Francie, style is simply your calling card. You could have stepped right out of *Cosmopolitan* or *Vogue*." She craned her neck to see the seamstress, who again worked on the netting at Mrs. Wilson's back. "I'm sure you know, Celeste, that Mrs. Wilson will be showcased at the tableau. Which means, of course, that your dressmaking skills will be showcased."

"It's exciting, all right," Celeste said. She had been hearing for months about how Mrs. Wilson would be presented as an officer of her Mardi Gras society at a grand processional, or tableau, before the ball. It was a huge event, the pinnacle Mrs. Wilson had sought. "I will be proud to have you model my work."

"Oh, but, Celeste, sweetie, it's as much how you *wear* a dress as how it's made," Mrs. Wilson said. "More, even. Let's face it. Anybody and their sister can make a dress. Lord, I bet retards make them in factories all the time. I mean, the real flair is in the *wearing* of it, don't you think?"

"Yes. Of course." Celeste, practiced in the art of appearing unruffled by insensitivity, began unpinning and re-pinning the gold netting around the back of the dress.

She had tried to tell Mrs. Wilson that the netting would clash with the texture of velvet and had urged her to pick a grainy satin for the skirt of her gown, but Mrs. Wilson would have none of it. Mrs. Wilson had been looking for a specific effect, "a Marie Antoinette effect," she had said, "all swooped out on the sides, you know, but add a part hanging down the back. Almost a train, you know. A French queen for the Mardi Gras ball—le bon temps."

French like a New Orleans whore, Celeste had thought.

Mrs. Wilson had been coming to her dressmaking parlor for over twenty years, as had an entire parade of ladies and little girls carrying mounds of satin, Chantilly lace, dotted Swiss, peau de soie, crêpe, velveteen—fabrics that cocooned their social station in life like spun silk. She threaded embroidery into fine linen christening gowns, stitched the smocking across toddlers' dresses, sewed red-and-black velvet cuffs onto tartan plaid Christmas dresses, secured pastel netting over bridesmaids' skirts, and attached mother-of-pearl beads and Irish lace onto wedding gowns. She ran her tape measure around the busts, waists, and hips of the women, down the lengths of their backs, an intimacy ripe with irony. She aided well-dressed ladies in elaborate deceptions, drawing and cutting patterns for designer copies, that part of the business that was the most lucrative, and she deposited the women's folded bills and personal checks into her own burgeoning bank account. The stock market investments she made had doubled, tripled, and quadrupled the fees provided by the ladies who commanded her services. In recent years she had begun to look forward to a very comfortable early retirement. Now, in the midst of her forties, she was finally winding down, putting the last of her children through college, coming upon her own time in life. And she had taken more abuse than she would have ever predicted when she ran away from home at the age of seventeen, from wealthy parents in the Mississippi Black Belt, just to be with the man who loved her briefly, and very well, indeed, before he died.

A couple of her clients were from not old, but *very* old, money—Old Mobile aristocrats who would never deign to boast as Mrs. Wilson did, but who maintained a slick silver barrier of aloofness, a more subtle reminder that Celeste's purpose in life was to be at their beck and call. Unlike the social unfoldings of Mrs. Wilson's Mystic Order of Mirthful Merry Makers, their Mardi Gras functions were written up in vast detail in the *Mobile Press-Register*. Their King and Queen were treated like the blue-blooded royalty they were born to be, their expensive crowns bought and paid for with money that had been seeded by robber barons, and aged in timber, shipping, and double deals. Celeste hated them, save for one or two, with a fierce purity. She hated the low esteem in which they held her. And, having refused her own inheritance, having put it aside for her grandchildren, she hated the inherited currency her customers bestowed upon her after she worked on the hems of their garments, bowed there at their feet like a penitent parishioner seeking absolution.

But she hated Mrs. Wilson and her ilk a million times more, hated their hungry grasps at that higher station in life she had shunned, their shallow little battles, the meager stakes they raised above their means. Mrs. Clark Hogan Wilson epitomized it all, and Celeste had watched her for over two decades, coming up a notch or two here, down one notch there, her long, futile climb tearing at what little potential for a soul had ever rested in her in the first place.

Mrs. Clark Hogan Wilson talked about the local aristocrats—the Fillinghams, Dolans, McColloughs—as if they were more than passing acquaintances of hers. "Who will be the next Queen of Carnival?" she would ask. "Of course, we knew Maxine Dolan would have it this year, but next year there's going to be a huge battle between Lexus Dolan and that Mary McCollough. Their daddies are likely to come to blows. Isn't it delicious?" Celeste thought this talk of hers analogous to those pathetic women who discussed TV soap opera characters as they would friends or family members, filling their empty lives with the escapades and tribulations of the fictional characters portrayed by third-rate stars.

Mr. Clark Hogan Wilson was a merchant who had made it to the top of the floor-covering market in town, complete with television commercials on the local stations—"Let Hogie make your home homey," the jingle went—bringing in plenty of money, though never enough, in Mrs. Wilson's eyes, to erase his lack of a college education. As he aged, his wife shaded the truth about him by degree, until he became "an honorary Kappa Sigma at the University," and "an honorary member of the Wolf Landing Hunting Club," and "an influential player in city politics."

No one seemed willing to call her on her lies. Celeste, as always, chose to keep her stoic, perfected silence and her fruitful livelihood, for the sake of her children. Sometimes, though, she featured herself treading silent black waters, gasping for air, grappling for a lifeboat captained by Mrs. Wilson, whose history was the antithesis of her own prin-cipled past, an impostor of a captain who all the while pushed down on her, shoving her head under the waves, beating her back from the vessel with an oar.

"It will be nothing short of magnificent, Celeste," Mrs. Dixon was saying.

"What is that?" Celeste silently cursed the stiff netting.

"The tableau, of course. The tableau." Mrs. Dixon squirmed and gig-gled like an antsy kindergartner. "I know it's supposed to be very top secret and all, Francie. And I know it's going to be my first time as a guest at the Mystic Merry Makers' Ball, but can't I please tell Celeste just a little? Just a little about the tableau?"

Celeste pulled another pin from the shiny red satin wrist cushion.

Mrs. Wilson sighed. "Oh, all right. But Celeste had better not go blabbing our secrets to just anybody, because not just anybody gets to come to our ball for a reason."

"Celeste won't tell, will you, Celeste?"

"No," the seamstress said.

"All right, then." She set her handbag on the floor and sat up very straight. "First of all, there will be the most elaborate costumes you can imagine. All two hundred and forty members will be in the processional. Their husbands will be seated along the edges of the arena, in white tie and tails, of course. And the members will wear these gorgeous costumes. But naturally you know they are gorgeous, because you made lots of them yourself."

"Yes, I did," said the seamstress.

"Anyway, the theme this year is 'Let the Good Times Roll All Around the World,' so each group of ten or twelve ladies will be dressed in costumes native to a particular country. And they'll do a dance to some taped music—related to that country, you know. And this will go on and on and on. Until the big moment."

Celeste fingered a sequin that had worked loose from the bodice. "I'll have to fix this," she murmured.

"The big moment is when they introduce the five officers, one by one. And these spotlights follow them down from the stage and across the arena. And they do a Mardi Gras dance to some New Orleans jazz and the president introduces the queen and the queen commands the ball to begin and, oh, I am so excited!"

"My goodness, Camilla, get a Xanax out of my purse and calm your-self down," Mrs. Wilson said. "But I admit it will be a thrill to be followed across an arena by spotlights while hundreds of people seated in the audi-ence watch. Kind of like being Miss America. And to think it might have been that Jewess Mitzi Stanton instead of me, if not for that tacky Hawaiian luau she threw. Goodness, I'm tired of standing on this step-stool."

"You can get dressed now," Celeste said. "I think I see what needs to be done."

Mrs. Dixon babbled on and on about the tableau while Mrs. Wilson changed clothes. "I mean, I've been to balls before, and they were nice. But this is the Mystic Order of Mirthful Merry Makers. They are known to have the best ball, besides the top two societies, of course. And you have to practically marry into those, you know."

Celeste almost said, "Yes, I know about marrying into even more money, because that is what my father expected, only I chose not to take my father's fortune and double it by merging assets with another family. I did not prostitute myself to a man I did not love." She often wanted to spit the truth at them, tell them what a sham it all was, their desperate bid for upward mobility. "When you marry for money, you earn every penny," her husband used to say, and Celeste knew that these women could only have reached their desired level by marrying into it, and they had certainly not done that. Marrying up would have been a long shot, at best, for women like them, shallow and unbeautiful as they were. No, the heart-pine core of aristocracy they lusted after was a closed society, and they would never be allowed into the club. Not that club, the one in which she had been reared. Never that ultimate club.

Mrs. Dixon caught Celeste's gaze, pointed at a scrap of the gold net-ting on the floor, and mouthed the words, enough of a whisper that Celeste could hear her. "That just does not *go*," she whispered, shaking her head, wide-eyed.

Celeste shrugged.

"Remember to bring your shoes to your next fitting," Celeste said again when Mrs. Wilson emerged from the hallway that served as a makeshift dressing room.

"Yes, I know. I don't have to be told a thing forty times," Mrs. Wilson huffed, rolling her eyes at her friend.

"Oh, Celeste," Mrs. Dixon said. "My cousin Martha is coming down from Brannon to visit this weekend. I'll tell her hello for you."

"Yes. Do that," the seamstress said.

"And I warn you, Miss Mysterious. My cousin Martha will give me the scoop on you and yours. So if you have some big old juicy secrets, well—look out."

"I certainly will," the seamstress said. "Goodness."

"I know what, Francie. You *must* do the dance," Mrs. Dixon said. "Before we go, you must do the dance for Celeste."

"Yes, our little Cinderella," Mrs. Wilson said, in mock sympathy. "Our poor little Cinderella who needs a fairy godmother to transform her for the ball."

Celeste gathered the cast-off gown into her arms, gold netting stiff and scratchy. "What sort of dance?"

"The Mardi Gras dance. You know the one. Like this." Mrs. Wilson began to strut, the familiar Mardi Gras strut so common on the streets of New Orleans and Mobile. "Da-da-*da*," she sang, dipping and swaying. "Da-da-*dadada*. Da-da-*da*. Da-da-*dadada*. And here comes the good part." She did a half turn and broke into a backward strut while Mrs. Dixon joined her in the song. And they both danced their way out the front door, laughing a rowdy chorus of anticipation while the seamstress pressed the crisp gold netting to her cheek and contemplated their reverie.

When Mrs. Wilson returned the following week for her final fitting, gold shoes in hand, she was sans her usual appendage, the fawning Mrs. Dixon. She was also oddly quiet, the sulk lines in her forehead grooved in a fixed petulance as she stood on the small platform. Celeste re-pinned the hem and double-checked each seam, the zipper, the hook and eye, the malignant gold netting all webbed out like a cancer around the skirt. The room was a jumble of sparkling gold, yellow, green, purple—fluffs of flounces, bolts of beaded and brocade fabrics for the Carnival season. Last-minute gowns lay about in various stages of glitter, some gaudily playful with festive flashes of rhinestones, others like garish Las Vegas neon, ready to play out to a night all boozy and sour with stomach-turning dances and sloppy, slathered-on kisses from strangers.

"You don't wear your gown on the float, do you?" Celeste asked. "It could be a problem getting—"

"Well of course not," Mrs. Wilson snapped, breaking her silence in two. "Don't you know anything? We have to wear masks and costumes that go with the theme of the float. My God. Why would you even *have* a float if you weren't going to have costumes? Just why?"

Celeste tugged at the sequined shoulder strap. Mrs. Wilson's flaccid skin pooched around it; more flesh spilled over the top of the scoop-necked back. "This seems fine," the seamstress said.

"I'll tell you what *seems*," Mrs. Wilson snapped again. "It *seems* to me that you often ignore what I say. It seems to me that you often behave rudely. Like now. You do not show one bit of interest in the workings of the float."

"I never cared much for Mardi Gras parades. I only went when my children were small." Celeste made gentle rearrangements in the gold netting that swept around the sides of the velvet skirt.

"And I admit I don't care much for the parades, either, so don't think you're anything special," Mrs. Wilson said. Her voice had an angry, tense tone that Celeste had not heard before. "I don't want to be gobbed up in those hordes of people on the sidewalk, that's for sure. The unwashed masses." She shuddered. "I'm telling you, you get a bird's-eye view of the dregs of Mobile from high up on a float."

Celeste uttered her favorite of her standard remarks. "Goodness."

"You can't tell me you wouldn't like to be a float rider. You can't tell me you wouldn't like folks to be yelling to you for beads or Moon Pies. It's like being a queen. It's like being Cleopatra coming down the Nile on a gilded barge. I don't understand anybody that wouldn't like that."

Celeste moved to the other side of Mrs. Wilson's skirt, to the other pouf of gold that accentuated her saddlebag thighs.

"No, I don't understand it one little bit," Mrs. Wilson went on. "Oh, I'm sure plenty of folks would *say* they didn't want to be a float rider, but those are the ones that are so jealous they wouldn't ever admit how much they deep-down want to take your place. But I can't for the life of me understand somebody that gets to be a float rider and then walks away from it like it's nothing. Like it's not worth a damn thing. Do you understand somebody like that?"

"Well, I suppose it's—"

"Somebody like that is just mean or crazy or stupid is what I think. Somebody like that maybe has brain cancer or some kind of schizophrenia to walk away from what counts."

Celeste knelt at Mrs. Wilson's back, checking the hem of the faux train, seeing how it lined up with the glittering three-inch heels she wore.

"It's a disgrace is what." Mrs. Wilson huffed and blew like a spooked pony. "It makes me want to spit to high Heaven."

Celeste stood. "I'll send this over to Lawson's Dry Cleaning to have it pressed for you as soon as I get it hemmed. You can pick it up there on Thursday."

"You do that," Mrs. Wilson said in a voice thick with sarcasm. She stepped down, wobbling on her heels. Celeste caught her elbow, but the other woman jerked it away and stomped off to the hallway dressing room.

"I guess you see that Camilla Dixon, my little pilot fish, is no longer at my side," Mrs. Wilson, still boiling, shouted from the hallway. "She's like to have a breakdown, too, because I have officially uninvited her to the Merry Makers' Ball. As an officer I am allowed to do that. You see?"

"Oh?"

"Some people just don't know when to shut up. Some people say more than anybody wants to know, that's all."

"Yes. They do," the seamstress said.

"But not you. No. Never you. You don't do a damn thing to let on what cards you've been dealt, do you? You keep your trump hand right up against your chest, don't you?"

Celeste smiled. "I don't play cards."

Mrs. Wilson burst through the door, flushed and trembling. She flung the dress across the room. "See that you get this finished right away," she commanded.

"Of course," the seamstress said.

Mrs. Wilson snatched several bills from her purse. "I have your money. And, oh—here's something else." She dug down into her handbag, coming out with a handful of throws. "Since you won't be at the parade," she said, and threw beads, bills, doubloons, and a lone Moon Pie across the room, the dinging and clattering of the cheap trinkets like a percussive curse against the hardwood floor.

Celeste watched her priss her chubby frame through the front door, where she turned and scowled her best, deepest-wrinkled sneer at the seamstress. "Camilla was right about one thing, though."

"Really?"

"Yes. Really. She was right about how you ought to experience at least one of my parties. Maybe you could serve hors d'oeuvres for me sometime, or pop out of a cake or something equally cheap, like what you have chosen in life."

"Oh, I don't know," Celeste said. "I'm really only good at sewing. But you might consider asking my son, Hollis. He does a little private bartending to help with college expenses."

"Is that so? Well, I'm sure I am honored that you chose to reveal something about your personal life to little old me. A son. And in college, no less."

"Just finishing medical school," Celeste said. "But he won't be available much longer. He'll be doing his internship. And he's engaged, too. A very nice girl, very down-to-earth. Mary McCollough."

For a split second it seemed to Celeste that Mrs. Wilson's sneer would be wiped away by utter shock, but it held steady, set there in the grooves of her face, her eyes ripe with pure hatred.

"You go to your choosing and rot like a trashy beggar in hell," Mrs. Wilson said, slamming the door hard enough to rattle windowpanes in the adjoining room.

Celeste retrieved the throws and the cash, then picked up the mangled purple velvet with its clashing Marie Antoinette gold netting. She walked over to her time-worn Singer sewing machine, spread the skirt back and out, and then set to work on the hem, the stabbing and clicketing of the piston-borne needle sealing her resolve.

The Mardi Gras season came to a drunken climax on Fat Tuesday and faded into the confessions of a hungover Ash Wednesday, and the ladies who came into Celeste's place of business were abuzz with the tales of intrigue, subterfuge, strife, and backbiting that so often accompany large social gatherings.

But by far the most buzzed-about tale was that of the bizarre and shocking occurrences at the Mystic Order of Mirthful Merry Makers' events. All along the parade route, it was told, Mrs. Clark Hogan Wilson would go missing for an inordinate while, only to be found in the Port-o-Potty hidden in the bowels of the float, miserably shoveling Moon Pie after Moon Pie into her jowly little face, eyes glazed over in a sugary, chocolate-induced haze. She would be brought up to her place high at the top of the float, a facsimile of a pink Matterhorn with purple clouds towering above the crush of the crowd, above the masses who were corralled back like sheep by grilled metal barricades. She would throw a few handfuls from the large box hidden behind a cliff in the Matterhorn, then, when no one was noticing, would make her way again to the Port-o-Potty, another stash of chocolate Moon Pies hidden deep in her bra and in the folds of her emerald-green satin Swiss Alps costume.

Mrs. Wilson's mood picked up later, most agreed, as the members of the Mystic Order of Mirthful Merry Makers retired to the Civic Center to prepare for their tableau. Everyone agreed it was a beautiful tableau this year, maybe even better than any society in town. The China Dolls, Flamenco Dancers, Hula Girls, Belly Dancers—group after group, they waltzed, twirled, and waddled their way across the arena to the applause of the crowd, the ceremonial flash and swoop of spotlights, the twinkling of sequins on satin.

Then the arena fell silent as the officers, in various states of elegance and preeminence, took the stage. Mrs. Wilson was announced first, illuminated by three white lights that tossed the glitter of her sequined bodice out to the audience as she began her walk down the stairs to the Mardi Gras song. The three spotlights brushed her round frame, the deep-purple velvet skirt netted over with gold. When she reached the arena floor, she broke into the traditional strut while the onlookers clapped hands to the rhythm.

And it was told all over town what happened when she turned to execute her signature flair, to strut her backward strut. It seemed, they said, to happen in slow motion, that the heel of one gold shoe caught in the netting, and, in that instant, all that followed became inevitable. Her arms flailed, the crowd sucked in a collective gale of a gasp, the other foot stepped back, even farther into the netting, pulling the first shoe completely off, and pulling her the rest of the way down. She tumbled to her ample buttocks with a padded thud, sitting in the middle of the arena floor, legs outspread, all dignity seared away. Even worse, the jolting force of her landing, it seemed, had liberated one lone Moon Pie from the brassiere prison where it had resided since her chocolate binge on the Merry Makers' float. The chocolate-covered disc of cake and marshmallow hit the floor beside her, cellophane glinting as it spun in the Miss America spotlight. And it did a twirling little dance of its own before coming to a rest on the waxed floor of the arena next to her cast-off shoe. From the hushed audience came a twitter or two, but these were hurriedly shushed by others, who then twittered a bit themselves. A long forever of stunned silence passed before a couple of the escorts—not her husband, who was frozen with embarrassed horror—leapt to their feet to help her up. One of them gallantly and discreetly pocketed the Moon Pie in an effort to restore a fraction of dignity to the occasion. Then, like an awkward Prince Charming, he bent down to hold the sparkly gold shoe as she wiggled and worked her plump foot into it.

Of course, the music swelled again, and the processional went on. The other officers were introduced, and the president introduced the queen, and the queen commanded that the ball begin. And, after crying on the shoulders of her most bosom of friends, Mrs. Clark Hogan Wilson danced all evening with a smile fixed to her face, fixed like the grin of a stalked and trophied animal from a taxidermy establishment, attempting to make light of the ruination of her vertical advancement.

Efforts to put a gag order into effect for the members of the Mystic Order of Mirthful Merry Makers were futile, and the events of that evening were carried from function to function by wagging tongues, received with doubled-over laughter, and passed on. The story was unstoppable, and it grew exponentially, on its inevitable course of becoming a Mardi Gras Legend. The Moon Pie, too, became an icon, was auctioned off at charity events, passed from Mardi Gras society to Mardi Gras society and beyond, along with the tale of Mrs. Clark Hogan Wilson.

And the tale was told again and again, at bridge clubs and teas, in nail salons, beauty parlors, and shops. It was told at the country clubs of the nearly elite and at the exclusive clubs of the most elite. And it was told in the fitting room of the seamstress, Celeste, who bowed at the feet of the ladies, working the fine fabrics of their choosing. It was told over and over, while the seamstress, she with the most vindicated of hearts, turned bland bolts of material into crisp summer blouses edged in navy blue piping and full, cinch-waisted skirts swirling the colors of stained glass windows between her practiced and nimble fingers.

Dog Days

Jamie Kornegay

D oc returned from lunch around one o'clock. There was a note
from his secretary, Dorothy, taped to the office door: "Got
hungry. Be back later. Call Mr. Chatham. Urgent." The door was
unlocked, and the magazine-strewn waiting room was empty. The big
tooth chair, yellowed by years of scrambling children, sat overturned in
the corner. Doc closed the door and went behind the counter to
Dorothy's desk, where he sat down and flipped through patient files to
get Royce Chatham's phone number. Curiously, it wasn't there. Come to
think of it, he'd never worked on the retired farmer's teeth. It was mighty
sad, Doc thought, how even his own neighbors wouldn't patronize his
office. These days they didn't trust you if you weren't a clinic or an ortho-
dontist.

He tracked down the number through the phone book and mashed
out the combination. A gruff man Doc took to be Chatham answered in
a deep, exasperated whisper.

"You called me, Chatham?"

"Goforth?"

"Yessir."

The man exhaled in a disapproving huff. "Goforth, you better get
over here and collect your dog. One of 'em's done got run over and its
blockin' my drive."

"Oh, dear Lord…" Doc couldn't take much more punishment today.
He had gotten into it with his son-in-law that morning. Then at work
he'd nearly blacked out while drilling Mona Chuckworth's bicuspid. Doc
desired that this news of his dog would prove to be false, but he'd been
around long enough to know better. He knew Royce Chatham wasn't the
type to play a joke, only to deliver the truth in a way no one cared to hear
it.

"I mean it, I got errands to run," Chatham wheezed into the phone.
"If it ain't cleared outta here by two o'clock, I'll run the sucker over

again."

"I'll be there just as soon as I goddamned can," Doc spit. "And I better not find out you run it down, or else I'll pay you a visit late at night."

Chatham hung up directly. He wasn't the type to listen to such sass, nor was he the type to argue about who had done what to whose dog and what the repercussions might be. He was famous for delivering guff, but loath to receive it.

Doc flipped Dorothy's note over and scrawled out: "I'm gone. Cancel all appts." He doubted there were any appts, what with the slick new dental complex on the highway, and he didn't care to find out. He retaped the message to the front door, slammed it shut without locking it and headed for his truck, which was parked around back. The steering wheel was as hot as a griddle in the midday sun, so Doc sat for a minute and let the air conditioner run. What dog could it be? Turd or Steve or Muffin? Damnit all anyway.

Despite the warm freedom of his afternoon reprieve, Doc was in mourning. Not necessarily for the animal—the dogs were old, like him, and mostly uninterested in human companionship—but for something deeper and unexplainable. Something like his spirit, though he'd never confess to that. It was a dull ache that seemed to rise with the temperature of the day.

Out Highway 16 on the cusp of town was Keating's Run, a beer store specializing in fishing supplies, snacks, and certain ice-cold beverages unavailable in the two adjacent counties, where unrepealed blue laws prohibited the sale of cold beer. The store was close enough to both county lines to make it a destination for hot and thirsty traffickers, and back in his day, Doc had sought incalculable relief there. That relief had accounted, in no small part, for the trouble with his spouse and her moving in with their daughter and her second husband and their merry-go-round of stepchildren whose names he could never keep straight. It had been a year since he last stopped in to say hello to his pal, proprietor Deke Keating, who would surely be glad to see him, if not a tad disappointed to watch him climb down off the wagon again.

Doc pulled into the cracked lot and parked catty-corner by the ice machine. There was no sign of Deke's truck. Instead, behind the counter sat a frowning young girl with a sun-coated face and frantic blond hair, wearing little to nothing of a halter top and her mouth going ninety to nothing. "Where she at?" the girl called to a young man whose front end was up in the beer cooler. Doc stepped past him and dug around in the cooler for a six-pack. He eyed the young man, who bared a patchwork of fresh scars on his face and lingered in the swirling coolness.

"You still with her, then?" the girl behind the counter yelled out to him. The young man closed his eyes for a moment, then tucked a case of beer under his arm and proceeded to the checkout counter in front of Doc.

"That's it then?" the young woman asked, indignant. "You still with her, ain't ya? I knew it!"

"We're gonna see 'bout it," the sheepish boy replied, his red face glistening with salve. He rifled nervously through his billfold as she sized him up and down.

"I know if I was goin' with somebody who took after me with a beer bottle, some hell would have to be paid!" she demanded, refusing still to ring up his beer.

"How much I owe you?"

"You ain't scared she'll try it again?"

"How much?"

"A-ight. Just let her whup your ass. Pat it and prick it and mark it with a B for Budweiser." She finally tallied up the charges and he paid it and walked out.

"See ya," he called and was gone.

"Wouldn't no man put scratches on my face with no damn beer bottle, ya hear me?" she cried. Doc didn't know if she was talking to him or the boy who was now outside climbing into his truck. "Nu-unh, not no motherstuffer!"

Doc had his beer on the counter, waiting patiently for the sale. "Where's old Deke at today, on the lake?" he asked the young woman, still fuming over her previous customer.

"Huh?" she asked.

"Deke. Don't he still own the place?"

"Yeah."

"So where is he?"

She stared at him as if she didn't speak his language, then rolled her eyes while her fingers scuttled across the keys. "Six fi'ty-seven," she said.

Doc stared at her.

"Six fi'ty-seven."

"Where's Deke?" he tried again, pulling two fives from his billfold.

"Up in Memphis in the hospital," she said, snatching the money, scandalized by this conversation.

"Hospital, well what's a matter?"

"Ugh-uh," she moaned in ambivalence.

"You don't know what's wrong with him? Or you ain't at liberty to say?"

"I don't know!" she pouted, like she was the only one privileged to talk. She thrust his change back in a lump. Clearly she was still stuck on scarface.

"Well, what hospital is he in?" Doc asked, trying beyond his patience to talk her out of her funk.

"All's I know is Memphis and hospital. Shit, he might even be home now."

"That's all you can tell me?"

"Look, all I got is the who and the what. I don't know no where, no what because of nor hidey-hide. You're barkin' up the wrong tree, mister. Now—"

Doc slammed both hands down on the counter, shaking the whole apparatus and commanding a quiet that swept over the store. "Wake up and join life, lady!" he wailed. Little drops of spittle flew out of his mouth and across the counter. The young woman was shocked into silence.

"A man pays you a good wage to sit up here and priss all day, take some chip and beer money, you'd think you'd know where the hell he is and how he's doin'! See if he's gettin' along all right! Get your head out of your damn butthole and pay the world your dues!"

He snatched his beer and strode out of the store. He heard her screaming as soon as he hit the parking lot.

Back in the truck, Doc's heart was thumping like the nervous rhythm of treads on patched road. Muscles all the way to his groin had been strained. He hadn't raised his voice like that to a stranger in years. Hadn't felt the call to. As the truck idled and his pressure lowered, he felt a twinge of guilt come on about the way he had yelled at the beer-store girl, and how he had spoken to Mr. Chatham, who had always been a respectable fella, despite his orneriness. Doc groped around in the sack and retrieved a beer, popped it open and guzzled. Hopefully six would be enough to dull the guilt and all the other worrisome thoughts bound to crop up.

As Mr. Chatham's place appeared on the horizon, Doc's stomach seized up like a provoked rattlesnake. *Which dog would it be?* he wondered. *And Lord please don't let me have to get mixed up with that old goat.*

Doc pulled off onto the gravel shoulder and stopped before the mailbox just off Chatham's drive. The dog was sprawled out across the foot of the driveway, two of its legs flopped over and its neck twisted. It was Steve. Damnit all. He'd had him since he was a puppy. Ten years or better. You could put as much faith in that dog as you could just about anybody. Sure was a shame to see him end up here, a nuisance, dead on somebody else's property. Doc got out and walked over to him, knelt down in the dust as fumes rose from the steaming blacktop. The long crack of a rifle shot sounded from Chatham's place, set far back off the road. He could just make out the little man standing by the house, the gun aimed at the sky. "I ain't comin' down there, you old goat," Doc said to himself, then yelled half-heartedly down the way to Chatham, "This ain't my dog nohow!"

There was no collar, and the markings were different. This dog was young still. His bloody teeth were bared as if in final affront to whatever vehicle couldn't slow down, couldn't make time for this starving beast to back out of the way. Dried blood had crusted around his ears too. Probably his brain had gone to mush in the heat. A logging truck sped by in the opposite direction, throwing up dust and bark. Stealing his county's trees and barreling through it like a hellhound. Another car was coming his way, small in the distance. It seemed to speed up the closer it got until it zoomed past with such force that it made Doc a little dizzy. No wonder this dog got the life creamed out of him. Who or what beast could survive such a terrible onslaught?

His dog or no, Doc was sad all the same. About the violent repudiation of life that had occurred here in these rocks and sand, along this strip of combative road. This, he recognized, was the dog he'd seen munching on a dead vulture earlier that morning on the way to town. So much for sweet, short-lived justice. "He probably woulda turned rabid anyhow," he said, and hefted the mangled dog out of the dirt and carried him and placed him in the back of the truck. He climbed in and shot off some gravel getting back on the highway, headed toward home.

Just about a half mile up ahead, he turned onto his property and pulled up to his banished corner, where he lived alone in his old Airstream trailer while his wife and daughter and all the kids lived in the house on the hill. He fetched a shovel, then drove off into the uncut pasture to a little hollow on the backside of the property where several other pets had been laid to rest. He noted all three of his dogs tumbling along the horizon, coming off cool shade at the big house to investigate. Over the tree line, smoke rose from the stump burners and trolling bulldozers carving up the adjacent lot, which had been recently surrendered to developers. Doc pulled into the back corner beside the makeshift pet cemetery. A few wooden sticks tied in crosses and plywood headstones marked the weed-ravaged graves of forgotten pets. He reached back and grabbed his shovel as the three dogs came bounding up, tails wagging with curiosity. Immediately they knew something was up. Turd tried to climb into the bed of the truck to inspect. "Go on, y'all durn old fickle beasts," Doc cried, waving the shovel at them. "There ain't nothin' here for you to see, ya nosy curs. Now get on." They scampered away briefly, but hovered together a short distance away. Doc searched the ground for rocks to throw, then quickly gave up, ignored them and commenced to digging a grave beside the other plots. He worked the spade through the rock-hard soil, which deeper down turned to red clay. It came away in hard chunks, streaked in various hues of red and brown. The sweat beaded up on Doc's brow, and as it trickled down his eyelashes, he thought he saw an arrowhead in the clay. He bent down to retrieve it, but it was only a bone. He kept on, his smock becoming drenched, his pants rising with the heat, and his leather shoes becoming scuffed and red from the soil.

He stopped for a break and another beer, then noticed a buzzard circling overhead. He watched its pinwheel trajectory, hypnotizing him from the sky with its patient arcs. "You'll have to eat me first to get to him," he called to the bird, which dipped lower and lower in taunting swoops. He reached behind the seat of the pickup and retrieved a .44 pistol. It was hard to sight the swooping menace, but he squeezed off two rounds that seemed, for the time being at least, to frighten the bird away. He stared down at the nice wide plot he had carved out and crawled down in it himself. He lay on his back, staring up at the sky. The only clouds were wisps of yellow haze from the fires. As the cicada choir warmed up in the trees, Doc began to warble a eulogy:

> He was a good ole dog
> But he ain't no more
> Got run over by a four-by-four
> Oh, Lord, have mercy on me

The dogs sat on the hill and watched and raised their ears and scratched themselves, all privileges of the living. Doc closed his eyes and reached over for a handful of dirt and piled it up on his face. The coolness of it provided a pleasant mask, and the scent was like the sweat of earth.

A sustained shriek arose from up the hill at the house. He tried to ignore it. Probably his daughter, Candace, had seen a snake, or her boys had been acting up. He had grown too comfortable in his prone position to get up right away, but his imagination soon played hell on him. He staggered to his feet and inspected the silent hill. There was no movement coming from the house. He snatched the dead dog out of the pickup, placed him in the hole, and began covering it up furiously. He got about halfway done and decided to check out the scream. He'd make one of the boys come down and finish the job. He climbed into the pickup and crawled up the slope, approaching the back of the long brick house with the plastic swimming pool and a litter of plastic toys strewn over the backyard.

The truck crunched over the gravel drive, and Doc killed the engine near the carport. He got out and walked up to the house. Just then Irene came bursting out of the house and stopped and howled when she saw him. Her trembling hand covered her mouth and she'd been crying. It looked like the scene of a tragedy, or the scene of relayed news of a tragedy.

"R.L.!" she cried. She looked as if she wanted to run up and hug him, but it was an awkward, distant gesture. "R.L., what happened to you!"

"Whatcha mean?" he asked, dumbfounded. "What's all this hollerin' about?"

She stumbled a bit and sat down on the front steps, then buried her face in her hands and cried. Doc walked to her slowly. He didn't have the stomach for any bad news. *What had happened?* he wondered. *Was it one of the boys? Candace's car was missing. Was it her? Did Jack wreck?*

"What is it, Irene?" Doc asked, agitated at being ignored.

She looked up, her face a mess of suffering. "Just look at you."

Doc looked down. He was a muddy mess from top to bottom. Soaking wet and stained with mud.

"I thought you'd run off and killed yourself," she wept. "I called the office and Dorothy said you'd left, then I heard gunshots in the pasture. I looked down there and you were lyin' in the dirt."

"Suicide?" he asked, more agitated still. The faint whir of ambulance sirens emerged from the distance. "Aww, shit!"

"Well, I didn't know what else to do," Irene blubbered.

"Damn, damn, damn!" Doc protested as the siren grew louder and louder. "Couldn't you just have hollered out to be sure?"

"I didn't want to waste any time!" she cried out in frustration. "I thought you might have buggered it so I didn't have time to waste. Plus Candace is off in town. I told the boys to go hide in their closet."

Doc looked up at the screen door behind. Three nosy kids were peeping through the glass. "Y'all boys get out here and get this yard picked up," he hollered to them. They disappeared in a faint rustle of scurrying footsteps and giggles.

The ambulance turned down the long driveway, creeping at a humiliating pace, as if unsure this was the right place. If he truly had shot himself and somehow botched it, he would still be lying there in the clay, hemorrhaging as the ambulance braked down the drive. Doc looked at Irene, bawling away and distant now from this situation, then back to the ambulance, moving at a snail's pace.

As it happened, the EMT crew, two young guys, were relieved there was no messy suicide attempt. Doc waved them away before they could even get out of the vehicle. He apologized, blamed it all on his wife's misunderstanding. They asked him to hop in the back and took his blood pressure just in case. It was a little high, and Doc told them it was the heat. He didn't mention the beers.

HOMECOMING

William Gay

Winer in unaccustomed and more opulent surroundings. A house of near palatial proportions rising above him, yellow light from its windows spilling out onto slashed red earth tilled and seeded and strewn with wheatstraw. She peered down at him through the glass of the storm door, her blue eyes limpid and myopic, a solemn and inquisitive owl's face. Then he saw recognition form there as if she were reconstructing his child's face in the lines of his older face and he heard the latch slick.

"Sure it's me," he said. "Who did you reckon it was?"

"Come in, come in. Well, I didnt think it was anybody in particular. It's just been so long since I saw you you look like you're standing on a box or something. Lord, I haven't seen you in years."

He entered into a high foyer where to his left carpeted stairs curved upward out of sight. Above his head a glittering chandelier hung from a gilded chain. She guided him into a large room with subdued lighting. The room was more cluttered than opulent, high ceiled, the walls papered with what appeared to be black and red velvet. "Well, well," he said awkwardly, looking about the room. He seemed unaccustomed to such splendor. Expensive pieces of furniture set at random about the room showed a predilection for the same rich wines and purples, the plusher fabrics. The room seemed happenstantial, undirected, as if too much money had been spent to no good purpose.

He brushed magazines aside and seated himself on the edge of the sofa, weight on his calves and ankles, as if he must soon be off again. The room held a vast profusion of truestory magazines. They littered the tables and chairs, their covers and titles as lurid as the furniture they adorned, perhaps she'd won a lifetime supply of them in some obscure contest.

"Is anything wrong?"

"Not that I know of. Why?"

"Well, I didn't know," she said. "I never see any of the family unless somebody's dead or in the hospital; my own first cousin and I can't remember when I saw you last. How's your mama?"

"All right. I was just in town and I thought I'd come by and see you a few minutes."

When she sat beside him on the sofa he could smell a strong scent of gin on her breath and he recalled talk that his mother's niece had been wild when she was growing up, before she had married well; but if she had there was no vestige of it left in her face, she looked placid and almost matronly, though she could not have been over thirty. She took up a pair of glasses from the table and put them on, her face altering with the addition, becoming somehow more confident. She was a bigboned statuesque woman, yellowhaired, and there was something intimidating about her. Winer sat with his hands in his lap, seemingly lost in a deep study of his fingers. When he looked up she was smiling at him.

"What's so funny?"

"You are. You talk as if you came all the way cross country instead of three or four miles out of town."

"I just don't get out much."

She was studying him appraisingly. "My guess is that's going to change before long. I'll bet you've got a lot of little freshman girls with their caps set for you."

"If that's so it's been kept mighty quiet."

"And modest on top of it."

He was already wishing he had not come but could think of no reason for leaving so quickly. He could not remember what he had once liked about her or what kind thing she had said to him: what her face would be like with ten years gone from it and he could see little resemblance between the photograph of a smiling schoolgirl and this woman sitting beside him. There was some vague memory of his father's leaving, the slight weight of her forearm across the back of his neck.

"You want a Coke or something? I think I'll have a nice glass of icewater."

"I'll drink a glass of water if you don't mind."

She arose and passed through a curtained doorway into an adjoining room. The curtain was gold plush, tassels of satin depending from the doorway, a gold fringe that swayed against the passage of her yellow hair. For no good reason he thought of history books, of the decadence they said was Rome. He picked up two or three of the magazines and thumbed idly through them. Raped and strangled, they said. Beaten, assaulted by their fathers, unwed and pregnant. Bereft, orphaned, dragged screaming to their stepfather's beds. Mad confessionals here of the reviled, the undone, hard times on the land.

He laid them aside when she came in with two iced glasses. He drank water from the glass she handed him, mildly surprised to discover it was indeed water; he could smell the juniper scent of the gin in her glass and he felt a cynical sort of disillusionment about her, it seemed a needless and shoddy attempt at deception. It was her house, she was three times seven, it was none of his business if she chose to drink kerosene.

She had pictures that she would show him.

"Here," she said. "Have you ever seen this picture of you and your daddy?"

He studied it. He laid it face up on the coffee table, sat staring at the image of himself, four or five years old. The picture seemed curiously and profoundly prophetic. His eyes were held by the image of his childhood eyes, calm, unquestioning. They seemed already at some cold remove from the scenery that locked them. From the big man holding his hand. The man towered above him, dwarfed him, the face stern and flinty. He wore a black slouch hat and as he stared into the sun the shadow of its brim fell across his eyes like a bandit's mask so that he appeared already a fugitive of the order of this life or of life itself.

"Wasn't you the cutest thing?" she asked. "I always thought you were anyway. Still do, for that matter. Look, here's one of me, wasn't I the ugliest girl there ever was?"

There were others. Old folks he barely remembered or never knew. Snippets of time like souvenirs saved from some vague wars, moments preserved in perpetuity that seemed better let alone and forgotten. Ultimately the pictures seemed to depress them both and she laid them aside.

She picked up one of the magazines, let it fall. "They keep me company," she said. "I'm by myself a lot with George running the restaurant and movie house both; it's generally late when he gets in."

"Is that where he is tonight?"

She sipped the gin. "It's where he's supposed to be. I couldnt say for sure where he is."

"I guess he has a big night Fridays. The football game and all."

"George has a big night every night," she said obscurely.

This didn't seem to call for a reply and Winer made none. She seemed different, as if she had passed some unnamed border down whatever road the gin was taking her. Winer realized it had been foolish of him to come here, the past was here no more than it was anywhere else. It was dead. He could not imagine anything they had ever had in common save some idiosyncracy of the blood. They sat in a deepening silence, for Winer realized he had nothing to say to her, nor she to him. He wished bitterly he had not come, had let the random debris of the years lie undisturbed. All this was was a soft sofa beneath him and a cold glass in his hand. The silence did not seem to bother her, she seemed in some manner used to it, nourished by it, and there was an undercurrent of tension beneath her placid flesh, she seemed to be waiting for something to happen.

"Has the cat got your tongue? Surely you didn't come all this way for a glass of water."

"I wasn't even sure you'd be here. I knew you used to cook at the General. I figured George would have you frying hamburgers."

"George says it's unseemly for me to fry hamburgers," she said. "George finds many things unseemly."

Winer could smell her. He could smell her makeup and perfume and the gin and beneath all these separate fragrances the almost indefinable female smell of her.

"How is George?" Winer noticed she had almost finished the gin.

"I don't know. He has to go to the doctor now and again and get a little something cut out of him. His stomach I guess." She was silent for a time, then as if in reply to something Winer should have been perceptive enough to ask but was not, she said, "So I sit. And every once in a while I get up and look in the mirror and watch myself get older."

"He's built you a fine house here," Winer said nervously. He shifted his weight to the edge of the sofa. He seemed to be making ready to go.

"I suppose," she said, dismissing it with the words. "George's folks all had money you know, and I reckon it's George's ambition to spend it all before he dies. He lost money on that theatre he put in. He's losing more on that damned cafe. He doesnt care; it makes him feel important. George likes businesses where he gets to hire little highschool girls with short skirts he can look up."

"I got to get on," Winer said. He set his glass atop the table. He did not need or want any of this. He was finding he liked certain doors better left closed.

"Why you haven't been here but a few minutes, Nathan. Lean back and rest a while, you look tired out. I'll hush about George. You leave now and you won't be back for another four or five years."

When he saw the face at the window he jumped involuntarily and knocked the tumbler of water over. "Hell fire," he said. The face was pressing itself against the fogged glass, a cheek and one eye, then as he watched it turned full face to the room, two blue eyes and hands coming up to shade them, the nose twisted onesided, two rubbery lips misshapen with the weight of the glass. He leapt up. "Somebody's trying to break in," he told her. "I'll see if I can catch him."

She had a hand on his arm. "Oh, it's just George. Sit back down and act like you don't see him. He does this sometimes."

"What's the matter with him? Why would a man sneak around looking in his own window?"

"I guess he's drunk," she said. "He thinks folks come here to see me, you know, menfolks. He thinks I entertain men when he's not here and he's always sneaking back and peeping in trying to see something." She laid an arm around Winer's neck. "You want to give him a thrill?" Her head rested against Winer's cheek.

"Not so's you'd notice it," Winer said.

The eyes opened wider then blinked closed in a solemn dual wink.

They opened again and Winer pulled away from her and began to pick the icecubes from the carpet and put them back in the glass and when he looked back toward the window he was gone. George must have run all the way around the house for almost immediately there were two loud raps at the front door and then Winer heard it open and close. "Crazy crazy crazy," the woman said to herself. She was agitatedly smoothing back her curly hair. The curtain parted and George came into the room. He flipped a wall switch and the room sprang into bright relief. He stood there watching them and batting his eyes rapidly.

He was smaller than Winer remembered, wasted, dried up. He had on a plaid sportcoat and gray flannel slacks too large for him. He appeared to be very drunk. He swayed from the knees up and his left eye showed a tendency to wander, as if it must see all the world at once and refused to be confined. His left cheek bore a mauve birthmark the size of a woman's hand: the area where the fingers would be cleft the hairline and his smooth hair was brushed to cover it. From across the room the birthmark stood out in livid relief. It looked like purple velvet or yet some fungoid growth spreading outward from his face. He stood slowly twirling his hat in his hands, watching Winer.

"Figured I better knock," he said. "Liked to caught you anyway, didn't I?" He laughed dryly through his nose, wandered toward them across the room, sidestepping such furniture as he chanced to notice. "Ain't I seen you around town, boy? And what are you doing on my couch, you little cockhound?"

"Oh shut up," the woman said. "For God's sakes, George, this is my cousin Nathan. You remember Nathan."

"Yet another cousin," George said. Then as if he hadn't heard he said, "Oh yes, I liked to caught you. Don't think I didnt see you with your hand run up her dress there. Ahh yes," the voice went on, slurred and somehow mechanical, like a voice issuing from a tape played too slow. The voice had the singsong quality of litany, a child repeating an oft-told story to hurry sleep. "Yeah I seen you with your hand between her legs, rubbing the straddle of her drawers."

Winer started toward him. The coffeetable banged his shins and he kicked it viciously out of his way without looking down.

George threw his hands up before his face. "No young man, you hold up a minute. You're in my house. You lay a hand on me and you'll wake up in the jailhouse. How do I know you ain't broke and entered? How do I know you ain't raped my wife or vice-versa?" As if he had suddenly remembered Adell he whirled to face her. "What have you been up to?"

"I'll tell you what I haven't been up to," she said. "I haven't been humped up in a hot little broom closet peeping through a hole I bored in the ladies' room wall."

"You whoring slut."

"You pathetic drunken sot."

Winer was looking aghast from one to the other. George seemed momentarily to sober himself. He squared his narrow shoulders and adjusted his tie and smoothed a hand across the bird's wing of his gray hair. "All right," he told Winer. "I apologize. I'll go back out and you go right ahead and do it to her. All I ask is for you to let me watch through the window."

"All I ask is to be out of this crazyhouse," Winer said. "Just move the hell out of my way." He turned to his cousin. Her face was convulsed and he thought at first she was crying but she was not. She was laughing. "By God you're as crazy as he is," Winer told her shaking shoulders. She was laughing uncontrollably. Her glass tilted, gin pooled like oil on the satin pillows of the sofa. An icecube slid, fell soundlessly to the carpet.

George had his wallet out, he was peering shortsightedly at its contents. His weight shifted drunkenly, the floor was adrift on uncertain waters. "All right, you cockhound," he said, "I've got your number. Now what's your rockbottom dollar?"

"I dont know what in hell you're even talking about."

Adell had brought her self under a semblance of control. "Don't pay him any attention," she said. "He's sick."

"He sure as hell is," Winer said. "And I think it's contagious."

"Why sure you do, son. You know you been settin' here wantin' to screw her like all the rest of these little cockhounds around town. All right then, go ahead. Here's...twenty dollars for you. Go on and get started and I'll ease on out. All I want to do is watch through the window."

"All you'll get is a basketweaving course up at Bolivar," Adell said. "And me living high on the hog spending your money. You better get a grip on yourself or you're going to be in a place where the rooms got rubber walls."

Winer stepped past George and George grasped his arm. "Thirty's my absolute top dollar," he said. Winer turned and slapped the wallet out of his hand. George fell, fumbling for the money on the carpet. His glasses fell off. He felt for them, pale hands weaving like drunken spiders above the nap of the carpet. Winer kicked the glasses out of his way and started for the door.

"You ought to go on and take the money," Adell told him. "You've got to humor him."

"You humor him," Winer told her. "You married him." He went out the door without looking back.

"Come back sometime, Nathan," she called after him, but he heard the voice through the wooden door he'd already closed behind him. He went on down the steps.

It was late. He paused in the yard, filling his lungs with fresh cold air, holding it, his chest swelling, expelling it slowly. It had grown chill and he could see the vapor of his breath. He looked up. The sky was full of stars, broken jewelry slung in anger against a velvet backdrop. The moon rode high above the rooftops of town and the distant woods were a constant presence he divined rather than saw. In the distance a few scattered tin rooves winked back the light but here the dark shingled rooves sucked the darkness to them, they were mere negations of the moonlight.

He walked on. Here slept the rich, what would their dreams be like? Their untroubled scions reposed as well, their lives assured, they slept clutching roadmaps to the future. The daughters of the well-to-do lay in tousled musky darkness. He went past porch and facade, stone lions that watched him go with silent contempt. The town was sleeping, curtains drawn, the houses of the monied fell away and here were tacky porches steeped in dark silence, pockets of deeper night, watchdogs that watched from the shadow of hedges with wary surly eyes.

He rested once where Mill and Holly intersected, sitting on the curb, his feet in the street. Above him the traffic light blinked red to green unnoticed save by the moths flailing blindly at it. He wondered what time it was. He was tired, exhaustion was a weight he carried that grew heavier and heavier. He got up and walked on listening to the hollow sound of his footfalls.

After a while he smiled to himself and shook his head. Crazy son of a bitches, he said. As he walked toward town his weariness seemed to leave him little by little, and a sense of elation seized him. The world he was moving toward seemed infinite in its possibilities, the lives he could lead, the people he could be, limitless and complex. The world was full of places he could go to, people he could meet, emotions he could make his own.

About the Authors

GREGORY BENFORD is a working scientist and author of 23 critically acclaimed novels. He received two Nebula Awards, including one in 1981 for *Timescape*, a novel that sold over a million copies. A native of Fairhope, Alabama, Dr. Benford received the United Nations Medal in Literature in 1992. He has also been a professor of physics at the University of California at Irvine since 1971.

LARRY BROWN was born in Oxford, Mississippi, in 1951. His work has appeared in many magazines and anthologies, and he is the author of nine books of fiction and nonfiction that have been widely translated. He lives in the country outside Oxford, where he fishes and writes.

JILL CONNER BROWNE is THE Sweet Potato Queen and bestselling author of *The Sweet Potato Queens' Book of Love*, *God Save the Sweet Potato Queens*, and *The Sweet Potato Queens' Big-Ass Cookbook (and Financial Planner)*. She lives with her husband, Kyle Jennings, in Jackson, Mississippi.

JOHN T. EDGE writes for, among other publications, *Gourmet* and the *Oxford American*. He has a number of books to his credit, including *A Gracious Plenty* and *Southern Belly*. Edge is director of the Southern Foodways Alliance and lives in Oxford, Mississippi, with his son, Jess, and his wife, Blair Hobbs, a poet and painter.

BEN ERICKSON grew up in Mobile, Alabama. He is an award-winning furniture maker and has contributed to magazines and books on the subject. His first novel, *A Parting Gift*, was published by Warner Books and chosen as a BookSense selection. He now lives in Fairhope, Alabama.

BETH ANN FENNELLY's first book of poetry, *Open House*, won the 2001 Kenyon Review Prize for a First Book and was published by Zoo Press. Her second book, *Tender Hooks*, will be published by W. W. Norton in April 2004. She is an assistant professor of English at the University of Mississippi.

FANNIE FLAGG's writing career began behind the scenes of television's *Candid Camera* and progressed to the *New York Times* besteller list with *Daisy Fay and the Miracle Man, Fried Green Tomatoes at the Whistle Stop Cafe, Welcome to the World Baby Girl,* and *Standing in the Rainbow.* She lives in California and Fairhope, Alabama.

JOE FORMICHELLA holds degrees in Medical Technology and Creative Writing. He is a former Hackney Literary Award winner whose work has appeared in *Mobile Bay Tales, Grassland Review,* and *Red Bluff Review.* He lives and works in Fairhope and has a wife and two sons.

TOM FRANKLIN is the author of a story collection, *Poachers,* and a novel, *Hell At The Breech,* both published by William Morrow. A 2001 Guggenheim Fellow, Franklin teaches at Ole Miss in Oxford, Mississippi, where he lives with his wife, poet Beth Ann Fennelly, and their daughter, Claire.

DAVID FULLER is a 55-year-old real estate developer recently turned poet. He now uses images of ink instead of asphalt to express his creative urges. His first book of poetry, *Ordinary Moments,* was privately printed.

ROBERT GATEWOOD is the author of the novel *The Sound of the Trees,* published by Henry Holt & Co. and Picador USA. The novel was a Book-Sense 76 selection and a Southwest book of the Year. He lives with his wife, Sara, in New Mexico, where he is finishing his second novel.

WILLIAM GAY is the author of the novels *Provinces of Night* and *The Long Home* and the short story collection *i hate to see that evening sun go down.* The winner of the 1999 William Peden Award and the 1999 James A. Michener Memorial Prize and the recipient of a 2002 Guggenheim fellowship, he lives in Hohenwald, Tennessee.

CHARLES GHIGNA (aka "Father Goose") is the author of more than thirty books of poetry for children and adults. His poems also appear in numerous textbooks, anthologies, newspapers, and magazines. He lives in Homewood, Alabama. For more information, please visit his Web site: WWW.FATHERGOOSE.COM.

W. E. B. GRIFFIN, whom Tom Clancy calls "a storyteller in the grand tradition," is the author of the current bestseller *Final Justice*, one of more than 30 epic novels in five series, all of which have been listed on the *New York Times*, *Wall Street Journal*, *Publishers Weekly* and other bestseller lists. Over forty million of his books are in print in more than ten languages, including Hebrew, Chinese, Japanese, and Hungarian. His website is WWW.WEBGRIFFIN.COM

DONALD HAYS is the author of two novels, *The Dixie Association* and *The Hangman's Children*. His stories have appeared in various literary journals. He teaches fiction writing at the University of Arkansas.

FRANK TURNER HOLLON is the author of *A Thin Difference*, *The God File*, and *The Pains of April*. His novels have been selected by BookSense and Barnes & Noble's Discover Great New Writers program. He lives with his wife and family in Baldwin County, Alabama, where he continues to practice law.

SILAS HOUSE is the author of *Clay's Quilt* and *A Parchment of Leaves*. He is a recipient of awards from the Southern Fellowship of Writers and the National Society of Arts and Letters. He lives with his wife and two daughters in Eastern Kentucky, where he is at work on his next novel, *The Coal Tattoo*.

SUZANNE HUDSON took first prize in an international writing competition sponsored by the National Endowment for the Arts in 1977 while she was an undergraduate. She subsequently gave up writing until her short story collection *Opposable Thumbs* came out in 2001. Her first novel, *In a Temple of Trees*, was published by MacAdam/Cage in 2003.

CASSANDRA KING's second novel, *The Sunday Wife*, was released by Hyperion in September of 2002. *The Sunday Wife*, currently in its fifth printing, is a BookSense, Literary Guild and Book-of-the-Month Club selection, and a *People* Magazine Page-Turner of the Week. Her third novel, *The Same Sweet Girls*, is scheduled for release in 2004. A native of L.A. (Lower Alabama), she lives in the low country of South Carolina with her husband, novelist Pat Conroy.

ERIC KINGREA, an avid reader of comic books, is a student at the College of Charleston and one day hopes to fully comprehend *Ulysses*. Until then, he writes short stories, plays, and poetry. This is his first published work.

SUZANNE KINGSBURY is the author of *The Summer Fletcher Greel Loved Me* (Scribner, 2002) and *The Gospel According to Gracey* (Scribner, 2003). "Panama" is the seed-story from which her third novel grew.

JAMIE KORNEGAY lives and writes in his native north Mississippi, where he raises barnacles and works at an independent bookstore in Oxford. "Dog Days" is a chapter from a novel in progress.

MICHAEL MORRIS is a native of rural Northern Florida and currently resides in Fairhope, Alabama. His first novel, *A Place Called Wiregrass*, was a BookSense selection. A second novel, *Slow Way Home*, will be published by HarperCollins in October 2003.

JACK PENDARVIS is from Bayou La Batre, Alabama. "Escape by Zebra" is an excerpt from his just-completed novel, *The Big Whitewash*.

RON RASH is the author of six books of poetry and fiction, his most recent being his first novel, *One Foot in Eden* (Novella Press, 2002). His second novel will be published by Henry Holt in 2004. He lives in Clemson, South Carolina.

MICHELLE RICHMOND is the author of *Dream of the Blue Room* and *The Girl in the Fall-Away Dress*, winner of the AWP Short Fiction Award. A native of Alabama and a former James Michener Fellow, she lives in California and teaches in the MFA Program at the University of San Francisco.

GEORGE SINGLETON is the author of *The Half-Mammals of Dixie*, which was a SEBA Awards finalist for Fiction of the Year, a BookSense pick, an Amazon.com Top Ten Editors' Award winner, and included in *Book* magazine's Top Five short story collections. He lives in South Carolina.

LES STANDIFORD, of Miami, is the author of more than a dozen books, including *Last Train To Paradise: Henry Flagler and the Spectacular Rise and*

Fall of the Railroad That Crossed an Ocean (a BookSense selection), and the best-selling John Deal thriller series, including *Bone Key* and *Havana Run*.

SIDNEY THOMPSON's stories have appeared in *The Southern Review*, *The Carolina Quarterly*, *New Delta Review*, *Louisiana Literature*, and *Stories from the Blue Moon Café (Volume One)*. Originally from Memphis, Tennessee, and a former resident of Fairhope, Alabama, he currently lives in New York City with his wife, Jennifer Paddock.

LEE GAY WARREN has completed two novels and is working on a third. This is her first published work. She lives in Hohenwald, Tennessee.

BRAD WATSON is the author of a novel, *The Heaven of Mercury* (Norton, 2002)—a finalist for the National Book Award—and a collection of short stories, *Last Days of the Dog-Men* (Norton, 1996), from which the story in this edition of *Stories from the Blue Moon Café* is taken. "This story was never published in a magazine, and I've always regretted that," Watson says. He is on the graduate faculty of Spalding University's brief-residency MFA in Creative Writing. He lives on the Alabama Gulf Coast and is at work on a second novel and a second collection of stories.

DAVID WRIGHT, a native of a small town in Texas, currently teaches writing at the University of Illinois. His first book, *Fire on the Beach* (Scribner 2000), a narrative history of the only black crew in the nineteenth-century Coast Guard, was chosen by the *St. Louis Post-Dispatch* as one of the "Best Books of 2001."

STEVE YARBROUGH, a native of the Mississippi Delta, lives in Fresno, California. He is the author of five books, including *The Oxygen Man* and *Visible Spirits*.